To the Moon and Back

Reviewers Love Melissa Brayden

"Melissa Brayden has become one of the most popular novelists of the genre, writing hit after hit of funny, relatable, and very sexy stories for women who love women."—*Afterellen.com*

Love Like This

"I really have to commend Melissa Brayden in her exceptional writing and especially in the way she writes not only the romance but the friendships between the group of women."—*Les Rêveur*

"Brayden upped her game. The characters are remarkably distinct from one another. The secondary characters are rich and wonderfully integrated into the story. The dialogue is crisp and witty."
—*Frivolous Reviews*

Sparks Like Ours

"Brayden sets up a flirtatious tit-for-tat that's honest, relatable, and passionate. The women's fears are real, but the loving support from the supporting cast helps them find their way to a happy future. This enjoyable romance is sure to interest readers in the other stories from Seven Shores."—*Publishers Weekly*

"*Sparks Like Ours* is made up of myriad bits of truth that make for a cozy, lovely summer read."—*Queerly Reads*

Hearts Like Hers

"*Hearts Like Hers* has all the ingredients that readers can expect from Ms. Brayden: witty dialogue, heartfelt relationships, hot chemistry and passionate romance."—*Lez Review Books*

"Once again Melissa Brayden stands at the top. She unequivocally is the queen of romance."—*Front Porch Romance*

"*Hearts Like Hers* has a breezy style that makes it a perfect beach read. The romance is paced well, the sex is super hot, and the conflict made perfect sense and honored Autumn and Kate's journeys."
—*The Lesbian Review*

Eyes Like Those

"Brayden's story of blossoming love behind the Hollywood scenes provides the right amount of warmth, camaraderie, and drama."
—*RT Book Reviews*

"Brayden's writing is just getting better and better. The story is well done, full of well-honed wit and humour, and the characters are complex and interesting."—*Lesbian Reading Room*

"Melissa Brayden knocks it out of the park once again with this fantastic and beautifully written novel."—*Les Reveur*

"Pure Melissa Brayden at her best…Another great read that won't disappoint Brayden's fans. Can't wait for the rest of the series."
—*Lez Review Books*

Strawberry Summer

"This small-town second-chance romance is full of tenderness and heart. The 10 Best Romance Books of 2017."—*Vulture*

"*Strawberry Summer* is a tribute to first love and soulmates and growing into the person you're meant to be. I feel like I say this each time I read a new Melissa Brayden offering, but I loved this book so much that I cannot wait to see what she delivers next."—*Smart Bitches, Trashy Books*

"*Strawberry Summer* will suck you in, rip out your heart, and put all the pieces back together by the end, maybe even a little better than they were before."—*The Lesbian Review*

"[A] sweet and charming small-town lesbian romance."—*Pretty Little Book Reviews*

First Position

"Brayden aptly develops the growing relationship between Ana and Natalie, making the emotional payoff that much sweeter. This ably plotted, moving offering will earn its place deep in readers' hearts."—*Publishers Weekly*

Praise for the Soho Loft Series

"The trilogy was enjoyable and definitely worth a read if you're looking for solid romance or interconnected stories about a group of friends."—*The Lesbrary*

Kiss the Girl

"There are romances and there are romances...Melissa Brayden can be relied on to write consistently very sweet, pure romances and delivers again with her newest book *Kiss the Girl*...There are scenes suffused with the sweetest love, some with great sadness or even anger—a whole gamut of emotions that take readers on a gentle roller coaster with a consistent upbeat tone. And at the heart of this book is a hymn to true friendship and human decency."
—*C-Spot Reviews*

"Read it. Embrace it. Do yourself a favor and provide it to yourself as a reward for being awesome. There is nothing about this novel that won't delight any reader, I can guarantee this."—*FarNerdy Book Blog*

Just Three Words

"Another winner from Melissa Brayden. I really connected with Hunter and Sam, and enjoyed watching their relationship develop. The friendship between the four women was heart-warming and real. The dialogue in general was fun and contemporary. I look forward to reading the next book in the series, hope it will be about Mallory!"—*Melina Bickard, Librarian, Waterloo Library (London)*

"A beautiful and downright hilarious tale about two very relatable women looking for love."—*Sharing Is Caring Book Reviews*

Ready or Not

"The chemistry is off the charts. The swoon factor is high. I promise you this book will make you smile. I had such high hopes for this book, and Melissa Brayden leapt right over them."—*The Romantic Reader Blog*

By the Author

Waiting in the Wings

Heart Block

How Sweet It Is

First Position

Strawberry Summer

Beautiful Dreamer

Back to September

To the Moon and Back

Soho Loft Romances:

Kiss the Girl

Just Three Words

Ready or Not

Seven Shores Romances:

Eyes Like Those

Hearts Like Hers

Sparks Like Ours

Love Like This

Visit us at www.boldstrokesbooks.com

TO THE MOON AND BACK

by

Melissa Brayden

2020

TO THE MOON AND BACK

ISBN 13: 978-1-63555-618-6

This Trade Paperback Original Is Published By
Bold Strokes Books, Inc.
P.O. Box 249
Valley Falls, NY 12185

First Edition: March 2020

Credits
Editor: Ruth Sternglantz
Production Design: Stacia Seaman
Cover Design by Jeanine Henning

Acknowledgments

You may not know this, but in my past life (and sometimes my current one), I was a theatre professional. There's something extraordinary about that mechanism of storytelling, and perhaps that is why I've come to write about it a second time. I fully believe that the exchange of energy between a performer and a live audience is a unique experience, never again to be repeated. Magic in a bottle. I never tire of it and hope you take away a little bit of that magic in the reading of this tale.

Now for the thank-yous. This is my fifteenth novel with Bold Strokes Books, and I fully believe we have many more stories to tell together. I want to thank my editor, Ruth Sternglantz, for confidence along the way and helpful direction, not to mention her friendship. I feel strongly that Sandra Lowe needs more credit for the immense amount of strategic work she does, so I shout out to her for her wisdom, insight, and savvy business sense. Radclyffe, as you can imagine, is a fantastic mentor, boss, and visionary all in one and I'm eternally humbled to be in the BSB stable of authors.

To my friends in the writing community, especially Georgia, Rachel, Nikki, Carsen, Kris, Paula, Barbara, Fiona, Jenn, and Elle, I've never felt your friendship more than this past year. My heart is full and I cherish each and every word of support and act of friendship you've showed me when I needed it. The pep talks, the work sessions, and the dinners and drinks all go such a long way. To many more!

Alan, Everett, Mom, Dad, Becki, Krissy, Sean, Danielle, Shauna, James, Emma, and Weston, and of course, Apple and Ryder, you guys are my steady ship and anchor. I realize it humbly on a daily basis.

To my readership, I have to extend both cartwheels of gratitude and warm hugs. The messages and emails keep me going and my imagination firing. I'm excited to get to work each day because of our give and take and look forward to our social media interactions. I hope you enjoy this book and the next!

For anyone who thought it was too late to shine.

CHAPTER ONE

"No one died today," Lauren Prescott said out loud to herself. It was a glorious statement, and she proclaimed it proudly. She hadn't killed anyone, and no one had keeled over on their own. She punched the air a few times in a Rocky-like victory dance. That accomplishment was a pretty big deal for a Saturday night sold-out show with a cast who had a penchant for drama, hijinks, and tantrums. As she began her final stage managerial duties for the night, she longed to include that sentence on the performance report she would momentarily email to her entire production team, as well as the designers, director, and front office staff for The McAllister Theater. She decided, instead, to add that knowledge to the celebratory wine column. In other words, all the reasons she'd earned a great big gulping of a glass once she returned home to peace, quiet, and serenity. God, she longed for that wine. She might even chair dance like a boss once it was in her hand. After all, celebratory wine time was her most favorite of all the times, which was why she reserved it as her daily after-show reward. Lauren dreamed about it now, lustily. She could be in the living room she very much missed in under an hour if she played her cards right and was expeditious with her daily paperwork.

Thank God the tumultuous night was finally winding down, and only two people had cried. Well, two and a half, if you count misting up and fanning your face like it was on fire. Most of the actors were already out of costume and makeup and out the door following the performance, likely signing Playbills for the patrons who'd lingered for photos and a chat with their favorites. Lauren's two assistant stage managers were busy tending to their nightly housekeeping responsibilities. Janie, who decked the show at the stage level, was busy organizing the props and giving Milky White, the cow puppet they used in the musical, Sondheim's *Into the Woods*, a good brushing to get the makeup stains off her shoulder. At the same time, Trip Hooper, her right-hand man and the closest friend she had, swept the stage in that very methodical way Trip was known for. When he spotted Lauren watching him, he offered a playful salute along with a jovial dance.

"You're totally Bert right now," she told him and began to hum a few bars of "Chim Chim Cher-ee."

He spun in a circle with his broom.

"You need soot though, or you're just the poor man's version, and who wants that?"

He kicked his heels together in full chimney sweep mode and grinned. "I'll work on that for ya, Mary," he said in his best Cockney.

"Brilliant." Lauren adored her staff. She was lucky, because this was not the kind of job you waded through alone. That's actually how she and Trip had become so close. In stage management, you needed soldiers to help you crawl through the battlefield of high maintenance performers and irate designers. Later, you had a cocktail together and toasted days like today when *nobody* died and said all the things you could never say in the actual rehearsal room, even though you desperately wanted to. She and Trip had been through many such battles and were closer than ever because of it. They always had each other's backs and always would.

"Night, Lauren," Jesi, their wig mistress, said as she headed home. "Almost to the end of this one, and I don't know about you, but I'm ready. This group is a handful."

"They're definitely on their own journey. I pray for them," she said with a wink. "One more to go, and we're out. Oh, hey," Lauren said, pausing Jesi's exit. "Did Cinderella's act two wig sit far back tonight, or was that just me?"

"It did." Jesi shook her head ruefully. "All because Alicia keeps tugging on it when she's gabbing with the princes in the wings. It's how she flirts. I've talked to her, but I can't hold her hand all night. She's a man-crazy lady."

Lauren nodded, knowing how much Alicia hated being wigged. She was a kind person, but the brand of actress who didn't understand why everything wasn't simpler for her specifically. When she'd asked

Lauren to run lines with her, part of her gig as stage manager, Alicia actually asked if she could rewrite a few of them. Sondheim and Lapine would be *so* pleased. Alicia had also argued to use her own hair for the show but lost that fight to the design team when it was pointed out quietly in a production meeting that she didn't have a ton of hair to work with, as it had thinned out considerably once she'd entered her thirties. The costume designer had made the right call, in Lauren's opinion, and Alicia was much more glamorous in the wig. Now, if they could keep the princes, who happened to be gay anyway, away from her for one more day.

They were so close, Lauren could taste it. *Into the Woods* was in its final weekend of performances at The McAllister Theater in Minneapolis, where Lauren was one of two resident production stage managers. Her job was varied and intense, but she wouldn't trade it for any other. It fell to her to oversee the assistant stage managers and keep everything about the production moving forward in a timely, healthy, and organized manner, and that came with a long list of responsibilities. Lauren called each cue of the show personally on the headset from the stage manager's booth. She worked with actors on any problems, both personal or performance based, arranged for their understudies to step in when they were sick, and made sure the production team was informed about nearly every detail of each performance. She filled out electronic paperwork on every performance. She coordinated with the house manager. She made sure the director's vision remained intact once the show opened. She booked doctor's appointments, arranged for rides, and acted as therapist and counselor. In short, there was nothing Lauren Prescott didn't do in the scope of her job to make each and every performance better, and she did it calmly with a smile.

And while she loved her gig as stage manager, she loved The McAllister even more. With a season of six productions annually, every one had to be top-notch. Lauren generally stage managed three or four of them, making the pace of her life incredibly busy. Sure, she'd love to date, socialize, or maybe make it to the gym on occasion. Hell, she'd settle for time to drink her coffee before it got cold. Yet she didn't have time.

"And *send*," she said, striking the key on her silver Mac with the rose-gold casing that would blast the performance report to everyone who worked behind the scenes in any position of status. They'd run three minutes longer than the night before, which meant that The Baker was milking his dramatic moments again. She'd pass on the note, knowing the director's wish for him to keep the pace of those emotional moments in act 2 aloft.

Most of the forty-eight performances of *Into the Woods* had been sold out, and the reviews had been relatively positive. Yet the production had devolved into a backstage circus because of the dramatic nature of a few choice actors. Nothing new, but not Lauren's favorite type of ensemble. Her goal was to get them to the end of the run the following evening without The Baker's Wife killing The Baker, without Little Red Riding Hood wandering away to Instagram her face eighty times a show to the world while missing her act 1 entrance, and without The Narrator, a functioning alcoholic, performing so soused that audience members noticed. She could do it! She saw the homestretch in front of her with a glass of wine blinking like a 7-Eleven sign on a lonely highway at midnight.

God, she couldn't wait for this trip.

She'd earned this vacation. Dreamed about it. In forty-eight hours, this production would be another successful entry on her already impressive résumé, and The McAllister would bring a new show to the main stage, and enter rehearsals for another. The system was in constant motion.

"Mona—the dresser for the princes?—hit on me tonight," Trip said, leaning against her table in the booth. "She grabbed my ass, and it hurt like hell. Mona has traumatized me."

"Do you want me to write it up?" Lauren asked with a sympathetic grin. She was also the first step to Human Resources for such claims, before the union got involved. "Call it aggressive ass grabbing?"

Trip rubbed his right cheek. "I do not. This time."

"I'd do that for you, Trippy. I'll say Mona's an ass grabber."

"Nah. Maybe next time. I just want my boss and friend to sympathize with me."

She offered him puppy dog eyes and blinked slowly. "I'm so sorry your ass is sore, and that Mona thinks it's so cute she has to harm it."

"That's it," he said, nodding, warming to the characterization. "I have a harmed ass. I'm glad you're finally acknowledging my pain."

"Always, Trip. Always. Want to go home now? Cuz it feels like it's three a.m. and I'm close to death."

"Quarter to midnight, but yes, please," he said, snapping out of martyr mode. A thought seemed to pop into his brain. "Excuse me. Lala?"

"Yes?" Lauren asked, smiling at the use of the nickname he'd assigned her years ago.

"Will you be at the after-party tomorrow night? Please don't say you need to have lonely wine time at home. Lonely wine time is really sad wine time, and you don't want to be that lady."

She nodded and ignored his judgmental observation. "I'll be there. I'm exhausted, numb, and ready to clock out of this one, but it wouldn't feel right to skip out, you know?" She'd never missed a closing party and didn't plan to now. There was something important about the cast and creatives coming together socially to say their good-byes, and send the show off into the history books as a united group. Say what you would about a drama-filled production, but once the curtain was down for good, everyone forgot the tumultuous details and fell in love all over again. The glory of theater.

"Perfect. I'll need you to keep me from flirting with Gregory. It's your job." Gregory played Rapunzel's Prince in the show, and Trip had been drooling over him since they'd started rehearsals. Gregory, however, was the love 'em and leave 'em type, and Trip was more the fall in love and get married type, so Lauren had done her best to run interference.

She raised an eyebrow. "We're still on that?"

Trip covered his heart. "Can you support my endeavors sans judgment?"

"I can." He bowed, and she laughed. "Now get out of here, so I can finish my paperwork by five a.m."

"You mean midnight."

"It's whatever. I'm barely alive."

"One day more!" he sang loudly, giving her his best *Les Mis*. She had the decency to grin. When he disappeared from sight, she heard several more voices join his chorus. She laughed quietly. Theater people, man. Their world was a unique environment, full of unique individuals who Lauren happened to love, flaws and all.

Just before leaving The McAllister that night, Lauren paused to watch one of her most favorite rituals. A stagehand placed the ghost light center stage and wandered away. Gorgeous. She folded her arms across her chest and let the image affect her. There was no visual she loved more. Something about that solitary light keeping watch over the theater, until they could come back and tell more stories the next day, stole her heart. She leaned into her goose bumps, offering herself a small hug. She stayed another minute and stared at the light, internalizing it, appreciating it, before packing up her bag and heading out. When she arrived in the staff parking lot, she turned back and regarded the looming white building with four long regal columns in front. The amount of theatrical history inside those walls was not lost on Lauren. She carried a great deal of reverence for the theater, and never tired of its demands. They were friends, she and The McAllister. She leaned back against her car. She'd once dreamed about performing on that stage herself. She didn't dust off those old dreams too often, because why harp on the past, you know? She wasn't meant to be an actress and clearly understood that now. But there were times when she allowed the twinge of envy to creep in, when she saw others doing what she once longed to do herself and felt the loss. She batted back those wistful thoughts before they got too far along. Hell, she was Lauren Prescott, and holding everything together was her specialty. No time for those kinds of indulgences.

She stood and gave the theater a final nod good night. She'd be back in just eleven short hours for the final Sunday matinee. That meant older patrons and children would cram the house in a jumble of red wine and peanut M&M's.

First up, her after-show celebratory wine gulping, when she could put her feet up, relax into her own life, and leave the stage management professional on the shelf for another day. Bring on her real world, namely: her dog, her house, and her leggings purposefully purchased one size too large for this very occasion.

❖

Whoa. Carly Daniel lowered her banana-razzmatazz-kale smoothie and set it on her white marble kitchen counter in sunny Los Angeles. The man servicing her infinity pool stared at her in her baby blue bikini through the automated open wall between her backyard and kitchen. She turned away from him, killing his view, and stared at her phone's readout in disbelief. Her agent was calling for the first time in months. She wasn't calling Alika. Alika was calling *her*. At long fucking last. She picked up without hesitation, hoping silently for an offer, an audition, anything to get her feeling like she was working again. Alika Moore had been dodging her calls for weeks, so to have her reach out now had Carly's heart hammering with anticipation.

"Hey, Alika. Just catching some rays." Carly forced a smile because she knew it would make her sound happier. She always made a point to sound breezy and successful, even though they both knew her career was circling the toilet. "How's your day?"

"Been busy out there," Alika said. She had a lot of clients, and Carly was now probably low priority after her star had fallen so publicly. She was lucky her agent hadn't dropped her altogether. "I'm calling because, wonder of wonders, we have an offer on the table."

Carly closed her eyes and thanked heaven above. "Tell me it's Barrow's latest film. I don't even mind auditioning for him, which we both know I haven't had to do in a while. Plus, he loves me, so it would just be a formality." She and director Jay Barrow had been talking about working together for the past two years, and his new film had the perfect role for her. She'd read the script three times, reveled in the dialogue, the rich characterization, and the fantastic plot twist toward the end that would have audiences talking for weeks. She was ready to report when and where they needed her.

"I called on it already. They passed."

Carly started to speak and stopped. She turned around and stared at her white cabinets with the glass insets. That didn't make sense. Jay told her she was a favorite actress of his and he was dying to work with her. "Did you tell them I'd audition? I'll prove what I have to prove."

"I told them you'd audition. I told them you'd be in bed every night by eleven. I told them they could have your firstborn. They passed, Carly. They're all passing, and if we don't do something to turn this around, this whole hands-off Carly Daniel policy that's circulating the studio system is going to be permanent."

Carly frowned. She'd behaved badly, partied too hard, and taken advantage of her status in Hollywood, imagining she'd be solid no matter what she did, including holding up production when she'd failed to make her call times. She'd fallen into the Valley of the Stupid and was paying for it mightily. It wouldn't have been such a big deal if that hotheaded director hadn't run to every media outlet who would listen and exaggerated all that had happened. It didn't matter how sorry she was, or how vehemently she planned to be different moving forward. No more late partying. No more late arrivals, no more pushy opinions, and definitely no more hookups who would tell all to the tabloids. She truly regretted that one night with the Norwegian woman who sold compromising photos of them to *The Inquirer*. Her kingdom for a time machine. Yet she'd been on the straight and narrow for months now, and no one cared. Well, maybe until now. She backtracked to the important part, leaving the Barrow news in the past. "But there's an offer?"

"Not one you're going to be thrilled with, but if you ask me, we're lucky to get it." There was a weariness in Alika's tone, and the words themselves didn't bode well, either.

"Okay, I guess. Tell me about it?"

"The McAllister Theater in Minneapolis is mounting a production of a new play, *Starry Nights.*"

Carly squinted and noticed absently her tan was in great shape. That was a bonus, at least. "Like the Van Gogh painting?"

"The script is inspired by the painting, yes, and I've gotta be honest with you, it's good. The director, Ethan Moore—no relation, by the way—has offered you one of the two lead roles."

Carly shook her head, picked up her smoothie, and walked. "But stage work? Think about it, Alika, no. That's not who I am. It's not what I do." She sighed dramatically. "If this offer was Broadway, then maybe. I could at least think of it as a bonus on the old résumé, but some dusty old regional house?"

"It's not just *some* regional house." Alika seemed frustrated again. "It's the fucking McAllister. Well respected. Coveted in artistic circles. It attracts top echelon directors, actors, and designers, all because everyone wants to work at The McAllister at least once in their career. Don't just blow this off, Carly. I can't guarantee there'll be another offer."

"You honestly think I should do this?"

"If you want to reestablish yourself, this is a fantastic way to do it." Alika had put on her serious voice, the one she used when she tried to get Carly to see things from her point of view. The serious voice tended to be right, so Carly paid attention. "Go back to basics. Act your ass off in this play, and let the reviews sell you to Hollywood all over again for the credible work you did. Remind them you're an actress and not a headline."

Carly dropped her head back and stared at the ceiling. Not only did stage work not appeal to her, but she'd never done any theater. Zilch. Not even in her tiny high school back in Oregon. Her first audition had been for a television guest spot when she was nineteen, and that had quickly led to her first film cameo at twenty. Since then, the water had been warm in Hollywood, and her star had continued to rise until she was the name selling films. Nine years later, as she approached her thirtieth birthday, she could definitely say that star had fallen. And hard.

On the other hand, how hard could it be to transfer what she did to a live performance, right? She was a good actress. She knew that much, and acting was acting. "Can I think about it?"

"You can, but why?" Alika drew out the last word. Carly could imagine Alika's hair vibrating the way it did when she was frustrated. "Would you rather float around in your pool some more and sip mimosas? I can let you get back to that. I have other clients who are interested in working." One of Carly's favorite things about Alika was that she rarely sucked up and instead told it like it was. "Or we can begin building your career back to what it was, one brick at a time. The McAllister is a brick, baby girl."

Why did Alika have to be so tell-it-like-it-is? Carly sighed and tapped her countertop about eight hundred times. Her pool guy stole another glance at her in her bikini, and she closed her sheer cover-up tighter around her body. "Fine. Take the offer. There's a dude gawking openly at my breasts, and I'd like to say something positive happened today."

"Gawking at you? What else is new?" Alika chuckled. "Report his ass to his supervisor immediately. Also, as your friend, I'm happy you see the light. I'll send over the contract as soon as I have it. This is the right move. The McAllister is big."

"When do I have to be in—I'm sorry, where the hell am I going, again?"

"Minneapolis. They want you there for the first rehearsal next week. The theater will be in touch to arrange your travel once we've signed. Start flexing that acting muscle again."

"On it. Maybe you'll visit?"

"Doubtful. I must wheel and deal so we can all eat."

Carly sighed as she tried to keep up, tried to imagine waking up in Minneapolis next week, and tried not to swear in frustration at her agent, who was merely the messenger. "Alika. Level with me. Is this whole thing really necessary? I mean, can't we just send Warner Brothers a fruit basket and hope they tell the others?"

"Baby girl, if you want to see your career ever again, then I'd say yes, you need to pay some dues. Fruit baskets can be for later."

It wasn't how she'd imagined she'd spend the next three months of her life, but then when had life ever been predictable? She'd go to Minnesota, of all places, hang out at an old boring theater, and show everyone in show business that, after everything, she was a safe bet. That was right. Carly Daniel would play ball, and she'd play it well. Maybe she'd even make a new friend or two in Minneapolis. That part, she'd never had trouble with.

She harnessed all her energy. "All right. Next week it is. Do you have a script for me?"

"I'll send it right over. And Carly? This is the right move. You gotta trust me on this. It's a desert out there for you. You're crawling on your hands and knees in search of water."

"Jesus, that's a depressing image."

"It's your life. Seek out that oasis. It's in Minneapolis."

Carly clicked off the call and caught her reflection in the glass. She pulled her blond hair from the clip holding it back and felt it tumble down past her shoulder blades. She stared out at her infinity pool that overlooked all of the Hollywood Hills. It was August. She had maybe six months until she couldn't afford this house any longer, unless something changed. Life was about to shift dramatically for her, but Carly was up for it. She wondered what Minneapolis was like in the fall.

❖

Ten minutes to actor call time and every single last one of them had already signed in. What had Lauren done to deserve such a smooth final performance? Her little stage manager heart swelled with pride. No phone calls to make. No one to track down. No tardy entries on that performance report. She celebrated the victories when they happened.

Following today, *Into the Woods* would fade into history and Lauren had some time off. She would take a weekend trip to Cancun, lie on a beautiful beach, take in the crystal blue waters, and who knew? Maybe she'd meet a nice woman at a bar for some after-hours fun. The other resident production stage manager, Matthew the Great, would take over the driver's seat as PSM on a new play going into rehearsal at The McAllister, *Starry Nights*, scheduled to run for four weeks in the fall. She'd return to PSM the Christmas show, which would go into rehearsal in just over a month, once *Starry Nights* moved to the stage. Between now and then, she'd find out what it felt like to be a person again, a real live one with a life.

"Got a sec, Lauren?"

"Hey, Wilks." Nolan Wilks was the artistic director of The McAllister and responsible for keeping the whole engine moving. In other words, her boss, and a very capable one. "What's up? I'm approaching half hour so I don't have a ton of time to talk, unfortunately."

He straightened his polo shirt as if it were a tie. She smothered an affectionate grin. "You're going to hate me, but you might just have to hate me. Are you ready to hate me?"

She stared at him, checked her watch, and held up one finger to place him on hold. She pressed a button on the microphone in the booth and leaned toward it. "Ladies and gentleman, half hour until curtain. This is your half hour." Refocusing on Wilks, she prepared herself. "Please don't make me hate you. I much prefer celebrating you as headmaster over all of Hogwarts." She smiled at him but wondered what in the world was going on if he was storming the booth at half hour.

"I need you for *Starry Nights*."

She swallowed. "No, you don't. You and I both know I'll be on that much needed vacation. That means me, a beach, and the tiniest of umbrellas in my glass. Picture it, and please don't say any more. This is my time away, and I'm in love with it. We're getting married."

"Time you very much deserve." He paused. She stared. They repeated the process. "But I need you, and you know I wouldn't ask if it wasn't that important."

She took a moment. "I don't understand. Matty's on it. Matty is fully capable." Matthew the Great was a decent enough production stage manager. Reliable, focused. True, he didn't always know the best way to defuse a hot-button situation, but his organizational skills had earned him his nickname. His series of personally developed charts and spreadsheets had changed Lauren's PSM life for the better. Plus, Matty could track a prop's journey onstage like no one she'd ever met.

Wilks rubbed his forehead. "I'm not sure he's right for this one. We have a high-profile cast member, and I need someone with a delicate touch."

Lauren frowned. "But that's not at all unusual. Pretty much every other production has someone famous headlining. We've worked with Meryl Streep, for God's sakes. Matty can handle famous."

"It's not unusual, no," Wilks said. "But from what I've read this morning of Carly Daniel, she can be a handful."

Lauren blinked. Carly Daniel? Of course she knew of her. She'd been a much talked about film actress who was everyone's favorite in Hollywood until recently. It all came back to her. Sometime last year, a series of articles about her misbehavior on sets swarmed the gossip rags, and as a result, she'd been MIA onscreen. Lauren looked to Wilks, incredulous. "Who's directing *Starry Nights*?" The real question was who the hell had cast a party girl to come and headline at a show at the esteemed McAllister Theater, of all places?

"Ethan Moore, who I've been trying to get on our season for years. I finally managed it. He's a fabulous director who knows what he's doing. He'll do great things here, but he wants Daniel. Insisted."

Lauren could understand, to an extent, why. She was a good actress, layered, and watchable as hell with how pretty she was. Lauren couldn't argue that fact. Lauren wished she had half of Carly's talent— maybe things would have gone differently for her. As far as Ethan Moore, of course she'd heard of him, too. He'd directed multiple times on Broadway in the past five years but would be new to The McAllister space. "Okay, so Carly Daniel, problem child, is starring in our next one. Sounds like a done deal. Keep her from dancing on top of tables and you'll be fine. Why do you want me?"

"You can handle her, and I want more than anything for Ethan to have a good experience here. I'd love to foster this relationship with him for future projects, and if Carly Daniel comes in and makes this production unsavory for him, he'll always remember his time here as… undesirable. Ultimately, we'll pay the price for it."

She closed her eyes. "And Matty can't make that happen for

you? I'm hours from a beach and a piña colada, Wilks. Hours," she practically squeaked. Anything to not have to lose her vacation. She needed this vacation. She'd planned for it for over a year now. She had a bundle of little brochures all in a folder.

"Not the way you can, Lauren. No one has your cool head and skill with people. I was nervous about not having you with Ethan already, but now that Carly Daniel has been attached to the project?" He shifted and stuck his hands in his pockets. "I really need you and will buy you eighteen piña coladas when this is said and done."

She glanced at the clock apologetically. "I need to get this performance going."

"Of course. I'll scoot-scat out of your way." He did a little dance to lighten things up, which Lauren appreciated. Wilks, who had to be in his late sixties, could be cute despite his otherwise distinguished persona. She wanted to pat him on his head while still carrying great respect for him. "Think about it? You'd be the hero of this place." He backed away. More scoot-scatting. "And you'll be compensated appropriately."

"You should have led with that."

He pointed at her. "I will next time. And Lauren?"

"Sir?"

"You're the best goddamned stage manager in the business."

"I will remind you of that someday when you forget." He nodded and snuck away so she could do her job for the next three hours and give this show a proper closing. The compensation part of his offer didn't sound half bad. As a stage manager, she was a member of Actors' Equity, and there was a minimum pay scale in place. Hearing Wilks say he'd go above and beyond did carry some weight. Maybe if she put off her vacation a bit, she could take a few extra perks for herself. Fly first class. Upgrade her reservation to one of those upscale all-inclusive places with private cabanas and butlers that brought the fruity drinks. She closed her eyes and imagined herself in a bikini, the sun caressing her skin. God, could she really give that up?

"Lauren, we're at fifteen," Trip informed her.

"Right, right, right. My fault entirely." She made the fifteen-minute call to everyone backstage and checked in via headset with her house manager, who reported everything out front was on schedule for an on-time curtain.

Twenty minutes later, they were wandering their way through a

Sondheim journey, the audience on the edge of their seats. From the booth that overlooked the house, where she called each and every show, Lauren could occasionally catch a glimpse of an audience member's face as they went along for the ride, gasping and glancing at their seatmate for each plot twist or turn. She loved that about theater. Back when she used to be an actress herself, she'd taken great pride in affecting those who took in her shows. When an audience member cried or laughed loudly, she carried that energy with her and brought it back out again in appreciation of that relationship. That actor-audience connection was like nothing she'd ever experienced. Those kinds of thoughts always made Lauren's heart squeeze.

She missed life onstage. Not to say she didn't love her job. When acting hadn't panned out after college, she'd made a choice for herself that would keep her in the business she dearly loved, working to tell stories every day. Her skill set fit nicely into stage management. She'd started as a production assistant at a lower level regional theater in Missouri, worked her way up to assistant stage manager after a couple of years, and eventually became a PSM. Landing a resident gig at The McAllister had been a dream come true. Well, a second-choice dream come true after that first dream didn't pan out. People could have multiple dreams, couldn't they? And she didn't take anything for granted. No, sir.

Four and a half hours later and Lauren swirled her lemonade margarita and adjusted her burgundy cocktail dress. The cast party, always traditionally held at the upscale Argyle Hotel, was fully underway. Everyone was doing that thing where they reminisced about how far they'd all come together, hugging everyone else to excess, and professing how much they were going to miss each other. Though it was definitely a routine process for the closing of a show, it didn't make the sentiments any less sincere.

"Lauren, I don't know how I would have survived without you," Emily Heitner said with a flutter of dramatic hand gestures. She was a well-respected actress who'd played the role of The Witch. Kisses and kind words followed.

"Oh my goodness, Lauren. I might miss you most of all," a male cast member gushed. More kisses and kind words. There was a welcome predictability to it all that she truly cherished.

They danced and sang with the music as the beverages flowed

more freely, and when most of the cast and creatives cleared out, Lauren did, too.

She walked to her sky blue Mini Cooper with the white top just after eleven that night and heard footsteps behind her. When she turned to see who followed so closely, she wasn't surprised.

"Hey, there," Tinsley said. "That was a lot of fun."

"Hey, Tins. It was. Headed home?" Tinsley Worth was an up-and-coming scenic designer who was currently working under their head of department. She lent her artistic talents to their main stage sets and got to design some of the smaller children's shows in the adjoining space.

Tinsley leaned against the Mini and smiled. "I was actually seeing where you were headed. Thought maybe you'd want to grab a drink?"

Lauren considered the offer. Tinsley was cute, and friendly, and her crush on Lauren seemed apparent. Lauren just wasn't sure she had the time in her life to offer to someone right now. It was possible all Tinsley wanted was a hookup, but wasn't that a bad idea with people you worked alongside? Hadn't she just given Trip that same advice? As tempting as it was, Lauren decided to sidestep the offer.

"You're sweet, but I've had such a killer day, you know?" She tapped the top of the Mini. "Gonna head home and play sock tug-o-war with Rocky IV, and maybe have a Baileys on the rocks before bed. Still debating whether I'll wear the footie pajamas or not, wild child that I am. No photos, please."

Tinsley laughed. "You definitely have the pajama fashion down. So, I've been wondering about something. Is Rocky your fourth dog named Rocky?" Tinsley asked, flashing her smile again. Yep, she was looking for some action, and Lauren just wasn't prepared to go there with her. She was a pretty girl, and friendly, and gay as hell, but that didn't necessarily mean Lauren wanted to take her up on the apparent offer. Maybe her romance mechanism had busted somewhere along the way. She should be all over this chance yet wasn't. That said something.

"No, I just prefer the fourth movie. Rocky just wants to retire, but then his friend needs justice. Then there's Adrian having all these feelings, and Dolph Lundgren is a fantastic villain, and I'm here for it. Does that make any sense? My brain is compartmentalized."

"I think I translated." She nodded. "A very cute explanation. I'll let you get to those footie pajamas."

"I better hurry. Have a great night." Lauren slid into the driver's side and wondered if that had come off as rude. She'd tried to explain the *Rocky IV* origins with a grin attached, but maybe she was just awkward. After her long day, who knew what her face said to Tinsley? To help punctuate her lightness, she waved through the windshield just before speeding away. It would have to do.

Her favorite snuffling pug, Rocky, did his famous front paw dance as she opened the door to her home, at long last. She dropped to the ground and mimicked his prancing back and forth. "Rocky, Rocky, Rocky," she said to each landing of his front paws, exciting him all the more. The more he snuffled, the more thrilled he was. Finally, she toppled him onto his back and rubbed his belly and his sides vigorously, his favorite. "Do you know how much I missed you? There was this cow wandering around onstage, and it reminds me of you every time, you wiggle worm of love. I will kiss your face eight times to celebrate our reunion." More snuffling as he was kissed. He loved kisses.

Lauren scooped up her best friend and carried him into her living room where they collapsed together on the couch and channel surfed until her adrenaline from the day receded. She did go ahead and pull that cup of Baileys, which tasted like a lovely chocolate shake in liqueur form. Before consuming it, she took a moment to straighten the blanket on her couch and make sure it was folded neatly. Everything in Lauren's life came with order, her lifeline.

Once she'd accomplished her goal, she was able to breathe a little easier in her well-structured home. Magazines on the coffee table, but books on the shelves. Mug handles faced to the right, and dish towels were folded into squares. Everything had its place, and that made her happy.

The more Lauren relaxed, the more her mind began to turn over the events of the day. More specifically, one important event. She thought on the offer before her. The question was, did she have another three months left in her? Could she push pause on a vacation that she'd already booked and pined away for in order to go back into the rehearsal room all over again?

As she drifted off to sleep with Rocky snoring at her side, the answer was clear.

Hell no.

CHAPTER TWO

"What do you think of me in plaid?" Carly asked and held a shirt up to her chest. "I feel like in Minneapolis maybe I should embrace my plaid side. Are there lumberjack types there? I feel like I remember that from school."

Her best friend, Fallon, sat cross-legged on the floor of Carly's enormous walk-in closet, one of her favorite rooms in all the world. "I think you look great in plaid, and isn't Minnesota where *Little House on the Prairie* took place? Plaid worked for Walnut Grove, though I think they've industrialized quite a bit since then." She said it with a semisarcastic grin and turned another page of the *Cosmo* she'd found on Carly's bedside table. "Did you know that blueberries are a superfood? I feel like my day just made progress."

"I did know. I have some in my fridge if you're hungry." She was struggling with what to pack for this unplanned jaunt across the country. "What about sweaters? I feel like sweaters are making a strong comeback."

"I didn't know they'd been banished."

"The heavier ones certainly were. Chunky heels were also temporarily on the no-fly list. I never know who decides such things, but I wish they'd slow down a little bit with all the shifts."

"I kinda feel like you and your fellow starlets do." Fallon shook her head. "Leave it to me to be on the wrong side of fashion for the twenty-ninth year in a row. I'm five years behind at all times. It's almost a badge now."

"You always look great, Fal. I'm serious. I love your sense of style."

Her friend looked up with a soft, genuine smile. "Thanks, Car. I appreciate that."

Carly and her best friend Fallon Mendez met once upon a time on the set of an early indie film that had helped put Carly on the map. Fallon had been a production assistant and Carly had a small but memorable role in the film, that had come with a dramatic death scene, blood packets and all. They'd bonded at the craft services table over their mutual nervousness about possibly losing their jobs. A friendship blossomed, and they'd never looked back. Other than her mother, who was less than reliable, Carly didn't have too many people she would consider close to her. A million acquaintances? Sure. But she tended to keep people in that category on purpose. Fallon was different, and she treasured their friendship.

Fallon set the magazine aside and blinked at Carly. She had her jet black hair pulled back in a ponytail which accentuated the earnestness in her eyes.

"It looks like you have something on your mind," Carly said. "I may be crazy, but I've known you a while."

"I'm worried about you," Fallon said simply.

Carly tossed the plaid shirt into her open suitcase, deciding if nothing else, she could always tie it around her waist. "That I'll be in Minnesota when autumn hits? Oh, me, too. I'm not built for extreme cold. I'm a cabana in the summer kind of girl. Maybe you can send me igloo building instructions."

Fallon inclined her head to the side as if waiting for a loud noise to cease. "I know that it's your instinct to joke your way through most anything serious, but that's part of the problem. I love you, so let me say this."

Carly paused midfold, with an ache in the pit of her stomach. If anyone could make her shut up for a moment and listen, it was her best friend. Fallon was grounded, kind, and intelligent. Because her thoughts were important, Carly took a seat on the plush beige bench in her closet. "Okay. Sure, Fal. I'm listening."

"Don't screw this up. I know you think that Hollywood sidelining you is temporary, and it's only a matter of time before you're on *The Tonight Show* again, but it's not." Fallon now read scripts for a major studio and was in a good spot to have her ear to the ground. She would know, which Carly found sobering. "You need to get your act together and show the world that you are a wise investment again."

Carly smiled. "I get that. But, Fallon, this is some little stage production that no one is going to see or talk about. How hard could it be?"

Fallon pointed at her. "I love you, and you have a kinder heart than most people realize, but it's that kind of thinking that's going to bite you in the ass and have you doing informercials to pay the mortgage on a house that could fit in a tiny corner of this one." Fallon pushed herself up and placed her hands on Carly's knees. "Take this very seriously, and do the best work of your life."

Carly offered a mock salute and a smile. Her goal was to reassure Fallon, but honestly, she wasn't concerned. This play should be a cakewalk, and then she'd get back to the business of her real life. She gave Fallon's hair an affectionate ruffle. "You got it. My best behavior."

Fallon sighed. "You're doing very little to convince me."

❖

"Wow, so you're doing the show," Trip said, sliding in next to Lauren on the first day of rehearsal. "I was shocked when I heard. Twizzler?"

"No, thanks." She sighed, then reconsidered and snatched a rope. "I put my entire vacation on hold. Can you believe I did that? I still can't. I'm in mourning and still tanless." She made a circle in the air with her Twizzler. "It's a whole thing."

"Noted." Trip, who'd make a great PSM someday, grinned. His mop of brown curls seemed to contribute to his enjoyment. In fact, his hair had a way of communicating emotion in the most rare sense. Lauren had never seen anything like it. When he was happy, his hair bounced. When he felt depressed, it fell softly against his forehead. When he partied, it stood straight up. She wasn't sure how in the world he managed to personify emotion so perfectly.

He gestured back with his Twizzler. "Must have made you quite the deal because you were dead set on getting out of here for a while. Still can't believe anything was able to keep you from the beach. You've been talking about it for a year. Not that I'm cataloging you."

"You have no idea how badly this hurts." She shrugged. "But I'm human, and I saw the dollar signs and leaped. I could use that cash, and now I'm an official whore in stage manager's clothing, and you should feel free to call me such." She pointed with her Twizzler. "Daily." Lauren shook her head as she reflected on the large bonus Wilks had tacked on to her normal paycheck. He must have had a rainy day fund stashed away somewhere. She grinned at Trip and did her best to shift gears. "But—and I say that with an exclamation point—happy to have you on board for this one. Didn't mean to gloss over that very important fact because I adore you forever."

"Thanks, Lala. I plan to do you proud." Trip would be the perfect assistant stage manager for the show, and because the production was not a musical and had fewer moving parts, he'd be the only ASM, aided by a band of production assistants. Trip could anticipate her moods like no one else, and that made him incredibly valuable. He'd come up from the stage management program at University of Michigan and hit the ground running from a young age. He was professional, fun loving, and kind, a hard to find combination, so she planned to keep him. If she could just get him to be a little more organized, and turn the lust meter to low, he'd be the full package.

Lauren stapled the last of the *Starry Nights* company contact sheets and dropped them in the pile that contained the rest of her paperwork. With their first rehearsal underway in just a few minutes, she now had all her ducks in a perfectly assembled and well-behaved row. Nothing gave her more satisfaction than order and structure. She lived by it. Now she was ready to get this show on the road.

Over the next ten minutes, members of the eight person cast filed in one at a time along with members of the design team, who would sit in and make individual presentations to the cast. She watched as Ethan Moore took a moment to greet each person with either a warm handshake or a hug. He'd worked with some of them before, she realized, listening in on their small talk. Her initial meeting with him, after finally taking the gig, had left her with a strong impression of him as both an artist and a director. Each director was different, and understanding how they worked helped Lauren anticipate problems on the road ahead. Ethan seemed the type to know exactly what he wanted and, beyond that, came with a strong vision for the show. She didn't pick up on any hothead vibes either, which was a blessing. God, Lauren loathed working with short-tempered directors motivated by ego. No, this guy gave off a kind, thoughtful, warm vibe that made Lauren feel like he was going to be a good guy to work alongside. Plus, his creative reputation preceded him. He was a visionary.

"What's your favorite part of the process?" Ethan had asked her toward the end of their coffee meeting a few days prior. They'd already gone over all the logistics of how he wanted the rehearsals run and how she would notify him of union-required breaks, and laid out the rehearsal calendar, among other agenda items.

She took only a moment to think on her answer. "For me, it's always been about off-book day, where the scripts are tossed away, and the actors face each other fully. That magical connection from one character to another is established for the first time and...I don't know. You can feel it in the room." She shook her head and lifted her shoulders. "I just don't think I'll ever get tired of that."

"That's a pro answer. That earns you big points." Ethan ran his hand through his sandy blond hair. He had it short on the sides but longer on top, which allowed the curl to take hold. She had him pegged in his late forties. Maybe the type who'd been married a couple of times, but who really knew? "You're somebody who gets it, then, Lauren."

"You say that now," she said, playfully.

"Ever done any acting?" he asked, casually. "You have that look about you. You *look* like an actress."

She had no idea what that meant but answered honestly. "Back in the day, sure. I auditioned full-time for a year, ate ramen, and pounded the pavement."

"And what happened?"

She shrugged, feeling the pang all over again. "The time limit I gave myself before moving on finally arrived. My acting career hadn't gone anywhere, and I'm a realist."

"Ouch. You just gave up? How is that possible?" he asked, with a challenging smile.

"I don't think of it as giving up. I evaluated the situation and made the best call. I'm type A. What can I say?" She shrugged.

"Do you miss it?"

God, did she ever. "Once in a while," she said, downplaying the reality. "But I found my calling in a stage manager's booth one night and never looked back. It's a better fit for me anyway. My refrigerator is in alphabetical order."

"Fuck me."

"Yeah. I'm a bit much when it comes to processes and procedures. They get my fur up."

"I guess that's good for me, right?"

"You just hit the lottery. I keep it all together, so you don't have to," Lauren said, with a proud grin.

"A former actress turned stage manager on crack. What the hell will they think of next?"

"You ready to do this thing?" She gathered her belongings as he did the same.

"More than you know. See you soon."

"I'll be there. Early."

"I had a feeling." Ethan smiled, picked up a second coffee to go, and headed out. She had a feeling this professional relationship was going to be a valuable one. If this was the guy Wilks wanted to keep happy, she didn't think it was going to be too terribly difficult.

Well, until one of their two lead actresses was late for the first damn day of rehearsal. Really? The drama had started already? Lauren surveyed the long table she'd assembled for the first read-through and the polite, smiling faces gathered around it, all with scripts in front of them, ready to go. So where in the world was Carly Daniel? She checked her watch. It was five past. Nothing to panic about yet, but it wasn't ideal. She exchanged a look with Ethan to see what he wanted to do. He mouthed back, *Let's give her another five.* Lauren nodded and listened to the polite getting-to-know-you conversations happening all around her. She said hello to an actor she'd worked with before. At twelve minutes past, she did what any good stage manager would do—she excused herself and placed a call to Carly's cell phone, which rolled to voicemail.

"Hi, Carly. This is Lauren Prescott, stage manager for *Starry Nights*. Checking in on your estimated time of arrival, as we're now at thirteen past our go time. Please check in with me when you receive this voicemail, so I know when to expect you. See you soon."

She clicked off the call and headed back to her seat where she looked to Ethan, who was seated to her left. "Why don't we get started and Ms. Daniel can join us when she arrives," Lauren said quietly to Ethan.

While it was ultimately Ethan's call, it was Lauren's job to make suggestions that would keep rehearsal running in a timely manner, and putting any more of their allotted time on hold for a late actress was not in the production's best interest. Ethan nodded his agreement and opened rehearsal. He introduced himself and allowed the cast of eight, well, seven in its current state, to introduce themselves. When they got around the table to Evelyn Tate, the other lead actress in the play, the door to the rehearsal room opened with a noticeable bang and none other than Carly Daniel appeared. She wore distressed jeans, heels, a V-neck white T-shirt with a short floral kimono top hanging open, all accentuated with a long silver necklace. She was gorgeous, a vision straight out of a magazine. Her blond hair fell several inches past her shoulders, and she had large sunglasses perched on her head. In her right hand, she carried an oversized iced coffee, halfway consumed. Everyone swiveled in awe. While it wasn't Lauren's first choice to pause the introductions for a late arrival, it seemed Carly had the entire room's attention regardless, which meant Lauren needed to pivot from her plan of plowing forward.

She turned to the table. "Ladies, and gentleman, Carly Daniel. Thank you for joining—" But Lauren didn't get to finish her sentence because the cast burst into happy applause, and Carly did a makeshift curtsy, extending the iced coffee outward as she lowered her body.

The applause seemed to encourage her, and she beamed as if greeting her adoring public. "Hi, everyone. I'm Carly, and I'm so thrilled to be here, to meet each one of you and make this the best experience possible." Most of the room beamed right back at her, honored to be in her sunshiney presence, and nodded in welcoming agreement. All but one, that was. Evelyn Tate sat tight-lipped and sour, as if waiting for the moment to pass.

The little late ball of sunshine that was Carly Daniel was going to be a force to wrangle. Lauren could already tell. People clearly adored and responded to Carly, and she was used to that kind of lavish attention. In a production like this one, where ensemble work was so important, Carly might not blend. Something to take note of. Plus, Lauren had done her research since taking the job. The headlines hadn't been forgiving. "Carly Daniel Delays Production," "Studio and

Director Argue Over the Costly Decision of Daniel," and her personal favorite, "Carly Daniel Billed 10K in Hotel Room Party Fiasco." What in the world had gone on in that hotel room that had cost ten thousand dollars? One could only guess, as the article didn't say. Lauren had let her imagination run wild, cringing at each possible scenario.

Carly, who was more beautiful than should have been allowed, turned to Ethan and Lauren with a hand over her heart. "I am so sorry I'm a few late. Crazy morning for me."

"No problem," Ethan said. "You're here now and we can roll."

Lauren forced a smile. If Carly knew she was running late for rehearsal, why had she clearly made a coffee stop? Those ice cubes were fresh. Instead of belaboring that point in her brain, she shook it off. At this early a juncture, she decided not to go there. Lauren would give Carly the same benefit of the doubt she gave everyone, and she at least had the courtesy to apologize with a smile. Maybe it had all been a fluke. A miscommunication of their start time.

"Am I here?" Carly asked, pointing at an empty chair next to Evelyn, the one actor at the table who still looked like she tasted something unpleasant. That said something, and Lauren mentally clocked the disdain.

"Yes, that's you," Lauren said. Carly slipped into her chair and waved at Kirby Bonner, the young actress seated across from Carly, who was clearly starstruck. Carly put out a friendly vibe, at least. "We were in the midst of introductions when you arrived."

"Oh. Sorry," Carly whispered loudly and bowed her head as if to make herself invisible. The room laughed. Lauren didn't.

"Evelyn, please continue," Lauren said, holding out her hand with an encouraging smile.

"I was wrapping up anyway," Evelyn said. "I'm thrilled to be working with Ethan, as I have nothing but the highest respect for his work, and look forward to a great run with all of you." She held up the script. "I think this play is an important one. It's about the love between two women, and we need to see more of that in live theater. If we do this thing right, it's going to touch a lot of people."

That comment resonated with Lauren. She'd read the play upward of ten times at this point and adored it. It was the story of Ashley and Mandy, who experienced a sliding doors moment. Down one path, they found themselves stranded together overnight at an airport when their flight was canceled. They argued, got to know each other, stargazed until the wee hours of the morning, and eventually, over time in the coming weeks, fell deeply in love. The other path, played out in act 2, had Mandy making the flight, and Ashley missing it. Their lives took separate, more tumultuous turns. In the end, they passed each other in a grocery store and took a long searching look back, feeling something unspoken tugging at them. The final scene had them abandoning their carts and taking a step toward the other, ending the play on the question, is fate real? It was a hopeful ending, especially having seen how fantastic the two were together in act 1, once they got past their differences.

Lauren broke out in goose bumps each time she read it. She couldn't wait for Ethan to work his magic, along with Evelyn and Carly, of course. Carly, who would play Ashley, a blond knockout, and Evelyn, who would play Mandy, a redheaded everygirl, made a great physical pairing when she saw them seated next to each other, a perfect looking couple. Once the first read-through began, Lauren clicked the stopwatch and sat back to listen in eager anticipation of hearing the play come to life. It was good, but at the same time, she felt like something wasn't quite…there.

Probably just because this was the first time they'd heard the words, out loud. Together. The character of Ashley was a driven, focused hedge fund manager. In the read, Carly tackled those characteristics with gusto. Evelyn played the character of Mandy, a kindergarten teacher who understood the value of stopping to smell the roses and appreciating the little things. Lauren missed the lighthearted portions of Evelyn's reading. Carly's Ashley was real, raw, and identifiable. But Evelyn brought an edge to Mandy that kept her from feeling relatable. While it wasn't at all Lauren's job to worry about those kinds of things, she loved the play so much that she'd taken a silent interest. She thought about how she would have delivered those lines, identifying moments of comedy for Mandy that were entirely missed or glossed over in the read. Luckily, she had a feeling Ethan would be working on eliminating some of Evelyn's bite in the coming weeks. He'd been furiously scribbling notes as they'd read, stealing glances at the two of them. The six other members of the cast had tracks in which they would play all the other roles in the show. Some would take on as many as seven different characters before the journey was done. This was going to be a ride.

On their first official break, Carly stopped by Lauren's chair. "You're Lauren, right? From the voicemail."

Lauren stood and offered her hand. "Yes, I'll be the PSM for the production. Nice to officially meet you." She was caught off guard by the vibrancy of blue in Carly's wide Disney princess–like eyes once they were up close for the first time.

"Likewise." Carly quirked an eyebrow. "PSM? Sorry, you may have to help me out with the theater lingo. I'm still stuck in camera speak. I have very little experience with stage work." She closed her eyes. "That's not even true. I have zero experience."

Aha. She was *that* green when it came to live theater. "Not a problem. Stands for production stage manager. Think of me as head stage manager, and Trip is my number two." She pointed at Trip, who poured himself a cup of coffee. "I'll be organizing and helping Ethan implement a rehearsal strategy. I'll also be in charge of maintaining the show once he moves on after rehearsal. I also do a myriad of other things. For example, if you ever need help with your lines, let me know. We can set up a session."

"You have a lot going on."

"I do, but I'm no stranger to the job."

Carly pointed at her and smiled, exposing how her whole face lit up when she did. "Above all other stage managers. Got it. Anyway, sorry for that late entrance. I'll try and be better." She held up a finger. "Scratch that. I *will* be."

Lauren liked those words a lot, because they were not off to a great start. At the same time, she wasn't sure Carly understood the importance. "Well, that's good to hear. I know Ethan is thrilled to have you on board."

Carly nodded. "I'm grateful to be here. Trust me. I needed this." Lauren took a moment because Carly's beauty had *not* been exaggerated. She could see why Hollywood put up with her wilder ways for so long. Not to mention the fact that she was also crazy talented. A one-two punch that couldn't be argued. "You okay?" Carly asked.

"Me?" Lauren shook herself out of it, embarrassed and attempting to recover. "Very much so. Yeah. Why?"

"You seemed to lose your focus."

"Oh no. Just always thinking two steps ahead. Another part of being a stage manager." It was the lamest answer, but she couldn't very well tell Carly that she was stunned silent by how pretty she was. Not really the message she wanted to send in the moment to a colleague in her workplace.

"Anything I can do to help?" Carly also had a really nice tan going that made her skin look incredibly smooth. Likely very soft. Okay, what the hell was she doing? Lauren didn't recognize herself or her own ridiculous behavior. She never crushed. And she still wasn't, damn it. That's not what this was.

"No. We only have seven minutes left on that break."

"Good call." She touched Lauren on the wrist as she passed, which caught Lauren off guard. She stared at Carly's hand, briefly on her arm. "I'll let you enjoy it then. Really nice to meet you." Then Carly Daniel and what was left of her irresponsible iced coffee glided through the room, speaking with the other members of the cast, laughing with them, and remaining a palpable presence.

She was a force, that was for sure. Lauren just hadn't yet categorized what kind: good, evil, or somewhere in between. Regardless, the temperature in the space had changed noticeably when Carly arrived, and Lauren had a feeling that working on *Starry Nights* was going to be a handful. Nothing she was wasn't up for, however. She'd better buckle up.

❖

Good God. That stage manager, Lauren, didn't mess around. That's what Carly had come to understand in just the few days she'd known her. When she'd arrived for their third rehearsal six minutes late, only six minutes, Lauren had pulled her aside and felt the need to point *that* out, too. How important were six minutes in the scheme of life? That was actually a great step in the right direction. Why had Lauren not noticed that? The progress. The day before she'd been twelve.

"We need to talk about your tardiness," Lauren had said calmly to Carly during a quiet moment the day after that. "This is the third time in three days. It's eating into our rehearsal time, and I need you to make more of an effort to be here before we begin. Shoot for fifteen minutes early, maybe? And if there's anything I can do to help the process, please tell me. That's what I'm here for."

"Are you offering to wake me up in the morning, Lauren?" She'd said it playfully, because let's be honest, Lauren was really cute, a little too serious, and Carly was a harmless flirt. The comment fell flat. Ouch. Not that kind of environment, apparently. A shame, too. Lauren was probably very straight, and likely taken. She was a looker with all that thick brown hair paired with a really pretty pair of green eyes, or were they hazel? No, definitely green.

Lauren blinked patiently. "If that's what you need, I will happily be your wake-up call. I'm serious about making sure we're able to begin on time each day."

For the love of a good martini! She'd been only six minutes late. Since when did that constitute a crisis? Their play would still come together. In fact, she'd been impressed with herself lately when it came to focus and responsibility. She'd been *hours* late for film shoots and heard less about it. People tended to give you whatever you wanted when your name was on the poster. The theater world, she was finding, was way less forgiving and uptight as hell. She swallowed her reaction, however, remembering Alika's advice to be good.

"Got it, coach. I'll work on punching the clock more to your liking, so you don't have to worry about me so much. I mean, unless you *want* to."

Lauren smiled. If the coach nickname had rubbed her wrong, Carly never would have known. Lauren-the-organized-beauty was a puzzle, never giving away too much of what she was feeling. It made Carly want to find out and unwrap that mystery one piece at a time. There was a real girl underneath all of the business, and maybe one day, she'd get to meet her.

An hour later and here Carly sat, waiting for notes from Ethan Moore on what was turning out to be a more complicated character than she'd ever anticipated.

Ethan met her gaze with a thoughtful one of his own. "Carly, I love the frustrated sink to the floor, but can we try it again, the moment where Ashley notices Mandy nearby just after?"

Carly nodded at Ethan and reset herself in the scene. "Yeah, of course. As in a fleeting glance, or something more meaningful?"

"Let Ashley's stare linger a moment before she recesses into her thoughts again. Notice something about Mandy. You choose what that is. Oh, and I love the action of you blowing your hair off your forehead. You did it earlier."

"Great. I'll keep it." She studied Evelyn, who sat waiting on the floor of the faux airport for them to pick up again. Evelyn, Carly had decided, was a decent enough actress, but certainly not very giving within their scene work. Carly didn't have a lot to play off emotionally. They were supposed to be constructing this deep, destined-to-be relationship a little at a time, but with Evelyn as her counterpart, they were falling flat. Surely Ethan felt that. Hopefully, they still had time.

This whole process was a trip. Carly had never been allotted this much rehearsal on any one project or character. With screen work, there was rehearsal, sure, but it was short, and then you shot the scene, moved forward to the next, and never looked back. The rehearsal process for the play, however, came with a never before experienced intensity for her. It blew Carly's mind how deep they were going with each nuanced moment, how much time they invested in just two minutes of the play. The technique allowed her to sink her teeth into this role like she'd never done before. The jury was still out on whether this had been a good move, career-wise, but on the plus side, she was learning a lot from working with Ethan Moore. He damn well knew his stuff. They'd gone over objectives, tactics, line-by-line intentions, all of it, and they still had over three quarters of the play ahead of them. Mind-boggling.

"You good, Evelyn?" Carly asked before beginning. Evelyn nodded politely and looked away as if choosing not to engage further. "Before we start, do you need anything more from me in the scene? Or less, for that matter? I'm open."

"I'm good," Evelyn said coolly.

Inside, Carly sighed. The two of them definitely had different processes. Carly liked finding the moments in the rehearsal room, taking a more organic approach. Evelyn showed up with every choice already made in advance. What you saw on the first run-through of the day with Evelyn was often the same set of choices she ended with. Didn't allow for a ton of collaboration.

As Carly reset herself for another run of the scene, she stole a glance at Lauren Prescott, who sat at the table next to Ethan, complete with her clipboard and series of file folders, all neatly laid out. She was studiously scribbling something in her production book. From the moment they'd first met, she'd noticed Lauren. She came with a quality that was hard to look away from. She carried herself with confidence, and while she seemed friendly, there was also a removed quality that drove Carly nuts. She'd tried several times to break through that shell, to only fleeting success.

"Lauren?" she'd asked on their last break of the day, because she was apparently five years old and simply couldn't seem to leave it alone.

"Yep. What can I do for you?"

She rested her chin in her hand, hoping Lauren would make eye contact. "How many tickles do you think it takes to make an octopus laugh? I'm just curious. I've been dying to figure it out. Up all night. It's a problem." She flashed what she hoped was a killer smile.

Lauren looked up from her laptop with confusion in her green eyes that quickly dissolved into what could best be described as slight amusement. Not a full-on smile, no, but the start of one. "I don't know, Carly. Why don't you tell me how many? I have a feeling you know."

"Ten, Lauren. *Ten tickles* to make an octopus laugh. Can you imagine?"

Lauren shook her head and laughed silently, returning to the solace of her production book. "I can't believe you just said that," she murmured. Her dark hair, when Carly studied its length, fell just above her breasts, not that she knew much about them. The clothes Lauren wore to work, while professional enough, didn't offer too many glimpses of the body beneath, which she had a feeling was being undersold.

"Oh, but I did. I did say it. And there's more where that came from. I'll hit you up tomorrow."

"If you're on time, I'll consider it," Lauren said casually, this time not glancing up from her work.

"Now you're just tempting me."

"I'm entirely fine with that."

Carly noticed that Lauren didn't socialize with the cast much during their downtime. She maintained a professional distance, which made sense given how she was not only the person who kept them moving forward but, in a way, the disciplinarian as well. Kind of like their very put together camp counselor.

Carly stole another glance. The really, really hot kind you made out with before summer ended.

CHAPTER THREE

O ver the course of the next week, several things became clear to Lauren. Number one: Carly Daniel was single-handedly breathing life into each scene without much help from Evelyn Tate, who was still holding back, and turning in a stiff interpretation of Mandy. Number two: Carly Daniel was proving herself to be a total thorn in Lauren's side. She was chronically late and had twice now organized the cast into a late-night gathering at the bar down the street, leaving them all slower and hungover the next day. She hadn't memorized any of her lines and didn't seem to care about simple requests like returning a prop to the prop table when not in use. Number three: she was, conversely, always upbeat, positive, and actually kind of fun to have around. Sigh. Carly Daniel was an interesting problem to have.

"Hey, Lauren?"

"Yep?" Lauren said, looking up from her production binder to see Carly standing next to her with an anticipatory grin. She had some slight blocking corrections to add to her notes, based on the changes Ethan had made at that day's rehearsal, and hadn't even heard her approach.

Carly slid a strand of hair behind her ear and flashed the dimple that resided in her right cheek. "I was wondering if you wanted to come out with us tonight? Everyone's going to meet at Put Upon Pete's for mango martinis. My treat."

Oh, man, she hated having to shoot people down, but that outing wasn't in her best interest. She would celebrate with everyone at the closing party. "Very nice of you, but I have to decline." The reply was automatic. There was probably a good *Dateline* waiting for her and a warm bowl of popcorn. She looked back down at her binder, prepared to jump back into work.

"Why?"

She glanced back up at Carly. Lauren hadn't been prepared for the question. Did she have to explain herself, include the *Dateline* bit? She stared at Carly, who blinked back at her with big, sad blue eyes. Those eyes were incredibly hard to argue with. It became apparent that this woman wasn't moving from her spot until Lauren gave her more.

"It's been a long week. I need to decompress."

Carly nodded. "But it's Saturday. No rehearsal tomorrow. Do it. Come be bad with us."

She sighed. "I'm not sure it's always the best idea to fraternize with the cast. It's better for a stage manager to keep a professional distance when possible."

"But it's not possible, because your lead wants to see you mingle in a really bad way." Carly knelt next to Lauren, which showcased the dip of cleavage down the front of her aqua-blue ribbed tunic. Well, that was certainly…attention getting. She quickly glanced away out of respect, but her eyes apparently did what they wanted and slowly drifted back. She was going to hell for this. She'd never objectified an actor before. She had more control than that! What was happening? "So, what do you say?" Carly asked.

Lauren blinked and opened her mouth to try to answer. Didn't go so well.

"What's happening right now?" Carly furrowed her brow and followed Lauren's gaze, glanced down at her shirt, then slowly back to Lauren with eyebrows raised and an intrigued look on her face. Nope, now it was amusement. "Okay. Okay," she said quietly, like the cat who'd gleefully found the stash of catnip. "I see."

"What?" Lauren asked, doing her best to play it off. "I don't think there's anything to see."

"No?" Carly asked.

Lauren shook her head. Her face felt hot, and she reached for her water bottle, pretending to study the group in conversation across the room from her table. Yep, something important was clearly going on over there that needed her attention. She needed to make sure all was well. There could be a fist-fight at any moment. Inside, she berated herself for being highly unprofessional, and weak to boot. No wine gulping for her later. She was grounded from the gulp.

"Martinis, then?" Carly asked, standing again.

Lauren glanced back at Carly as if she was an afterthought. "Yeah, I guess I could stop by Pete's." What in the world had she just said? Damn it. Yet there had been no other choice but to give Carly what she wanted, or she'd never go away. In that moment, Lauren was so mortified by her own behavior that she desperately needed Carly to walk away and give her a moment to breathe and experience the unrelenting self-recrimination in peace. Luckily, she did just that.

Tops of tan breasts were hard to scrub from one's brain, apparently. Lauren knew firsthand. The fact that Carly had likely come by them by sunbathing topless was an image she probably shouldn't imagine. Yet she damn well did, to traitorous response from her body. She spent the rest of rehearsal trying to stop that image from infiltrating her brain. Failure struck. Her mouth was chronically dry, and her temperature remained warm. Lauren focused on her job as best she could, but one thing was clear. Carly affected her and not always for the good. She also hadn't had sex in over seventeen months, so maybe that played in to things a bit. Not like she was counting or anything.

Once everyone had left for the day, Lauren and Trip put the room back together, moving bits of stand-in rehearsal scenery back to their assigned spots in the room. Though the rehearsal studio belonged entirely to The McAllister, so no production except for *Starry Nights* would use it, it was important to keep the room in top condition for when they arrived back to work on Monday. "Hey, I've got the rehearsal report pretty much ready to send. Can you update our end times and projected daily for Monday?"

"On it," Trip said. "You going to Pete's? Carly's throwing another bash. Say yes. She's a lot of fun."

"That's what TMZ says."

"Don't be uptight, Lala. You can have fun, too. There's no law. I checked."

She sighed. "Fine. Nine tonight, right?" She was trying to come up with some way to get out of this thing. Court TV was back, and they likely had a killer to put on the witness stand. She wouldn't want to miss crucial testimony from a killer. She mentally winced at her own line of thinking. God, she'd become boring. A lonely little shut-in.

"She says nine, but no one will be there until ten."

"Ten? Is she trying to kill me?" she squeaked. "I'm a grandmotherly thing."

"You're thirty-one, Lala, and no one's nanny. Carly Daniel is a girl who knows how to turn it up, and you could use a little of that in your life." He sat on top of the table and did the gesture he did with his hands that said she had to hear this. "You should have been there Friday night. She literally danced on the bar. It was all over Instagram, and then Perez Hilton jumped on the bandwagon and ran a story with the photos. Not your typical McAllister kind of coverage."

"Wait. She danced on the bar at Put Upon Pete's?" Lauren wasn't sure she'd ever seen anyone dance on the bar at Pete's. "It's not really that type of place."

"It is now. Lala, you should have seen it. She had half our people up there with her in thirty seconds flat. Everyone was in sync and working it. I felt like I'd stumbled upon the middle of a performance of *Rent*. It was epic."

"Sounds epic," Lauren said blandly. Inside, she scoffed. She knew how to have fun, but it had been a while since she'd kept show-people hours. She turned in when the theater folk headed out because she was Lauren. Maybe she missed it a little bit, though. The old days. She could admit that.

When Lauren arrived at Pete's at precisely ten, she found Carly and Kirby, who played Ashley's assistant in the show, among other roles, doing a pink colored shot at the bar. The rest of the group populated the small tables that dotted the main floor, an oasis in which drinks and pub food flowed. The lighting gave the place an overall red tint, and a variety of ball caps—each sporting the word *Pete* somehow worked into a slogan—dotted the walls. The other room was furnished with dartboards and pool tables under fluorescents. Five restored jukeboxes lined the back wall. Pete's was known for two things: drinks and billiards. Lauren happened to be better at one than the other.

Deep breath as she approached her colleagues. She relaxed, smiled, and left her metaphorical clipboard at the door. Hell, if she thought about it, she was supposed to be on a beach right now. Tonight, she planned to embrace that relaxation, unwind, and maybe even get the tiniest bit tipsy. Who knew? The night was young.

❖

"Did I mention that I love martini night?" Kirby enthused. Kirby Bonner was an up-and-comer who couldn't have been more than twenty-two, twenty-three at most and had the cutest little pixie cut. From the moment they'd met, she seemed to really look up to Carly, even after all the bad press. Maybe not the wisest role model choice, Carly thought, but she also understood that her celebrity did tend to attract people. "Let's do them every Saturday. God, I live for a good martini. Don't you? I'd love it if we made it a thing. Do you want to make it a thing?" She also liked to talk. A lot.

"We can totally make that happen," Carly said, accepting the mango martini from the bartender. Orange and beautiful and well earned. Carly touched her glass to Kirby's. With her brown hair and doe-like brown eyes, she would surely be cast as everyone's cheerful younger sister. At least for the next five years. Carly turned back to the group, and would you look at that? Her stomach muscles went tight, and she shimmied against the tingle that crept up her spine. Lauren Prescott had just walked in. "Well, well," she murmured to herself. *Dreams do come true.*

Kirby followed her gaze. "I feel like she gets on you a lot," Kirby said, surely trying to make it clear that Carly's enemies were hers. "Who cares if you missed the off-book deadline for the first three scenes. You're a professional. You're going to be fine on lines."

"Lauren? Nah, she's just doing her job."

"She should get who you are, though, you know?"

It was possible the same thought had occurred to Carly. Yet she could forgive Lauren for being so uptight and stuffy and hell-bent on following a clock. It was apparently what she was hired to do.

"I'm not always easy to wrangle," she told Kirby.

"My boyfriend says that about me. He's six three."

"Is he now? Amazing." Carly sipped her martini and let the nearly too loud music wash over her. Saturdays were for letting off steam, and that was exactly what she planned to do, especially with a day off tomorrow. She was already a drink in and her muscles felt a little looser. She inched her way slowly to that point of tipsy with each new sip. God, she loved the gradual feeling of that unravel. She wasn't a fan of drunk, but tipsy she could do. "Be back soon," she told Kirby and headed across the bar, following the magnetic pull that wouldn't seem to let up.

"You came," she said to Lauren when she arrived at her table near the front of the bar. "I honestly wasn't sure you would."

Lauren gasped and smiled. "Why? Because you think I'm uptight?"

"No. Because I know you are." She tossed in a wink for good measure.

"Don't be so sure you know everything."

"I'll work hard," Carly said. "Let me buy you a martini. Please. I've never seen you outside that rehearsal room, so this warrants a celebration. Deal?"

"I'm in." Carly stole an extra few seconds to absorb this new version of Lauren. Her dark hair was down and she'd added a subtle curl to it which came off as fucking glamorous. Carly loved it. Lauren wore jeans and a white cold shoulder blouse. Yeah, those bare shoulders were really doing Carly in. Lauren was hot with her shoulders covered, but this just seemed cruel. The straitlaced thing only fueled that fire.

"One martini for my stage manager," Carly said five minutes later, depositing the drink next to Lauren. She picked up her own martini and offered a toast. "To a kick-ass show."

Lauren touched her martini glass to Carly's. "I will sincerely second that. As soon as you meet your off-book deadlines." She added a wink.

"Is it really that big a deal?"

Lauren stared her straight in the eye. "It really, really is."

"For you? I will put in the effort."

"It should really be for you, but I'll take it." Lauren passed her an amazing smile, and that made everything better.

The music in the bar portion of Pete's was loud, but by now Carly's ears had acclimated. Yes, they had to talk louder than usual to hear each other, but that was part of the fun of being out and about. God, she felt like dancing, but one-on-one time with Lauren won out.

"Do you live near here?" Carly asked. It wasn't small talk. She wanted to know more about Lauren, and geography seemed like a good place to start.

She nodded. "Only a couple of miles north. Easy commute to the theater, which is nice, given I have to be there at odd hours."

"I feel like your job is never ending. You're there before all of us, and you leave after we do."

Lauren sipped her drink, which, okay, was off-the-charts sexy to watch, and considered the statement. "There are definitely a lot of responsibilities that fall into my lap, and they take time."

"Then you have Hollywood assholes like me, who show up and ruin your life."

That one apparently hit home and pulled a laugh. Carly liked Lauren's unabashed smile and wanted to do more to inspire it. "God, it's rough."

There was a pause as they grinned at each other. The moment felt...tentative. Carly wasn't a fan of those and decided to shatter the hell out of it.

"If you think I'm attractive, blink twice."

"I don't have to. Everyone thinks you're attractive. It's ordained and universally agreed upon." Lauren set down her martini like it was a period at the end of her sentence.

"Everyone is not you. I happen to think you're beautiful, and the alcohol gave me the courage to say so outright. Look at me go."

Lauren laughed, and then laughed some more.

Carly watched, mystified. "What? I don't see why that's funny." But because Lauren was laughing, she was now, too. "Tell me. I want to be in on the joke."

"It's bullshit." The laughter ebbed slowly, as Lauren sat back in her chair. "Since when do you need alcohol to say what's on your mind? I've never met anyone as confident as you are. You own every room you walk into and know it. Sometimes on purpose, other times, I think it just happens."

Carly paused and took a moment to sip her drink. Lauren watched her do it, making Carly hyperaware of the things she was feeling. Correction. *Craving.* "That's fair. Is it a turnoff? You can be honest."

"Not entirely." She suspected the three-quarters of her martini Lauren had consumed made that admission possible. Daytime Lauren wouldn't have said that in a million years. "Another drink?"

"You're having a second?" Carly raised an eyebrow. "This is a downright scandal. That's what this is."

Lauren met her gaze evenly, almost in challenge. It inspired an enjoyable shiver. "Uber is real, and I'd like more. Is that a bad thing? I can go."

Carly stood. "It's the best fucking thing I've ever heard. In fact, allow me. Don't move."

When she returned to the table, she found one of the scenery people sitting next to Lauren. One of the ones she'd seen painting in the theater. She forgot what they were called. The woman, who sported a dark blond ponytail, turned when Carly sat down.

Lauren gestured to the woman. "Tinsley Worth, meet Carly Daniel. Tinsley is our assistant set designer."

"Very cool to meet you," Carly said, taking her hand.

"Likewise. I'm a fan. Loved you in *Race the Night*," Tinsley said, but Carly was unable to tell if that was true because Tinsley turned her attention immediately back to Lauren, and began chattering away as if they were alone in the world. It took only two minutes for Carly to understand that this Tinsley girl had a crush, which she totally identified with, but Carly made three and wasn't the type to nip at heels.

"You're just always so great with people," Tinsley gushed to Lauren. "I've always thought so. And this shirt looks great on you. Really."

Lauren glanced down. "Just trying to blend."

"It's working. Wait. No. I mean, you never blend, but—"

Lauren touched Tinsley's arm to steady her. "I translate you."

Yep. There was a definite adoration vibe happening. Bummed to have lost the moment, Carly slid the mango martini across the table to Lauren and headed off in search of fun because the night was too short to waste. She found Trip and TJ, who played the gate agent who informed the main characters that they missed their flight. She'd already decided TJ was good people. The two were in the billiards section of the bar, contemplating a game of pool.

"You want in?" TJ asked her.

"I'm not from around these parts, you know," she told them, batting her eyelashes like a naïve little lady. She wasn't half bad at pool, though, and was prepared to flaunt the hell out of that. She was competitive to a fault.

"All right," TJ said. "You and me versus Trip and—"

"Me."

She turned to see Kirby sidle up next to Trip. The two high-fived and exploded their hands.

Carly put her hands on her hips. "Well, this should be interesting."

It wasn't, though. She and TJ cleared the table on the other duo in under six minutes. Losers bought drinks, and to slow her roll so the night would last, Carly opted for a dressed Dos Equis she could sip slowly.

"Who's taking us on next?" TJ asked. "Where are the brave souls? Step right up. That's right."

"I'm out," Kirby said. "Gotta call Joe. He waits up to say good night. He's a doll."

"I'll partner with Trip," a voice from behind said. Carly turned, and her beer went still on the way to her lips. Lauren.

Trip walked to her and offered a high five. "All right, Lala. You and me. Let's do this."

"Lauren, do you know the rules?" Carly asked with a small smile. "I can explain them."

"I was hoping to figure them out as I went," she said with a hopeful wince. "Think that might work?"

Carly laughed. "Let's give it a try and see."

But she was a damn liar, because after just sixty seconds she'd made quick work of three-fourths of the table.

Carly blinked as Lauren sank another, like the secret pro she apparently was. "What in hell?"

Lauren straightened and admired the results of her own shot before raising her gaze to Carly. "Wow. It turns out I'm a quick study."

Trip laughed. He, of course, would know all about Lauren's prowess with a cue. "I think the shark just got out-sharked." Lauren shrugged at Carly and touched her glass to Trip's in reverence. Carly spent the next few moments with her jaw on the floor as Lauren took them to school.

The end result? Carly had to buy Lauren another drink. Not that awful a prospect. When she delivered it, she caught the soft scent of her perfume. Hints of vanilla and maybe lavender. Subtle, but very effective.

"I'd love a rematch," Carly said. "Now that I know who I'm dealing with, I'll be sure to focus fully."

"Oh, you weren't before?" Lauren asked in a teasing voice. "Because it looked like you were trying extra hard. It was sweet."

The drinks were working. Lauren had relaxed, stepped away from her always-put-together demeanor, and was just…a person. A really witty one, too. It had Carly on a high, and she wanted to soak up every minute until the guard went back up again. What was it about Lauren that had her all hot, bothered, intrigued, and willing to take her clothes off? Part of the fun was not knowing.

"If you don't want to go again, we don't have to," Carly said with a grin. She turned to TJ. "We'll just chalk it up to a fluke." He nodded and touched his longneck to hers. "Everyone gets lucky once in a blue moon."

Lauren also turned to TJ. "Rack 'em."

And it was on.

As "Cherry Pie" pulsed over the speakers, Lauren studied the table from one angle, then another, before sinking three balls in a row. Carly and TJ rallied, Trip barely made a difference, but it was Lauren who once again owned the table. While Carly had paid more attention to her own shots this go-round, thought them through, and taken her time, that hadn't been the reason she'd asked for a second round. No, she'd wanted to watch Lauren, who was clearly in her element. She was something to behold, too. Her eyes shone bright when she spotted her shot and then darkened as she concentrated. Her lips, shiny with gloss, parted slightly just before she delivered her shot, and *sigh*, the cleavage she glimpsed each and every time Lauren leaned over the table… *Do not get me started.* As competitive as she was, she'd agree to lose a thousand times over to have that multifaceted sense-inspiring experience again and again.

"So, what's your secret?" she asked Lauren after the second trouncing. "Do you have a secret pool hall below the theater that you sneak away to and practice through the night?"

Lauren met her gaze with a smug smile. "If I told you my secret, then you wouldn't sit up and think all night about what it could be." She took a delicate sip from her martini that did something wonderfully uncomfortable to Carly's midsection. The skin of Lauren's shoulder called out to her, and she noticed how ridiculously smooth it was. She wanted to run her forefinger across the curve and follow up with her tongue. Yeah, it was that kind of night.

"Then the least you can do is teach me how to break like you do." Lauren straightened. "I can help if you want."

Carly reached behind Lauren and grabbed a cue, inhaling the vanilla lavender scent once again. That perfume flirted with her all on its own. Who'd invented this stuff? She met Lauren's gaze. "Oh, I want."

Lauren followed her to an empty table and racked the balls. "Secret number one. Make sure the rack is tight." Carly blinked and held her tongue, but the insinuation was not lost on Lauren, who blushed. She made a rewind gesture. "Taking that back. Just heard how that sounds."

"You don't have to on my account," Carly said with a playful wink and joined Lauren on her side of the table. She made it a point to lose the shenanigans for the rest of her lesson. "What's step one?"

"You want to make sure the cue ball remains in the center of the table." She placed it on the felt and pointed to the corner pocket. "If it breaks off and bounces back over here? You're in bad shape."

"And I won't be able to clean the table like you just did, which is now all I want to do in life. Well, almost."

Lauren inhaled and blinked. She seemed to decide to plow forward. "Exactly. It's all about that initial positioning after the break."

Carly studied Lauren in the midst of their lesson. "And how do I make sure it remains centrally located?"

"Easy. You have to connect with the ball in front by tapping the cue ball right *here*." Lauren pointed at a spot on the cue ball just above the center point. "If your aim is off, you're going to have a rogue cue ball and probably miss an easy side pocket sink. Why don't you give it a try?" Lauren cleared the area.

"All right." With cue in hand, Carly lowered her body and surveyed the table, focusing on what Lauren told her was key: the sweet spot on the cue ball. "Like this? Am I doing it right, Ms. Shark?"

"I prefer Madame. But, oh…" Lauren laughed quietly. "Your stance is off."

Carly straightened. "What do you mean? I've always been told I have a great stance."

"Because they're probably looking at your ass."

"Were you?" Carly asked playfully. Okay, she was also half serious because the combination of alcohol, the perfume, and the way Lauren had cut loose tonight had her in the friendly land of lust. She loved it in Lust Land, where she could frolic with anticipation, hope, and longing. God, if only Lauren would join her there, they could have a little fun while she was in town. Ride a few of the rides.

"Checking out your ass?" Lauren paused before answering, meeting Carly's gaze. A ball of tension coiled tight and wonderful in Carly's stomach, and she felt the slightest tingle between her legs. "Unfortunately, no. My mind was on the break shot." She fluttered her eyelashes, which told Carly she left room for fibbing. "Now, about that stance." Carly, always one to help, took up the position once again. "See your back arm?" Lauren asked. "It's angled wrong, and it's screwing up your shot line. Here."

And before Carly could scream *Hot damn!* Lauren's body was at her back and Lauren's arms came around hers. "Well, hello," she said to Lauren quietly.

"Hi," Lauren said back. "Pay attention."

"Trust me. I'm riveted."

Lauren let that one go, too. "Level this back arm out so you can draw a perfect line between the cue ball and the front ball. That red one there, see?"

Carly nodded but was in no rush to take the shot, not with Lauren this close, turning Carly the hell on with the warmth from her body. She hadn't been wrong about Lauren having a killer body. She could see it in her mind's eye, the way it pressed against hers. The tingle from earlier was now a full-on throb, and she relished it.

"Ready?" Lauren asked quietly in her ear. Her breath tickled wonderfully.

"Ready," Carly said. Lauren stepped back and allowed Carly to take the shot, which in the end came off perfectly. She nailed the front ball, sank another in the side pocket, and watched as the cue ball hung in the center of the table, just like Lauren had promised it would.

"Well, now who's a shark?" Lauren asked, as Carly tossed her hands in the air and held them there. The room broke into applause, and that's when Carly realized that the crowd had nearly tripled in size, and all eyes were on her…in addition to five or six cell phones. That meant someone had likely tweeted or Instagrammed her location. It happened often, actually. She smiled and nodded to their onlookers as she passed by to retrieve her drink. She remained hyperaware of Lauren's location in the room, however. She sipped slowly, posed for a few photos, signed the back of a guy's jean jacket, and watched as Lauren seemed to grow more and more unsteady. Carly got the feeling that she didn't go out much, and maybe the night had gotten away from her. She was using the backs of chairs to maneuver the space, and that was Carly's signal to check in and make sure she was okay.

She touched Lauren's shoulder. "Hey, you. Are you a little drunk right now? Because you're looking a little unsteady."

"No," Lauren shouted over the music and grinned. Totally was.

"Okay," Carly said with what was probably a disbelieving smile.

"I'm a *lot* drunk right now." She followed that up with the most adorable laugh. "I need to get an Uber so I can…" She trailed off the way drunk people sometimes do and instead stared glassy-eyed at the grooves on the tall wooden table next to them.

"Tell you what. Why don't I take you home?"

Lauren blinked and raised a drunk eyebrow. "I'm not going home with you. You're not going home with me, I mean. Not that kind of thing. You're an actress, ma'am, and I haven't forgotten."

"And you're a stage manager. Ma'am," she added for good measure. "We have our jobs all sorted out, so let's get you home safe. I'm in good shape."

"Okay," Lauren said, her eyes now looking heavy. "Listen, I'm in no condition to argue, even though we probably would argue real, real good."

"Real, real?" Carly couldn't help but wonder if *argue* was a euphemism. She decided it was. "I have a feeling you're right."

Six minutes later, they were in an Uber on the way to Lauren's, where Carly would get her situated, then do the gentlewomanly thing and head back to the apartment the theater had rented for her.

"We have arrived," Lauren said. She stumbled out of the car. "I wonder if Rocky can make me another martini."

"Oh." A long pause. "Rocky is your…boyfriend?" Carly closed one eye as she awaited that little piece of unfortunate news. She imagined a muscle-bound ex-football player appearing on the front porch any moment, looking for his girlfriend. If sexy Lauren was taken, who was she going to have fun with while she was here?

"Rocky is not my boyfriend. He's tiny." She held her hand just slightly above the pavement. "He's complicated, means well, and is very snuggly. I miss him." Lauren sighed wistfully.

Aha. An undefined love interest who was apparently very small. This was complicated, indeed. Lauren was right.

"He's also a really good dog. Mostly."

Carly froze on her way up the walk. "He's a dog? Rocky is a dog?"

Lauren laughed. "Yeah. What did you think he was? A hamster? Hamsters are no Dolph Lundgren."

"You're going to have to explain that one later," Carly said, watching Lauren try three times to pull her keys from her bag. "Here. Let me do that."

"You are really nice tonight." Lauren leaned against the brick and stared at Carly, who felt Lauren's gaze boldly roam her body. It sent a flash of heat all over. "God, you're pretty, Carly Daniel. Just like the movies. No. More." A pause. "Maybe you should come in after all."

Damn it. Lauren might actually be into her, and because she was too drunk to decide, Carly couldn't do a damn thing about it. "I think I'll just get you in there safely and take off."

"Okay, if that's what you want. Is that what you want? You're free to say, you know."

Carly chuckled, just as the key turned in the door. She opened it for Lauren and stepped back. "If I went after what I wanted, this night would end very differently than it's about to. Not that you'll necessarily remember all of this conversation tomorrow."

"Right? The world is a little...spinny, which is the most fun word. Spinny." A pause as she marveled at the sound. "Spinny, spinny, spinny." Carly laughed. Lauren was cute and made her smile. "Thank you for seeing me home safely, Supergirl. I'm going to drink water and sleep, okay?"

"Sounds like a great idea to me. Maybe the spinning will stop."

Lauren walked past Carly into her home, paused, walked back out, and stared at her with those luminous green eyes. She didn't say a word.

"Lauren? You okay?"

She nodded, grabbed the material of Carly's shirt with one hand, and kissed her. Well, hello. Carly didn't have time to think, to stop Lauren, because her body had taken the lead and had elbowed wisdom in its boring face. It was a simple kiss, but Lauren's mouth was warm and wonderful, and she tasted a little like mango. Her tongue touched Carly's lower lip and made her shiver. When Lauren stepped back and steadied herself with an arm to the doorjamb, all Carly could do was blink and smile. Well, that was settled. Not straight. Lauren Prescott was one hundred percent *not straight*. This was big. This was a victory, but it also had to be over for tonight. Lauren was drunk. Not that she could articulate that at this point. Carly, on the other hand, reveled. She bit her lower lip and let her tongue run over the same spot Lauren's had, still tasting the sweetness from Lauren's lips.

Finally, when her language skills drifted back to her, she passed Lauren a soft smile. "You certainly know how to say good night to a girl."

Lauren grinned. "I just…wanted to. Oh, man. I'm going to regret that tomorrow, aren't I?"

Carly backed up down the walk a few steps, her lips still pleasantly buzzing. "I think this is when we wait and find out." She pointed at Lauren. "Drink some water. Pop a couple Advil, and I'll see you at rehearsal."

CHAPTER FOUR

What the hell had she done? That was the question of the day, and it played over and over in Lauren's brain from the second she opened her eyes the next morning. Her head throbbed like someone was beating a bass drum inside her skull, but she couldn't pay that any attention, because somehow she'd kissed Carly Daniel on the steps of her home, and if her memory served correctly, it had been really, really good.

"Lauren, are we going from act one, scene three, or are we starting at the top?"

She blinked, not at all thinking about a pair of full, kissable lips beneath hers that never should have been there. Trip was speaking to her. Had it been important? She had no clue because she was too busy reliving a kissing scene from a movie starring Carly Daniel, only it wasn't a movie. It was her own life. "I'm sorry. What?"

"Rehearsal setup? We go in half an hour, and I was double-checking where Ethan wanted to begin. Did you chat with him?"

"Oh. Yes, top of the show. Sorry."

"It's okay. You in there? You need a Red Bull or twelve?" He touched her shoulder lightly as he passed.

She laughed ruefully. "I'll take the twelve. Just a crazy weekend."

"Oh, right. The Carly thing. Wow."

She froze. How in the hell did Trip know about Carly? There was only one explanation, which of course she should have anticipated. Carly had told someone in the company, maybe multiple someones, forever tainting Lauren's stellar reputation as a professional in the field.

Stage managers didn't engage with actors currently in their shows. That was just basic.

Trembling slightly, she turned around and faced Trip as he arranged the rehearsal furniture for the top of act 1 to simulate gate nineteen at the airport. "It was a passing moment. That's all. I don't even know how it got to…that. It never should have."

"Oh, I know. But talk about attention, right? Otherworldly the way these things take off."

Lauren chuckled along with Trip, because she had no idea what that meant but didn't want to appear totally daft. But then, forget it, because she needed to know, and right the hell now, what he was referencing if she had any hope of squelching this thing early and fast. "What attention? I'm sorry. Slow today." Her heart thudded as she awaited what would surely be a catastrophic reply.

"On Instagram. The post that rando put up got a lot of play."

Lauren made a gesture as if to erase the board because she had an urgent need to understand what was happening, and it felt acutely like Trip had adopted another language entirely. "Can we start over? I think we're talking about different things. At least, I hope we are, for the good of all things sacred."

He squinted at her. "I'm talking about the Instagram post that went up Saturday night of you and Carly getting cozy over the pool table. The one where you were all up in her space, teaching her your break shot, looking like a total badass."

Her mind stuttered to catch up. She remembered putting her arms around Carly to teach her to break properly. It had been a little intoxicating. "How is that online?"

He stared at her like she should know this. "Cell phones were everywhere that night. One of her adoring fans snapped it, and it got shared about a million times."

"Right," Lauren said, squeezing the spot between her eyes.

Trip continued to talk as he prepped the set. "She's crazy famous, and people are clamoring to know who she's dating. She stays tight-lipped in the press about it."

"How do you know so much?"

"I collect gossip for a living, Lauren. You know me. Flip on an episode of *Access Hollywood* once in a while. *TMZ* can be fun."

"Gotcha," Lauren said, numbly. While learning that the ill-advised kiss wasn't public information provided Lauren a small measure of relief, the photo wasn't exactly fantastic news. That kind of cozy relationship with her lead actress wasn't the image she wanted out there. Her cast would see that, not to mention the wider world. "Can I see it?" She had an Instagram account but rarely opened it these days.

It took Trip only a few seconds to produce the image. "It's not... awful," he said, clearly doing his best to minimize the perceived fallout. "Actually, it's a really hot photo of the two of you. People will talk about it for a few days and then move on to something else."

She looked down at the photo on Trip's screen. She was crouched over Carly, their faces very close together, their bodies touching back to front. It looked like she was speaking quietly into Carly's ear. Carly was smiling. *Wonderful, Lauren.*

"They should fire me now," she said with a sigh and tossed the phone onto the table in front of her.

Trip abandoned his task and headed over. His hair seemed sympathetic, having lost its festive bounce, and that helped.

In favor of the larger issue, she shoved aside the *other things* that viewing the photo did to her, the tightening of her stomach muscles, the warmth that started at her hairline and moved rapidly down her body, making her fingers tingle and dance nervously. She'd never really had to deal with dancing fingers before.

She remembered the moment itself clearly, how Carly's blond hair had tickled Lauren's collarbone as she'd spoken quietly. She swallowed.

"Lauren, my noble leader, you're blushing profusely."

She glanced up. "Am not."

"And now you're telling outright lies, and it's me." He turned a chair backward and sat next to her as if in down-to-business mode. "Lala, you have a thing for Carly Daniel? You wouldn't be the first in this life, so it's not at all a surprising thing. Let me tell ya. She's a lesbian. You're a lesbian. Sometimes lesbians get together and do lesbian things."

"Please, Trip. I was drinking and trying to be...I don't know, fun?" She sighed. "Look where it got me. Definitely not a mistake I'll make again. I need to keep my distance. Decided."

"Stop it right now, or I'll hurl this chair through a window like Patti Lupone in a rage."

"Dramatic."

"When it comes to this? Yes. I loved that you came out with us. It's been a while since you've attended any kind of gathering outside of the ones that come with formal invitations, and you're not a nun. Yet."

Trip's pep talk fell flat, ineffective in the face of her own minor freak-out. Lauren blinked several times, waiting for her emotions to settle. Any moment now. When they did, she would take full grip of the reins, and conquer this situation the way she did all others. She was type A for a reason, damn it.

Because she didn't respond, Trip punched her in the arm. Hard.

"Ow," she said, rubbing the spot. "Why are you beating on me, you lunatic?"

"Because you need to snap out of it. We have a rehearsal to get to, and we can't do it without you." A pause. "Our resident Casanova pool shark."

She gasped in outrage as Trip bounded away. His upbeat, lighthearted demeanor helped alleviate some of her stress. As did his hair.

It didn't last long.

Ten a.m. came, and with it, the entire cast gathered. Well, except for one. Carly was MIA again, and this time Ethan seemed to truly take notice. "Why are we waiting on her again?" Ethan asked Lauren with an unusual bite in his tone. Even he was growing weary, which said something.

"I'll call," she said, offering him an apologetic glance. Not that this was her fault, but stage management often took the brunt of the disdain for rehearsal not going according to plan. That came with the gig. Carly didn't pick up her first call, or her second, nor her third either. It was now forty minutes into rehearsal, and her understudy, Nia, had taken over to keep them from losing any more valuable time.

"Shall I go bang on her door?" Trip whispered in Lauren's ear. Normally, that would be the protocol. She'd keep things moving in the room, and her ASM would search out their problem child. Today felt different. Already angry and resenting the hell out of Carly's presence after what happened this weekend, this behavior only multiplied her frustration.

"No. This is her fourth late arrival, and this one is flagrant. I'm going personally."

Trip's eyebrows touched his hairline. He hadn't expected that response, and she hadn't expected to give it. "Gotcha. I'll take over here."

"I appreciate it," she said, quietly, scooping up her bag.

Ethan moved to her, having overheard their discussion. "And Lauren? Make sure this doesn't happen again."

"I hear you," she said, swallowing her hatred for this day, and it wasn't even noon.

She was familiar with the apartments the theater retained for housing out-of-town talent. She hopped in her Mini, blasted the radio, and headed there. She rode the elevator to the fourth floor of the building, stared down the number 406 that matched the paperwork she had on Carly, and knocked three times with maybe a little extra force. No one answered. Wonderful. She knocked again, this time vigorously, and when that didn't work, she knocked with her key to the theater, generating a much louder, grating sound.

"What the hell?" Carly said, swinging the door open, bleary-eyed. She stared at Lauren, then craned her head around the corner and stared down the hallway. Then back to Lauren.

"Carly, you're an hour late to rehearsal, and that's if we were teleported to The McAllister right this moment."

More blinking. Carly ran her hand through her hair, which was tousled, but in that shampoo commercial way that only certain people—people who were not Lauren—could pull off. When she opened the door more fully, Lauren took in her whole outfit. A tank top and what appeared to be a baby-blue thong. She looked away from the expanse of skin available to her gaze.

"Fuck. I didn't mean to oversleep." She glanced behind her for answers, flashing a bare cheek at Lauren. "I was up late and probably didn't set an alarm."

"Probably?" Lauren asked and turned back to Carly, because thong or not, this irresponsibility at work was unacceptable.

"Yeah. Sorry about that. Let me get myself together." Lauren nodded and folded her arms. "What? You're just going to stand there? Is your plan to escort me?"

"I thought we'd ride over together, yeah." Damn right she was going to escort her. She was not walking back into that rehearsal hall with word that Carly would be there soon, while they all watched the door and crossed their fingers.

"Lauren," she said with a dramatic sigh. "I'm a successful adult. You don't have to babysit me."

"Apparently, I do."

"Fine," she said coolly. Carly let the door fall open as she headed back inside. "Then do so inside. Less weird that way. Plus, it might help you relax."

Lauren followed quickly behind Carly, hostility flaring. "Please don't insinuate that I need to relax. That's rude. I arrived on time for my job. You're the one who kept twenty people waiting and made both of us look bad."

"I said it was a mistake." Carly raised a shoulder as if to telegraph this was no big deal and they should move on. "Why can't you understand that things happen."

"To just you? Because everyone else made a point to arrive on time, prepared. I think we all deal with alarm clocks. We all have the same traffic to battle. Hell, this apartment is ten minutes from the theater."

"I'll be early tomorrow. How's that? I'll add a little investment to your time management bank account, because you're clearly keeping track. Doesn't clock-watching get boring?"

"That's not enough."

"Fine. What is it that you want from me? Why don't you just spell it out and save us time? Because I'm starting to feel like it's my head on a platter."

"That's not at all what I want." Lauren clasped her fingers in front of her to keep her tone calm, reined in. That had never been difficult before. Why was she struggling? "You have to make changes to not just your punctuality, but your approach to life. At the very least, to your work."

Carly stared at her with fire in her eyes. The anger turned them a deeper shade of blue. Yep, she'd finally upset Carly. "Oh, I need to change the way I approach my work? Because I haven't achieved any kind of status in a cutthroat town like LA. Got it. Thank you so much for your unsolicited wisdom from…where are we again?" She looked around. "God, it's good you're here now to steer me back onto the right path."

"Well, if I wasn't, you'd still be asleep. So there's that."

Silence hit. "It was an accident," Carly said, biting off each word before disappearing into the bedroom in a beautiful flutter of anger.

Lauren stifled an eye roll and stepped inside Carly's apartment, as she'd left the door ajar for her. Wow, okay. Once inside, she took note of the fact that the space was definitely a lot neater than Lauren would have predicted, given hurricane Carly. The entirely gray and white kitchen and modern living room both gleamed. The granite countertops sparkled. No clothing bombs or pizza boxes to be seen. Everything appeared neat, tidy, and organized. Carly Daniel, who wasn't capable of organizing her life if it killed her, was neat? No. Who was this person? That's when it hit her. Carly *was* capable. She just had to care enough. "All right. I see how it is."

"Did you say something?" Carly called from in the bedroom.

"Nothing important," Lauren called back.

Now alone, she had a moment to get herself under control again. She was at Carly's apartment on business, and her job was to keep the polished stage manager veneer in place. She tried to cut herself a small break, however, because her feelings were edging to the surface, making it all feel like a messy, jumbled ball of competing emotions she had trouble separating. Plus, she was in a strange state both mentally and physically, and it all began Saturday night. Carly got her all worked up and bothered in too many ways to keep track of. Instead of trying, she forced herself to focus on the important issue at hand. Carly missing her call time wasn't charming or endearing. This was bad behavior and nothing new for Carly Daniel, according to the headlines, which made it worse. But then there was the Carly with the confident swagger at the bar, the sweet smile she afforded anyone in the rehearsal room. She never said an unkind word to anyone, well, until today, and—

"Are you having a conversation with yourself?"

Lauren looked up from Carly's couch, where she'd apparently sat down at some point, to see Carly studying her like an interesting science experiment. "I was just sorting out all I need to get done today. It's a lot, so we should get going."

"Well, the warring expressions that just took turns on your face tell me that your day must be pretty dramatic. Conflict ridden, in fact." Carly paused and placed one hand on her hip. She now wore slim-fitting jeans, a really soft looking long-sleeved pink T-shirt with a dip at the neckline, and short lace-up boots. Sigh. The universe was taunting her with a gorgeous movie star who kissed like a goddess and had little regard for professionalism. What a combo, indeed. That's when she remembered that Carly was still regarding her expectantly.

"I don't know what my face was doing. I can't always worry about my face's agenda. I was busy." Lauren did her best to make sure her face now appeared perfectly blank. She couldn't decide if she'd succeeded and glanced around surreptitiously for a mirror.

Carly eyed her knowingly. "It's just that we haven't seen each other since the other night. Is that where your mind went?"

Chita Rivera, were they really doing this? Right now? On the heels of a disagreement when they should be racing back to work? "Carly, we're due at The McAllister yesterday."

"Good point."

Lauren stood and walked to the door.

"We can talk about the porch kiss in the car," Carly finished.

Everything came to a screeching halt, including Lauren. "No. No, we definitely shouldn't do that. In fact, I don't think we should talk about it at all. Ever."

"Oh," Carly said. Her tone was soft, and the knowing smile dimmed. "Got it."

Lauren sighed at the pang of guilt that slammed her and tried to explain. "It's just that the whole thing, everything that night, was alcohol fueled, and skewed, and not a good representation of who I am as a person. As a stage manager, I mean. This"—she gestured between herself and Carly—"never should have happened."

Carly blinked once, and a distance settled between them, her eyes glacial. "Understood. A total mistake to erase from the history books." Carly breezed past her out of the apartment, seemingly unaffected.

While that should have been a good thing, an appropriate conclusion to their interaction, instead, it left Lauren feeling…listless, unsatisfied, and full of a tugging she couldn't quite name. Just erased from the history books, huh? Wasn't that what she wanted, though? Suddenly, she wondered.

Didn't matter. They had a job to do. When her gaze drifted to

Carly's ass as they walked the length of the hallway, she reminded herself of just that.

It didn't work.

❖

Carly was over the judgmental attitude. Since when did being a stage manager come with such a healthy dose of superiority? She was quiet in Lauren's care on the way to the theater. To cover the awkward silence, she sang quietly along with the radio, stealing an occasional glance at Lauren, who had her hair pulled partially back today, with the ends in a lazy curl. Nope. She would not crush on Lauren any longer. She shook herself out of it and watched the road instead.

What a complete cluster the morning had been. Though she was not thrilled with herself for staying out with Kirby and her boyfriend so late and missing her call time, she was equally annoyed with Lauren and the way she'd approached the situation. Not only that, but now her head wasn't in the game. She'd had trouble connecting to anything meaningful in the scene work with Evelyn as of late and felt like a fish flopping in the sand when it came to her work on *Starry Nights*.

"You want to take our ten a little early?" Ethan asked her wearily, three hours later. He'd had a chip on his shoulder ever since she'd arrived to work, part of which she attributed to her absence, and part to the lack of cohesion between her and Evelyn. They simply weren't in sync. He rubbed his forehead in a way that said his frustration with the scene was at a peak. They'd worked on the motivations leading up to the couple's first kiss in act 1, but everything they tried seemed to fall flat.

Carly turned to Evelyn for her opinion on whether to take the break but was met with only a half-hearted shrug.

"Yeah, let's do that," Carly said to Ethan. She watched as Evelyn immediately fled the space they shared like she couldn't get out of there fast enough. Evelyn had mentioned several times that she was straight, and maybe the female romance was harder for her. But based on the speech she'd made about the importance of such a play, it couldn't have been the whole reason. Evelyn didn't like *her* and had made it abundantly clear, which would be fine, if she would set it aside for the work. She hadn't. Her contempt for Carly read in every moment they shared onstage together. The no-good morning had Carly in a mindset to look into it.

"You have a second?" she said quietly to Evelyn, who was engrossed in something on her phone.

Evelyn raised her gaze to Carly's. "Sure. What do you need?"

"To talk." She leaned against the wall next to Evelyn and geared up. Suddenly, she had a shot of nervous energy move through her, but this was too important a conversation to sidestep. If they could get past whatever conflict was between them as actresses, then maybe they could still turn this thing around. "I feel like we're not connecting in the scenes."

"You don't, huh?" She glanced back down at her phone, making Carly feel about two inches tall. "Trust me. We're doing fine. We still have two weeks left, and you're just out of your element."

Interesting response. "What's my element, exactly?"

Evelyn gestured wildly with her phone in the open space before settling on a phrase. "Hollywood. La-la land. None of this is your speed, but it's what I do for a living. I happen to have great respect for the process."

"And you think I don't?"

"No, I know for a fact you don't. I think you've shown all of us that you're a spoiled, pampered celebrity who cares more about herself than the larger good of the production." She let her phone arm fall to her side as she straightened. "Go back to Hollywood, little girl. Let us handle the hard stuff."

With that, Evelyn strolled back to the rehearsal set, leaving Carly clutching the wall and reeling. No, she wasn't just clutching and reeling. She was also crying. Tears had pooled in Carly's eyes, which mortified her no end. Only six-year-olds cried, and she would not let Evelyn see the effect of her words.

"And we're back, everyone," Lauren announced to the company. Carly stayed right where she was, still in the room, but removed from the action. "Carly, you all set?" Lauren asked in a quieter tone.

Carly didn't move. She couldn't, out of sheer humiliation. She wiped the tears that now stained her cheeks, but she wasn't making much progress in shutting down the waterworks. This was awful.

She heard footsteps behind her and Lauren appeared. "I think we're ready to get—What's wrong?"

"Nothing. I just need a minute. Is that possible?" she whispered, doing windshield wiper hands. "Maybe I could go wash my face?"

Lauren nodded, squeezed her arm, and moved back to the larger group. "Can we maybe skip to the Mandy at work scene, act one, scene four?"

"Not a problem," she heard Ethan reply quietly. "Is she...?"

"She'll be fine," Lauren said. "Just needs a minute. Allergies." For the first time, Carly was overwhelmingly grateful for Lauren's professionalism and owed her big-time for running cover. "Carly, why don't you take fifteen, and then we'll regroup."

"I'll be back in under ten," she said, trying to keep her voice from cracking. This wasn't like her, but the pressures, the insecurities, the fear that she was continually letting everyone down weighed on her like a two-ton brick upon her chest. This whole process was so much harder than she'd anticipated. She was a good actress, but this required a level of depth and commitment that had her on her heels.

She stared at her red-rimmed eyes in the bathroom mirror moments later, as she splashed some water onto her face. The cold helped zap her out of her paralysis and self-pity. She had to be honest with herself. She'd been horrible since she'd arrived, and it was no wonder veterans of the stage like Evelyn had taken offense. This was her crossroads moment, however, and it was Lauren's voice she heard in her head. *You have to make changes to your approach to life, to your work.* The sentence repeated over and over, and each time she heard it, it resonated more powerfully.

She somehow made it through the remaining hours of rehearsal, even cradling Evelyn's face in her hands and looking into her eyes as if she was the most precious person in the world. She'd survived. Ethan had given her a shoulder pat on his way out at the end of the day, which hopefully meant she'd been forgiven. Evelyn had breezed the hell out of the room, apparently standing by her earlier assertion. As for Carly, she lingered, taking her time changing her shoes, packing up her belongings.

After a few minutes, it was down to just her, Trip, and Lauren in the room.

"You got this?" Trip asked Lauren. "I promised Wilks I'd back up the house manager for tonight's performance. He's a fill-in tonight and not entirely sure of our procedures."

"I got it," Lauren said. "Go play house manager." They then engaged in some kind of secret handshake that made her smile to herself.

Once they were alone, she dropped her bag and approached Lauren. "I can help." She didn't wait for an answer but instead went about assisting Lauren as she reset the rehearsal furniture for the scene they were scheduled to start with the next day.

"This is unexpected," Lauren said, tossing her a glance. "I don't generally have my lead actors schlepping the furniture. You okay? Feeling any better?" She said it with kindness, and it meant the world to Carly.

She felt the uncomfortable lump rise in her throat again. Something about Lauren checking in on her made her crumple, like when her mom used to pick her up from school after she'd had a bad day. She'd just blurt it all out in one giant release. Her safe place. "I've had better days."

Lauren straightened, abandoning a chair midtransit. "Did Evelyn say something to you earlier? You can tell me, you know." The soft green eyes made her believe it.

Carly exhaled slowly, and it all came gushing out. "Only that I was out of my league, spoiled. She called me a little girl and told me to go back to Hollywood."

Lauren's head dropped. When she raised it again, her features carried compassion. "I'm sorry she said those things to you."

"But you agree with her. You said so earlier. Sometimes I wonder what the hell I'm doing here. I'm a joke."

"Don't say that. You're keeping this production afloat. That's what you're doing here." She picked up the chair again and went on her way.

Carly laughed beneath the dark cloud still looming. "Yeah, you and I both know that's not true. I'm trying to pass as someone who knows what she's doing."

"You're a good actress," Lauren said plainly. "You bring a lot of bullshit with you, and people put up with it, for that one reason. You're amazing at what you do."

A tiny breeze could have blown Carly right over. "Wow. Thank you."

"And after our trouble today, it means a lot that I'm complimenting you. It means that what I'm saying is true. So you have to ignore Evelyn, because the play is blossoming with the work you and Ethan are doing. She's been the problem, the one not committing to character."

Carly was mystified. It was so rare to get to hear Lauren's actual take on things. Carly wanted to know more, needed to. She longed to know what music she liked best, who her early influences were, what she did at night when she left The McAllister. There was so much ground to cover, but first she needed to internalize the words Lauren had just gifted her. "Thank you for saying that. I feel like I keep trying to connect with her, but it goes nowhere, and it's hard to develop an onstage relationship if you're getting nothing back."

"Let me know if you ever need someone to run lines with you. That's actually part of my job, believe it or not."

"Really? You do that? I thought when you said so that first day of rehearsal you were just being polite."

"I wasn't. I do it all the time. Most stage managers do."

That pulled Carly up short. Running lines would actually be incredibly helpful. She'd worked on her own in her apartment, but she hadn't had that extra person to read with her. The only time she'd been afforded the chance to work on a give-and-take was opposite Evelyn, and that had been only stressful.

"It's not uncommon, actually. Especially with wordier shows, like this one. The playwright had a lot to say."

Carly sighed. "You have no idea. When are you free?"

Lauren glanced around. "As soon as I'm done putting the room in order."

Carly couldn't believe her luck. "Well, then I will help you in repayment." She spent the next few minutes following orders and enjoying seeing Lauren in her element, in charge, and with a plan. Just when she thought Lauren couldn't get any more attractive, she had to go and own a very simple task.

Once they slid the rehearsal couch up against the wall, Lauren grabbed her script, grabbed a spot on that couch, and tucked her feet beneath her. The overhead fluorescents in the room were off and a floor lamp provided soft illumination. "What scene would you like to run?" Lauren asked.

"The last scene we ran today, with the teakettle, and the talking a lot line?"

"Act one, scene four."

"Yes, that one. I felt like I was all over the place and not zeroing in on my objective or the connection to Mandy. At that point? It should be undeniable that these two are meant to be, and it just…isn't." It was the last scene before intermission, when the first version of the couple was at their peak of happiness, the moment a romance novel would have come to a close. The goal, as Ethan had described it, was to build the couple up as so in love, destined to be together, that the audience is dumbstruck to see them miss out on the relationship entirely in act 2 and instead witness how their lives play out if they'd never met. "If there's no lost relationship, the narrative fails. Nobody will care."

"Got it," Lauren said, as she located the scene. Carly, newly off-book for act 1, didn't need her script.

She looked over at Lauren, who would be reading the first line in the scene. "Whenever you're ready."

"So, we're doing this?" Lauren said, reading the line as Mandy.

Carly, as Ashley, took a deep breath. "Do you know what you'd be getting into? I let teakettles whistle too long on the stove. I scream when spiders show up. I know I'm not the easiest person to love. I'm pretty sure I just lost my job, and my cat moved out. I'll probably be homeless myself in a matter of—"

"Ashley?"

"Yeah?"

"You're talking a lot."

Carly grinned. She liked the way Lauren said that line, with a kind of playful affection. She'd never heard it delivered that way. It gave her a shiver. She kept going. "Should I stop now?"

"You should definitely stop," Lauren read. "I have a lot of things to figure out, but one of them is definitely not you. You're staying." She'd lifted her gaze to Carly's for that last line and inspired another shiver. Carly was struck—this was what it was supposed to feel like between them.

As they got farther into the scene, Lauren brought warmth, comedy, and a very human vibe to the character of Mandy. Carly felt like she'd stumbled upon a gold mine with this rehearsal session, as it informed so many new choices she hadn't yet considered. When they finished their fourth run-through of the scene, she stared at Lauren, who still sat on that rehearsal couch against the wall.

"Why are you looking at me like that?" Lauren asked, with a curious grin.

Carly shook her head. "I just didn't see that coming. Have you ever acted before?"

Lauren sighed. "It's all I ever wanted to do when I was younger. Be onstage, tell amazing stories, hear the audience applaud." She shrugged. "Wasn't meant to be."

Carly didn't understand. She moved to the couch and took a seat next to Lauren. "Why do you say that? You're fantastic at it."

"I don't know that I would go that far. Didn't get many jobs. Make that one. A voice job for a nightclub commercial that aired only on the radio. I played the part of a happy college girl, thrilled with the drink options."

"I'd buy those drinks based on what I just heard." This whole concept was blowing Carly's mind and her entire perception of Lauren. "You were out there auditioning? What happened? Why would you give up if it's what you wanted?"

Lauren nodded, and embarrassment flashed. "I tried to make a go of it. Didn't work out." She shrugged, as if stuffing down the regret of what had never been. "After a while it became clear that I was on my way to being a professional waitress and part-time out of work actress. What I really wanted was a way to pay my bills in the midst of something I love." She gestured to the space around them. "And here I am. The learning curve was steep, and I started at the bottom, but I like to think I'm damn good at my job."

"You are. Don't get me wrong." Carly tucked a knee beneath her. This new information had her keyed up and intrigued on top of the high she'd just received from the nuanced scene work. "Tell me about a favorite role of yours."

Lauren laughed. She was so pretty when she did that. "I can tell you about the time I received my first lead role. We did *Peter Pan Jr.* in middle school. I was cast as Wendy, and it was the best thing that ever happened to me. I'll never forget the afternoon I saw my name posted on the cast list."

Carly was rapt. "Get out. What happened?"

Lauren beamed. "I rehearsed night and day and counted the moments until the curtain rose. Not to mention, the entire town would be there, including my extended family who'd driven in."

"And you were a hit," Carly supplied, imagining Lauren wouldn't settle for anything less than perfection.

"No. Actually, my performance was fine, but my nightgown snagged on the set during the flying sequence and brought the whole thing tumbling down. Children and nightgowns and Lost Boys scattered for safety as I swung back and forth, dragging the wall." She grimaced as Carly laughed. "I probably should have taken that as a sign it wasn't meant to be for me. Unfortunately, it took a little longer for me to get the message."

Carly tried to stop laughing, but the image of young Lauren sitting in a pile of rubble while an audience looked on in horror was too much. "Was anyone hurt?"

"I wish *I* had been! Would have pulled attention away from the disaster." She exhaled and relaxed against the couch with a tired smile. "The boy playing little Michael was traumatized, though. We'd brought him in from the elementary school. Broke into tears and cried in the arms of Tiger Lily. I'm hopeful the therapy he required helped, some."

Carly was dying. Wheezing. Gasping for air. Yes, she was punchy already after such a roller coaster of a day, but the images Lauren painted certainly contributed. "Please tell me there are photos."

"Oh, there are *videos*," Lauren deadpanned.

"My kingdom for this video. What is it you want? A car? A house? I can make your dreams come true. Except that's a lie. My movie money is dwindling."

"I wonder why," Lauren mused with a grin. She extended her arm across the back of the couch between them, which made things feel extra cozy. "If we survive this production without you single-handedly causing me to pull my hair out, I will make that video happen for you."

Carly tapped the top of Lauren's hand with her finger. "Promises, promises."

A pause. "But I remember what it was like to take on a role, rehearse, and lose yourself for a little while. There's nothing like it."

Carly touched Lauren's knee. "You should give it another go sometime."

"I'd be a liar if I said I didn't miss it a little, but I think I'll stick with my steady paycheck, and organizing all of you people. How's that?" She stood. "It's getting late. We should clock out before we have to be back in the morning."

Carly nodded, feeling so much lighter than earlier in the day. This was the first time she and Lauren had just…relaxed together. Chatted about life. She found it refreshing and couldn't help but crave more.

"And this is okay? To run lines with you again in the future? Because I'd really like to."

"Completely. Just let me know."

"Before rehearsal tomorrow? I can come in early and we can—"

Lauren held up a finger. "You're a liar and you know it. You're incapable of the word early." She'd said it in a bossy but playful tone, and hand to her hip. Carly wanted to kiss her right then and there, then lose herself with Lauren on that couch, slowly. Very slowly.

"I'll be here at nine tomorrow," Carly informed her, as she headed to the door. "I can help you and Trip set up as we run lines."

"Sure you will."

"You're gonna be shocked. Wanna walk out with me?"

Lauren gestured to her laptop. "I better get that rehearsal report out before heading home."

Carly shook her head. "You work too hard."

"Do you think that's it, or do you think maybe you don't—"

"You don't even have to finish that sentence," Carly said, pointing at her. She softened. "Good night, Lauren. You saved me today."

Lauren studied her. "You're welcome."

"You can bet I'm not going to forget it, and you know something?"

"What's that?"

"You're an awesome person. I may not make that clear in how I behave, but I'm spoiled and working on a recovery strategy."

"I appreciate that," Lauren said, with a twinkle in her eye. "I have all the faith in you."

As Carly walked to her rental in The McAllister's parking lot, it was already dark outside. That extra hour she'd stolen with Lauren had been the most productive of the rehearsal day, and entirely unexpected. She'd gone from furious with Lauren that morning, to eternally grateful to her this evening. What a difference a few hours and some alone time made.

Carly had already known Lauren was many things, but a decent actress hadn't been one of them. She closed the car door behind her and sat in the cold car. She'd enjoyed tonight. She'd made friends since she'd arrived in Minneapolis. She and Kirby and a couple of other actors from out of town had gone out for dinner a few times, and of course, the meetups at Put Upon Pete's had been fun. Yet they'd all paled in comparison to the time she'd just spent with Lauren Prescott, when it felt like everything was right with the world. She was leaving for the night fulfilled, invigorated and inspired by the story of the younger Lauren's love for the art. Perhaps, if she paid enough attention, she'd walk away from this experience with that same kind of passion. She already felt it blossoming. Maybe there was something special to this whole theater thing. Maybe there was something special about Lauren Prescott.

She looked back at the large white building. Maybe it was both.

CHAPTER FIVE

I brought doughnuts."

Lauren nearly jumped out of her skin at the sound of the cheerful voice behind her. Her hand flew to her heart and grasped the fabric of her shirt as she turned around to see none other than Carly, standing in the doorway of the rehearsal room, holding a greasy looking white bag. Lauren checked her watch, and checked again to be sure it actually was Carly and not an apparition. Yep, still her. "What are you doing here at nine a.m.?" She placed a hand over her heart. "Oh God. Did hell actually freeze over? I never even got to see it."

"You're funny."

"Rarely. But I do keep trying." Lauren eyed her. "What gives?"

Carly inclined her head to the side and dropped off the bag on the table next to Lauren. "You said we could run lines."

"And we can."

As Carly breezed past, she smelled fantastic, like lemon and maybe…cupcakes? The same scent Lauren remembered from the billiards lesson. If Carly smelled amazing, she looked even better, wearing perfectly fitting jeans and a lime-green flowy blouse, paired with boots with a modest heel. She topped off her outfit with a long, intricate silver necklace that might have been expensive. "Great," she said, flipping around to Lauren. "I was hoping we could back up to the beginning of the play and run those scenes." She glanced around the room with her hands out, like she was figuring out what to touch. "I can also help with your stage manager-y stuff."

Lauren laughed. "My stage manager-y stuff?"

Carly grinned, and when the sunlight touched her skin, her face glowed. Lauren wasn't sure she'd ever seen anyone glow quite like that. It stole her next breath. To cover, she reached for the bag of doughnuts.

"Yeah, you know, all the furniture moving, and laptop typing, and cross-referencing, and highlighting. We can do that while we run lines."

"Where in the world did you get these doughnuts?" Lauren asked, amazed at the flaky goodness she was tasting. They were still warm. These doughnuts weren't just any doughnuts—they were perfection, and from her own city? How? She'd ordered a million doughnuts for her companies over the years. None had been these.

"Oh. I read about them on Yelp. Danny D's Donut Diner on Donato Street. Heard of them?"

"No," Lauren said, around a heavenly mouthful of dough.

"Tiny place. No tables. Couple of guys behind the counter, working hard." Carly pointed at the stand-in airport chairs. "Shall I place these for act one?"

"Yes. That would be fantastic." Lauren's brain hadn't quite caught up. "Wait. So, you're telling me that you woke up early, got dressed, drove to Danny D's Donut Dynasty."

"Diner. But you're right. They missed a great naming opportunity."

"Drove to Danny D's Diner and made it here an hour before rehearsal is set to begin?"

Carly slid the chairs onto the blue spike tape on the floor that marked their intended home. "That's exactly what I'm telling you."

"How?" Lauren asked in amazement. "Why?"

"Because I wanted to run lines. Why aren't you listening to me?" Suddenly, it became crystal clear. Carly needed proper motivation, and when she had it? She responded in spades.

Lauren nodded her head sagely. "So with a little carrot waving, you're up and at 'em."

"I do lots of things for the right carrots." Carly made the statement as if it was the most basic of understood facts. Well, it was now. "Lines?"

"Let's do it."

They went back and forth on the first scene between Ashley and Mandy at the airport when they first met.

"Wait. So we're stuck here. As in overnight?" Carly balked.

"That's what I'm telling you," Lauren said gently.

"No, no, no. I have a presentation in Boston in the morning. I need to be on that plane."

"We all have somewhere to be, but sometimes you have to accept defeat. Cinnamon pretzel bite?"

"What are you doing? Why are you getting comfortable with the pretzel things? We should argue. Or call someone. Someone important."

Just like Lauren had noticed the night before when they'd read, Carly's version of Ashley came alive. Not that it wasn't good before. It was. But the readings they did together were other-level for Carly. *It's because she has something more to respond to.* So Lauren continued to give, and Carly continued to come up with new and exciting line deliveries. By the time they'd worked their way to the end of the scene, Lauren noticed that she'd abandoned her stage management duties and had lost herself in the world of *Starry Nights* and Ashley and Mandy. The result was her standing face-to-face with Carly when the scene ended.

"You have no concept of how helpful that was," Carly said quietly. Lauren's focus fell to Carly's bottom lip and the subtle pink lip gloss that gave it a small shine.

"Well, that's what I'm here for. To help."

"Then you need a raise," Carly said sincerely. "I really feel like last night and this morning have amounted to a major breakthrough for me. I can see the path to this character now, and it's because of you."

"Good. That makes me happy."

They stared at each other.

Lauren closed her script and remembered herself, heated cheeks or not. She had only a short amount of time to finish her rehearsal prep, yet she found herself completely out of sorts. She wasn't complaining. The buzz she got from reading lines with Carly reminded her of the days she used to act herself, and with such a capable scene partner, her enjoyment level only doubled.

Reading Mandy's and Ashley's lines as they discovered each other in the play reminded Lauren so much of her personal journey with Carly, who she had yet to fully figure out. Just when she thought Carly was a spoiled, entitled starlet, Carly would do something to showcase her humanity and kindness. She was beginning to care about this production, and seeing her cry yesterday had been eye opening for Lauren. No, she hadn't pinned Carly Daniel down just yet, but Lauren also understood that was part of her appeal. Carly was a lot of things, some of them unexpected.

"All right. I'm back with some scheduling details from Chuck." Lauren blinked. Ah, yes, she'd sent Trip to speak to The McAllister's resident technical director about their transition to the theater. Chuck was known for his grumpy side, and she'd come to learn that Trip's cheerful disposition offset it nicely.

"What did he say?" she asked, trying to ease back into her PSM role, despite the fact that the back of her neck felt warm and she could still feel Carly's gaze all over. She stole a final glance at Carly but felt that connection from minutes ago still very much intact.

"He said that if the scenic folks would speed the hell up, we're on time to move in this week. Yet he's grumbling about Tinsley demanding more money for paint."

This wasn't the first time those two had butted heads. "Tins is always very particular about her mixing, and sometimes that requires additional coats we didn't budget for."

"Sounds like she's our holdup. Other than that, we're good to go."

Lauren set out the sign-in sheet and nodded. "I'll talk to her." It wasn't technically her job to wrangle an assistant designer, but if Tinsley was going to be a monkey wrench in the works, she could always mention it to Wilks so he could get ahead of the problem.

"So, this is yet another thing you do," Carly said, grinning. "You look ahead to any problems."

"Part of my job. Yes." The answer seemed to intrigue Carly, who stole a doughnut and wandered a few feet away to study her lines.

Trip pointed at Carly silently with a shocked looked on his face and his jaw fully dropped. Lauren nodded back at him wordlessly with wide oh-my-God eyes, as if to say, yes, an early Carly Daniel was something to behold. The morning had been a unique one. Yet Lauren couldn't wipe the never-ending smile off her face. Their one-on-one work sessions invigorated her just as much as they did Carly.

In fact, she wondered when they'd find some alone time next. She told herself that the thought was a harmless one and allowed it. Underneath, concern crept in, because with Carly, Lauren felt out of control, and there was nothing Lauren craved more in life than structure and control.

"You okay in there, Lala?" Trip asked quietly, as the cast members began to trickle in.

Lauren grinned at him. "I think so." She didn't have time to dwell on her status, however, as her phone danced in vibration where she'd left it on the table. They were two minutes from the official start of rehearsal and the actors who had been called were already engaged in vocal warm-ups. "This is Lauren."

"Lauren. Evelyn."

She glanced down at the sign-in sheet and saw that she'd yet to sign-in. "Hey, there. Everything okay?"

"Definitely not."

"Okay. What's going on?" Lauren walked a few feet away, out of earshot of the group, sensing this might need to be a private conversation.

"I'm not coming in today. Food poisoning. Really bad."

"Oh no. Do you need anything? What can we do?"

"I'll be fine," Evelyn said in a curt voice. Even sick, she apparently wasn't the warm and friendly type. "Just can't quite keep anything down, so I better...Oh no. I have to go." Lauren winced as Evelyn clicked off the call out of clear necessity. She made a note to check in on her later in the day, and moved to plan B. "Evelyn's out today. Food poisoning," she told Ethan.

"Fan-fucking-tastic. I get Carly here on time, and Evelyn can't make it."

"I know," Lauren said sympathetically. "But we have Nia ready to step in." Nia Blankenship had been cast as the standby for both lead roles. She was a sturdy understudy, which was why The McAllister recommended her readily in the casting sessions. You could always count on Nia, and with a wild card like Carly Daniel in the mix, having a solid backup was key. No, she wasn't the most charismatic actress, but she was serviceable.

Ethan sighed. "All right. Put her in."

After briefing an eager Nia, rehearsal was finally off and rolling. Their agenda was a run of act 1, and with only a few hiccups, they stumbled their way to the end, blandly. Carly looked defeated by then and walked away to a quiet corner alone. Ethan appeared weary, almost as if he hadn't slept in a week. Nia looked nervous as hell. Apparently, working with a celebrity rattled her more than Lauren would have guessed. Today was feeling like a wash.

"And that's lunch, everyone," Trip announced to the company. "See you back here in an hour."

Lauren could feel the low energy in the room as the cast quietly filed out. The run-through had run flat without Evelyn, but honestly, it hadn't been much stronger with her. The production, while still afloat, wasn't exactly thriving, and she could feel Ethan losing his patience as the days went on. They opened in just over two weeks, and while the set, costumes, and publicity were all on track, the narrative needed a jumpstart. Even Lauren could see that much.

"Hey, guys?" Kirby said, returning to the rehearsal hall. "Nia's in the women's restroom in really poor shape."

"What do you mean, poor shape?" Lauren asked.

"I think it's her stomach." Lauren deflated and exchanged a look with Trip. It was starting to look like they had a stomach bug on their hands, not the food poisoning Evelyn suspected. This was not good news at all.

"Aren't you two friends?" Lauren asked Kirby, who nodded. "Would you be able to help her into an Uber? I don't think it's a great idea for her to be around the other actors." The idea that she'd already been in such close proximity to Carly was a bad thing, and Lauren was now in save-the-cast mode.

"Yeah, I can do that. No problem at all."

"If you're late back from lunch, it's okay. We'll make it work," Ethan said. Once Kirby headed out, Ethan turned to Lauren and Trip. "I'm thinking we work everything that doesn't involve Mandy's character, and then call it a day."

"Can I make a suggestion?" Carly asked from across the room. She leaned against the wall with her arms crossed over her chest.

"Of course," Ethan said.

Carly pushed off the wall and straightened. "Have Lauren fill in. We've run lines together, and it's always gone smoothly."

Lauren felt her cheeks heat. "No. I don't think that's a good plan. I need to be on book for lines, and—"

"I can be on book," Trip said.

Ethan waved them off, still not over his catastrophe of a rehearsal. "If that works for Carly, I'm fine with it." He stalked away with his hands shoved into his pockets, probably already conceding defeat.

"Is that okay?" Carly asked her quietly.

Lauren nodded. "It's fine. Whatever you need to salvage the afternoon. We're down two Mandys and have to get creative, right?"

Carly squeezed Lauren's wrist and smiled at her with gratitude. That smile filled Lauren's half empty cup to full. She was happy to help and would do her best for Carly and Ethan.

When the company returned from lunch, they moved backward to act 1 at Carly's request. Lauren played the role just as she had in her two rehearsal sessions with Carly, only this time, instead of just the lines, she followed the set blocking. As stage manager, she was intimately familiar with Mandy's path in the show, as it had been her job to track and record it. Rehearsing the scenes face-to-face with Carly was at first a little jarring. She found herself staring into those light blue eyes and losing herself in them as Mandy, something she'd never allowed herself, as Lauren, to do. The liberties she could take as Mandy were startling, freeing. She could reach out and touch Carly briefly, study her when she spoke, smile like Carly affected her, and even lay her head down in Carly's lap when Mandy was called to do so. She loved every second of it so much that she lost herself in the afternoon. Before she knew it, they were done with rehearsal for the day.

She sat up from Carly's lap, where they'd concluded, and turned to face her. "Was that okay?"

Carly chuckled. They were the only two left at rehearsal apart from Ethan and Trip. The others had been released one by one. "I'd say so. Wouldn't you?" She stood and moved toward her belongings with a triumphant smile on her face. Lauren wasn't sure what that meant, until she turned to Ethan, who still sat behind his director's table, beating a pencil against the top of his lips.

She joined him and Trip at the table and opened her laptop, prepared to record Trip's times for the day and get Ethan's input about who to call first thing tomorrow.

"We have a problem," Ethan said, finally turning to her.

Her heart sank. She couldn't take any more setbacks. If one more person was struck ill by this virus, they'd be hobbling along at best. "What's wrong?"

He pointed at the makeshift set with his pencil. "That was fucking amazing."

Lauren blinked. "Today?"

He swiveled in his metal chair to face her. "Yes, today. The whole thing lit up like a Christmas tree. The story came alive. The relationship mattered. I know the whole fucking story word for word, and even I was rooting for them, and this was only the first portion of act one."

Where was she supposed to go with this? On one hand, Ethan's words were incredibly flattering. On the other, they didn't really matter. She was the fill-in for the fill-in. "Well, maybe we can talk about why it worked so well today with Evelyn and recreate—"

"Do you really see that going well?" Ethan asked, now up and moving with purpose, except he didn't seem to be going anywhere. Just extra energy he needed to burn off.

Lauren grimaced. "Not exactly, no. But if she's a professional, she'll try to take the notes."

"I've given her eighteen thousand notes since we've started," he said, with a hand extended outward. "She's cold and unfeeling when playing a character who should be warm and lovable, which I've seen her pull off nicely in a dozen different roles. She hates Carly and it reads all over the scene like spilled blood on a white carpet."

She watched Trip wince at the reference.

Ethan noticed, too, and pointed at Trip. "What did you think? You were here."

Trip hesitated and passed Lauren a look, as if to ask for permission to speak honestly. She nodded at him, granting it. "I loved everything about the run today. They had fun together, but there was still this ball of sexual tension that kept me engaged. It's the first time I've been sucked in by the story since we started."

Ethan snapped his fingers and pointed at Trip. "Thank you. That's what I'm talking about, too."

"Ethan, I'd be happy to keep running lines with Carly."

"Can we do some right now?" He looked at his watch. "I know we're off the clock and rehearsal is officially over, but if you'll show me the final scene of act one, I can know more." He ran his hand over his scruff as he waited for her answer.

Technically, according to Equity rules, rehearsal was over, and asking Carly to work longer went against good standards and practices. She couldn't do it. Lauren opened her mouth to advocate for Carly, when Carly herself turned from across the room. She'd been engrossed in her phone and had seemed to be out of earshot. Apparently, that had not been the case.

"I'm happy to run the scene, Lauren."

Lauren stared at her, and then back at Ethan, running out of options. "The last scene?" she asked.

"If you don't mind, that is. I don't want to put you on the spot if you're uncomfortable in any way," Ethan said, more gently.

It was a big scene, the happily-ever-after fake out that got ripped away from the audience after intermission. There was a kiss in that scene, a pretty serious one. She closed her eyes and did her utmost to appear unaffected. She was a professional, and she could do this. It was for the good of the show. "I don't mind," she said, retrieving her script.

She joined Carly onstage.

"You good?" Carly asked and gave her hand a squeeze. That did it. The nervous energy, the self-doubt, the overthinking all seemed to slide away with that one moment of contact.

"I'm great. Shall we?"

Carly nodded.

"So, we're doing this?" Lauren asked, as Mandy. She went for timid, excited, and fully in love.

Carly stepped into her space, hands at her side, confidence on full display. "Do you know what you'd be getting into? I let teakettles whistle too long on the stove. I scream when spiders show up." Her proximity alone sent a series of tingles across Lauren's skin. She didn't try to move herself out of it, however. She put it into what the character would feel. "I know I'm not the easiest person to love. I'm pretty sure I just lost my job, and my cat moved out. I'll probably be homeless myself in a matter of—"

"Ashley?"

"Yeah?"

"You're talking a lot."

Carly grinned and cradled Lauren's face with one hand. "Should I stop now?"

"You should definitely stop," Lauren said. "I have a lot of things to figure out, but one of them is definitely not you. You're staying."

Just as the script dictated, Carly brought her lips to Lauren's and kissed her with determination, and tenderness, and love. Lauren's entire body went instantly warm, and she had to steady herself or her knees would give out. What was abundantly clear was that they kissed really well together, the perfect amount of give and take. Lauren's limbs felt like Jell-O when she pulled her lips from Carly's. She opened her eyes slowly and smiled. Just another day at work, right? She opened her mouth to speak, but couldn't for the life of her remember her next line. That's because she was supposed to be reading from the script. "Oh, um, one moment," she said, flipping the page, her cheeks on fire with embarrassment.

Before the scene could continue, Ethan's voice cut them off. "I think we can stop there. I'm going to chat with Wilks about the future of the production. I want to thank you both for such a committed rehearsal." Ethan didn't dwell or stick around for chitchat. He left notes for Trip about the breakdown for the following day and was out of there.

"You did great," Carly said quietly in Lauren's ear. She kissed her cheek quickly and gave her some space. "I'll see you tomorrow."

Lauren nodded, still in a haze of what the hell was happening. She turned to Trip, who sat behind the table, arms folded with a big old grin on his face.

"Little Lala," he said. "Who knew?"

She stalked back to the table, disconcerted, excited, and turned the hell on.

CHAPTER SIX

Lauren sat in one of her favorite spots in all of The McAllister, the long hallway off the grand lobby. At the end stood Wilks's office, but along the way were framed photographs of some of the most noteworthy shows put on by the theater. The faces of Broadway legends dotted the walls, just a sampling of the many great actors who'd performed at The McAllister, the theater Lauren now inhabited on a daily basis. She carried such reverence for the place and sometimes had to pinch herself to remember that she actually worked here. Oh, and down the hallway a little way, they'd even added a framed shot of one of their most recent shows. Yep, that was Gyllenhaal she saw in a serious moment from a new play that had been very well received.

"Ready for you, Lauren," Wilks said, opening the door. He did a little ballerina twirl as she passed in attempt to lighten the mood.

She chucked. "Nice one."

"I'll spare you my twerk."

"And now I'm sad."

It wasn't very often that they met in his office. Their working relationship had always been more informal, with him crashing her space as they quickly hashed out daily details like scheduling, budget, or interpersonal matters. The more official meeting in his rarely visited office intimidated Lauren, which was downright ridiculous. This was Wilks! Her Wilks. That reminder didn't calm her churning stomach, though the twirl had helped.

Once inside, Lauren took a seat. As he walked around to his side of the desk, she nervously grabbed the Rubik's Cube in front of her. "Mastered this one yet?" she asked. He grabbed the cube, worked the whole thing in under a minute, and tossed it back to her. She whistled. "I'll take that as a yes."

"What do you think I do all day in here?"

Just another testament to Wilks's ability to deliver. She sat up straighter, because this felt like she'd been called to the principal's office.

"Well, here's the crazy thing." He sat back in his fancy leather chair. "Ethan wants to make a change in his cast."

"Okay. What kind of change?" It wasn't a real question. She already knew where this was headed. Hell, it had kept her up all night. What Ethan was angling for was unprecedented. Fear struck first and it landed hard. She was an imposter. For some reason, they seemed to think she was this amazing actress, when in all honesty, she wasn't. She hadn't booked a decent job in all the years she tried. Then, the fear danced away and swapped places with a twinge of excitement that twisted, turned, and vibrated pleasantly. She ordered the dueling emotions to stand the hell down, and take twenty. Given it was her job to remain calm at all times, she luckily had the ability to mask the cascade of emotions in front of Wilks. Yep, that was her, completely not in control.

"I don't know if this is going to shock you or not. It shocked me."

She nodded but said nothing, probably because she was holding her breath.

"He wants you to step into the role of Mandy effective today. There's an official offer on the table." He held up a hand before she could speak. "I know it's a little out of left field, and I told him so myself. We went over it from every angle last night. Took hours, but we came up with a deal for everyone that makes sense."

Lauren exhaled slowly. "Wilks, I haven't acted in years. I was just filling in for our sick cast members."

"But you have acted before." He held his hand out as if presenting a very obvious point.

She shook her head. "Not at this level. Plus, I'm rusty." She gestured behind her. "These people are…pros. I couldn't even land a toilet paper commercial on my own, and trust me, I tried. Too many times."

He waved her off. "We both know the industry is tricky. It's not about how good you are in the beginning. It's about who you know, and being in the right place at the right time. Then suddenly your talent matters."

He had a point. She nodded. "I guess that's what yesterday was." "I'd say so."

Wilks leaned forward with a kind smile. He seemed more personable, like the everyday Wilks she was used to. "Here's the thing. I know you, Lauren, and you're nothing if not a professional yourself. Are you willing to step in? This is quite the opportunity." He held out both hands. "These kinds of things don't happen that often in the business."

Again, he was right. You heard about Cinderella stories like these, but never in a million years did Lauren think it could happen to her, especially after she'd carefully tucked those hopes away. She never dared imagine. After years of schlepping from one audition to the next, she'd just been offered a major role, the kind she used to lie in bed dreaming about. And she'd done so via her stage management career? It really was about being in the right room. How strangely the world worked.

She clenched her fists several times, to discreetly burn off some of the nervous energy coursing through her limbs, and stared Wilks right in the eye. "I'll do it," she said quietly, feeling something long forgotten in her click into place. "I've never been more scared of anything in my life, but how can I not?"

"I thought you'd eventually get there," he said with a wink. He picked up a folder from his desk. "I have a contract all drawn up, and since you're already an Equity member, there's less red tape to fuss with."

"What about Evelyn?" Lauren tried not to wince at that particular side effect. She imagined her being sat down and let go officially, followed by the to-be-expected ire Evelyn was known for.

"She'll be fine. She works fairly steadily and will move on to the next project in no time. Part of the business."

Lauren nodded. This would be a setback for Nia, as well. Though she was never guaranteed replacement status, she would likely wonder why she was passed over. But she still had her original standby gig. Nothing had changed on that front, and she'd still have a job.

"We'll need a new stage manager. How do you feel about giving

Trip a shot as PSM?" Trip had been a faithful assistant stage manager for over two years now and, in Lauren's opinion, was the perfect one for the job. Not only had he earned it, but he was already familiar with the show and its specific needs.

"I'm glad we agree. I have an appointment with him next to make it official." Lauren closed her eyes, knowing how thrilled he was going to be. "I'll see if we can get Janie to ASM."

Lauren nodded. "Great. I know she's off this slot and was worried about employment."

He picked up his phone. "We're about to make her day." He glanced at his watch. "Rehearsal in an hour. You better grab a coffee and learn your lines."

"Oh. I need to get over there and set up."

"Not anymore you don't," Wilks said sternly. "You're an actress only now. Make your call time, and be ready to work. That's all you have to worry about. Trip will do the rest."

The concept left her dumbfounded, almost like she'd left home without money, keys, or her phone. Just show up and be prepared to delve into Mandy? The concept seemed so foreign to her when she was used to managing so many details.

The smile was small when she left Wilks's office, but as she walked the long hallway, passing one historic McAllister moment after another, it steadily blossomed. Her body hummed with a slow-growing excitement that started somewhere in her midsection and radiated out.

An adventure was about to begin, and this time, she wasn't Lauren Prescott, standing with her clipboard on the sidelines. She was part of it. As she reached the end of the hallway, she had to steady herself. The smile reached its full bloom as she allowed the understanding to settle.

A dream was about to come true. She was an actress again.

❖

When Carly's alarm went off at seven thirty, she wanted more than anything to hurl it across the room and put out a hit on the clock and all its distant relatives. Instead, she remembered the new leaf she'd decided upon. "One foot on the floor," she mumbled, and slowly made the request a reality. Now, as she lay there, half off the bed with the bottom of one foot touching the floor, she had to figure out how to get the other one there, too. "Not just yet," she said to her ceiling and let her eyes slowly close again. "Just three minutes. I just need three."

Once they passed, she blinked. "Two feet on the floor." She slid the second leg out, banishing it from the warmth of the covers and placed it flat on the floor next to the other one. Now only her body remained in bed, perpendicular and clinging to slumber like a life raft in a storm at sea. "Gotta sit up," she whispered in defeat, but damn it, she made it happen. This whole routine was a production, yes, but for two straight mornings in a row, it'd worked. She'd not been late, and the day had been better for it. She'd also been afforded some extra time with just Lauren, and that made it all worthwhile. Lauren was so much more pleasant when the two lines between her eyes weren't creased and angry. Carly sighed, naked and wrapped in her snuggly comforter, because those little lines were actually really cute, too.

She could admit it. She was more than smitten with Lauren Prescott, and she'd thought about that sexy stage kiss nonstop since yesterday. Yes, it had been Mandy and Ashley, and she knew the difference, but the physical chemistry had been all theirs. Carly didn't know if what they'd shown Ethan would give him the motivation to actually talk to Evelyn, or maybe even let her see Lauren perform the scenes in person. God, if only uptight Evelyn could see how likable Lauren was as Mandy, how funny and kind. She didn't know the protocol for those kinds of practices in the theatrical world, but she hoped for her own career's sake that yesterday hadn't been for nothing.

Two hours later, she stood in the rehearsal hall, iced coffee secured—without being late, mind you—waiting on Ethan. Lauren and Trip were behind the stage manager's table passing a lot of pages back and forth and nodding. Evelyn was still out, apparently, which was great for at least one more rehearsal with someone else.

"Ladies and gentlemen," Ethan said, breezing into the room with a noticeable extra spring in his step. "Lots to do today, but first a brief announcement." All eyes were on him. Heads quirked. Glances were exchanged. "There's been a change to our cast. Effective today, the role of Mandy in *Starry Nights* will be played by Lauren Prescott. Trip will be our new production stage manager, and Janie will join him tomorrow as assistant. You'll meet her then." The room was silent for a moment. Carly's gaze flew immediately to Lauren, who smiled demurely at the table, continuing to work and avoiding all eye contact. Finally, when she did look up, it was straight back at Carly, who sent her the biggest smile of encouragement. This was better than anything she'd hoped for. Carly couldn't believe it. Her toes were numb and she wanted to jump up and down. They'd given Lauren the role? Unable to take it, she raced across the room to Lauren, as the rest of the company chatted quietly in shock.

"I don't believe it. This is fucking awesome," Carly whispered, her arms around Lauren.

"Is it?" Lauren asked.

"Yes! You're in the show now. You're starring in the show, Lauren. Do you get that? Why didn't you call me?"

"I just found out." Lauren smiled. Her usual confidence didn't shine through, however. "And I didn't really see this coming. Yet here I am." She lifted her arms and let them drop to the side in demonstration. "I think I have you to either thank or kill." A pause. "So…thank you."

Lauren was afraid, Carly realized. She was a quieter individual, who had dealt with a lot of rejection as an actress. Carly needed to remember that. "Well, all I did was put you in front of Ethan—you did the rest. Besides, when do people around here pay any attention to me, anyway?"

"More than you realize."

Carly shook her head, still on a high from the news. "This was all you and your talent."

Lauren exhaled slowly, as if she was about to board a really intimidating roller coaster.

"Places for act two," Trip announced to the room with gusto. Carly passed him the thumbs-up and slapped his shoulder.

"You're gonna kill it as the production stage manager-y thing."

"Thanks, Carly D. Working on it." He winked and ran a hand through his bouncy curls, which, strangely, seemed even bouncier than usual. It was almost like they knew he'd been promoted.

Kirby raced over. "Oh my God. This is the best thing ever. Lauren, you're perfect for this. Do you need anything? How about I help you with lines? Oh, wow. This is huge. I gotta call my boyfriend later. Oh, do you want to get drinks after rehearsal tonight? Maybe we can all get drinks," she said, indicating herself, Lauren, and Carly with a circular gesture.

"Kirby?" Carly asked.

"Yeah?"

"Let's give Lauren some space."

Kirby beamed and pointed at Carly as a light bulb appeared. "Got it. Say no more. You're doing great, Lauren. Gonna smash some faces, which is a good thing. It's like the new break a leg."

"Is it?" Carly asked. Because that seemed aggressive.

"Yes, and that's exactly what Lauren is going to do," Kirby said, with confidence.

Except, once they got started, Lauren wasn't herself onstage. There was a stilted quality to her delivery that hadn't been there in days past. She didn't hold eye contact with Carly for very long during any of their scenes and seemed unexpectedly clumsy all of a sudden.

"I am so sorry," Lauren blurted to TJ, as she turned and ran right into him on her downstage cross.

He steadied her by the shoulders, in character, and continued on. Company members seemed tense yet supportive as they watched, only exchanging a few looks when the same moment had to be restarted six different times. Carly felt responsible for Lauren and reassured her every time she apologized.

"And that's lunch. See you back in one hour," Trip announced.

Lauren's face was red and flushed as she moved to the door. She kept her head down in what looked to be mortification.

"Hey, Lauren, wait up." Lauren paused her exit and glanced back at Carly. "We're grabbing lunch."

"No, no. Thank you, though," Lauren said. "I'm just gonna dash back to my house and freshen up."

Carly allowed her face to fall. "No, you're coming with me. Say yes." She batted her eyelashes at Lauren and hoped she hadn't lost her touch.

Lauren opened and closed her mouth before finally settling on, "Well, when you look at me like that."

"Then I will always look at you just like that." She grabbed Lauren's hand and dragged her out of the building to the parking lot.

"Where are we going?"

"To Pete's."

"To Pete's?" Lauren squeaked, mid-drag, in the cutest voice. "That's kind of a bar, more than anything."

"Yes, I've been there and I'm dying to go back. Killer fries."

Carly secretly had another motive, however, and knew exactly what Lauren needed to get through this day and loosen the hell up. When they arrived at the dimly lit pool hall, Carly headed straight for the bar. "Fries for all?"

Lauren shrugged as she slid onto a stool at the bar, not as engaged in this field trip as Carly was. It was clear she was carrying a lot of disappointment in how the morning had gone. "Sure."

Carly took the stool next to her and signaled the bartender, who moseyed over, towel on his shoulder.

"Carly Daniel is back. We need to get you to sign the wall before you head out of town."

"I'd be happy to." She beamed. "We'll take a large order of fries, a side of nacho cheese, two Diet Cokes, a shot of whiskey, and a pickle. No, two."

Lauren raised an eyebrow. "Normally, I would question that whiskey decision, but I'm not your stage manager anymore."

Carly laughed. "Except the whiskey isn't for me."

"Who's it for?" She balked, knowing the likely answer.

"That liquid courage is for you, my friend."

Lauren backed away from the bar, hands out. "No, no, no. I don't drink during the workday. Ever. Strict rule."

"I applaud your resolve, and you're right. Not advisable. But you're nervous, and you're in your head, and just for today, let's help you out of it. Your rule can go firmly back in place tomorrow. What do you say?"

Lauren let her head fall back as if she was a teenager who had just been asked to clean her room. "Fine. I surrender to your wisdom." She popped back up. "Not on everything. You struggle with decorum, responsibility, and arriving on time."

"I also suck at singing, doing my taxes myself, and figuring out how to get the thermostat in my apartment to do what I want it to." Lauren stared at her. "Well, it seemed like you're keeping a list, so I thought I'd contribute." Lauren seemed to relax a little bit. A little self-deprecation went a long way, apparently. Carly met her gaze. "I also get nervous, you know."

"*Pshh*," Lauren said. "You absolutely do not. I've been watching you for a couple of weeks now."

"Do so. Why do you think I get caught up with parties and staying out late and—"

"Outrageous riders? I heard you had it written into your last film contract that there had to be a fluffy white bearskin rug on the floor of your trailer in addition to a fresh tray of European cheeses, but that Brie would not be tolerated."

Carly grinned. "You googled me. Does that mean you like me? Can't stop thinking about me?"

"Common problem," the bartender said, interjecting with a wink. She smiled at him as he deposited their Diet Cokes, but didn't encourage him further.

Lauren seemed focused on her drink. She looked so beautiful today. Dark blue jeans and green crocheted blouse that looked perfect for September. "I googled you to know what kind of human I was about to have on my hands."

"You mean, in addition to liking me." Carly bounced her eyebrows playfully.

"Yes, I happen to like you. There."

"Also? That rider is completely exaggerated. That's not at all what my rider looks like."

"Huh. Well, who would have guessed the gossip magazines weren't truthful?" Carly nearly spat her Diet Coke across the bar. Lauren laughed.

This was progress. She had fun bantering with Lauren. They were so different in their takes on the world. She never got bored with her. "By way of correction, I asked for cheese cubes, chocolate covered pretzels, and a fluffy blanket because I get cold. No bears were harmed in the making. What do you take me for? I love all adorable creatures. Don't believe everything you read about me, Lauren."

"I no longer will."

Their fries arrived hot out of the fryer, and Carly popped one, closing her eyes as it practically melted in her mouth. She moaned quietly and felt Lauren's gaze on her. When Carly turned, purposefully catching Lauren in the act of checking her out, Lauren quickly feigned interest in the fry basket. "So, the partying you were talking about?"

"The recreation. Ah, yes." Carly chewed her food and tried to figure out how to explain. "It was a way to take my focus off the work. If I thought about the film all day, whatever part I was trying to tackle, it consumed me and wound up undoing any and all progress. When I started goofing off, I thought about work less and just did my job when I got there. It seemed to work until…"

"Until?"

Carly shrugged. "I got spoiled and greedy. You were right when you pointed that out. I didn't take other people, or their goals, into consideration and just did what worked for me." She shook her head. "And now, I'm trying to climb my way back out, and do better."

"I've seen a difference."

"Yeah?" Carly bumped Lauren's shoulder with hers and took a pull from her soda.

"Yes," Lauren said, meeting Carly's gaze. "Your head is definitely in the game a lot more than when you first showed up for that table read."

Carly winced. "That was a pretty awful entrance. I get that now that I have a feel for the culture here. God."

"You've rebounded." Lauren shook her head and stared at the array of bottles that lined the shelf behind the bar. "I hope I do."

"What has you out of sorts? You were fine yesterday."

Lauren shook her head. "I'm Wendy and I'm going to bring the set tumbling down all over again."

Nope. Carly wasn't letting that kind of defeatist talk fly. "That mentality will leave you on your ass."

Lauren sat back in a huff. "It's not like I can help it. You saw me this morning. I was a mess."

"First day nerves. You just gotta get past 'em, and tell yourself how awesome you are. Say it. Right now."

"I'm awesome," Lauren said, in the most underwhelming voice possible.

"No, you're not. You're lame. Say it again."

"I'm incredibly awesome."

"Better. But I want to feel it here." Carly placed a hand over her heart. "I can help. You're awesome at interacting with people. Organizing things."

"That one is true. I'm like the Marie Kondo of theater."

Carly continued her list. It honestly wasn't hard thinking of things Lauren excelled at. "Pool. Multitasking. Creating likable characters onstage."

"Thank you for that. I needed to hear that."

"Making people feel important. Kissing."

Lauren blinked at her, opened her mouth and closed it. Her cheeks pinked up until she was a rosy shade of adorable. "Should we let that one go?"

"If you want," Carly said, casually. She loved affecting Lauren in any way she could. It was her favorite new pastime. That blush was worth its weight in gold, and now Carly was all hot and bothered. "Doesn't change the fact that I believe it. I've had multiple opportunities now to find out." She took a sip of her Diet Coke. "Stop me if I'm out of line, but you have really nice lips."

Lauren didn't say anything for a moment or two, and Carly gave her that space. "So do you," she said finally, with a shy grin.

"And you really know how to use them." Carly slid the rest of the fries to Lauren. The rosy cheeks remained.

"You make my head get a little crazy when you say things like that."

"You're not my stage manager anymore, you know."

"I know."

"Does that…change the rules at all? Can I file some kind of official request with a union to flirt with you on occasion?" She made a show of glancing around the bar for a spot to do just that.

Lauren smiled. "I can admit that there's…something indescribable there."

"Lust," Carly said matter-of-factly.

Lauren choked on a fry. Carly laughed and handed her a pile of napkins. "I was just kidding. Well, only kind of."

Lauren finally swallowed and rebounded. "Sorry. Wasn't expecting that. Man, you just get right to it, don't you?"

"Life is short, Lauren. I happen to like living it."

"I don't live life that much," Lauren said to her drink. "I was going to take a vacation. My first one in years. In fact, I'm supposed to be on a beach in the Caribbean right now. Instead I'm starring in a major production and having lunch at a bar with a very famous movie star." She shook her head and smiled. "I'm not complaining."

"Neither am I. I'm at Put Upon Pete's in Minneapolis with the most intriguing woman I've ever met. Also, the most beautiful."

"Oh, look at you, working it hard." Lauren laughed.

"You haven't seen anything yet." Carly glanced at her watch. "Shall we? We need to allow five minutes for the drive and another five to pay our bill. Listen, I wouldn't want you to be late. Good thing you have me to look out for you."

Lauren gasped. "Is this the Upside Down? What is happening? Where's the starlet I came here with?"

"She could be the one you go home with," Carly said, with another playful wink.

"Carly!" Lauren covered her eyes.

Carly chuckled to herself as she paid the bill. "Drink that." She slid the untouched shot toward Lauren. "It will get you out of your head and through your first day. Our little secret."

With a dramatic sigh, Lauren downed the shot with one gesture at the same time that old eighties song "You Give Love a Bad Name" blared through the speakers. Sexy as fucking hell and entirely apropos.

"This was a good lunch," Carly said, marveling.

"Agreed." Lauren smiled. "C'mon. Let's get back to work."

The rest of rehearsal had to be the most satisfying four hours Carly had spent in her entire acting career. Lauren opened up, bringing all kinds of levels to Mandy, which only inspired Carly's own emotional creativity. Under Ethan's guidance, they tried one approach, then another. As the day went on, Ethan released each cast member individually, until only Lauren and Carly remained. That's when they really dug in and made one fruitful discovery after another. Carly laughed, cried, and lost herself in Ashley, leaving her a satisfied bundle of excitement by the end of rehearsal.

"That's the day," Trip said to the three of them. "Check your email for tomorrow's rehearsal call."

Carly felt everything in her go slack as Janie moved about, tidying the rehearsal space. Productive or not, the day had taken a lot out of her. There had to be a glass of champagne and a cool mask for her eyes waiting back at her apartment, which luckily had a concierge for hire downstairs.

"I feel really good about what we did this afternoon," she told Lauren as they packed up. "We really got into it." She shook her head, still amazed at the attention to detail that went into each scene. So different from the rehearsal process for screen, which was fast and furious.

"No kissing scenes today," Lauren said, as she changed from her rehearsal shoes into her street shoes. She said it as if it was the most casual thing in the world.

Carly swallowed, as a shot of longing she hadn't been expecting rippled through her. "Nope."

Lauren straightened and slung her bag over her shoulder. "A shame. See you tomorrow, Carly." She squeezed Carly's shoulder as she passed, leaving Carly's mouth dry and her focus squarely on the spot on her arm Lauren had just touched. Yes, they'd had physical contact all day, but as Ashley and Mandy. This was Lauren's touch and it felt…purposeful.

She turned to see Trip looking on with an amused smirk. With Ethan across the room out of earshot, she stole this opportunity. Hooking a thumb behind her to the door, she asked Trip a question that she was pretty sure she already knew the answer to. "Does Lauren… flirt very often?"

Trip didn't hesitate. "I've never seen it once." A pause, as his grin widened. "Until now."

Carly, by most people's standards, wanted for very little. She was lucky in that sense. She had money, the adoration of millions of fans, and a job that she enjoyed. But that little bit of attention from Lauren made her feel like the sun was shining on her face for the first time. She stared at the door and placed a hand over her heart, wondering how it had been so boldly stolen.

Chapter Seven

L auren was on fire, and the throbbing between her legs had her breathing labored. She stared into Carly's eyes, aching to be touched. Alone in the rehearsal room, they only had a few minutes before the rest of the company would return from lunch, but it wouldn't take half that long to send her tumbling over the edge. She could already tell. She rocked against Carly, lost in the sea of the blue of her eyes.

"Please," Lauren whispered. She'd never been so turned on. Kissing Carly throughout the morning rehearsal session had done that. She loved the feel of their lips coming together, again and again. Sinking into the warmth of Carly's mouth and exploring every inch of it with her tongue left Lauren in a dizzy haze. With her jeans lying on the floor next to where she stood, Carly moved the square of fabric between her legs to the side as Lauren hitched in a breath.

She blinked, and looked around. But it wasn't the rehearsal studio at all. She found herself in the center of her own dim bedroom, just touched by morning light. She blinked again, realizing she lay in her own bed. The throbbing remained, but her surroundings had shifted drastically. "Wait. It was a dream," she murmured. Disappointment settled. Her libido didn't.

She took a shower, and as the hot water caressed her sensitive skin, she closed her eyes and relived that very vivid exchange. The circumstances might have been left to her imagination, but the way it felt when Carly touched her skin, kissed her lips was something she could rely on her memory to supply. That part was entirely accurate.

Lauren's love life hadn't been entirely barren. She'd had girlfriends here and there. She thought she'd been in love once with the owner of a small coffee shop in Ithaca, where she'd gone to school. Brenda had been five years older and highly influential in the awakening of Lauren's sexuality. She once imagined they'd get a cute little place and start a life together. Lauren would become a working actress, and Brenda would run her café. They'd meet back home for wine and dinner and curl up in bed. None of that happened, because she'd been naïve. The relationship eventually fizzled when it became apparent they didn't truly like each other outside of the bedroom. Since then, there'd been a couple of casual relationships, but nothing that really held Lauren's attention in the midst of her busy schedule.

Nobody had quite the effect on Lauren that Carly did. She had the ability to get under Lauren's skin in eighteen different ways. Even when she was annoyed with Carly, she was focused on her fully, engaged, and connected to her. It was the most unnerving thing. Yet she was beginning to crave that connection more and more, and that felt…dangerous. They lived very different lives and had very different goals for themselves. Plus, Carly had a million different people in love with her. She could have her pick. There was no way that a woman like Lauren would hold her attention for too terribly long. Not when there were so many other exciting options out there.

Wanna ride to work? Lauren stared down at the text that had just arrived as she prepared her bag for rehearsal. Water, snacks, her rehearsal shoes, and headphones for when she wasn't needed and wanted to zone out and focus on her trajectory in the show. What she hadn't prepared for was seeing Carly this early or the way her skin tingled at the thought.

What in the world was she supposed to do now? Giving in to her guilty pleasure, she typed back, *If you can be here within ten minutes.*

I'm in your driveway with two vanilla lattes. Send me away or get the hell out here so we can drive to work together.

Lauren laughed, still not quite believing Carly's new commitment to responsibility. She headed down her sidewalk with her bag and slid into Carly's upscale rental, a red BMW convertible with the top down. The morning sun shone brightly on Carly, making her blond hair pop with color.

"This is a really nice car," Lauren said, looking around. "The theater actually rented this for you? How is that possible?" While they did their best to accommodate celebrities in residence, the budget only went so far.

Carly handed over a latte. "Let's just say I upgraded." She popped her oversized black sunglasses onto her face, then hit the road with the wind in their hair.

"Of course you did."

"Hey, I can't have people taking photographs of me in a Buick."

"The world would end."

"Or my career would." Carly glanced over at her. "You look so pretty today. I've thought that eight times since you got in the car, but I feel like I should say it."

"Thank you. You're okay, too, I guess."

Carly gasped as she studied the road. "You're hard to impress. I'll have to do more with myself in the future."

"I know. I mean, look at you." She laughed and shook her head because Carly was beyond beautiful, and the entire world knew it. In fact, today she seemed like a new kind of attractive, the California girl kind. Something about the sun and the open air. The only thing missing was warmth as evidenced by her already frozen ears. Didn't matter. Lauren got an uptick in energy just being near her.

"Did you sleep well?" Carly asked.

Just the mention had Lauren remembering the desperate state she woke in, and the very detailed dream of Carly doing decadent things to her in the rehearsal hall. "I did okay," she said conservatively. "Wild dreams."

"About me?" Carly joked.

Lauren's mouth went dry. "Oh. Um, rehearsal."

"Gotcha. One of those dreams where something goes wrong, or you don't know your lines. The worst. I had them when we first started rehearsal, nearly every night."

"No, it was..." She didn't know why she'd even started the sentence, and now she didn't know how to end it. "Different than that. I love this song." She tried to move them off the topic by feigning intense interest in the radio. In fact, she turned up the volume and jammed out to it like an idiot.

Carly looked over at her curiously as she applied her turn signal. "Why are you being weird? Are you Mick Jagger all of a sudden? What kind of moves are those?"

"This is how I dance in the car." Well, hell, she had to commit now. She tossed her arms around, threw them over her head, and pushed her lips out, trying to stay on beat, which, hello, was not easy for her.

"You've got duckface down. Wow. That's impressive. Do it some more. Yes! Just like that, you sexy party animal." Carly brought the car to a stop at a traffic light and relaxed. She turned to Lauren calmly. "So do you want to talk about this sex dream, or pretend you always flail around in the middle of the morning to music you don't actually love?"

Lauren blinked and slowed her dance break. "Wasn't a big deal. Have you tried that chicken place right there? It's amazing. Get the extra green sauce. I want to say it's tomatillo. Watch out for the slight kick, though."

"Oh my God. You did have a sex dream, you little minx."

Lauren's jaw dropped. "You acted like you already knew. You didn't know?"

"Of course I didn't know. How could I know?"

"I don't know."

"Neither did I! I wondered, but then you fell completely for my trap, and it's one of the most gratifying things that's ever happened to me." They pulled into The McAllister. "I'm crazy impressed with myself right now. I feel like I might be beaming." She pulled off her sunglasses and checked herself out in the rearview mirror, dimples on full display. "I totally am."

Lauren scoffed, doing her best to downplay. "Like I said, it wasn't even that big a deal. We should just focus on our day. I finally have my act one lines down."

"Not a big deal? Really?" Carly turned off the ignition and regarded her. "I thought we'd be, you know, good at it."

God, cue the unasked-for blush once again. She felt the heat spread over her face. Lauren hated how suggestible she was in Carly's presence. "I didn't say we weren't good at it." She looked Carly square in the eye when she said it, having bundled her courage. It felt good.

Carly's lips parted, and she blinked. Her tongue touched her top lip and Lauren felt it. "It was a good dream then," she said quietly.

Lauren nodded.

The upbeat music still played from the car's stereo, and for several long moments that remained the only sound. Finally, much to her own surprise, Lauren was the first one to speak. The spark between them was undeniable. She knew it. Carly seemed to know it. While they still worked together, it was in a different, less regimented capacity. What was Lauren waiting for? "Maybe we could have dinner sometime. Only if that's something you'd be interested in. You can say no." She felt like a vulnerable and awkward teenager, asking the cool girl out.

"You're asking me on a date." Carly said it more like a victorious statement than anything else. Lauren held off exhaling for a moment until they were through this part. "What about right now?"

"Right now? What? No, we have rehearsal." She gestured to the theater.

"They can't get too far without us. Let's play hooky and go to breakfast. We can find a place with champagne and eggs Benedict."

"You're crazy." Lauren laughed. "Absolutely not." She pursed her lips. "What about tomorrow night?" She was on some sort of adrenaline high now, and it apparently supplied courage.

Carly tucked a strand of hair behind her ear, and Lauren took in the smooth column of her neck. She had flawless skin, perfect for a cinematic close-up. Lauren wanted to run one finger down that neck, to her collarbone, down the center of her chest to the round—

"I'm free tomorrow night. You pick a place. I'll drive." Lauren gave her head a tiny shake to wake herself from the fantasy. Carly quirked an eyebrow and glanced down at her chest. She wore an open collared Henley, and yes, there was a hint of cleavage. "Please tell me you were checking me out."

Lauren sipped her latte in a very obvious, playful manner. "Fine," she confessed. "I was, a little."

"Am I going to be objectified at work today?" Lauren exited the car with a smile, as Carly called after her. "Do I need to report you to my stage manager? Is there a union rep to call?"

"Maybe." She shut the door to punctuate her point just as Carly's laugh escaped. Lauren couldn't remember the last time she'd had such an invigorating morning. She felt alive and ready for all that lay ahead.

As they walked from the parking lot to the theater, the sizzle between them was almost palpable. Lauren felt like she could reach out and touch it. Carly looked back at her with a sly smile. Yep. They were on the exact same page. She didn't know what this was—a flirtation, a fling, or something legitimate. What she did know was her life sparked into color every time Carly Daniel was around, and she was really looking forward to the rest of their day together. Honestly? That's all she needed to know.

"Lauren?" Carly said, pausing in front of the door to the rehearsal hall.

"Yes?"

"Just so you know, I plan to objectify you right back."

❖

Carly couldn't remember the last time she'd gone out of her way to pursue a woman. She'd have to study a calendar, but it had definitely been before she'd become a recognizable name in entertainment. Generally, women wooed *her*. They chased her. They sent her gifts and made huge overtures to win her attention. Sometimes, she let them. Other times, she said thank you, but passed. Just part of the hookup game in Hollywood.

Lauren Prescott was different.

She didn't care who Carly was. She paid no attention to Carly's status in Hollywood, and she certainly wasn't easily impressed. Not only that, but Carly couldn't quite put her finger on what it was she wanted from Lauren. Yes, she was attracted to her and daydreamed about kissing her languidly in a variety of settings. But she also wanted to talk to her nonstop, make her laugh, figure out what made her tick, make her a plate of fluffy pancakes, and then kiss her face off some more. What did *that* mean, exactly? She didn't recognize herself lately. This was new territory for Carly, but she was up to the task of wooing.

"I can woo," she said out loud, inside the apartment that, after weeks, was beginning to feel like hers. Over the next half hour, she tried on seven different outfits, none of which felt worthy of her date that night with Lauren. Failures, all of them. Unsure what to do and close to downshifting entirely, she lay on her back in the middle of her bedroom and called the one person who could help.

"Hey, Car, what's up?"

She closed her eyes and smiled at Fallon's voice. They talked every other day or so, but she'd yet to confide in Fallon about Lauren and her swirling, confusing feelings. "I have a date and need help because I'm a train wreck and look stupid in everything I try on. Do you have time? It's okay if you don't. I can just cry in a corner and hope someone finds me later."

She heard Fallon chuckle. "Your timing is perfect. Just left the office at Sony. There was a birthday, so cake and spiked punch abounded."

Carly laughed. "Your favorite combo."

"So, you're a stupid train wreck. Who is this date with?"

"My stage manager, who is now my costar."

"Wait, the super strict one who lectures you?"

"That's the one. She's in the show now, which is a whole separate story. Her name is Lauren and she has semi-long dark hair and amazing green eyes with these tiny flecks of gold, and she sometimes keeps me up at night thinking about her. That's a lie. Lots of times. Is this normal? It doesn't feel normal."

"Wow, Carly-bear. Do you have a crush? A real one?"

"Yes," she said, drawing out the word, and throwing her arm above her head. She knew she was bringing the drama, but just hearing Fallon's voice allowed her to let all her feelings come tumbling out. Fallon was her safe place to fall. "She makes me smile, and she gets me hot."

"Those are two important things."

"She's also smart, and kind, and flirts in these subtle little ways. There's more, but I should leave in twenty. She doesn't like it when I'm late."

A long pause on the other end of the phone. "I'm sorry. You're showing up places on time? I thought you said this was Carly earlier, but clearly I misheard."

Carly sat up and spoke animatedly to her wall, pointing at it. "Very funny. But yes, she's had that kind of effect on me. It's wild, and I like it."

"Whoa."

"Whoa is exactly it. Double whoa. Hold the pickle whoa. Thank you for getting that. So I need advice." She scanned the room, wondering if she should maybe jot a Lauren to-do list. This was all so beyond her experience level.

"Hit me," Fallon said. "I'm ready."

"First of all, what do I wear?"

"Well, do you still have a tan?"

She checked out her arms. "It's fading, but yes."

"Anything to accentuate it. Light colors. Whites, beiges, pastels."

A burst of energy hit. She had an idea. "A yellow chiffon blouse with a slight ruffle in the cuff, light wash jeans, and my beige block heels?"

"Now we're talking. Where are you two going?"

"To dinner. I plan to pay, and open doors, and be genuine and charming."

Fallon chuckled. "You're always charming. You don't even have to try at that part. People love you, Car. That's never been your problem."

"What is my problem? I should probably know."

"Really? Right now?" Carly heard a car door open and close. Sounds of Taylor Swift drifted on to the call. "I'm not sure this is the best time to go into—"

"Yes, really. Put me on speaker and let me drive home with you while you tell me all the things I need to work on. What's my biggest problem? I can take it."

She heard Fallon sigh. "Fine. It's consideration. You tend to think about the effect your actions will have on other people only after the fact."

"Go on." Carly tapped one nail against her top lip nervously as she listened.

"You take what you want first and let the chips fall where they may. Oftentimes, it's other people picking up those chips after you."

Carly sobered. Lately, she'd been trying hard to listen in the midst of harder conversations and truly internalize what she heard coming her way. This wasn't the first time she'd heard the sentiment Fallon described. It wasn't even the first time from Fallon. Yet she was at a point in her life when she truly wanted to do better, behave better, and think of others first. Not because her career was in trouble, but because something in her was changing. She wanted to be a better person.

She nodded. "You're right. I'm going to work on that. And Fallon?"

"Yep."

"If I've ever taken advantage of our friendship, your kindness, and I have a feeling I have…Well, I'm really sorry."

The line went quiet for a moment. "I appreciate you saying so. You're a good egg, Carly. I've always known that part."

Carly smiled at the wall. "Not as good as you, but I'm going to work harder. Thanks for the chat."

"Anytime. Call me tomorrow with all the noteworthy details, and don't you dare leave out the sexy parts."

"Try and stop me."

Carly clicked off the call and felt her heart rate slow. Fallon had pointed her in the right direction, helped her come up with the perfect outfit, and had been a friend to her when she needed it. She smiled and took a deep breath. Tonight felt important, but that didn't mean it wouldn't also be fun. She'd been looking forward to their date since the very moment Lauren had asked her out.

Now all she had to do was put on her chosen outfit and go and pick up her date.

CHAPTER EIGHT

Rocky looked up at Lauren and snuffled as she took a final glimpse at herself in the mirror, happy with her look. She'd left her hair down, liking the way it fell across her forehead today. Rocky snuffled some more and lifted his feet. She grinned. He was a big time snuffler, always using the sound to express his emotions, which were varied and complex. "You got something to say?" she asked. "I put your dinner down already." She returned her focus to the mirror and ran a finger along her bottom lip to apply a little more gloss. Snuffling. "You don't want your dinner?" She glanced down at him.

He picked up his feet, set them down, and snuffled some more in response. Aha. The shuffle-snuffle combo. He likely knew she was going somewhere and demanded to know who with. Rocky IV had always been her protector, defender, and right-hand man. She scooped up the pudgy little guy, carried him with her to the kitchen, and plopped him in front of his full dish to see if he'd get back to regularly scheduled programming. He glanced up at her, snuffled, but obliged, shaking his little curlicue of a tail as he ate.

When the doorbell rang, he trotted dutifully behind her to scope out the new guest. Lauren opened the door, prepared to apologize for Rocky's likely bark, only to have the words stolen from her lips. Carly stood there in a yellow top that had her glowing and a sexy pair of heels. Her hair was half up and half down, and came with lazy waves, the kind they had on TV but Lauren could never seem to master when she tried. "Sorry."

Carly grinned. "Why are you sorry? And hi."

"Hi." She swallowed and found herself again. "You look so

beautiful. Sorry, again." She shook her head to emphasize how silly she felt. "I wasn't expecting to lose my ability to communicate."

"That's okay," Carly said and chewed on the inside of her lip. "Thank you. I was about to say the same to you. Oh, and I got you these." From behind her back, Carly produced a bouquet of flowers in a variety of oranges, yellows, and purples. They were gorgeous, and the perfect fall arrangement.

"Wow." She accepted the flowers and marveled at their beauty. She didn't receive flowers too often. They made Lauren feel special, knowing that Carly had gone out of her way for her. "Thank you so much."

"You're welcome." Lauren took Carly's hand and tugged her inside. "And I'm on time," Carly said triumphantly as she passed.

Lauren smiled to herself. "I noticed that." She followed behind Carly, taking in how she wore those jeans as if they were tailored to her perfect body. "Among other things," she murmured quietly.

"What other things?" Carly asked, turning around.

Caught! Lauren hadn't meant to be overheard. "Oh. I just meant that I'd noticed how thoughtful you were to bring flowers."

Carly stood a little taller, as if she'd won the spelling bee. It was adorable. *She* was. "It's what you do on a first date."

Rocky, seeing their new guest, lifted his feet and wagged his whole stubby body in Carly's direction. Lauren gaped because he usually took a moment to warm up to people, but then it was Carly, after all, and she'd never had trouble making friends. "This is my dog, Rocky IV. He wants to sniff you all over and then make snuffling demands of your time."

Carly plopped right on the floor and held out a gentle hand to him. "Hey there, buddy. You are a little man with a plan, aren't you? I like your little scrunched face." Rocky sniffed the outstretched hand several times for good measure and then crawled into Carly's lap. Lauren shook her head. This dog was no fool.

"Are we friends now?" Carly asked Rocky. His back leg started to kick like a drumstick when Carly found his favorite spot, the one right underneath his collar.

"Should I give you guys some privacy?" Lauren asked.

"No way." Carly kissed the side of Rocky's face, which warmed Lauren's heart, and stood right up. "While Rocky IV is cute, my date is cuter." She paused. "Was that a dumb thing to say? You make me nervous. Well, dating you does."

Lauren played that sentence back because she had a hard time believing it. Carly came off as the most self-assured human, comfortable in her own skin and proud of it. "No, you're not."

Carly nodded, and her smile dimmed, showcasing a glimpse of vulnerability. "It's true. You're...different than the women I generally go out with." Carly held out a hand. "In a good way. That's why I have the nervous thing. Am I talking too much?" Carly took a deep breath.

Wow. She was serious about the nerves and seemed actually off-kilter. "Not at all," Lauren said, finding her own confidence now that she understood she wasn't alone. "It's just dinner. We can get away from the theater and just hang out. Shoot the breeze. Count white guys with blue ties."

"Are there a lot of those?"

"Too many."

Carly nodded. "I'd like that."

"Me, too." A pause. "Shall we?"

"After you."

Lauren gave Rocky a good-bye series of scratches and led the way out. Carly, to her surprise, hurried past and opened the door in grandiose fashion. Okay, Carly was bringing the full charm, which resonated with Lauren. She felt significant and cared for and was so into Carly in this outfit that every inch of her screamed for contact. *Relax*, she commanded every last nerve ending. She had a date to enjoy.

"Where does your mom live?" Lauren asked. "You mentioned the only child thing, and that the two of you are close."

Carly sipped her after dinner coffee and Baileys, the house specialty at the little bistro Lauren had picked out for them not far from downtown. "She's in Portland and works at a boutique winery owned by a really great family. They take care of her. She handles tastings and merchandise, things like that. Tangle Valley Vineyards."

"I love that. I had no idea you knew about wine."

"Well, she knows a lot more about it than I do. I can tell you the best places to hide in a vineyard. It was a great place to grow up. Hidden away and beautiful."

Lauren leaned her hand on her chin. "But somewhere along the way you got the acting bug."

She nodded. "From the beginning. I used to act out my own stories with my friends at that very vineyard. My good friend Joey and I would divide up parts. Whichever role I was given, I would always make sure to infuse it with some kind of dramatic twist not indicated in the script. My costars wanted to throttle me."

"But knowing you, I'm going to predict they didn't."

Carly set down her glass mug. "No. People let me get away with too much."

Lauren appreciated the self-awareness that came with that statement. The Carly of just a month ago would not have been so quick to admit that. "You're lucky, if you think about it."

"Yes, but maybe I've ridden that train as far as I should. It seems to have done damage." She sat back in her chair. They'd each had a glass of wine earlier in the evening, which had helped relax them into easy conversation. There was a flirtatiousness flitting between them every so often, too, that seemed to elevate everything. Lauren's senses were on high alert. She could feel the air against her skin, smell the amazing aromas wafting in from the kitchen, and appreciate small things like the purple ribbon tied around the candle on their table.

"I think you're doing an admirable job of turning it all around, though. Maybe that will extend to your career back home as well."

"That's my hope."

Lauren met Carly's gaze. "I really like tonight," Lauren confessed.

Carly leaned in and squeezed Lauren's hand across the table. "Me, too."

Lauren stole a bite of the cheesecake they shared and sank into glory. Clearly, it was sent from an army of angels on a mission from heaven. "Oh, Carly. Here. You gotta try this."

"Yeah?" Carly asked. She had this way of smiling sometimes that was actually more half a smile. One side of her mouth would pull, revealing the dimple on her right cheek, and it was the sexiest thing. Lauren had seen it at rehearsal, midscene, but seeing it now for her benefit came with a whole new level of appreciation. Lauren couldn't resist. She prepped her fork with another bite and held it out to Carly, who smiled and moved in. Watching her eat that decadent dessert was downright erotic. Her lips pulled away from the fork slowly, and she sank into wonder and enjoyment once the cheesecake hit her taste buds. Lauren blinked, imagining her in the throes of another brand of pleasure, which made her uncomfortable in her own chair.

"Amazing," Carly said and dabbed her mouth with her cloth napkin.

"It really was." They stared at each other, and Lauren swore the temperature in the room doubled.

"I didn't get to see much of your place," Carly said, finally. Lauren was an adult and knew the implication. She didn't hop into bed easily and wasn't sure she was ready, even with the surprising feelings she already had for Carly. Okay, the lust factor wasn't helping her keep a clear head, either. Carly must have picked up on her hesitation. "But we can just hang out. I don't want you to think that I'm trying to seduce you."

"I like you a lot. Let me emphasize the *a lot* part."

Carly grinned. God, she had the best smile when she responded to something that made her genuinely happy. This particular smile was different than the others, the ones that were polite, or friendly, or fun-loving. "I like you, too. I want to keep liking you."

"Then, yes, come see my place, and hang out," Lauren said.

Their bill arrived and Carly snatched it up. "I'd like to pay for this one." She opened the leather portfolio and deflated. "Already taken care of."

Lauren quirked an eyebrow. "They comped the check because you're Carly Daniel? Does that happen a lot?"

Carly looked forlorn. "Yes. But I was hopeful it wouldn't tonight, outside LA. I really wanted to buy you dinner." Anguish flashed in her eyes. "That's part of this."

"This?" Lauren squinted. "You'll have to explain."

"You know." Carly stared hard, like it was apparent. Finally, she lifted a shoulder. "The wooing."

"Oh. The wooing." A pause. Lauren frowned and had to run that by herself again. "You're wooing me?"

"I was trying. How's it going? Be honest."

Just when Lauren thought Carly couldn't get any cuter, she got an eager look on her face that made Lauren want to kiss all over it. Instead, she maintained her composure. "I suppose, on evaluation, I would say it's going well. There were flowers, doors opened, and now an attempt at paying the bill. Yes, now I can see the wooing quite clearly."

Carly leaned in. "Sorry for the epic check failure. Next time, it's on me. Trust me. I'm good for it."

Lauren nearly spat out her Baileys. "I've heard that somewhere. Oh yes, I think it was *Fortune* magazine." Underneath her amusement, Lauren was beginning to understand that Carly had a very specific idea of what would impress her, when really, all she needed was a nice night out with Carly, talking, laughing, stealing glances. The kind of date they were having truly fed her soul. "You know what, though? You don't have to woo me. I'm happy to just sit with you."

Carly exhaled. "Good. Wooing is hard. You have to think several steps ahead, which I must admit, has never been my strong suit." She glanced at the door. "Shall we get out of here?"

Lauren nodded. Once they hit the parking lot, it was clear a cold front had moved in. She scrunched her shoulders to her ears and took Carly's hand in hers. Whoa. How was it that they fit together so effortlessly, as if those hands had been holding each other for a long time now?

"Hey, Carly D, marry me!" a man yelled from the window of a passing SUV. Carly ignored him, focusing entirely on Lauren, and when Carly focused on someone, it felt like they were the most noteworthy person on the planet. Lauren felt that way now.

It wasn't a long drive to Lauren's place, but now that the sun was down, it was getting colder by the minute. They were expecting rain that night, and Minneapolis was ready to introduce Carly to its infamous lower temperatures. Carly's jacket was light at best, and she seemed to cling to it for dear life. Lauren cranked the heat and placed a hand on Carly's knee. "You okay?"

"Just getting used to what September can feel like here. I'm not in California anymore, Toto."

"That's for sure. Do you miss it?"

Carly nodded. "Would you want to visit me there sometime?"

Lauren took in the question. She hadn't imagined that whatever this was would extend beyond the here and now of the show. Like it or not, she knew the game. She saw the showmances crop up, and she saw them recess as soon as the show closed. Everyone moved on to their next project. Sometimes, the inevitable breakup left one of the two heartbroken. That was the hard part. "Could be fun," Lauren said, keeping it vague, guarding her heart, but underneath thinking how much fun it would be for Carly to show her around LA. She decided to amend her answer. "I'd like that."

The temperature seemed to have dropped even more as they made their way up Lauren's walk.

"Holy hell full of icicles and frozen witches." The first cold front of the season was not messing around, but Carly was also a bit hyperbolic in her reaction.

"I wouldn't go that far," Lauren said. "You're kind of a baby."

Carly did a freezing little dance up the walk. "I don't even care. It's Santa's workshop weather. Are the elves in the bushes? Send them out here."

Lauren laughed. "While this is cold for a Minneapolis September, there's no ice or snow to be seen." Lauren estimated the temperatures to be in the forties. Not a big deal.

"I think Minnesota is hazing me," Carly shouted, as the wind whistled past. "Minnesota is laughing with its northern friends about my frozen ears. They're probably tossing back hot toddies and high-fiving." The wind picked up and the branches of the trees in front of Lauren's house swayed noticeably. "Ahhh! Get me inside. I'll die!"

"Working on it." Lauren landed on the front porch just behind Carly and put her key in the lock. "Do you think it's possible that you might be overreacting just a little bit?"

"No," Carly said, her expression dialed to panic, and her nose red. She shifted from one foot to the other in a ridiculous looking march, waiting for Lauren to get the door open.

Lauren laughed. Actresses were dramatic. She'd always known that part. She liked it on Carly, though. It felt playful, and fun. "Well, then come inside. I hear there's no wind." With the door unlocked, she held it open for Carly, who raced through as the wind howled behind her. Lauren closed the door and joined Carly in the dimly lit entryway, bringing them to silence, having left the escalating weather outside. Well, silence except for the very quiet sound of Rocky snoring on the couch on top of his favorite plaid blanket.

"You lived," Lauren said quietly. Her smile receded and her heart thudded.

"You saved me." Their voices seemed so quiet, the air thick and heavy. She could almost hear the snap, crackle, and pop of the tension coiled between them. "I owe you for that. Come here." Carly held out her hand, and Lauren took it, allowing herself to be pulled in. Every part of her hummed with wonderful anticipation. She wanted to be close to Carly, to take in her scent, and touch her skin, and feel Carly's lips beneath hers. They'd kissed in rehearsal, and one drunken night out. Nothing came with the same level of intent as right this moment.

Carly was shorter, but with her wearing heels, and Lauren in flats, they were square. Carly made the move. She turned her head to the side and hovered just shy of Lauren's mouth. "You do things to me," she whispered.

Lauren closed her eyes, waiting for the kiss, desperately wanting. "You do them to me, too," she whispered back. At those words, Carly's lips were on hers, softly at first, and even that made Lauren's knees shake and her muscles melt. When Carly deepened the kiss and ran her tongue along Lauren's bottom lip, requesting entry, Lauren thought her brain might explode in the best way. She parted her lips and accepted Carly's tongue, which lightly explored her mouth with soft, fleeting touches. It was like everything Carly did was designed to make her crave more, and oh, she very much did. Carly, clearly on a mission, walked Lauren backward as they kissed until her back met the wall of the entryway with a soft thud. Her hands moved up Lauren's body to her shoulders, her neck, until they cradled her face. With her thigh pressed between Lauren's, they made out like fourteen-year-olds against that wall. It was so different, kissing Carly this time. Yes, she knew what she tasted like, how their mouths fit, but this kiss? Had no destination. Outside, the wind sang. Inside, the heat tripled. Somehow, without fully planning on it, she was pulling Carly's yellow blouse out of her jeans. This hadn't been the plan, yet here they were. Carly pulled away from the kiss and watched her do it. God, she had such a sexy look on her face. Her eyes were dark and her lips were swollen from all the kissing.

A crack of thunder hit, loud. Carly stepped into her space and slid her arms around Lauren's neck. She kissed just below her ear and down, sending a shiver all through Lauren. "I want you so badly," she murmured between kisses. "I can't stop thinking about you, touching you. God, you smell so good."

Lauren's eyes fluttered closed again as she attempted to deal with the sensations that flooded her from every direction. She could feel Carly's breasts through her shirt. She wanted to see them, touch them, lick them. Another crack of thunder. What were they doing? Was this maybe too soon? This was technically just a first date. Carly felt amazing in her arms, warm and sexy and ready. *Should we stop?* She wanted to get her out of these clothes. She cupped Carly's ass, which was firm and tight. Not at all surprising from the way it looked in every pair of pants she wore. *Maybe we should log some more time together first.* Lauren was on fire. Her bikinis were wet and her center throbbed. She slid her hands up to the small of Carly's back and under her shirt. Carly gasped quietly when she touched her skin. *Maybe slow down.* There was her brain again, ruining all her damn fun. She pulled her mouth away and turned to the side. She heard the sound of her own ragged breaths, of Carly's.

"You okay?" Carly asked, touching her lips.

"I need just a minute," Lauren said, walking down the hall into the kitchen, and holding up one finger over her head. Carly waited a moment before following. Lauren could hear the soft click of her heels and turned to her, speaking across the granite island in her kitchen. Rocky raised his head, surveyed them, and dropped it again, returning to his midevening snooze. "Is it bad that I'm not a quick hookup kind of girl?"

Carly blinked, and rolled her lips in as if waiting for her wits to return after all the kissing. It was also possible she had whiplash from Lauren's about-face. "No."

"No? Okay, good, because as much as I want to…keep going, I'm worried I'm not her." Lauren ran a hand through what had to be disheveled hair, from the wind, and the making out. She attempted to fluff it back into place.

"Your hair is sexy like that. Don't touch it?" It was a request, not an order. Carly was watching her with interest. No, that was appreciation. But she also gave Lauren space, and that helped Lauren's mind slow down.

Finally, Lauren gestured between them. "This is…good." She

blew out a steadying breath and leaned one arm on the counter in front of her. "The way we kiss…" Lauren shook her head in wonder.

Carly nodded.

The rain that she'd predicted was on the way was here and began to pelt the side of the house. They were in the midst of a storm, and Lauren could identify. Why wouldn't her brain just shut up and let her enjoy this woman whom she very much wanted to undress?

"Lauren? We don't have to jump into bed."

"I want to."

Carly grinned, but her eyes also held understanding. "But you also want to get your feet underneath you when it comes to me."

"Is it that obvious?"

"It's how you work. You like order, and processes, and all your pencils sharpened for the day." Carly had been paying attention. Lauren, as stage manager, started every rehearsal with four sharpened pencils. When she'd taken on the role of Mandy, she'd kept the practice. Carly came around the island and faced her. "I'm not quite sharp yet." She shrugged. "I'll get there. Hopefully. But I'm not in a hurry."

With Carly so close to her, Lauren's body began to wake up all over again. She moved closer and touched Carly's bottom lip lightly with her thumb. "Maybe we could wait a little bit?"

Carly nodded. "We can wait. I can wait." She nodded about eight times and Lauren had to laugh and kiss her again. And oh, that led to a lot more kissing. God, they were advanced placement when it came to it. She'd never enjoyed kissing another human so much in all of her life.

"I'm regretting that decision about now," she confessed between kisses.

"It's okay. We can do this instead. I really like doing this." Carly breathed, and dove back in, this time backing Lauren against the counter.

"You like me up against things."

"Because you're fucking hot up against things." A kiss. "And up against me, too." Another kiss. "Really anywhere, you're hot." More kissing. "Have you seen yourself play pool? God. It's hard to stop kissing you. Distract me."

"Tell me a joke," Lauren said.

Carly paused mid-kiss. "That's your solution? Stand-up?"

Lauren ran her hands up and down Carly's shoulders. "I'll try anything."

"Who do you call when you need your pants hemmed tomorrow?"

Lauren's gaze drifted to Carly's collarbone. She touched it and traced it lower, to the glimpse of cleavage peeking out of her top. "I don't know. Who should I call?"

Carly watched the progress of Lauren's finger, her breathing rapid. "Taylor Swift," she said and offered a half-hearted smile followed by a desperate swallow.

Lauren grinned and a portion of the tension eased. "That was a pretty good one." She dropped her finger, knowing she'd been playing with fire and should back away from the ready-to-ignite flame.

"New idea," Carly said. "Separate countertops, one fact each." Carly pointed to the counter across from her. "Your back goes there. Mine will stay here."

"Bossy, all of a sudden. I thought I was the stage manager." She did as Carly commanded and stood across from her, back against the opposite countertop.

Carly mirrored her stance against her own counter. "Tell me one fact about you."

Lauren looked to the ceiling as she combed her brain. "Office supply stores turn me on."

"Really?" Carly nodded and touched her temple. "Filing that one away."

"Your turn. One fact."

Carly didn't hesitate. "I love it when food is burned a little."

"Oh, you mean like cookies."

"No, I mean anything. A little bit of char on my vegetables, my fries, my burger, anything."

Lauren balked. "Blasphemous. Your burger? No, no, no."

Carly extended her hand and shook her finger. "No judgment. Only facts. Go."

She was being bossy again, and damn it, it made Lauren even hotter for her. "I love matching underwear sets, but I've never been able to master a thong." She watched as Carly's lips parted. Yeah, that one had affected her, and Lauren enjoyed the response. "Your turn."

"I'm wearing one right now."

Lauren squeezed the countertop behind her. Her body had been on high alert since they'd arrived at her place, but that last comment sent her to a whole new level of arousal.

Lauren blinked. "I've always wanted to have sex in public but have never had the courage. Go."

"When I first met you, I thought you were uptight and a buzzkill. Your turn."

"When I first met you, I thought you were self-involved and overrated." Carly's jaw fell. "No judgment, remember? Your fact?"

"But now, I think you're the most intriguing, most beautiful woman I've ever been involved with."

Lauren sucked in a breath. Those words settled over her, and she felt like she might float away. She refocused, remembering the game. "I was wrong about you, too, and the sex dream I told you about? Impactful as hell. I still haven't been able to shake it. Go."

"Whether it's days, weeks, months, or years, I will probably think about undressing you until the moment I get the chance."

God, was her heater on high? Her cheeks were warm and she felt a little drunk on desire. "Kissing you in rehearsal is the best part of my day."

"Same. Staring into your eyes at the end of act one is everything. I always end that scene with a slight tremble because you affect me so much. That's not acting. That's you."

Lauren let go of the counter and took the two steps that brought her to Carly. With one hand under her jaw, she slowly kissed the woman who'd walked into her life out of nowhere and made her feel so much. Call it lust, infatuation, or even a damn showmance. It didn't matter. Lauren felt alive, and that meant everything.

"Look at that," Carly murmured. She smiled as she kissed Lauren back. "We're at it again."

Lauren pulled back in Carly's arms and met her gaze. "It's like you're this magnet, pulling me in. I can't stay away. Plus, these lips are addictive."

"The best part is you don't have to stay away." She caught Lauren's mouth and melted into the kiss.

That's how the night ended.

With kissing, more kissing, and a side of wandering hands. She walked Carly to the door, still touching her as much as possible. The small of her back, her hand, her cheek. The kiss at the door was the longest yet, and when Carly stepped back onto her porch, she glowed like an angel under the porch light.

"I'll see you at work tomorrow."

"Carly. Thank you for all of this. It was a fantastic night."

"For me, too. Maybe I can woo you again in the future? Maybe?"

Lauren laughed. "God, yes. The more wooing the better, I always say."

"Good night, Lauren."

"That it was. Good night."

CHAPTER NINE

Carly was half giddy, half terrified. The key lime yogurt she'd had for breakfast was a nice temporary distraction from the very big day she had ahead at work.

They had seven rehearsals remaining. Seven. Luckily, they had moved to The McAllister's main stage for the remainder of them, and that meant they'd have an entire set to get to know and work with. It also meant there'd be new spatial relationships and technical elements, like lights and sound, that would make their way into the show beginning today, during their ten out of twelve rehearsal.

As Lauren had explained it, the ten out of twelve was for the addition and tweaking of each and every technical cue in the show. Each of the designers would sit in the house with stage management as they adjusted levels, intensities, and timing of each cue. They'd work ten hours out of a twelve-hour day, with two hours allotted for meals.

"I can't believe we're finally here," Kirby said, looking up at the theater's architecture. It reminded Carly of a beautiful outdoor theater, complete with the illusion of a night sky overhead, stars and all. Cherubs lined the proscenium, and newly upholstered red seats filled the house. Nearly fifteen hundred, she'd been told. Kirby turned in a reverent circle. "I've wanted to work at The McAllister since I was twelve, and I'm finally here, in the room."

"Kinda makes you want to pinch yourself," Carly said. Though she'd once underplayed the entire experience, Carly now understood how special this all was. She just didn't want to do anything to screw it up, and there was lots to learn about working in the space.

Lauren arrived with her bag slung over her shoulder, and Carly turned. If she'd been aware of Lauren's presence in the past, before their date, she was hyperaware of it now.

Lauren waved at the room with two hands. "Happy ten out of twelve, everyone." She wore fall boots, taupe and up to her midcalf, gray jeans, and a navy hooded sweater. Carly blinked back a too noticeable reaction to how fantastic she looked. The idea that she now got to spend the rest of the day with this woman and would be paid to do so was a surreal concept. Her job certainly did not suck.

"Did you catch anything I said?"

She turned absently and looked up at Trip, who must have been speaking. "I'm so sorry. I didn't."

He looked across the room to Lauren and smothered a knowing smile. "Right. Got it. Well, I was just offering to walk you through the different danger zones on set for when we go to black between scenes. I've marked them with glow tape, but you'll want to be aware for safety."

"Good idea. Lead the way." She glanced over her shoulder one more time to Lauren, who was busy signing in with Janie. For whatever reason, in that moment, Lauren intuitively raised her gaze to Carly's.

"Hi," she mouthed.

Carly offered a wave back. The connection from the other night was still in full effect.

Bam. She smacked right into somebody. Tinsley. The set woman. "Oh my God, I'm so sorry," Carly said.

"Yeah. Probably best to keep your eyes forward." She flicked a look in Lauren's direction. "Instead of over there. Make sure everybody is safe."

Carly offered a salute. "On it."

Tinsley tolerated her at a minimum. Carly was pretty confident it was because of her own interest in Lauren. Jealousy flared, and she quieted it. She had no ownership of Lauren, even if she secretly hoped she had no interest in Tinsley, or anyone else for that matter. One thing Tinsley had over Carly—Minneapolis. She was a permanent fixture. Carly wasn't.

"When you make this corner, be aware of the edge right here. Use the tape as your guide."

"Got it." She followed Trip to their next destination. Carly generally considered herself a casual dater, never getting too serious, never demanding too much of the other woman. She was young, and out to enjoy herself. Why did this feel like the stakes were so much higher? A Tinsley in the mix should never have bothered her.

"Any questions?" Trip asked. He looked at her. She looked back.

"No, I think you covered everything. Very thorough." She pointed at herself. "Impressed." She realized, lamely, that she'd probably only registered about half of Trip's instructions, which couldn't have been good.

It wasn't.

Two hours later, during a run of lighting cues, she slammed smack into an end table on her exit, which kicked her into one of those incredibly graceful foot shuffles, where you thought you might just remain upright, but no. "Ow," Carly mumbled as the pain arrived.

"Hold, please," she heard Trip say over the God mic. The lights came on and seven different people moved to Carly, who held up her hand from the floor that she was fine.

"I'm good. Just a very stupid exit is all." She chuckled and tried not to point out that the front portion of her right thigh throbbed from the collision with the hefty end table, and the ankle on her same foot hurt from where she twisted it trying to prevent herself from falling.

In the sea of faces crowded around her, it was Lauren's that pulled her focus. "Did you try to take that set piece out?" she asked with a grin.

"I don't really feel like it matches Ashley's taste," she said back with some sass.

Lauren's fingers went around her arm to steady her as she stood. "Seriously, are you okay?" The stagehands, seeing she was upright, stepped back.

Carly nodded. "I'm an idiot, but I'll live." She leaned in closer to Lauren. "But I'm not going to refuse any TLC. I'm no fool."

"I'll kiss it later," she said back in Carly's ear. Suddenly, this little injury didn't seem like such an awful thing. Her ankle throbbed like crazy through the remainder of rehearsal, especially when she put too much weight on it, but she chose instead to focus on Lauren and their scenes together. Today, more than ever before, their onstage chemistry seemed to come clawing out of the dialogue. Ethan, when she encountered him, seemed on cloud nine about the show's progress. It seemed like he couldn't stop grinning, which made her feel satisfied with the work she'd done. They hadn't even been in front of an audience yet, and Carly was already so fulfilled by this process.

"How's your foot?" Lauren asked, as they stood in the wings, waiting for the designers to be ready to move forward to the next cue.

"I'll be okay."

Lauren didn't seem convinced. "You don't have to be a badass. For someone so expressive, this is the time you choose to be stoic?" She tucked a strand of hair behind Carly's ear. "Tell me where it hurts."

Carly melted then and there. She also dropped some of her pretense, because Lauren was becoming her safe place to fall. "I don't think I'm officially injured, but I do think it's going to hurt for a day or two. My ankle especially. I turned it weird. I'm thinking it's probably a mild sprain."

"Carly," Lauren said in the most sympathetic voice, "you need to take it easy, okay? I'm going to let Trip know you'll be at half."

She put her hand on Lauren's forearm to stop her progress. "No, I don't want to be any trouble. I'm kind of known for it, remember? Let's just get through today and relax with some pizza and beer after."

"We will definitely do those things, but in the meantime, you need to take care of that foot. I have your back, okay? This is a legitimate concern." She took Carly by the chin and didn't seem to care who saw. "You're going to be okay."

Lauren left Carly in the wings, overwhelmed at how wonderful it felt to be looked out for, taken care of, by someone whose only intention was just that. Lauren was legitimately worried about her.

The behavior continued for the rest of the day. Lauren arranged to have Carly sit whenever the designers got into a discussion that didn't require the actors to stand. In fact, she ordered Carly to do so several times during their ten of twelve. She checked in on her with little questioning looks and offered her an arm for assistance whenever they exited the stage together.

"Let me look at it," Lauren said, during one of their official breaks. Sitting together in the greenroom offstage, Carly took off the shoes that were a part of her costume and allowed her foot to be placed in Lauren's lap.

"Oh, sweetie, it's swollen." Lauren ran her fingertips lightly over the puffy area.

Carly relished the term of endearment. Lauren had never called her anything but Carly before. She liked the sound of it a lot. "Not looking too cute there," she said of her ankle, playing it totally cool. "I look like a woman in her third trimester—if I was only pregnant on one side."

Lauren's mouth fell open and she turned to Carly in amusement as if the most interesting fact had just occurred to her. "You would be so sexy pregnant. I hope that's not out of line to say."

Carly liked that comment a lot, too. "Nothing you say to me is ever out of line if it's what you're thinking. I do want kids someday. Not today, mind you. But down the road. Once I'm a little more settled."

"Your kids are going to love you. They'd have the most fun mom on the block. I have a feeling you'd be out riding bikes with them until dark." Lauren smiled. Her hair, which she generally wore straight, had a slight curl to it. The stylists were tweaking their looks for the show.

Carly reached up and touched one of the dark lazy curls. Lauren had such soft hair. "Can you imagine?"

"I can. Adorable." Lauren ran her fingertips back and forth across Carly's ankle and calf. The tickling sensation, and the fact that it was Lauren touching her, had her warm.

"Thank you for being so nice to me."

Lauren offered her a soft smile. "It's hard not to be nice to you. Believe me. I've tried."

Carly chuckled. "I remember someone yelling at me in my apartment. Holding their arm out in indignation."

"I wouldn't say yelling," Lauren said, closing one eye. She smelled so amazing.

"Mm-hmm. I would. You're very effective at yelling without raising your voice. You could teach a class: How to Shame People into Doing What You Want Without Doing Much at All."

"Oh my God," Lauren squeezed her knee. "I could be a millionaire and buy the fancy house next to yours."

Carly laughed. "Then I'd have to buy binoculars. Do you sleep in the nude?"

"Yes."

She froze. "You do not. You're just saying that to get me all bothered." But Carly still hadn't moved. The sexy image was too much to let go of, so she awaited confirmation that it had, in fact, just been a joke, before real life could resume.

"I'm not kidding," Lauren said. She tickled the top of Carly's foot.

"Good God." Carly fell back against the couch. "How am I supposed to deal with that?"

Lauren laughed. "There you go, being dramatic again."

"What if I told you that I sleep nude?"

Lauren threw herself against the back of the couch silently, mirroring Carly's exact movements. Her face was perfectly red.

Carly laughed this time and turned her face to Lauren's. "See?"

Lauren sighed. "I do now. I really, really do."

"Do you wanna have a quickie in the coat closet?"

"What?" Lauren's jaw dropped. "No way. That's a scandal, right there. You Hollywood types, such a bad influence on the innocent theater folks." But Lauren was looking at Carly's lips with intent and gave herself the hell away.

"Hey, you two," Ethan said, as he strolled to the fridge. He pointed at Carly's ankle that still lay across Lauren's lap. "How's it feeling?"

"I'll live." She pulled her leg back and sat up, remembering Lauren's advice about working on her professional side. "Just need to take it easy for the next day or so."

"We can make that happen."

Sally, the assistant to the costume designer, stuck her head into the room. "Lauren, can I borrow you for adjustments to your act two dress?"

"On my way." She gave Carly's knee a slight touch as she departed, which gave Carly an uptick in energy. Everything about Lauren did. She watched her leave the room with appreciation. Lauren had amazing legs, and the slim black pants she wore in the show made that point over and over.

"You've come alive on those boards. You know that, right?" Ethan said.

She turned to him and refocused. "It's starting to feel really good. If I can just avoid slamming into furniture, you know. Gonna practice at home."

"I think you should be proud of the work. Your portrayal is deep as hell." Ethan turned a chair from the table backward and took a seat. She received feedback from him in their notes sessions, and during scene work, but they hadn't touched base one-on-one in a while. She was interested in his take.

"I feel it," she told him, leaning forward on the couch, her elbows on her knees. "I don't know how to describe it. It's as if I've really bonded with this character. I get her, Ethan, in such a crazy way." She sat back and scratched her head absently as she sorted out her thoughts, reveling in the exhilaration of this rehearsal process. She'd never been so fulfilled creatively. "I understand what drives Ashley forward, and I love everything about her, as different as we are."

He nodded. "That's all coming through. I knew we'd get there. It's why I wanted you for the part."

"Thank you for giving me a chance. Not writing me off because I was an out of control brat."

He squinted. "You had me a little worried early on."

"Rightfully so. I apologize. I had a stage management team who knew how to handle me, though. Kudos to Lauren and Trip. I'm trying to be more aware of…others."

"It shows." He nodded. "Speaking of Lauren, the onstage romance since recast?"

"Yeah?"

He shook his head as if in disbelief. "There's such a specificity to it now." He used his hand to make a mind-blown gesture and then opened the pop-top on his Red Bull with a crack. "I don't know how we've gotten there in such a short span of time with you two."

She smiled at the compliment and understood that he likely didn't realize fully what was happening offstage. She agreed with his sentiment, however. She felt it when they were onstage together. "She gives me so much to work off of. I feel like we have great chemistry."

"I gotta tell you. It's never been more apparent than today." He shook his head. "I don't know what you two did differently, but if we could find some way to bottle it and save it for our audiences, I'd be elated. There's a large amount of sexual tension there."

"You have no idea what you're asking of me," Carly said with a sardonic chuckle. She knew exactly what they'd done to create that tension—starve themselves of the one thing their bodies craved. Yes, they'd decided to wait for Lauren's benefit and peace of mind, but apparently the show was reaping an unexpected reward. They were dying to rip each other's clothes off, and somehow, that bled through to the characters' relationship.

"What do we think, Ethan?" Sally asked, leading Lauren,

wearing a sundress, back into the room. "I'm thinking if we cinch it right here"—Sally pulled the fabric a little more to reveal the lines of Lauren's waist—"we'll eliminate the droop we saw earlier."

"Looks great," Ethan said. "Are we set otherwise?"

Sally nodded. "After this last alteration, we should be prepared for full dress runs."

Ethan tossed a fist in the air, likely relieved to have one more thing squared away. Carly shook her head. She never would have imagined how many moving parts went into a play. She had severely undervalued the experience. Never again. In fact, she could imagine herself doing more theater in the future. How crazy was that?

As Lauren slipped away with Sally, Carly followed her to her dressing room and waited outside for her to change. When the door opened once again, she pushed off the wall and stuck her head around the door. "Can I come in?"

"You can." Lauren looked around. "Anyone can. I've spent countless hours chatting with actresses in this room, and I don't know that I'll ever wrap my head around the fact that it's mine. I'm acting, Carly. Weird."

"All of this is. In the best way." She fell back onto Lauren's couch. "Do you know what Ethan just said?"

"What?"

"That our sexual tension is now off the charts."

Lauren didn't hesitate. "He's not a wizard. I could not agree more. I'm now really regretting"—she glanced at the open door and closed it—"my decision at my place, because now I just have to stare at you and deal with the effects. And there are *effects*." She exhaled slowly.

"Door is closed. You can kiss me, you know." Carly batted her eyelashes innocently. She was aware that the top two buttons of her blouse were undone. She had a feeling the view wasn't lost on Lauren. At least, she hoped it wasn't.

Lauren's interest seemed piqued. "At work?" A mischievous smile crept onto her face. "You think…we could?"

"You said it yourself. It's *your* dressing room, right? I feel like a person should be allowed to do whatever they choose behind the closed doors of their private space."

Lauren's eyes darkened, and right on cue, her gaze dipped from

Carly's eyes, to her lips, and lower. The top two buttons were working. "Come here," she said and crooked her finger.

Carly closed her eyes at the tingling sensation that quiet command inspired, but she did as she was asked. She moved into Lauren's space and allowed her to slip her hands under Carly's blouse to her waist. Lauren didn't say anything before she kissed Carly and the only sound in the room was the quiet gasp of release. Carly was fairly confident it had come from her, as everything in her body responded to Lauren now. They'd barely gotten past second base, but Lauren controlled so much of what Carly's body experienced throughout their workday. With just the right look or toss of her hair, Carly was deep-swallowing and forcing herself to focus. She'd never had that happen with someone before.

"You taste good," Lauren said between kisses. She ran her tongue along Carly's lower lip, which had Carly turned the hell on. Lauren was taller than her today, with Carly not in heels, and that had her going up on her toes for better access to Lauren's lips, which, damn, she could not get enough of. She slid her hands around Lauren's neck and deepened that kiss, exploring with her tongue and pressing her body as closely to Lauren's as possible. The warmth between them had her breathing a little ragged, and her panties a little wet.

Things were moving very quickly. Hands had destinations. Hers landed on Lauren's chest, over her shirt. Having Lauren's breasts in her hands took Carly to another planet of arousal. Entirely new territory. She wanted to lick and suck and lavish them with attention. She imagined what they looked like, longed to see for herself. She pushed against them, felt the weight of them in her hands.

"We're about to take care of that tension," Lauren said, her head thrown back as Carly massaged her breasts. "Carly," she whispered, desperation lacing her tone.

"Is that bad?"

"Not for me. God." She bit her bottom lip.

"You're incredibly sexy. Do you know that?" Carly asked. Her legs were shaking. That's how badly she wanted to touch this woman, to be touched in return. If Lauren would just touch her, she'd ride herself to release. "Can you imagine if we waited until opening? My God." She kissed Lauren again, long and good.

"Should we?" Lauren asked. She cupped Carly's ass and pulled her hips closer. "No."

"No," Carly said matter-of factly. Her intellect was attempting to intrude upon this moment. "Maybe," she said, still understanding how powerful their chemistry onstage currently was. "No," she said decidedly.

"No. But maybe?" Lauren countered.

She loved the sound of Lauren's ragged, hot-and-bothered breathing. "Because I want to take these boots off you and then these adorably cute jeans, and then slide your underwear down your legs until you're mine to take."

Lauren rolled her hips in response to the potent words. "Okay, maybe no waiting."

A loud knock sounded behind them. They froze midkiss. Carly pulled her mouth back and they listened. Another loud knock.

"Yes?" Lauren called, though her voice didn't sound like it generally did. Carly smothered a proud smile.

"Lala?" Trip said. "I don't know if you're naked or what, but we're going for pizza tonight at Crazy Crust. You in? Listen, the crust is crazy. It's hard to say no."

"Yeah, um, sure," Lauren said, then winced, probably realizing she now had to go out for pizza.

"Carly, too. But I can't find her. Gee, I wonder where she could be."

"I think she ran to her car," Lauren fibbed, as she ran her fingernails up and down Carly's back. "I'll let her know, though."

"Cool. See you in five for notes onstage with Ethan? Tell Carly when she gets back from her car."

"We'll—I'll be there."

"Thanks, boss."

"I'm not your boss right now," she called back.

"You're always my boss."

Carly heard Trip's footsteps retreating and grinned. "I think you just told a lie. Lauren Prescott has a dark side? This is getting good."

"I'm an awful liar," Lauren said with a tiny wince. "I should work on it."

"No, you shouldn't. I like you the way you are." Carly held her tighter. "Please remain an awful liar, and always stay a little bit uptight, and don't you dare lose your cute little organizational skills that make my stomach tighten."

"You think my color-coded sticky notes are cute?"

"And hot. Those sticky notes get me going. It's embarrassing to admit that, but entirely true."

Lauren grinned and pointed at Carly. "Use that onstage. In fact, we could use all of this onstage."

Carly closed her eyes and dropped her head back like a child on the verge of tantrum. "You're thinking we should wait until we're through opening, aren't you. Just say it."

Lauren lifted a shoulder. "Well, if Ethan thinks our chemistry is suddenly exponential, it's something to consider. At least through the reviews. Then, maybe…we reward ourselves, but hang on to that muscle memory of what it felt like. To…want."

"And I do. Desperately." Carly headed back to the couch, needing some distance between herself and Lauren if she wanted any hope of clarity on the topic. "I feel like I'm in high school all over again, trying to be good, when I just want to be really bad. Behind the gym. With you."

Lauren mock-gasped. "There was a time when you tried to be good?"

Carly threw a pillow at Lauren who laughed and caught it. "I'm not a total screwup, you know."

"Well, you are meeting people behind the gym." Carly lobbed another pillow, this time smacking Lauren on the shoulder. "But you do have a great right arm."

Carly stood. "Me, my arm, and my newfound teenage abstinence are heading to our notes session. Coming?"

"Apparently not until we open," Lauren said with a sly grin.

Carly shook her head and paused. The comment alone had her turned the hell on. "Let's get out of here before that whole plan flies quickly out the window."

"Right behind you. Just need to grab my sticky notes."

Carly blinked. "You're going to be the death of me."

"Maybe it won't be the worst way to die," Lauren said with a wink.

Carly didn't know how she'd ended up here. One minute she was living in the lap of luxury with fans and friends fawning all over her. The next, she was in freezing Minneapolis, of all places, in a historic old theater with a woman who now held the strings to her mind, heart, and body.

She wasn't sure she ever wanted it to end.

❖

"Where will we pick up our tickets? I want to make sure I leave plenty of time in case there's any mix-up, and you know how your dad always putters when I'm trying to get somewhere."

"I know," Lauren said.

"That man is a putterer, and it's not going to ruin my chance to see my baby on her big night. You'll need to remind me where the bathrooms are, so I can beat everyone there during intermission."

Lauren smiled. She had her mom on speakerphone in her dressing room as she prepped for their second-to-last rehearsal. "The tickets are at the box office, and there will be no mix-up. Dad is definitely a putterer, but I have a feeling you're going to be able to light a fire under him. The restrooms are clearly marked, but I'll send directions."

"Good. That will help. How's the show going, Boop? I just can't believe this has all happened. I put it on Facebook. Did you see? I had sixty-seven of those *like* things, and also some hearts, and your uncle Gregory hit *share* on what I said, and now other people can see it who are friends with him."

"Wow."

"I was real happy you could share it. I really like that Facebook."

"Social media is a wondrous thing. It's going well, I think."

"You think?"

Lauren sighed. "I second-guess everything I'm doing and sometimes feel like a total fraud working alongside true professionals, but I haven't been fired yet, so I keep showing up."

Her mother made a *tsk*ing noise. "You're selling yourself short. You always do that, Ms. Type A. You're talented, kind, gorgeous, and my daughter. I just can't wait to see you shine. Uncle Frank is going to look down on this from Heaven with a smile."

"Thanks, Mama," Lauren said. "Knock my little brother in the head for me."

"How about I just ruffle his hair a little next time he stops by for spaghetti and garlic bread? Did you know he's up for junior partner at the firm?"

"I didn't. I need to call him."

"When you have a spare minute, you will. Right now, I'm just vibrating that the tiny being that lived in my tummy is going to perform in front of thousands. My Boop. Do you hear me? Vibrating. You can probably tell through the fancy phones they have now."

"Mom!" she said with a laugh, though it was every bit as surreal to her, too. "We can vibrate together. I'll see you soon, and don't worry for a second about the tickets. I've taken care of everything."

They said their good-byes, and Lauren clicked off the call and sighed. She felt a little better after speaking with her mother, but nerves were creeping in as opening night approached. There was a knock on her dressing room door, and a moment later, Carly peeked her head around.

"May I enter?"

"You may."

"You were so on today," Carly said, sitting on the arm of the couch.

"Do you really think so?" Lauren's stomach tightened in that uncomfortable way it had been all week.

"I know so." Carly wore jeans, a purple ribbed top with two buttons undone, and brown heeled boots. The beautiful color was not lost on Lauren who spent just as much time thinking about Carly these days as she did the play. She always looked forward to their quiet times alone. She'd grown so used to her presence. She tried to imagine her life before Carly. It felt so long ago.

"Here's the thing," Carly said. "You're so precise. I can always count on you to be a reliable scene partner, but you always bring the emotion right along with it." A small pause. "I'm flipping out a little bit."

Lauren took in the compliment but moved right past it to Carly's confession. "What do you have to flip out about? You're a professional actress. This is what you live for."

Carly's eyes were wider than usual, and she chewed on the inside of her lip nervously. Her fists were balled, and Carly wasn't someone who balled her fists. Ever. "No. Not at all. No. This isn't what I do. I don't have thousands of people watch me work. Film sets are filled with production crew, yeah, but they're not there to see me perform. They didn't pay money. This is wildly different." She slid off the arm of the couch onto a cushion, in defeat.

It made sense. Carly wasn't used to having eyeballs staring at her. "That part doesn't matter. You're just going to go out there and do the same show we just finished running today." Lauren knelt in front of her and rested her hands on Carly's knees. "You're going to get angry with me, and then confide in me, and we're going to laugh together, and kiss, and then get ripped dramatically apart so we can find our way back once again in a grocery store, of all places. It'll be grand."

"But the audience will be there," Carly said, as if she was informing Lauren of something she didn't seem to realize.

"That part is true. They might also be noisy. Gum wrappers, cell phones, and the occasional vocal participant are all things I've gotten used to, working here. The elderly crowd have some opinions." She shrugged and tried to send Carly a reassuring smile. "Just part of what makes live theater unique. I think you might actually like it."

Something unexpected happened. Instead of smiling back, Carly's eyes brimmed with tears. "Sorry," she said, trying to find her voice that seemed strangled and not entirely available. She paused to wait for it to return, and Lauren's heart squeezed. She slid her hands up to the outsides of Carly's thighs, trying to bring them closer. Her instinct was to shelter Carly in any way she could, even physically.

"Hey, look at me."

Carly did, though her bottom lip quivered.

"I'm right here. It's just us. You don't have anything to apologize for." Lauren had talked actresses down a million and nine times, but not a single one of those conversations had affected her as potently as this one was. She had a lump in her own damn throat.

"It's just"—Carly wiped her eyes—"there's always been this little part of me that's wondered if my success in film was because of how I look, you know? That my talent mattered less when they could send a makeup artist onto set to touch you up every five minutes, and give you fifteen takes to make a moment work. Here…" She shook her head and sighed. "It's so raw. There's no smoke and mirrors. It's going to be me just standing there, acting, sweating, and crying, and I'm pretty sure that's not going to be enough."

Lauren gathered Carly's hands in hers. "I don't know who in the world has gotten in your head and made you think that you're not talented outright, but let me be the one to set you straight. Can I be brutally honest?"

Carly laughed. "I feel like you're always honest. But yes, let's toss in brutal, for God's sake."

"I wasn't thrilled when I heard they'd cast you in this show." Carly nodded, taking it in. "I'd read that you were unreliable, into partying, and held up production with your antics."

"Most of that was true," Carly admitted. "Not all. But most."

Lauren wasn't finished. "Never once, however, did I doubt your talent or ability to completely master this role in every sense. Not for one second."

Carly blinked. "Really?" She touched Lauren's cheek. "Come on. That can't be true."

"Except it is. I've seen many of your movies and have always admired your work." She inclined her head from side to side. "I mean, if you think about it, the reason they put up with you in Hollywood for so long is because you're good. Otherwise? You'd have been blacklisted years back."

Carly laughed, and that felt like progress. "I never looked at it like that."

Lauren straightened. "That's me. Voice of reason."

"Isn't that the damn truth?" Carly said. "Come here, please. Let's see if some of that reason will rub off." She leaned in, her gaze dipping to Lauren's lips. Lauren, as if pulled by that ever-present magnet, met her halfway. "Hi," Carly whispered, just before kissing her softly. Lauren drank in every sensation that kiss brought with it. She'd learned to revel in each shiver, flutter, and hit of pleasure that came her way from being near Carly. If those things worried or scared her before, she'd now embraced the power that Carly had over her body. Touching her only intensified the effect times ten. Lauren joined Carly on the couch, first sitting alongside her as they kissed like lust-starved teenagers, then welcoming Carly into her lap as she straddled Lauren and cradled her face as their mouths battled and explored. With her hands on Carly's ass, she wanted nothing more than her out of those pants. She imagined Carly naked in the same position and had to pause their kissing to ensure she received enough oxygen for basic survival.

Carly waited while she took several necessary breaths. There was the air, slowly returning. "You okay?" Carly asked.

Lauren nodded. "Sometimes it feels like we combust."

"So I'm not the only one, then?"

"I don't know if you experience what I do, but I can tell you it's more than a little intense."

Carly nodded and traced the line of Lauren's collarbone. "You know something else?"

"Tell me."

Carly shook her head but held her gaze on the progress her finger made, not meeting Lauren's eyes. "I really like you. It's not just the attraction. It's…everything."

Lauren took a minute to absorb Carly's words because it was apparent how closely she held them. They heard voices of their castmates passing Lauren's dressing room and for a moment, she thought they'd lose this important exchange.

"I like you a lot, too. Maybe that's part of what makes this all so scary. We're in the midst of one of the biggest things that's ever happened to me, but I'm confident it wouldn't be nearly as gratifying if I wasn't experiencing it with you."

Carly's smile began small and then took over her entire face. "Do you really mean that?"

"Of course, I do." A kiss. Another one. Lauren laughed. "Did I mention I like you back?"

"You just did. Your lips are so fucking kissable," Carly murmured. "And when you wear autumn colors, I'm done. Everything about you makes my head spin in the best way. When you wear fall boots? I want to invest in a catalog company that specializes in them." Lauren laughed again. Carly touched her chest and eased herself off Lauren until they were sitting side by side on even ground. "Thank you for talking me off the ledge. Even temporarily."

"Anytime, slugger."

"Is that a new nickname? Because I could really work with that. Hell, I'm so sexually frustrated that if you called me Clarence I'd be here for it."

"Decisions, decisions." Lauren stood and offered Carly her hand. "Since we're not able to tear each other's clothes off quite yet, how about dinner instead? I know a pizza place with the craziest of crusts."

"Do they have red wine? I could use a glass."

"They do." Lauren inclined her head to the door. "Let's get outta here, Clarence."

CHAPTER TEN

Ethan smiled at the company, who stood together on the apron of The McAllister's main stage. It was close to eight p.m. and this was the last official moment of rehearsal. Lauren had been through a million of these moments, but never quite from where she sat now. She looked at Trip, who beamed up at her with pride from his spot at the SM's table, and turned back to Ethan.

"This is where I take my leave," Ethan told the company. "I'll be here for opening night, but as your cheerleader. The show is ready for the world, and I, for one, can't wait to see how it affects the ticket holders who will file down these aisles tomorrow night. We've come a long way." Lauren looked down the row of her castmates, from Carly standing next to her, to Kirby on the other side. TJ and Nia down the line. Her gratitude rose straight to the top.

Yet a new chapter was going to start very soon.

Lauren had planned to allow herself to sleep in the next day, so she'd be as fully rested as possible. Only that hadn't gone as smoothly as planned since she'd tossed and turned all night, imagining herself forgetting her lines, getting locked in her dressing room, or, worse, losing her lunch all over the stage in front of the world. She would make up for it by drinking several tall glasses of water, advice she always gave her own actors.

When she arrived at the theater for opening night, she took a moment in the parking lot to study the building that now meant so much more. As she made her way down the hall, she was greeted by friends and production staff, just as she would have been for any other opening night. Except instead of heading to her office for show prep, she walked to her dressing room. What was this life?

"I got you these," Tinsley said, from where she stood in front of Lauren's dressing room. Lauren accepted the bouquet of red roses, too lavish for their friendship. Yet she knew Tinsley had a crush, and Lauren refused to be anything but graceful about it.

"You are super sweet to have gone out of your way. Thank you." With her free arm, she leaned in and hugged Tinsley, who smiled.

"I just want you to know how amazing I think it is that you've done all of this. You're the full package, Lauren." A pause. "Could we do dinner before the show next week?"

"Oh, I'm not sure I can."

Tinsley nodded. "Because you're seeing Carly."

Lauren hesitated. She and Carly had not officially said as much to anyone, but they hadn't exactly hidden it either. "Yes," she said, finally.

"I can respect that, I suppose. But, Lauren?"

"Yes?"

"She's going to drop you once all of this is over. She's Carly Daniel. Her world is huge. We're different."

The implication was clear, and Tinsley was voicing a concern Lauren had tucked away in the back of her mind: Carly could get any girl or guy she wanted, and likely would.

"Thanks, Tins. I appreciate the advice, but I can take care of myself."

"I know." She shifted her weight to the other foot. "Sometimes, though, it can be hard to see it when you're in the midst of it all, you know? Trust me on this. Don't let yourself get hurt, okay?"

"I won't."

She let herself in to her dressing room and tried to shrug off the uncomfortable conversation and prediction. That's not what today was about. She looked around her dressing room instead to find an embarrassment of riches in the form of good show gifts. Custom coffee mugs, ball caps, more flowers, and even a show hoodie. Her company had gone all out. She'd distribute her own gifts, small survival kits with a celestial theme, soon enough. In the corner of her dressing room, something large caught her eye. She tilted her head and studied the strange arrival: a shrink-wrapped pallet of boxes of some kind. Lauren dipped into her stage manager's kit, always at the ready, grabbed a pocketknife, and tore through the wrap to spring open one of the boxes. What she found made her laugh out loud. Boxes and boxes of multicolored Post-its in all shapes. With her hands on her hips, she marveled at the volume. She'd not live long enough to use them all.

"Has anyone ever expressed their preshow affection via office supplies before?" She turned to see Carly standing behind her, sporting a triumphant grin.

"I can't say they have. You're definitely proving yourself to be memorable."

Carly wiped her brow to dramatically convey her relief. "Thank God. I can't compete with red roses." She pointed to the large arrangement. "I'll just blend."

Lauren walked to Carly and wrapped her arms around her neck, not even bothering to close the door. "You couldn't blend if you wanted to."

Carly looked skyward, pulling Lauren closer. "I feel like that's a challenge. What did you get me? Tell me. I can't take it."

Lauren pulled her face back. "You? Nothing at all. You're rich and need no further material possessions." Carly's bottom lip emerged in a pout for the history books.

"Don't level the Daniel pout on me. That's playing dirty." More pouting. "I'm not made of stone."

"Then kiss me and give me a gift because I love gifts." Carly looked so expectant in that moment that anyone would be an idiot not to fall for her immediately.

Lauren touched Carly's chin and offered her a slow kiss that she hoped communicated *Good show. I find you very sexy. Break a leg. I could kiss you for days.* Surely, she'd succeeded on all four counts. "Now, about that gift."

Carly grinned and clapped like a kid on her birthday. She went from beautiful to sweet to sophisticated to innocent and back again with such ease. The contradictions kept Lauren captivated. She went to her bag of survival kits and pulled out a separate gift that she'd wrapped up special for Carly.

"I believe this is what you're looking for," she said and presented the rectangular present.

Carly carried it to the couch, already enamored. "I was actually just kidding," she said, sounding nervous. "You didn't need to do anything special for me."

Lauren shrugged and sat next to her. "I wanted to."

The moment felt quiet, like the hubbub of the day had gone still for them for a few minutes. Carly unwrapped the gift and stared down at the inscribed frame that held a print of Van Gogh's *Starry Night*.

"Lauren," Carly whispered achingly, running her hand down the mahogany frame. That's when she caught sight of the inscription. *To the only other person I'd want to watch stars with. –L.* Carly shook her head in wonder and then touched her heart. "This is an amazing gift. I don't know what to say."

"Say it goes with the décor in your home and that you're not secretly scheming to ditch it in the deepest recesses of your garage. Which, of course, is very much your right."

Carly was still admiring the painting. "It's going someplace special where I can see it each and every day."

"Really?" Lauren felt her heart reaching. She needed to be careful. Maybe because it felt like she'd climbed to a very precarious height? Things between her and Carly had started rocky but had steadily built to something she never in a million years would have predicted. Yet here she sat. Caring. Wanting. Reaching.

"Really." Carly kissed her softly. "I will treasure it."

"You smell amazing," Lauren said. "How do you do that so consistently?"

Carly laughed quietly as she stood. "Magical shampoo. All part of my plan to woo you. You better get ready for Froot Loops in the morning. I make a mean bowl."

"Post-it notes, magical shampoo, and Froot Loops. Who knew I was that easy?"

"Easy?" Carly gasped. "I'm working overtime over here, killing myself in the name of the woo."

Lauren lowered her voice. "Do you want a tip? You don't have to."

"What if I want to? What if I like doing things for you? Because I do. I love the way the sides of your mouth quirk up when I say something funny. Makes me want to be a permanent comedian, and I'm amusing at best."

Lauren's chest swelled. She resisted the urge to place a hand over the pang. "Well, when you put it that way." A pause. Her stomach fluttered. "So, will I see you...tonight? You know, after the show?" She tried to play it cool, but she still felt vulnerable when she put herself out there with Carly, almost as if she was asking the pretty girl to prom, if prom involved tearing each other's clothes off, which, technically, it often did.

"I certainly didn't want to presume anything. But I hoped we might see where the night led. If it's to one of our places, then that's purely bonus. Plus, I need my Rocky IV fix at some point soon."

"That chubby little dog can't get enough of you."

"It's mutual. His tan curlicue tail alone is worthy of a visit."

Lauren studied Carly. She seemed herself, yet not. "How are you feeling about tonight?"

Carly blinked several times, which was a total tell. Yep. She was in her head, and just as nervous as Lauren was. "I'm trying not to think about what's going to happen in just a couple of hours. I spent the day buried in loud music to keep me from dwelling. My mind is a dangerous place." She pointed to the dressing room around them. "I dashed in here as soon as I arrived, to distract myself. You have a remarkable way of doing just that for me."

"So, it sounds like you're anxious."

"A basket case. You?"

"Nervous in a good way." She ducked her head and captured Carly's gaze. "I think you're going to be surprised by the energy you find coming back to you from the live exchange. There's nothing like it."

"What if what comes back to me causes injury?" Carly looked entirely serious. "What if they throw things? I was thinking about that at three a.m. What if one of them just gets angry and pelts a cell phone at our heads."

Lauren smothered a smile. "I can safely say that in my entire career I've never had an audience member try to take down an actor."

Carly appeared morbidly serious. "Tonight could be that night, Lauren." She looked around as if expecting ominous music.

Lauren's dresser, Maddie, arrived at her doorway with her act 1 costumes and a steamer. "Hey, there. All set for me?"

"Yep," Lauren said, swallowing her own fear. Maddie's arrival signaled.the official start of opening night. This would kick off her prep for the show, leaving little downtime before the curtain went up. She smiled at Carly, who offered a nervous smile back.

"See you out there," Carly said and gave her hand a squeeze.

Lauren grinned back. "On the other side."

❖

"Actors, to the stage please. Places for act one."

Carly stared at the ceiling, glaring at Trip's voice floating in through the sound system to her dressing room. She made no move to obey his request. She couldn't. Her fear kept her glued to her chair, staring at her own seemingly distorted face in the mirror. Once she'd said good-bye to Lauren, she'd systematically come apart, realizing how ill-equipped she truly was. Even Lauren, who had been out of the acting game for a while now, was more prepared.

Moments later, Janie arrived at Carly's door, wearing her headset. "Hey, Carly? We're ready for you onstage. It's time."

Carly gripped the edge of the dressing table so hard she thought she might snap her fingers. Yet she couldn't seem to let go. "I'm not ready," she said quietly.

"I'm sorry. I couldn't hear you," Janie said. Carly couldn't seem to concentrate on anything except the dark waves of Janie's hair and the clear plastic framed glasses she wore that seemed to be so trendy now. She had a vanity pair of her own.

She tried again. "I need a minute."

"Okay." Janie watched her for a moment, her brows low and her lips pinched. "I'll let Trip know."

Carly was delaying their open of show, yet there was nothing she could do about it. She could hear Janie in the hall speaking in a hushed tone into her headset. Carly's shoulders ached with tension, her skin felt cold and clammy, and her brain wouldn't slow down for even a moment.

Trip appeared a moment later, his eyes wide. His hair seemed to be spelling out some sort of distress code with its various trajectories. Perhaps: *run.* "You feeling a little on edge, Car?" he asked, pushing a friendly smile.

Carly nodded. Trip was a nice guy. He might know what to do here, help her find the confidence she'd lost an hour ago. Or even more preferable, he'd just let her leave.

"I don't actually think I can do this," she confessed.

"I know it feels like a lot of pressure, but honestly? If you went out on that stage and gave half the performance you turned in on our last rehearsal, those people are going to love it."

He was flattering her for the sake of the show. She didn't fault him. Trip was executing his duties as PSM to perfection, dealing with the broken actress, attempting to wind her up and make her go. "How am I supposed to get out of my own head, though?"

"How about we take a few deep breaths?"

"How about I head back to California, and you put Nia onstage in my place?"

Trip's eyes went wide, which was probably high alert in stage management land. It all seemed so overwhelming now, and she thought back to the time she'd scoffed at Alika for bringing her this project when she felt so far beyond stage work.

"Guys, can I have the room?" The even-keeled voice was instantly familiar. Carly craned her neck around Trip to see Lauren in costume and makeup for act 1. That's when she found the air again.

"Definitely," Trip said. He exchanged a look with Lauren, snagged Janie, and was out of there. When the door clicked closed, Lauren turned to Carly.

"What you're feeling is totally normal."

Carly nodded, her heart rate easing. "Maybe. I just keep thinking about all the things that could go wrong. We can't just yell *Cut!* and start again, you know?"

"We should just go get crazy crust pizza." Lauren smiled as if the thought alone sent her to heaven. "I'd get extra mozzarella, fresh tomatoes, basil, and maybe some sliced meatball on top. God, that sounds amazing." It was the most random of statements, but the way Lauren described the pizza, Carly could almost smell the pies baking. "Should we go?"

Carly took a slow inhale and smiled. "Maybe. I'd love to watch you maneuver all that cheese."

"Because cheese and I have a sinful love affair I will not apologize for. Give me a minute to get changed, and I'm all yours."

Apparently talking casually about pizza, of all things, with Lauren was just what Carly needed. She stood. "Let's do a show first."

"Or that." Lauren shrugged nonchalantly, like she could take it or leave it. "Means we get to kiss in just a little while. I guess we could do pizza later."

"The extra cheesy kind."

"Strings of cheese for days," Lauren said. She glanced at the door. "We're doing this?"

Carly nodded, finding the floor had returned beneath her feet. "Let's give them the show they came for." She took a deep, centering breath, as she got her head on straight.

Moments later, she stood in the wings, listening to the recorded preshow announcement, as every part of her shook. She turned to Lauren, met her gaze, and received a squeeze from their joined hands. She smiled and let it all fall away. Lauren made her entrance, and Carly watched her sweetly argue with TJ, the gate attendant, about missing the flight. To her surprise, lines she'd heard spoken a million times were greeted with laughter. Whoa. The audience was actually enjoying their show. She stood a little taller, eager to get out there and participate. Her dresser handed her Ashley's attaché, and she made her entrance with purpose. When she appeared onstage, the audience applauded. Entrance applause because she was famous. Lauren told her this might happen. She paused until it died down and delivered her first line. Ashley was on a mission and so was she.

For Carly, the performance alternated between racing past, and plodding in slow motion. Lauren had been correct. Carly felt the energy from the audience, and it gave her life. The connection between all of them in that room, experiencing the same story beneath the same roof, was overpowering. She understood midway through, that live performance could easily become an addiction, like the best kind of drug. She loved the screen, but the theater was instantaneously rewarding.

That Tuesday night, she went on the same journey with Lauren that they'd gone on together every day in rehearsal. The audience only enriched their story and gave it texture. God, Carly could really get used to this.

When the curtain came down, the audience applauded and cheered loudly. Lauren fell into her arms. It was hands down the best moment of Carly's life, thus far.

"That was amazing," Carly whispered.

"You were," Lauren countered. "You're so talented, Car. Really. You broke my heart back there." There were tears in Lauren's eyes when she said it.

"It was you who stole the show," she said, as they dashed into the wings, hand in hand.

When the curtain rose again, the audience applauded enthusiastically for their cast members, and when it was Lauren's turn to bow at curtain call, Carly watched in awe as the audience stood in unison. A standing ovation. Because of her recognizable name, Carly had been given the final bow. As she stepped downstage before the audience, she looked into the faces of each and every person she could see through the bright stage lights. She took in the moment, then finally bowed, as her heart soared. Her year had been full of ups and downs, but this made it all okay again. She joined hands with Kirby and Lauren as they all took their company bow together. She waved to the audience and headed to the wings. The show was complete. She'd made it.

"What the hell just happened?" Carly asked, in the midst of the most intense rush of her life. She placed a hand over her chest. "Do you feel that?" she asked Lauren. "Because I do."

Lauren laughed, every bit as giddy as Carly. Trip raced down the hallway whooping. TJ put Kirby in a celebratory headlock. Lauren threw her arms around Carly's neck and hugged her. "That completely just happened, and it was amazing."

Lauren was in Trip's arms next as they all took turns hugging each company member. "Lala, my eyes only misted over eight times seeing you up there like a star." He kissed her cheek with a smack. "Maybe twelve. You dazzled." Carly couldn't have agreed more. Lauren had been versatile, charismatic, and lovable tonight, and the audience adored her.

"Cast party at The Argyle in an hour," Trip announced to the celebrating company.

Once alone, with the door closed behind her, Carly danced around her dressing room in silence, as one did when they'd just conquered a grave fear. She leapt onto the couch wearing her black pants and a bra and played air guitar in her private celebration. She couldn't wait to see her friends, eat some food, drink some wine, and maybe even dance a little bit more. Yet it felt so different from the partying she would do in LA. She couldn't get trashed. Didn't want to. Tomorrow, she needed to be sure she was fresh and ready for show number two.

"Are you coming?" Lauren asked, bag on her shoulder. Somehow, she'd opened the door without Carly hearing her. "Or do you have another guitar solo on the way." She held up a hand. "Don't let me stop you. It's an enjoyable view."

Carly glanced down at her nearly bare torso and the tops of the breasts she had on display. Never one to feel modest, she hopped off the couch and walked slowly to her clothing rack. "If I'd known my performance was being enjoyed, I'd have worked it a little more."

"I'm not even sure that's possible," Lauren said, with a lazy grin. She wore a tweed jacket with a black belt and black boots that made her appear both smart and sexy.

"Give me ninety seconds and I'm yours." Carly pulled a red sweater over her head and began to pack her bag. She joined Lauren, and they walked down the hall together, with Carly's arm around Lauren's waist.

"Shall I drive or would you like to?" Lauren asked.

"Well, if you're offering, how can I say no? I never pass up a jaunt in a Mini Cooper."

"And why would you?"

When they exited the stage door, a series of bright flashes nearly blinded Carly. She only stuttered for a moment. Though she'd been out of LA a couple of months now, she was still used to paparazzi. Yet the photographers weren't magazine guys at all. These were members of their audience.

"Would you mind?" a woman asked. She thrust a Playbill and pen at Carly.

"Oh, no problem." She signed her name and handed it back, realizing that there were lots more patrons where that one had come from. In fact, there was quite a crowd waiting for them. She moved down the row, just like any other autograph line, but this one felt a little more personal. They'd all just shared an experience together, and that bonded them.

"Hope you enjoyed the show," Carly said to a teenager. "It was certainly a rush for me. Did you know it was my first time in a play? Ever."

"I had no clue. I cried twice," the girl said with a wide grin. "Is the other actress who played Mandy coming out?"

"Yeah, she's right—Wait. Where did she go?" Carly glanced behind her and saw Lauren waiting off to the side, apart from the barricades separating the crowd from the actors exiting. "One minute. I'll grab her," Carly told the teenager.

She approached Lauren. "*Pstt*. What are you doing?" she whispered.

"I didn't want to leave without you."

Carly shot her a look. "You're not going to sign for them?" She hooked a thumb behind her.

"You're the famous one. They want you."

Carly scoffed. "They don't care about that. They just saw this show. That *you* starred in. In fact, they're asking for you." She gave Lauren a nudge. "Get over there and sign, or I'm going to make the crowd chant for you."

"Carly, I will kill you dead if you do that. Do you hear me?" Lauren appeared even more nervous than when they'd opened the show itself.

"Come on. This part I have down. You talked me off the ledge earlier, and I can help you through this part, in return."

"Okay," Lauren said and took a deep breath.

Carly took her hand and walked her to the teenager who lit up. "Oh my God. I loved you in the show. Like *loved*. Sorry, I'm Avery. Should have said that. Can you sign my Playbill?"

"Of course," Lauren said, as her cheeks dusted an adorable pink. "I'd love to. Do you come to a lot of shows at The McAllister?"

Avery nodded and gestured to a woman waiting in the background, likely her mother. "We have season tickets. I hope to audition for my school play." She shrugged. "We'll see what happens. I probably won't get it. You guys were amazing, though."

"Oh, don't say you won't get it," Lauren told Avery and passed the Playbill back. "You might be surprised."

"And if you do get it, don't knock the scenery over," Carly said, and inclined her head to Lauren, who winced and nodded.

"Get out. You didn't do that! You couldn't." Avery looked back at her mother gleefully.

"Oh, I certainly did. My family plays that video every time I have a birthday party. So if I can do it, so can you."

They moved down the line, and after a few minutes passed, Carly felt Lauren loosen up and come alive. "I can't believe I'm on *this* side of things," Lauren whispered as they departed the crowd and headed for her car. "I'm usually on the other side of things. That's who I am, an other-side-of-things person."

"What?" Carly balked. "No, you're not. You're definitely a mover and a shaker, no matter what your job is. It's silly to think otherwise."

"You can't call me silly." But Lauren was laughing.

"I can, too, but only when you're discrediting yourself, because you are kick-ass and amazing and talented and I really, really like you. You should like you, too, and believe you're worthy of the nice things people say."

"I'll work on that." Lauren shivered and shoved her hands into the pockets of that tweed jacket and looked adorable and fashion-forward at the same time, a killer combo.

"You talked about pizza earlier and what you would top it with. What's another favorite of yours in life?" Carly opened the passenger side door and slid inside.

Lauren joined her. "Total non sequitur."

"I want to know more about you. As much as I can."

"Okay, let me think." She started the ignition and pulled out of the parking lot, en route to The Argyle. "I like it when it rains, more than most people. It rarely depresses me. In fact, it makes me dive into my day and focus because I'm not being called outside."

"The rain makes me snuggly."

"You're a pleasure monster. It's…contagious." Lauren laughed. "I can't believe we just had one of the most amazing experiences not just one hour ago, and we're taking about liking rain."

Carly wasn't deterred. Maybe it was because of her high that she wanted to be even closer to Lauren. Hearing about what went on her head was part of that. "What else?"

"I color when I'm stressed in those fancy adult coloring books. I also really like yoga when I have the time for it, which is rare."

"Me, too," Carly said. "Not the coloring part. I've never tried that, but yoga has been amazing for my body and concentration. We should jump into a class together next week."

"We'd get kicked out."

"What? Why?"

"You in yoga pants? Not good for my reputation around town."

Carly laughed but loved that Lauren had just confessed to lusting after her. "Moving yoga pants to the front of my wardrobe."

"Don't you dare," Lauren said.

The Argyle was alive and humming when they arrived. Music played from a quartet in the corner, waiters walked past with full glasses of wine on trays, and everyone was smiling. The club, inhabited exclusively by The McAllister staff and the company from *Starry Nights,* broke into applause for Carly and Lauren as they made their way into the drawing room. Carly turned to Lauren and applauded for her, because her journey truly was an amazing one.

Lauren, in her typical fashion, waved them off and turned a bright shade of red. She finally covered her face. Carly's chest swelled with affection.

"Will you excuse me for one moment?" Lauren said, eyeing something across the room.

"Of course. I'll grab us drinks."

Carly watched as Lauren walked straight into the arms of a woman who simply had to be her mother. Same chestnut brown hair and light eyes, with just a few more lines on her face. The man next to her grinned just the way Lauren did when she was genuinely happy. When the women embraced, there were sentimental tears on both sides. Carly turned away to give them a moment and focused on snagging those drinks. She should have invited more people to the opening, she realized. Her mother likely could have gotten off work at the vineyard and made the trip, if only Carly hadn't downplayed the whole affair due to a lack of experience. If only she'd anticipated how important the show would feel to her.

Once Carly had their glasses of champagne, she turned to see Lauren beckoning her over.

Balancing the drinks, she maneuvered the crowd, accepting their congratulations on a good show until she arrived next to Lauren.

"Thank you," Lauren said, accepting the flute of bubbly. "Carly Daniel, I'd like you to meet my parents, John and Karen Prescott."

"Hi," Carly said brightly. "It's so nice—" It was too late. She was already pulled into a hug, very similar to the one she'd just seen bestowed upon Lauren.

"We know exactly who you are. Of course we do. And we're so excited to meet you in person." Lauren's mother released her from the hug but kept both hands on Carly's shoulders. "You stole our hearts tonight. First you were bristling and buttoned-up—then you were vulnerable and hurting." Karen pantomimed each of the actions. "We rooted for you."

"Thank you," Carly said, feeling all aflutter. She'd received tons of compliments on her work in the past, but this one carried a lot of weight. Karen said it with such unbridled, warm sincerity. Plus, she was an extension of Lauren, so her opinion was weighted heavily in Carly's book. "I was lucky enough to share the stage with an amazing co-star."

"I can't imagine who that could be," Karen said, in an overexaggerated tone that was so hokey, it looped back around to cute. "Oh, wait. That's you!" She released Carly and slid an arm around her daughter, who grinned, bashful at too much attention, as always. Lauren was the opposite of an attention hog, Carly realized, which was rare in an actress. Perhaps it was that selfless quality that held her back from success in her earlier acting days. Show business was cutthroat, and Lauren was a giver, not a taker. In Carly's mind, it was a compliment.

"Listen," Carly explained to Karen and John, "the minute Lauren stepped into the role, everything about my performance changed. Suddenly, I understood Ashley and what her journey had to be. Without Lauren, I'm not sure it ever would have clicked into place."

She and Lauren exchanged a private glance.

They'd been through a lot together. She almost couldn't remember what life was like without Lauren in it. In fact, everything before seemed unimportant, superficial, and so very far away. Her feet felt more firmly planted on the ground now, her self-awareness, though not always easy to swallow, was fully in effect, and she wanted things for herself that she'd never wanted before. Who was she exactly?

Karen latched on to Carly's wrist. "Seeing little Lauren, our Boop, up there reminded me of when she'd stand on top of her toy box and sing songs from *Annie* to her stuffed animals. She would even act out the group orphan scenes, playing all the parts."

Carly raised an eyebrow and faced Lauren. "Well, who knew?"

Lauren covered her face. "No more little Lauren stories, okay? Can I get you guys a drink?"

"No, no," John said, taking Karen's hand. "We're getting out of your hair. Let the show people celebrate without the parents. So proud of you, Laur."

Karen beamed. "Just wanted to stop by and tell you what a star you were tonight, my tiny baby Boop."

Lauren laughed. "Mother, you cannot call me that right now." She softened. "But thank you. Means the world that you were here tonight."

Carly's heart squeezed, and she felt like she'd wandered onto the set of a Hallmark movie where the parents were amazing and later, they'd light a Christmas tree in the town square. "Fantastic meeting you."

Karen squealed and cupped Carly's cheeks. "Come visit us someday, you famous person. We're just a couple hours by car. I'll make you chicken and waffles and a mimosa."

Carly laughed at the specificity. "How can one pass that up?"

"They can't," Karen said, triumphantly.

"Come on now," John said, with a gotta-get-her-outta-here look. "Past our power-down time."

Lauren walked her parents to the car, and Carly worked the room, feeling happy, warm, and connected to each person.

"You were amazing tonight," Kirby gushed.

"You were, too," Carly said, feeling the love.

"And I love your hair." Kirby touched a strand. "What did you do to it?"

"Thanks, Kirby. Just a few curls."

"I'm going to try that." Kirby stepped in closer. "So, are you nervous?"

"About tomorrow? No, I feel good."

"I mean about the reviews. They'll be out in just a few hours. I imagine people will be watching to see how you did, right? All eyes on you."

Carly went still. She didn't realize the feedback would be so imminent. A few hours? But Kirby was right. She'd come to Minneapolis to prove herself as a reliable, serious actress, but if the reviews hated her, what then? "Trying not to dwell on that part," she confessed.

Kirby looked extra serious. "Oh. I bet it will be fine."

"Of course," Carly said, blowing off her concern. "Plus, tonight is a celebration."

"Everything okay?" Lauren asked, touching the small of her back.

"Of course," Carly said. But she wanted to be out of there before those reviews hit. She didn't want anything to ruin her celebration. "Your parents are not real. You know that, right?"

"I'm a lucky person to have them. But the fact that she just impersonated my rendition of 'Tomorrow' from the running board of my dad's truck just as Ethan, of all people, walked past on his way into the club, tells me that they are very much real and embarrassing as hell."

"Stop complaining about your amazing life and drink this expensive private club wine." She handed Lauren back her drink that she'd taken custody of. They locked eyes and touched their glasses. Carly saw Kirby's eyes grow wide in her peripheral vision. Apparently, the intimate look they'd just shared had spoken to Kirby, who dashed off like she'd left the oven on. Everyone would know the nature of their relationship in just under six minutes. Carly was fairly confident.

They stayed through the toasts, standing next to each other. Lauren touched her pinkie to Carly's. They stayed through a second drink. Carly loved the little lip prints Lauren's lipstick left on her glass. She imagined herself kissing those lips later, tasting the remnants of that drink. They stayed through the quartet packing up and the party shifting into full gear when the loud recorded music began. She danced subtly with Lauren, who pressed her hips in close, behind Carly's.

"Wanna get out of here?" Carly whispered as she turned in Lauren's arms. Lots of eyes were on them, and she craved alone time in the worst way.

"Lead the way."

They didn't make a big deal of their departure. After all, they'd see everyone the very next day. Lauren quietly said good-bye to Trip, and with the formality of the gathering out of the way, all they'd miss was an abundance of dancing…and the reviews. They'd be there in the morning, Carly reminded herself.

"Take me home with you," Carly said, circling her arm through Lauren's in the parking lot on that chilly autumn evening. She stared up at the moon, the stars, and the dark expanse of sky in between. She felt intimately connected to everything in the cosmos, super aware of how all the events in her life had lined up to bring her to this very important day. It was already a night she'd never forget, and stealing away with Lauren was the perfect way to end it.

"Have you seen the moon tonight?" Lauren asked.

Carly gazed up at the luminous moon broadcasting its warm glow in the night sky. Appropriately, the stars were plentiful. "It's gorgeous. The entire sky."

"Almost like it's sanctioning our opening, looking down on us." She shook her head. "I've noticed the stars, the moon, the constellations so much more since we started work on the show."

Carly kissed Lauren's hand. "I don't think I'll ever look at them in the same way."

Lauren sighed happily. "Neither of us will."

Chapter Eleven

They were tipsy, but only a little, as they climbed out of Lauren's Mini that autumn evening, the one that had already changed Lauren's life. "Did you see the look on Trip's face when you told him to send Nia onstage?" Lauren asked, laughing. She waved her hand in front of her face a few times as she tried to get control. "Man, you made his first show as PSM a memorable one. I'll say that." She continued to laugh as she thought back.

"Who knew that all he needed was a little pizza porn and I'd be his?" Carly joined Lauren in her laughter and held out her hand. "Come here. I want to kiss you in the cold beneath this gorgeous moon."

Lauren grinned and leaned against the car. "The moon, I get. What's so special about the cold?"

"It's on my list." She caught Lauren around the waist and pulled her close. The streetlights in Lauren's neighborhood illuminated her driveway, but only slightly, allowing her to bask in the battle between shadow and light.

"What else is on your list?" Lauren studied Carly's expressive baby blues.

Carly looked skyward, still on the high of tonight. "I want to kiss you in the warmth of the West Coast, autumn in Maine, and on the beaches of Hawaii, Mexico, and Jamaica. We can negotiate European destinations next."

"Oh, we can?"

"I'm a big fan of Germany and the Black Forest. Once shot a film there and couldn't get enough of the food or the scenery. You'd love it. They sell schnitzel on a stick, Lauren. I'm not messing around."

"You take schnitzel very seriously. I can tell." Lauren laughed but quietly filed away that this was the first time Carly had spoken plainly of a future. She shocked herself at how happy it made her. Was it possible this wasn't just a showmance? It seemed ridiculous to think that someone with a life as exciting as Carly's might be happy with regular Lauren who liked a good Sunday morning crossword puzzle and a satisfying game of pool. Yet their connection seemed so authentic and effortless, she couldn't help but fantasize.

"Are we going inside?" Lauren asked. God, she hoped Carly said yes. Yes, their celebration was tons of fun, but in the back of her mind she just wanted to race through it all, hoping to have alone time with Carly, dreaming about taking off her clothes.

"If we're not, I might weep silently on the curb." Carly smiled, and waited. She rocked on her heels.

"We're definitely not weeping tonight. Follow me."

Carly's hands touched her waist as they walked, sending an anticipatory shiver across her skin. She was ready for Carly, and growing more so with each second that ticked past. She let them into her home, to the sounds of Rocky's tiny feet on the hardwood floors. "There's my baby," she said, scooping him up. He licked her face appropriately and shifted his attention to Carly. Seeing her there produced full on dog body-wagging, which required Lauren to place him back on the floor so he could wiggle around properly.

"I like that dance you're doing, Rocky." Carly knelt down and allowed him to take turns leaping up at her face and wiggling his body more, in festivity. She flipped him onto his back and gave his belly a ferocious rubbing, which yielded his customary snorts of appreciation. Lauren joined them on the floor and scratched Rocky's head, not wanting to be left out of the late-night lovefest.

"We opened a show tonight, Rock," Lauren said. He snuffled and wiggled.

"I think they liked us," Carly added. Rocky turned in three circles and trotted away.

Lauren faced Carly. "He's not really a night owl. He generally greets me after shows, but then heads back to his bed under the end table. He thinks it's his own personal fort, and I've done nothing to correct him."

"And why would you?" Carly asked, sweeping a strand of hair

behind Lauren's ear. That did it. She was back to stop one on the Lust Express and watched Carly with heated interest.

"Hi," she said softly.

"Take me to your room," Carly said back.

Lauren laughed nervously. "I really like that sentence." She took Carly's hand and walked through the house, turning off lights as she went.

"I have others," Carly said, as she was led down the short hallway to the master bedroom. "Here's one. I want my hands on you yesterday."

"A second truly good sentence," Lauren said.

"Another that comes to mind…my legs are shaking just thinking about you touching me."

Lauren sucked in a breath at that one. Touching Carly. God. Her own knees went weak. One look back when they reached the door to Lauren's bedroom told her everything Carly just said was true. Carly's playful side had slowly receded, and what Lauren saw in her eyes was inarguably desire. Heat flared, and the anticipation of what was about to happen engulfed Lauren. She was wet. She was in need. She was ready. God, they'd waited long enough.

She had her bedroom lights on a dimmer, which worked out nicely for them tonight. Dim enough for sexy, but enough to see all she'd been dreaming about for weeks. Lauren didn't have to wait long. Carly slid a hand behind Lauren's neck and kissed her with unmeasured passion. With Lauren gasping for air, Carly stepped back and, in full view, lifted her red sweater over her head, leaving her in black pants and a black bra so revealing Lauren had to swallow. She didn't move a muscle as Carly unbuttoned those pants and slid them down her legs. The matching lingerie underneath rode the curve of her hip and dipped between her legs. Lauren trembled at the sight of the gorgeous, confident woman in front of her.

"May I?" Carly said quietly as she approached. Her fingertips brushed against the skin of Lauren's collarbone, and she unbuttoned the top button of Lauren's red blouse. Lauren nodded, granting her silent permission to go farther. Carly stepped in closer and eased the top of her bare thigh up against Lauren's center through her jeans. She heard her own gasp and felt her entire body tighten. Carly's proximity did that to her, communicating her startling power. Lauren throbbed. She tried to concentrate. Carly continued to slowly unbutton her top, staring with interest as she revealed more and more. She let her hands drop after mastering the last button. Lauren's open shirt revealed a glimpse of her cleavage and the long sweep of her torso and stomach. Carly took her in as if studying the most beautiful of paintings. Finally, she reached up and slid the shirt off Lauren's shoulders, down to her elbows. She'd worn her yellow bra. She liked the way she looked in it best.

"God," Carly said and shook her head reverently. It seemed the yellow had been the right choice. She dipped her head and kissed the spot between Lauren's breasts, prompting Lauren to drop her head back in sweet surrender. Carly kissed up her chest to her neck and the spot beneath her jaw, all the while working the button on Lauren's pants like a damn professional. They were down around her knees along with her underwear before she could lift her head again. Carly would know how ready she was soon. Her bra quickly followed, and she watched Carly feast on that little reveal. "Finally," Carly breathed. She caught a nipple in her mouth and swirled her tongue, sending pinpricks of pleasure shooting through Lauren's midsection and immediately lower. God, it was the *lower* that nearly did her in. Carly palmed the other breast, clearly not at all shy in the bedroom. "You're everything I imagined and more, you know that?" Carly continued to bathe her breasts, sending Lauren's longing beyond anywhere she'd ever been before.

"I want to see you," Lauren whispered, running her nails up and down Carly's back.

"Mm-hmm. Soon." It was a torturous word. Carly slipped her hand between Lauren's legs and touched her softly for the first time. Lauren closed her eyes, melting, then jerking at the sensations that engulfed her.

"Carly," Lauren managed. She pushed against Carly's hand, asking for more.

"Yes, Lauren?" Carly said back, and smiled against Lauren's neck. Yet Lauren had no further words. Carly stroked her softly. Slowly. God, so slowly. Lauren moved in rhythm against Carly's fingers in pursuit of relief. She didn't get it. Carly withdrew her hand and instead eased Lauren onto the bed. From where she lay on her back, she watched as Carly put on the very best show, unhooking her bra and dropping it to the floor. Sweet heaven above, she had gorgeous breasts. Of course she did. She was Carly Daniel, and she was topless in Lauren's bedroom. Lauren thought of all the ways she planned to get to know them. Once

Carly straddled her stomach, Lauren reached up and started a soft exploration with her fingertips that ended with the gentle twisting of Carly's nipples.

"I had a feeling I'd come undone when you touched me. Good God." Carly dropped her head back which meant Lauren was on the right track.

Lauren sat up with Carly still in her lap, lifted one breast to her mouth, and dipped her head to taste. Heaven. She licked Carly's breast, her nipple, making a circle with her tongue. Carly murmured appreciatively, threading her fingers through Lauren's hair as she worked. She held her in place, which Lauren didn't mind at all. Touching Carly only made her own need escalate. Her own discomfort grew in the sexiest way possible.

Lauren reached between Carly's legs and grazed her through the fabric, making Carly moan, low and throaty. That did it. On a mission, she shifted forward and laid Carly down on the bed. She took her bikinis off in the blink of an eye, raked her gaze over all that was on glorious display to her now, and settled on top. Carly pulled Lauren's face down and kissed her, hungry and powerful. The sensation of skin on skin for the first time might have been one of the more satisfying moments of Lauren's life. She'd waited patiently for this moment, fantasized about this, and now it was all theirs. As they kissed, she settled her hips between Carly's legs and rocked. Carly gasped. Lauren rocked some more, firm and slow.

"God, yes," Carly said, arching into her, searching for more. Lauren pushed up onto her forearms as she worked her hips, watching as Carly's breasts lifted and fell with each thrust. Fiery desire flickered through her. She wanted Carly to come, and she wanted it soon.

Lauren crawled down the bed, parted Carly's legs, and kissed her between them sensuously, matching Carly's rhythm with her tongue. Slow, then fast, and slow again. She slid her fingers inside and listened to Carly gasp. "Lauren." Carly panted and made the best little whimpering sounds as Lauren pushed into her and out. She was a little drunk on those sounds, this whole experience more than she ever could have imagined. Her tongue circled and dipped, until the sounds only increased. With a final swipe, Carly went still and cried out, shaking all over as Lauren held her in place, protectively. She kissed up her body, treasuring it, memorizing each expanse of skin.

Carly took Lauren's face in her hands and kissed her, good and long. She flipped them easily, ready to take what she wanted. With fire in her eyes, she took Lauren's nipple into her mouth and sucked. She almost came. When Carly bit down, gentle yet firm, Lauren felt the sensation gathering from somewhere deep within. She couldn't stop it if she tried. Her hips pressed inward, and she tightened her stomach muscles, preparing for the tidal wave on the horizon. It built steadily every second that Carly touched her. "Almost," Lauren said, desperate. Taking the cue, Carly pushed her fingers inside. Lauren gasped and balled the sheets with her fists, as Carly moved her thumb back and forth, making amazing things happen to Lauren. Her body felt like hers, but it didn't. This was new. This was urgent. It was unhinged. The orgasm hit wild and hard in the best payoff of her life. Pleasure rocked her body and she bucked nearly off the bed, calling out. With her back arched and Carly still intimately joined to her, she rode out the waves that crashed one after the other. She'd been turned on for days—it was no wonder her body responded so powerfully.

Limp and happy, she pulled Carly to her and smiled. There were no available words left, but Carly nodded at the smile. "Right?" she said, settling a thigh between Lauren's, making her twitch with how sensitive she remained.

"Off the charts," Lauren finally murmured and ran her hand up the back of Carly's neck into her hair.

"That sounds like a challenge," Carly said with a twinkle in her eye. "We could see how far off we could go."

"Don't even think about it. You practically killed me just now."

Carly propped her head up on her hand and lay to the side, her gaze sweeping across Lauren's body. She touched her breast lightly, circling it. "Oh, I'll give it a few minutes. Don't worry."

Lauren laughed, happy, sated, and feeling wonderfully like a wanton harlot.

She could get used to this.

❖

Carly didn't have to open her eyes to know that she'd woken up in Lauren's arms. God, she loved the way Lauren smelled, like fresh cotton and soap and sunshine, if that was even possible. She didn't want to move from this spot. Ever. Her limbs felt heavy and comfortable. Her body felt the most rested it had for a long while. Lauren had seen to that expertly. Of *course* she'd be amazing in bed. She'd probably meticulously crafted her technique with careful thought, the way she approached every other aspect of her life.

Carly found herself lying in the wonderful crook of space between Lauren's shoulder and her collarbone, which gave her perfect access to place a soft good morning kiss on Lauren's neck, causing her to stir. "Are you awake?" Carly asked in her best stage whisper. When she got no answer, she smiled to herself and spent a few more minutes reminiscing about the night prior. The details were etched into her being for all time. It had been the single hottest sexual exchange of Carly's life, and in LA in her twenties, she'd experienced a lot. That was the thing, though. It wasn't always *what* she and Lauren did, but *how*. Their connection, their pacing, their ability to predict the other, their yin-and-yang vibe. All of it.

She absently traced the curve of Lauren's breast, loving the quiet of the morning with Lauren in her arms. Lauren stirred and shifted closer, pushing lightly against Carly's hand. Carly smiled at the signal and made her circles smaller, getting closer and closer to her nipple. Lauren, she'd learned just hours before, had very sensitive breasts.

"What in the world have I woken up to?" Lauren asked. She sighed contentedly. "Good morning."

"It really seems to be." Carly's forefinger, at last, landed on the nipple itself and teased it lightly. She pinched it and relished Lauren's quiet gasp. She ran her fingers between Lauren's breasts, down Lauren's stomach, and tickled the tops of her thighs, listening as Lauren's breathing pattern quickened and hitched. Things were starting to work, and fast. With her knee, she nudged one of Lauren's legs to the side and continued to lightly tickle her skin in a back and forth motion. When her fingertips reached the insides of her thighs, Lauren's cheek pushed against the pillow, and she squeezed her eyes shut. Carly continued to tickle closer and closer to the exact spot she knew would take Lauren deliciously over the edge, and when she settled there, softly moving her fingers back and forth slowly, it only took seconds for Lauren to tense, arch her back, and cry out quietly with pleasure. That's how Lauren did most things. Quietly and to perfection.

Unable to help herself, Carly slid on top so she could feel her skin pressed to Lauren's as she recovered. "Good morning, beautiful." She ran her hand through Lauren's luminous brown hair.

"That might have been my sexiest wake-up." Lauren shook her head. "Nope. I know it was."

"You came fast. Record time."

Lauren blinked. "I think we've established that I respond very well to you." Pink invaded Lauren's cheeks.

"Are you blushing? Do I make you blush?"

"No," Lauren said adamantly, touching one of her cheeks to cover it.

"But your cheeks are rosy and adorable. Just look at them."

"They are not. I checked. I love that you're naked in my bed in my home. I have no idea how this happened from six months ago, before I knew you, to here, but I really, really like you naked."

Carly straddled Lauren's thigh and rocked slightly, the whole process having turned her on in a big way. "We are in agreement about being naked together."

Lauren grinned and pulled Carly in tighter by her ass. "I had no idea you were this sexy minded in the morning. I mean, I definitely should have, because it's you."

"Do you know what I'm also a fan of, besides you naked?"

"What's that?"

"Lazy mornings. When there's no rushing, no agenda, no alarm."

Lauren rolled them onto their sides, which revealed a more perfect view of Lauren's body. Still not quite used to this intimacy, and loving every second of it, Carly let her gaze linger on the perfectly shaped, full breasts. "You are so sexy and alluring. Worthy of a painting. You need to know that."

Lauren pulled the sheet down farther, and Carly swore quietly.

"Do you know what else we agree on?" Lauren asked.

"What's that?"

"Our devotion to taking advantage of the lazy mornings you just described." Lauren slid on top and cupped Carly firmly, intimately. And they were off.

Lazy morning, indeed.

❖

Lauren made coffee to the sound of the shower. With her blue silk robe fastened loosely around her, she practically glided through the kitchen, pouring the grounds with flourish, adding the water to the rhythm of the imaginary song in her head, pressing start on the coffee maker, and gliding her way to Rocky's bowl for his breakfast. She felt like a sexed-up Snow White, bonding with all the animals and objects around her. Rocky quirked his pudgy little face at her as if to ask why she was so happy.

"Because I had an amazing night." He quirked his head to the other side, mystified. "It was so good, Rocky. I can't tell you the details because you're an innocent. Just know it was memorable in the best way." Her body tingled at just the thought of touching Carly, her own body still sensitive to the attention it had just been paid.

She deposited Rocky's breakfast in front of him. While he went to chow town, Lauren checked her phone to find only a million messages with smiley faces and congratulatory texts. There was also a series of links. Aha, the reviews. She took a deep breath, preparing herself, and clicked immediately on the one for Broadway World, knowing it would be an important one.

"Not a Cloud in the Sky as *Starry Nights* Shines Bright at The McAllister." That headline sounded promising. Lauren continued to read.

Audiences can rest assured that Starry Nights, *the new play by Mariah White premiering at The McAllister, will make you long for a telescope and a fated love of your own. Carly Daniel, taking her first bow onstage, delivers a serviceable performance as Ashley, but it's newcomer Lauren Prescott's Mandy that stole the spotlight. Prescott turns in a performance rich in charm, tenderness, and wit.*

Oh, wow. Lauren could hardly believe what she was reading. She revisited the portion about her performance over and over again. She wished they'd said more about Carly, though. *Serviceable* was a polite way of saying *fine* in the theater community, and Carly deserved much more than that. She skimmed the rest of the article in which the reviewer praised the direction, the set, and the lighting design. Tacked on to the bottom of the piece was a link that opened a secondary article separate from the review entitled "Spilled Tea and Starry Nights." She skimmed the content with a furrowed brow.

Insiders at The McAllister say that Carly Daniel, in line with past

rumors, was difficult to work with behind the scenes of the new play,
Starry Nights. *Daniel, a source said, became known in Minneapolis for
holding up rehearsals, making incredible demands of cast and crew,
and staging diva-worthy tantrums when she didn't get her way. Some
speculate it was Daniel's behavior behind Evelyn Tate's departure from
the project early last month. Tate, when contacted, declined comment.*

Lauren closed her eyes and set her phone on the counter. That
wasn't fair. Carly had been a pain to work with in the beginning,
and yes, she'd been late. However, she'd never spoken a rude word
to anyone and had put so much hard work into the show. To turn a
spotlight away from that and shine it on lies and rumors just seemed out
of bounds. Her chest ached.

"What were you reading?" Carly asked. Lauren turned to see
Carly standing across the room with wet hair, soft looking jeans, and a
pale yellow T-shirt. "The reviews?"

Lauren nodded.

"I'm ready. Lay it on me." Carly folded her arms and smiled. Yet it
wasn't her standard grin. There was a guarded, unsure quality, signaling
that she was nervous, vulnerable.

"They liked the show." It wasn't a lie.

"They did?" Carly let her hands drop. "That's such a relief. You
have no idea. What about us? I'm guessing if they liked the show then
we fared okay, right?"

"Yes, they were complimentary." She didn't mention that the
reviews seemed to favor her. It didn't feel right to say so, and it felt
even weirder that they'd written it. Carly was amazing in the show and
had come such a long way in terms of her work ethic.

"You're not saying much. Guess I better take a look." She squinted
at Lauren, headed back to the bedroom, and returned a moment later
with her phone, already engrossed in what she found there. She raised
her gaze to Lauren, beaming. "They love you. They absolutely do."

Lauren smiled back. "It's nice of them to say those things."

"I'm so proud of you." A pause. She held up her phone. "I don't
think they liked me as much." She shrugged but seemed a little smaller
as she stood there. "That's okay. I'm new at this theater thing, right?"

"They did like you. It's just that my late casting probably made for
an interesting spin on the write-up."

But Carly was continuing to click around on her phone now, and

Lauren watched as her supportive smile dimmed. Damn it. She'd run into the gossip reports.

"They think I started fights." She raised her gaze to Lauren's, dumbfounded. "But I didn't. I wouldn't. I like most everyone, and if I've been spoiled and shallow in the past, I haven't treated anyone poorly."

"You haven't. You were late and had a bit of a culture shock, but you were never hard to work with."

"Lauren," she said, looking helpless. "I never threw fits."

"No. You don't have to tell me that. I was there."

Carly kept clicking. Lauren's stomach turned over as she imagined what she'd find as she surfed from one link to another. Likely, much what Lauren had: other media outlets had picked up the same nugget of gossip, making it look widely reported that Carly had been a problem child yet again. When Carly set her phone on the kitchen counter and looked up with a crestfallen face, Lauren's heart broke for her. "I can't win."

"Don't look at it that way. Come here, please." Lauren held open her arms, but Carly hesitated and ultimately backed away from the gesture.

"I'm good. Not to worry." Instead of the embrace Lauren offered, Carly wrapped her arms around herself, resembling a vulnerable child protecting herself from other kids on the playground. She gestured behind her. "I should finish getting ready. Get out of your hair."

"I don't want you out of my hair," Lauren said to Carly's back as she retreated down the hall. No answer. She closed her eyes and let her emotions settle into a neat pile. Carly needed space to work through this atrocious rumor, which was the opposite of what she'd been hoping for. Though it was Lauren's natural inclination to try to fix everything, there was very little she could do about the media and what they wrote. She gave it some time, tidied up the kitchen, and eventually picked up Rocky IV and carried him, infant style, into her bathroom where she found Carly putting the finishing touches on her makeup.

"Someone wanted to say good morning."

Carly eyed her in the mirror. Her shoulders relaxed and the ends of her mouth tugged when she saw Rocky. It was hard to resist the face of a pug carried like a precious newborn. Rocky dropped his face over the back of Lauren's arm and regarded Carly from his upside-down position, content to be adored and fussed over like the little prince he was.

"Well, that's certainly an unusual greeting." Carly leaned down and let him swipe his upside-down tongue across her face. She scratched his head with both hands, and his curlicue tail set to wiggling, which was so much cuter than wagging. "I can't say I'd ever turn away a kiss from this fur ball of love."

"Well, who would?" A pause. "You okay?" Lauren asked quietly. "You fled the scene earlier. I was worried."

Carly leaned against the bathroom counter and considered the question. Her hair was shiny and her lips were perfectly adorned, but her soul likely hurt. "Yeah. I'm sorry about that. I'm doing okay. I can admit that those were not the words I wanted to read this morning, but do you know what I can't stop thinking about, the part that has stuck with me the most?"

Lauren set Rocky on the floor and watched as he darted back to the living room for more sun spot snoozing. "Tell me." She braced herself for Carly's disappointment, knowing she'd feel it as strongly as she would her own.

"What they said about you. I'm trying to be angry and feel sorry for myself, but all I can seem to do instead is smile about all the wonderful things they've said about you, because they're all true. And then I have to look in the mirror, because who am I? I'm supposed to be self-involved and throw a Hollywood tantrum, but I feel more like a woman who can't stop thinking about you."

"Carly." Lauren played those words back. They'd reached inside her chest and took hold. She hadn't expected them but now felt their warmth from the tips of her fingers to the ends of her toes and back again. She smiled, stepped forward, and wrapped her arms around Carly's neck. "Do you mean that? Of course you mean it, but do you?" That wreck of a sentence mirrored her scattered emotions.

Carly nodded and placed a kiss on the underside of Lauren's jaw. "I'm trying my hardest to be selfish, but I think you broke me. I'm Team Lauren now. Do we have T-shirts?"

"We definitely do not. Team Lauren is quiet and unassuming and tries not to steal attention from the real stars."

"I'm revamping Team Lauren," Carly said with a laugh. "It's okay to celebrate your reviews, you know. You've earned every compliment."

Lauren's heart and soul clenched, relaxed, and soared. "Thank you for saying that. I've never had a professional review before. This is new territory, so I'm not sure how to behave. I'm excited, though."

"And I'm excited for you." Carly lips brushed Lauren's. "I think we need to celebrate properly."

"And how would we do that?" Lauren asked.

"How about I take you to brunch and then bring you home and have my way with a celebrated actress? And I mean *thoroughly* have my way."

Lauren's entire body reacted in great favor of that statement. Today was turning around nicely, and she had Carly to thank. "I can get behind this idea."

She and Carly finished getting ready, sharing the space and touching each other here and there as they passed. When Carly returned to the living room shortly after Lauren, she was wearing a sky-blue hoodie on top of a white tank top with the word *Lauren* scrawled across the front in what looked to be a permanent marker.

"Did you steal that shirt from my closet?" Lauren asked, laughing.

"I have no idea what you're talking about," Carly said and slid her purse onto her shoulder. "But it's mine now. Shall we?"

"You're wearing that to brunch? *Nooo.*"

Carly turned to face her in proud challenge. "Try and take it off me."

Lauren blinked, and her stomach fluttered. She had a vision of doing just that. "Incredibly temping, given what I know is underneath."

Carly gasped and turned on her heel, as if hyperbolically shocked. "If you're going to objectify me all through brunch, then we're going to have a hell of a great afternoon."

Lauren laughed and watched Carly make her exit, hips swaying, blond hair flowing, sass on display. Just the way Lauren liked her.

CHAPTER TWELVE

Carly had been off her game. The performance she was capable of delivering had slipped through her fingers earlier that night, and she hated herself for it. As she lay in bed at her theater-supplied apartment, sleep mocked her. Instead, her brain took over, reliving each and every moment of her second live performance in gory and embarrassing detail. She'd flubbed lines, bumped into furniture, and was late for an exit because, like tonight, she couldn't stop thinking. She knew exactly what had gone wrong. The reviews had gotten into her head. She heard the word *serviceable* before each and every scene, and then, because she was truly masochistic, began to insert words of her own. Hack. Fraud. Nothing but a pretty face. All of them believable. None of them helpful.

"Coming over?" Lauren had asked after the show. She rested her cheek against the frame of the door. Her eyes were bright. Too bright for the end of a long day, but that was Lauren, always put together, and ready to take on the world. She envied her.

"I think I'm going to take a rain check and get some of that sleep we so desperately have been skipping over."

Lauren laughed quietly. "Oh yes, that old concept. I keep forgetting—sleep and I used to be buddies."

"But don't think you're getting rid of me that easily. Don't enter into a torrid affair with rest. I'd be so jealous."

Lauren came farther into the dressing room and took Carly's face in her hands. "Never." She kissed her sweetly. "Good night, Carly. I'll see you tomorrow when we get to do this all over again."

"Remarkable how that happens."

Lauren laughed. "Right?"

It turned out that rest had no interest in an affair with Carly. In fact, rest was an elusive bitch. Sigh. Lauren would have been the perfect distraction from Carly's scattered thoughts. She flipped herself over for the ninth, maybe tenth, time. She'd meant every word she'd said to Lauren the day before. She had been thrilled for Lauren's positive reviews. But when the exaggerated nighttime doubt crept in from behind the walls, Carly began to question her own self-worth in a way she never had before. Her career was in shambles, and as excited as she'd been for *Starry Nights* to help pull her from the trenches, it was looking less and less like that might happen. Fear arrived by her bedside next, and she hugged her fists against her heart as it raced out of control. What would she do with herself if her career ran out of gas entirely? Guest spots on game shows? Sure, until those invitations washed up, too. Her line of thinking felt irrational and premature, yet she struggled for air all the same. Gasping, she sat up and turned on the small lamp next to her bed, hoping to jar herself out of her downward spiral. She listened to the sound of her own ragged breaths. Finally, she reached for the glass of water next to her bed just as her phone rang. It was three a.m. Who in the world would be calling?

She checked the readout on her phone and quickly took the call. "Hey," Lauren said when she answered. "I'm sorry to call so late."

Carly closed her eyes at the sound of Lauren's voice. "It's okay." She swallowed. It was all she could manage.

"I woke up and, I don't know, felt like I needed to call. I was worried about you for some weird reason. Is that crazy?"

Carly looked up at the ceiling, her eyes filling. "No. It's actually not weird at all. I should have come over, I think. Rough night." Maybe Lauren had detected something earlier. Maybe she had some sort of sixth sense that pulled her from sleep. Maybe they were developing an intense connection. Whatever it was, Carly was grateful for the rescue call.

"How about Rocky and I drop by?"

"You don't have to do that," Carly said, but everything in her reached for that idea.

"I think we want to, though. We just took a vote. We're coming over."

Carly paused, releasing the remaining fist from its place against her chest. "Okay. I'll leave the door unlocked." She swallowed in enormous relief.

Fifteen minutes later, she heard the door click open and closed, followed by the sound of the lock. "Hey, you," Lauren said, dropping a backpack at the bedroom door. She slid into bed behind Carly, wearing yoga pants and a T-shirt, having never looked more snuggly.

"Hi, guys," Carly said to Lauren and an exuberant Rocky, who promptly licked her face six times and then curled into a ball at the foot of her bed. With Lauren's arms around her waist from behind, she felt everything in her relax. For tonight, she felt safe and solid. The *what-if* game still played in the back of her mind, but she refused to give it her attention. Lauren had her for now, and that was everything.

"Shall we sleep?" Lauren asked.

"Yes, please," Carly said. She switched off the light and let everything float far, far away.

❖

"Ms. Prescott, this is Elissa Newman from Telsey Casting calling again about setting up a meeting regarding a project you might be right for. Call me at your earliest convenience. Do you have representation I could get in touch with?"

As she sat at her dressing table before Saturday's matinee, Lauren shook her head in response to the voicemail. No. She didn't have representation. In fact, she'd never had an agent.

"You good, Lala?" Trip asked, popping his head into her dressing room. "All set for a wild two-show day?"

"I'm all good, Trippy. You're doing a bang-up job."

"You say that to all the first-time PSMs," he said and tossed his hair dramatically in departure.

Lauren scrolled to the next voicemail and hit play. "Hiya, Lauren. Dave Pell from *Playbill Online*. Would love to ask you a few questions about your Cinderella story working on *Starry Nights*. I think our readers would love to hear about it. Give me a ring."

She jotted down Dave's number for later, still not believing that *Playbill* was calling *her*.

Next message. "Good afternoon, Ms. Prescott. Jim Lawson from United Talent Agency calling to chat. Hoping to hear from you. I think we could do some great things if we worked together." Well, there was that possible representation Elissa Newman was asking about. UTA was a top agency. She took his number down, too.

Lauren smiled at the warm lips on the back of her neck. "Antonio, we have to stop sneaking around like this," she whispered. The nibbling didn't stop. "But I must say your kissing has improved. Your lips, they're amazing." She turned, gasped, and covered her mouth in mock surprise. "What? Famous actress Carly Daniel!"

Carly straightened. "Do I need to challenge this Antonio to a duel? I'll need to ask Trip for a sword."

"I think they use pistols for those things, but no way. I kicked Antonio to the curb the moment I felt those amazing lips." She fluttered her eyelashes dramatically.

Carly met Lauren's gaze in the lighted mirror. "Fantastic. Now talk dirty to me. List some office supplies."

Lauren laughed and dropped her voice as Carly kissed across her exposed shoulder blade. "Stapler. File folder. Rubber band."

"God, yes," Carly murmured. "More."

"Sharpened pencil."

Carly sucked in air. "I can't fucking believe it's sharpened. What are you trying to do to me?"

Lauren chuckled and pulled Carly into her lap. "How are you feeling today? Better?"

Carly's smile dimmed. "I'm good." She shrugged. "Talked to Alika about lining up some meetings for when I get back to LA. Auditions, too. I have no problem proving myself all over again. If anything, this experience has taught me about the value of hard work." She nodded. "I'm ready to do it."

"I know you are. Everyone else is going to know soon, too." Thinking about Carly going back to LA reminded Lauren that they were close to the halfway mark on their four-week run of the show. That put an uncomfortable lump right in the middle of her throat. Lauren didn't want this journey with the show to end, or her time with Carly. She also couldn't fathom not working with Carly every day. The concept of her returning to LA was one she hadn't quite examined fully. Maybe that was naïve of her, but it felt more like a guarding of her own heart, which she'd all but surrendered to Carly lately.

"Where did you go just now?" Carly asked, angling a strand of hair behind Lauren's ear. "You got that faraway look in your eye, and it's rare for you to drift away." She tapped Lauren's temple. "Always so focused."

"Thinking about when the show closes." She felt the wistful look creep onto her face right on cue. The future felt uncertain, and for someone who thrived on planning, that was a daunting prospect.

Carly sighed, mirroring Lauren's emotions. "You know, when I think about that particular topic, it always involves a side narrative where you come back to LA with me. Make a go of it out there. We fly through the streets with the top down on my convertible. We do some kissing, too. Maybe stop at Starbucks. Then, more kissing."

"Of course you drive a convertible back home, too. What kind?"

"I drive a 911 most of the time."

Lauren blinked. "I have no idea what that is. Is it bigger than a Mini Countryman? Does it have a siren?"

"No, and no. A 911 is a Porsche."

"Well, yeah," Lauren said, as if it was the most natural thing in all the land. "Everyone knows the names of all the Porsche models. So incredibly common." Lauren laughed in that hoity-toity way she imagined a rich person would.

"You're adorable." Carly shook her head, staring at Lauren with pure affection. "I'm keeping you and taking you to LA. Discussion closed."

Lauren opened her mouth and closed it. "I don't know." The concept was terrifying. She'd taken years to finally establish herself as a top-tier stage manager at The McAllister, a theater she cherished. Yet the attention this role had earned her propped open a door to a long-forgotten dream. She needed to figure out what the next step in her life would be. What did she want out of her career? At the same time, there was also Carly and their unexpected connection. "I think it's all terrifying." She held up her hand. "I'm even chewing my nails. I never do that. Just look at them."

"*Tsk.* Those are sad. Shall I schedule us a couples' manicure?"

"Would you believe I've never had one of those?"

Carly laughed. "Yes, because you're Lauren, and it's not all that practical. Manicures are a luxury. It's one of the things I love about you. You're not pretentious."

They'd both heard it. The L-word. No, it wasn't a proclamation of love, but it was the first time the concept had ever been entered into the record of their relationship. She watched Carly quickly gather herself, stand, and change the subject.

"I should get ready. Close to our half hour."

Aha, the word made her feel uncomfortable, daunted. Lauren felt the pang of disappointment, and a small part of herself screamed that Carly would never go there with her. Self-doubt truly sucked. Yet she lived with it daily.

"See you out there?" Lauren asked.

Carly leaned down, kissed her lips, and straightened. "Yes. Let's take these women on another twirl around fate. See you on the other side?"

"I'll be there. Break a leg."

Lauren watched Carly leave through the mirror. Since the reviews hit nearly ten days ago, Carly had carried herself a tad heavier, almost as if trying to escape a dark cloud following her around. She had fun moments, and sexy moments, and, as always, killed it onstage. Yet she'd get this faraway look in her eye that Lauren had come to understand originated from fear. That tugged at Lauren, who wanted to gather Carly up and keep her safe from the world, which had proven itself to be less than hospitable. Carly projected such confidence and bravado that it took a while to understand that beneath it all existed a well of vulnerability.

"Ladies and gentlemen, we're at half hour."

She smiled at the sound of Trip's ultra-professional voice. She'd only hear it for another two weeks of performances. She tapped the small notebook in which she'd taken down the phone numbers from the voicemails earlier. She wasn't on the schedule at The McAllister for the next show, as she'd been promised a true vacation by Wilks. That time was hers, and she wouldn't lose her job. Possibilities swirled. Uncertainty loomed. Above all, her heart squeezed uncomfortably. "What in the world am I supposed to do with myself now?"

The quiet of the room absorbed her question. She had a show to do first.

❖

Carly, in her act 1 business suit for Ashley, regarded herself in the mirror. She had ten minutes until places and had her hair, costume, and makeup ready in record time, which left a few minutes to spare. While in Lauren's dressing room earlier, she'd seen the names and numbers of several key industry players on her dressing table. That meant Lauren's phone was clearly getting a workout, while her own remained woefully silent. Not one to just accept her fate, Carly pulled her phone out of her bag and knew the only thing to do now. Call her agent. Again.

"Alika Moore's office. This is William."

"William. It's Carly Daniel. Is she available?"

"I'll put you right through." Only a small pause before Alika answered.

"Alika, do you know that it's the middle of autumn and forty-two degrees in Minneapolis? California is weeping for me and my lost tan."

Her agent chuckled. "Well, hello, Carly Daniel. How the hell are you today?"

"About the same as when we chatted last week. Show's going well. People seem to love it. We have huge crowds at the stage door and have sold out the entire run."

"That's fantastic news. I knew you'd kill it if we sent you out there. Right move all the way."

"You still think so?" A pause. Carly watched herself carefully in the mirror, insecurity creasing her features. She absently fiddled with the eyelash curler on her dressing table. "Just haven't heard from you. Wondering if you've had any bites since we last spoke. I'm ready to get going, line some things up."

She heard Alika shuffle some papers on her desk, which she knew from experience was always messy, stacked with file folders, and decorated with stray paper clips. Alika operated on a system of organized chaos which would drive Lauren insane. She smothered a smile just thinking about it.

"I wish I did, Carly. I had hoped that some good press would raise your demand a bit. The rumors that were published haven't been helpful."

"But the rumors weren't true. I got along with everyone, except the one actress who hated me from the moment I walked in the door. It was still a harmonious environment, though. We had a positive rehearsal period."

"Doesn't matter if you were Mother Teresa in that room if the opposite is what makes it to print. You know this business. The reviews are good, but—"

"Not amazing. At least, not for me." She placed a hand on her forehead, realizing her uphill battle. It was like she couldn't do anything right, even when she did.

"True." Alika sighed. "I could get you endorsement work, TV spots, but I'm worried that's the wrong move if we want to revive your film career. It's all about what you want your future to be."

"Film is where it's at, and it's where I want to be. Stage would be good, too. As long as it's high profile."

Alika didn't say anything. "The only thing might be, and don't grasp on to this yet, but—"

"Tell me." Carly stood up, needing something, anything to keep hope alive.

"There's murmuring down the hall among our theatrical agents that *Starry Nights* might make a Broadway transfer."

Carly held her breath. Was it possible? The McAllister was reputable, but Broadway was legendary. If they transferred the show, her visibility would soar. Not only that, but she felt like a part of *Starry Nights*, and it was part of her. She couldn't imagine the show making that leap without her and Lauren in their rightful roles. "Alika, my favorite agent ever"—she began to walk the length of her small dressing room, invigorated—"if that happens, it could be a game changer."

"I hesitated to mention it, as it could all just be rumor. Don't get your hopes up just yet."

Carly snapped her fingers. "Too late. How can we make this happen?"

"Well, I could always put the word out that you'd be interested. See if that sparks any momentum for the project."

"Yes, do that. I am."

"Ladies and gentlemen, five minutes, please. Five minutes to places."

"Gotta run," Carly said, glancing up at the speaker. "But let's talk soon. This is amazing, Leek. I'm sending a basket of bourbon. All the bourbon. It's yours."

"You might want to wait until the deal is done, but I will sip away in your name."

"You're making me misty. Showtime. Bye."

Carly clicked off the call and dashed out of her dressing room en route to the wings, where she planned to deliver the performance of her life and get herself and Lauren exactly where they needed to be. There was simply too much at stake.

Chapter Thirteen

Lauren stirred the big pot of homemade chili she'd made for herself and Carly to accompany the cold day, while the cornbread baked in the oven. It was after six and the sun was nearly down, a reminder that winter was not far off. Because it was Monday, they had the night off and were using it to unwind together.

"My mom didn't cook," Carly said. "She heated up at most. Chicken strips and those meals with the sectioned-off side dishes."

"TV dinners. Well, who would have imagined that Ms. Porsche 911 grew up on frozen foods?"

"What about you, Ms. Mini Cooper?"

"Homemade all the way." She tasted the chili. Perfectly spiced. "We would sit around the table and tell the high and low point of our day."

"So you essentially grew up on *The Brady Bunch*."

"Without the divorce part, but yes. Wholesome is a good word for it. Oatmeal cookies in a jar and all."

"Well, that explains it." Lauren offered a wooden spoonful of chili to Carly, who took a taste. She blinked. "That's the most amazing chili anyone's ever made."

"I have chili skills," Lauren said and shimmied her shoulders.

Carly grinned at her. "Please always dance while you cook. I would have to tell your family, if they asked, that your dancing was the high point of my day today. It's also kind of sexy."

Lauren bounced her eyebrows playfully, knowing full well she could capitalize on that shimmy later. "Wait. Explains what?" Lauren asked, returning to her stirring. "You never finished the thought earlier, and you're not off the hook."

Carly leaned her back against the counter. "Your upbringing explains why you're so put together."

"Does that get on your nerves?" Lauren scrunched one eye closed. "The organizing can be a bit much. I'm aware." She pointed at the cookbooks on her counter, arranged in height order.

"No." Carly shook her head. "There's something about it, all the little meticulous details you manage and move around and need to have a certain way, that gets me…hot. Even your calendar on the fridge with all the tiny writing." She braced against what appeared to be a shiver of pleasure.

Lauren chuckled. "Only you would feel that way."

Carly slid her arms around Lauren's waist from behind. "It's why we're drawn to each other like sexy moths to a romantic flame."

"I've always thought of us as sexy moths."

"Right?" Carly moved Lauren's hair to the side and placed a kiss on the back of her neck that sent a tingle. "Do you know what it is? Your family is the catalog family. The one advertising the matching pajamas that even the dog is wearing."

Lauren laughed. "We did have matching pajamas for Christmas morning."

"Oh my God, of course you did. I haven't met your brother, but he seems to fit, too."

"Oh, he does. He argues the hardest for which pair we should get."

Carly's hands traveled up from where they rested at Lauren's waist to her rib cage and then lightly circled her breasts through her sweater. Lauren was forced to close her eyes in sweet surrender, loving being touched this way by Carly.

"Have I mentioned how much I love your breasts?" Carly asked, just before kissing the side of her neck.

Oh, man. "I think…yes."

"Well, it's so very true today. Let me tell you."

Lauren opened her eyes and tried to pay attention to her very mundane chili task but was losing ground. *All you have to do is stir*, she told herself. Another open-mouthed kiss on her neck. Carly cupped her breasts more firmly, pressing them back against Lauren's chest in a slow massage. Lauren was supposed to survive this, how? Why did her breasts have to be so sensitive? As if reading her thoughts, Carly abandoned that practice and dipped her hands up the hem of Lauren's sweater, and then found her way into Lauren's bra, circling her nipples with two fingers, then pinching lightly. It was as if someone had turned up the volume on her body, and it was all she could hear or concentrate on. She felt that familiar tugging between her legs, as everything woke the hell up for Carly the way it always did.

"Wanna take a break for just a minute or two?" Carly whispered in her ear. "We don't even have to go very far." To tip the scale even further, Carly ran her fingers along Lauren's waistband, nearly causing her knees to buckle. "What do you say?"

Lauren nodded, because her voice felt far away in her haze of lust. She didn't recognize her life lately, in the best way possible. It was barely dark on a Monday, and she was about to have an amazing dinner and some action with a woman she was growing to truly care about. Okay, she could admit that Carly was also ridiculously hot and fun and taking Lauren's shirt off with skilled precision.

She allowed Carly to lead her a few feet away from the hot stove, her hands on the exposed skin at the small of Lauren's back. Carly turned her around and kissed her, flooding Lauren's senses. She tasted strawberry from Carly's lip gloss. She felt the soft tickling of Carly's hair on her own shoulders. She wanted Carly's hands on her soon, all the while inhaling the scent of the most wonderful pot of chili she'd ever cooked.

She drew one breath before Carly lifted the cups of her bra up and over, exposing her breasts. Lauren tried to control her breathing, but air was scarce. Carly pulled a nipple into her mouth as she unbuttoned Lauren's jeans with her other hand and slid them partway down. They didn't need or want foreplay. That wasn't what this was. They'd developed a shorthand like none Lauren had ever known. It was fun to take their time, and oh, they did often, but fast and good in a kitchen had its merits as well, Lauren had learned.

Carly slipped her hand down the inside of Lauren's underwear and touched her intimately. Lauren hissed in a breath and pressed back. Once the sensations settled, they began. She rode Carly's hand slowly, holding eye contact, losing herself in a sea of soft blue. It didn't take long. She said Carly's name, closed her eyes, and rocked her hips frantically. She came with a shuddering cry, rocketing to a wonderful oblivion of pleasure. She sucked in a steadying breath. She'd been innocently cooking just five minutes ago.

"You are so beautiful when you come," Carly said reverently, still touching her. With her other hand, she cradled Lauren's cheek and then kissed her softly. "Can there be more of that later?"

Lauren struggled to regain sentence structure, still in recovery mode. She nodded, however, imagining all the ways she'd even the score. The things she wanted to do to Carly entered her mind with gusto. It was shaping up to be a wonderful night off.

❖

Tiny details mattered. The early afternoon sunshine on Lauren's back patio caught the tiny hints of red in Lauren's brown hair. Carly wasn't sure she'd ever noticed them before and took joy in learning more tiny things about Lauren. She liked her coffee warm, but not hot. She liked to take walks in her neighborhood but preferred to do so at night after a show. She loved having her back tickled as she fell asleep and knew way more about football than Carly would have guessed.

"So I'm doing this?" Lauren asked, with a nervous smile.

Carly held up her palms. "I'm merely a supportive bystander."

She watched Lauren take the pen and sign her name with a flourish, finishing with a twist of her wrist. "There. Done." She raised her gaze in triumph.

Carly grinned back. "It's official. You have an agent. A really, really good one, too. UTA is top-notch." She shrugged extra-casually. "So, you're going to give your acting career a second shot."

Lauren hesitated. "Yes and no. I think it just means I'll dip my toe in the water and see if it's warm. My plan is to go on an audition or two and decide from there." She shook her head. "It's strange because I'm not unhappy stage managing."

"I could tell. You were in your element." The wind hit and Carly snuggled farther into her oversized sweatshirt.

Lauren winced and stared at the contract with uncertainty. "In fact, I really like it. But what if I like acting more?"

"I think you owe it to yourself to find out. One thing I know? You're really good at both."

"First world problems." Lauren shook her head, highlighting how torn she felt.

Carly's stomach tightened. They'd talked on and off about the possibility of Lauren coming back West with Carly, but she'd never quite committed fully. From Carly's perspective, she couldn't imagine anything better than the two of them in LA, the town she loved. Though she hadn't yet wrapped her head around what it all meant, she'd never had feelings as powerful as those she was experiencing for Lauren. While still mysterious, she knew they were too important to just wave to Lauren in her rearview mirror when she left Minneapolis in ten days. In fact, she couldn't.

"Pack a bag and come with me." There. She'd flat-out said it. Again. "Just think. You, me, palm trees, and blue water."

Lauren turned to her. Those sparkling green eyes carried hope and what looked to be interest. Jackpot. "I think that might be a nice idea. I think maybe that's what I'd like to do." Carly stared. So conservative. So cautious.

"I think *maybe* you should lose the *maybe*," Carly said and leaned in. She paused just centimeters from Lauren's lips, savoring the anticipation. Her favorite damn part.

Lauren closed the gap and kissed her softly, lingering. "Done. It's gone."

Carly's jaw dropped. She'd said yes. "We're LA bound. Look out, City of Angels."

Lauren took a deep breath and reached for her phone. "I guess I should look around for somewhere to live for a few weeks."

Carly shook her head. "You're impossible. Do you have any understanding of that?"

"Impossibly beautiful, sexy, and in charge, you mean?"

"Definitely, hell yeah, and"—she tilted her head back and forth—"all things are negotiable."

Another kiss. A longer one. Kissing Lauren, she'd learned, was a fantastic way to warm up in the colder weather. "I can live with those terms," Lauren said, with that sensual look she always got right after being kissed, almost as if it left her a little dizzy. Carly could identify. "How about before I race off to LA with you, we have lunch, then later meet in a fake airport and face destiny again?"

"You're on." Carly grinned.

"I could go for some fries."

Carly wanted to give Lauren the moon and stars. Fries shouldn't be so hard.

❖

No, no, no. Lauren was late for the matinee and she hated it with every fiber of her being. Traffic had clearly been out to get her, and she'd just barely make her call time, which was unheard of. She preferred to be extra early, and when she wasn't, she was automatically late, even though she was on time. It was a whole thing that made sense in her head, at least.

"Wilks, hi," Lauren said as she signed in. It wasn't unusual to run into Wilks backstage, as he liked to make himself visible, but it was rare on Saturday.

"There you are. Just the woman I was looking for," he said and kissed her cheek. He'd been her biggest cheerleader since she'd changed hats and stepped onto the stage instead of into the booth, attending three performances of *Starry Nights* that she knew about. "Just wanted to let you know that Jan Wendel attended last night's performance and loved what she saw."

Lauren squinted. "Wendel?" The Wendel family were well known Broadway producers. She didn't know any of their first names, but could one of them be Jan?

"Yes, that Wendel. She's a good friend of Ethan's. Told me that if you ever make the move to New York to let her know."

"Wow. As an actress?"

"As an actress. I thought about not telling you because you're the best stage manager I've ever worked with, but you should know how well your performance is being received." She understood that Wilks was also checking in with her, trying to assess if he was about to lose his favorite stage manager. The idea stressed her out, and she wasn't sure what to say. She hadn't made any plans...yet. She glanced down the hall that led to her dressing room. "Thanks for telling me, Wilks." She pulled him in for a quick squeeze. "I'm a little behind schedule." Which seemed like the lamest excuse when she heard it out loud. "Better get going."

"Just keep me updated," he said, and she headed down the hall. Her stomach turned a little at the idea of leaving her job, but it turned back at the thought of not exploring every opportunity. She ordered herself to take a deep breath and knew full well she might fall flat on her face as an actress once she stepped outside of this role. If so? She'd be no worse off. That helped a little.

"Hey, you," Carly said. She smiled warmly, leaning against the wall in the hallway. She'd done her makeup but had yet to get into costume. "What's going on? You signed in but weren't in your dressing room."

"Just a quick check-in with Wilks for a moment. No big deal. Logistical stuff."

"Oh," Carly said knowingly. "Is he trying to convince you to stay?"

"I get the impression he's worried."

"Good. Because if he's going to try and persuade you, I can certainly redouble my efforts." She tossed her hair playfully, but even Carly's silly side translated to alluring. If only she knew how little she had to work to be persuasive.

Lauren ran her hand down the back of Carly's hair affectionately. "Trust me. You're way ahead." She gestured down the hall toward her own dressing room, her stomach flip-flopping with uncertainty all over again. "I better kick it into gear. I've never been this late, and it's stressing me out."

Carly glanced behind her at the clock. "Yet you're not close to late at all. You still have time. What's it like to be you?"

"You don't want to know." She placed a quick kiss on Carly's lips and headed down the hall, never feeling more unsure of her future, and terrified of what that all meant.

CHAPTER FOURTEEN

L os Angeles has terrible traffic. You need to be prepared for that. Always allow extra time no matter where you're going." Lauren's mother looked at her quite seriously the way she always did when she was nervous. "Oh, and wear a seat belt, which I know you know, but I have to say it. I'm a mom."

Lauren returned to her bedroom from the bathroom, carrying her toiletries bag. "I will. As for traffic, I'm not taking my car, so Uber will be my friend. Plus, Carly apparently has a second one she doesn't drive too often that she says I can use." She tossed another shirt into her suitcase.

"Well, that's helpful of her." Her mother paused. "I like her, Lauren. She's...kind. Warm."

"I feel the same way."

Her mother sat on the edge of her bed and continued to help her pack. Lauren had a flight out West the next morning, and her mom had insisted on driving in to see her off and help get everything in order. No, she wasn't going forever. At least, not yet. But a few weeks away was a pretty big deal. Carly had already flown home, and though they'd only been apart a day and a half, Lauren already missed her like crazy. The distance made all the difference.

"The photos from curtain call looked so emotional," her mother said. "Was it as memorable as it looked? I just wish we could have been there for the last one. We almost bought tickets from a scalper."

Lauren laughed. "You were there for opening. That was enough. As for your question, the closing show was like saying good-bye to the most unexpected best friend." She met her mother's eyes. "You know, I still can't believe the whole thing was real. That any of this is."

She thought back on just a few nights prior, standing downstage, her hand firmly in Carly's as they took their final bows and said farewell to characters who they not only loved, but who had been instrumental in their own relationship. *Starry Nights* was what brought Carly to her and made Lauren step out of her comfort zone in a million different other capacities as well. The whole experience had been a dream come true, and Lauren was a different human for it.

"We'll see you back in a few weeks?" Wilks asked, as she performed the bittersweet task of cleaning out her dressing room the next day. Luckily, the stage management office was just down the hall, and she wouldn't have to travel far.

She smiled at him. "I have no reason to say no at this point."

"Until you do." His face held affection and understanding.

She shrugged. "This business, Wilks…I'm not sure I'll ever have a true handle on how it works, and I've been at it for years."

"That's because it's always changing, presenting one surprise after another. One of the reasons we love it." He opened his arms for a hug, and she moved easily into them. Since she'd started work at The McAllister, Wilks had been not only a solid boss, but a kind mentor. He'd shared his wisdom with her, and she trusted him.

"Thank you for everything," she said. "I mean that." This wasn't necessarily good-bye, but it felt like it.

He released her. "I feel I should be saying those words to you. You're a class act, Lauren Prescott." He shook his finger at her as he walked away. "And for selfish reasons, I'm going to pray you walk through those doors in a few weeks. I have a theater to run, you know."

"Good-bye, Wilks. I'll miss you." He kept walking. He was a sweet man, but sentimentality made him a little itchy.

Saying good-bye to Carly had been a different story. They'd be apart for under a week, but after the intensity of the last month and a half, she'd feel empty without Carly by her side. They'd become an inseparable team, both at work and after.

"Do you have something to put on in case you get cold?" Lauren had asked, as they stood outside of her place, waiting for the private car that would take Carly to the airport.

Carly gestured to her Chanel bag. "I have a cardigan tucked away, just in case."

"Good. What about snacks for the plane?"

"I'm flying first class, but if you want me to carry a sack lunch, I can. We can write my name in my clothes, too." She grinned.

"Cheeky," Lauren said. She was nervous, and when she was nervous, she overprepared. That apparently now extended to Carly, too. "I'm taking care of you. It's what I do."

Carly had held on to the sides of Lauren's unzipped hoodie. "You took very good care of me this morning," Carly said, alluding to their leisurely morning in bed. With Carly's housing running out when the show closed, she'd spent the last couple of days at Lauren's place, which had been the perfect way to decompress from the run of the show. Not that they'd done a lot of resting. "When does your flight arrive on Friday?"

"A little after four."

"Perfect." Carly got her idea face on. "We can go somewhere fantastic for dinner."

"I'll leave that planning up to you."

Carly took a dramatic step back. "Who are you? The Lauren I know plans everything. Get off her lawn."

Lauren laughed. "I'll miss you until then. Even your overly dramatic proclamations."

"I don't know. After a few drama-free days, you may decide life is easier without this girl. Who's going to lament loudly when you're out of milk?"

"No one as loud about it as you are. That's for sure." They heard the sound of a car pulling into Lauren's street. She glanced sadly in that direction and back. "Kiss me."

Carly hadn't hesitated. In fact, she'd wrapped her arms all the way around Lauren, making her feel cherished. Her eyes had misted, which was ridiculous. It was a few days, for God's sake.

Still, her heart ached.

"Do you have snacks for the plane?" Lauren's mother asked, pulling her back into the fold of the present conversation.

She laughed. "We're more alike than even I realized."

"Why do you say that?"

She squeezed her mom's hand. "Not important. Can I ask you something?"

"Is this about how to make your chili spices richer? I'm a big proponent of a longer marinating period."

Lauren laughed, fully aware that her mother was joking. "It should be about the spices, but no." She sat down on the bed, abandoning her packing for a moment. "When did you know Dad had your heart? As in, for good. Done deal. This was the guy."

"When he knew every fault and weakness in my arsenal and still craved me just as much."

"Craved," Lauren repeated. She could identify entirely with the concept.

Her mother held up a finger. "I'm not done."

Lauren bowed her head in apology. "What else?"

"The second part that told me was when I couldn't imagine my day without him. I didn't want to." She lifted her shoulders. "I love being here with you, my sweet girl, but I also miss him and can't help but wonder if he was able to heat up the chicken I left him for tonight without burning his fingers. Now, that's love."

Lauren closed her eyes, because that's exactly how she felt. Since Carly left, her days felt strange and empty. She spent more time counting the hours until she would be reunited with Carly than she did actually living. The imbalance was a lot to behold.

"I think I'm going to call him," her mother said, glancing around for her phone. She paused. "This is about Carly, isn't it? I don't think I'd realized it had gotten so serious. She's a celebrity, Lauren. That comes with a whole other set of obstacles."

Lauren smiled. "I know that. Sometimes I forget, admittedly."

"Does that…worry you at all?"

"Yes. It does." But leaving Lauren's world, and entering Carly's? It felt like a much larger issue now than ever before. Lauren wasn't sure what to expect. "I don't really know what her life is like."

"Well, kiddo, I think you're about to find out." She covered Lauren's hand with hers. "Do me a favor. You take care of yourself out there. No matter what kind of wheeling or dealing you run into with the new agent or your auditions, you remember who you are: Lauren May Prescott, the best human I happen to know."

She sent her mother a watery smile, as a mixture of excitement and trepidation took over. "That's my plan."

"And you're going to call me once a day for every state that now will separate us."

Lauren frowned. "I'll try." Lauren immediately winced at her error and prepared herself for the inevitable. "Don't do the Yoda voice."

"Me to excuse Lauren Prescott?" her mother said in an always startlingly accurate Yoda voice, which was prompted anytime Lauren used the word *try* instead of something more affirmative.

"You have to stop doing Yoda," Lauren said, with a laugh.

"*Hmmmm?*" her Yoda Mom said.

Lauren closed her eyes and grinned. "I promise to call."

That seemed to appease Yoda. At least for today.

❖

Carly clutched the autumn-themed bouquet of flowers too tightly, making the stems all mingle too closely. She couldn't seem to relax. This was it. Lauren would walk through those doors in a matter of moments, and she'd get to show her around her home city. She rolled her shoulders and swallowed the smile that kept bursting onto her face without warning. She'd never been the most patient of individuals, admittedly, but waiting on Lauren's flight to arrive had her stomach muscles fully employed and her skin all atingle.

To her right, a photographer snapped a couple photos of her, not even attempting to be discreet. There were three other paparazzi not far away. Having been out of LA for a few months, she'd not had to deal with those guys and had forgotten how awful it could be to feel like a fish in a bowl, always on display. She ignored the clicks of his camera. Yes, she could have allowed Lauren to take a car to her place, but she wanted to personally welcome her to California, whether it meant the whole thing would be documented or not.

"Who are you waiting for, Carly?" another paparazzo asked. She'd seen him before, always with a video camera, much like the one he had trained on her now. He was a piece of work. She didn't answer. It was none of his damn business. "You glad to be back in LA?" he asked. She watched the door instead, realizing sadly that he was only gearing up. She concentrated on the happy occasion and decided to pretend the paps weren't there.

A flight had clearly just landed as a new group emerged from the glass doors. She shifted her weight and watched the faces for Lauren, having missed her incredibly since they'd said good-bye earlier in the week.

"Sucks that no one wants to hire you anymore, doesn't it?" the man asked snidely. The others clicked a few photos of her response. Nope. She would hold steady and not let his words affect her. She was here because someone very important to her was arriving. This was a happy occasion. "Guess you're not pretty enough anymore to cover up the whole can't-act thing. Your last film sucked, by the way." More clicks of a lens. The video camera continued to roll. She closed her eyes momentarily until she found the strength she needed to maintain complete composure. She didn't know this man personally, so why did his words resonate? But she knew. They were the very words she heard in the back of her mind on a daily basis.

When she opened her eyes again, there was Lauren, moving toward her with the most beautiful smile she'd ever seen. She wore black pants, a green ribbed turtleneck, and a black and white plaid scarf. Her chestnut hair was down, and she looked absolutely amazing. Happiness hit instantaneously. Carly opened her arms, still clutching the flowers, and Lauren walked straight into her embrace, burying her face in Carly's hair. All was right with the world again. More clicks.

"Hi," Carly said quietly. "Hi." She said that second one with all the feeling bubbling inside of her. It was the most heartfelt *hi* of her entire existence. She squeezed Lauren again, inhaling her scent.

"Two *hi*s for me? I'll take it," Lauren said, still not letting go. "Hi back. Twice. God, it's good to see you. Don't go anywhere." Lauren let go and took a step back. They stared at each other happily, making *a sight for sore eyes* the most relevant phrase on the planet.

"I can't believe you're here." Carly practically bounced with excitement. "For you."

Lauren accepted the flowers and took a deep inhale. "I've never been given flowers on landing before. These are gorgeous."

"Times have changed." Carly wanted to kiss Lauren, greet her properly, but the sounds of cameras clicking not ten feet away stole her courage. Lauren looked over at the motley group. "Wanna grab your bag and get out of here?" Carly asked, trying to divert her focus.

"Yes, please. Show me your city. I would also kill for some food."

"Coming right up. All of it. I hope you like steak and lobster. I know a place."

Lauren melted. "You have said all the right words and in a really great order."

Carly held up a victorious fist in front of her chest. "Nailed it."

As they walked, Lauren stole glances at the paps who trailed them. "Is this normal for you?" she whispered. "All the cameras. I remember you saying they were around, but so close?"

"Usually not this bad, but they camp out at the airport. Anyone traveling has to come through here, so it's a good bet they'll spot someone noteworthy to harass on a daily basis. Today, they found me." She shrugged.

"I'm sorry." Lauren squeezed her hand just as video guy jumped in front of them, walking backward as he filmed. "Is she your girlfriend, Carly?" Carly tossed a *don't worry* glance to Lauren, who seemed understandably uncomfortable, but said nothing to the paparazzo. "Does she know you're washed up in this town? Maybe she wants to jump back on that plane."

Carly held tighter to Lauren's hand. "Could you give us some space, please? I know you're just trying to make a living, but we'd like to get my friend's bag and get out of here."

"Your friend, huh? Looked like more than that, a minute ago. Hey, I'm making a better living than you are these days, though, right? What do you say to a new line of work? I'll talk to the boss for you. But you don't look like you're smart enough to work a camera."

"Why would you say that?" Lauren asked, puzzled.

"'Cause your girlfriend here isn't doing so well. A washed up has-been who no one cares about."

Carly gave Lauren's arm a gentle tug to rein her in. The worst thing you could do was engage with these guys when their cameras were rolling. It was exactly what they were hoping for. Then you were raking in the views on the TMZ homepage having a meltdown, and no one ever saw what came just before to provoke you.

"What do you know about anything?" Lauren asked, refusing to back down. To her credit, she spoke with an impressive calm. "You're a slug with a video camera videotaping strangers in an airport." He didn't say anything, probably hoping she'd go on. Lauren sent Carly an apologetic look and went quiet.

"Oh, I get it. You're into washed-up women?" the same guy said. "Sad."

"Just stop," Lauren told him.

He didn't. "Cause I know a few folks who could show you what a real good time is." He grabbed himself provocatively with his free hand and laughed. "Wanna have steak and lobster with me instead? I'll make it worth your while."

That did it. Carly saw red. "You sad little asshole. Get the fuck out of our way, you sexually repressed piece of human waste. Do you hear me?" They stopped at the baggage carousel, and thank God, Lauren's bag was already circulating.

"No. Can you say it louder? Or are you scared now. I think I see you trembling." He walked in a circle around Carly, all the while filming. People looked on, clearly disapproving of his actions, but no one stepped in. Typical.

Lauren grabbed her suitcase, and Carly took the handle, pulling it behind them as they made their way out of the airport. The pap stepped into Carly's space, filming her from the side as they walked. "You're upset that your girlfriend knows you're a dumb loser, huh, Carly?" He stepped in even closer—and now his jibes felt threatening.

She let go of Lauren's hand, grabbed the lens of the camera, and gave it a shove. "Stay away from me." She wasn't happy with herself, but he'd gotten the best of her.

"Thanks, Carly," he said with a smug grin and took off. She'd just bankrolled the lowlife.

She sighed as self-recrimination swarmed. She knew full well they'd edit her words to go with that shove, making it look like a volatile, unprovoked outburst.

"I'm so sorry, Carly. You okay?" Lauren asked, once they'd made it to the parking garage alone.

Carly shook her head. "I wish I hadn't done that. It's going to be online the second he sells it."

Lauren looked back at the building. "I've never seen anything like that. That guy, he was so mean."

"They're like a pack of vultures. The second they sense a sliver of vulnerability, they attack. And I know better, dammit." Carly shook her head. "Guess I'm just out of practice."

Lauren kissed her cheek as they arrived at the car. "It was my fault. I engaged first."

"No. You've never experienced them before, and actually, you kept a very cool head. Color me impressed, as always." Carly popped the trunk and loaded them up.

"Wait." Lauren stared.

Carly turned. "You okay? What's wrong?"

Lauren took a giant step back. She pointed at the car. "This is it. This is the 911. The luxury vehicle you call when you have one hot emergency."

Carly laughed, which took her mind off the airport incident. "Live and in person. Did you just call me hot or the car?"

"You are the hottest person I've ever seen in my life, but this car is something else."

Carly touched her heart. "Don't leave me for a car. How would I explain that?"

"Between you and the car, you win," Lauren said, getting closer to Carly's lips with each word, and ending with the kind of hello kiss they should have been afforded twenty minutes ago. "God, I missed these lips," Lauren murmured. "Gimme more."

"You are such a good kisser," Carly said. She pulled away briefly. "I will never tire of the way you kiss. Do they teach kissing in stage management school?"

"Yes," Lauren said simply, going back in with a dreamy sigh.

❖

Sunshine for days. That's the best way Lauren could describe Los Angeles that early November. You wouldn't actually know it was fall unless someone pointed it out to you. The trees still stood tall, vibrant, and green. The blue skies seemed to scream, *Spend the day outdoors, you fool*. There was a chill in the air, but nothing near as harsh as Minnesota this time of year.

Lauren had traveled briefly to California when deciding where to pursue her career after college, ultimately deciding on New York City for a while. But this trip felt different. Low stress. Breezy. It was her second day in LA, and she planned to take it all in.

She woke just past eight, placed a kiss on a sleeping Carly's cheek, and snuck out of bed. She looked back because she loved the way Carly slept, with a fist tucked just below her chin. Lauren shook her head at the serenity of the image and marveled at how it made her chest squeeze happily. She wanted to bottle and store this moment. Instead, she took a mental snapshot and resisted the urge to climb back into bed with the beautiful naked woman before her. There would be plenty of time for that ahead.

Carly's house in the Hollywood Hills was modern, open, and expansive. It swam in natural light, which made the morning feel like a cheerful one. She made herself at home and started a pot of coffee, even though it took her fifteen minutes to figure out how to use the very foreign looking silver coffee machine. Much like she had in Minneapolis, Carly, and the hurricane she could sometimes be, kept a surprisingly neat house. Mail in a stack on the counter. Spices in a line on the rack. Only her refrigerator looked like the Carly she knew, as, for the most part, it sat empty.

"Are you stalking my groceries?"

Lauren turned at the sound of Carly's morning voice. She stood across the white marble countertop wearing a navy T-shirt with the image of a pink lip print across the top. She couldn't see the bottom half of her, but Lauren would wager that T-shirt was all she was wearing.

"You might need a few more. It's true. Good morning."

"I don't know what you're talking about. Grape jelly and pickles make for a great meal." She came around the counter and wrapped her hands around Lauren's waist. "Good morning. You're in my house."

Lauren glanced around. "Surreal."

"Isn't it? I suppose it's only fair. I've been to yours, land of full fridges and mighty pugs." She kissed Lauren sweetly and released her, heading over to grab a coffee cup from the cute little rack they hung on. "How's he doing?"

Lauren smiled. She missed Rocky IV, but he was bunking happily with his buddy, Trip, and she would see him soon enough. "Trip said he snored all night but woke up ready to play."

"I can identify," Carly said with a raised eyebrow as she doctored her coffee. "But you were out of bed before I could capitalize."

Lauren was now regretting that decision, especially as she caught sight of Carly's ass peeking out from the hem of that T-shirt. She squeezed her shoulders together at what it did to her.

"You have your meeting today?" Carly asked. She turned around, leaned against the counter, and took a sip of her coffee. Carly had amazing legs. And thighs, and—

"I'm sorry, what?"

Carly grinned. "Your meeting."

"Yes. I have a meeting with my agent at one, and an audition just after that."

"An audition on your second day? That's amazing. What's it for?"

"A rental car commercial. Apparently, I look like someone who might be capable of selling a temporary vehicle." She did her best *The Price Is Right* impersonation. "Who knew?"

"Me. You could sell me anything."

"Filing away. What do you have going today?" She watched as Carly's features shifted to blank.

"Just going to catch my breath, I think. Play hostess to my out-of-town guest. Fluff her pillow."

Lauren smiled, but understood she'd struck a sore spot. Carly was still struggling to be seen for the caliber of roles she was used to. "It's going to take time, you know, to get them to think of you as a viable choice again. But they will."

Carly offered a less than convincing smile. "Yeah. I'm sure you're right." A pause. "I hope you are." She set her coffee cup on the counter. "While the executives figure that out, I'm going to hop in the shower." To illustrate the claim, she freed herself of the T-shirt as she walked. Lauren blinked at her perfect, stark-naked body as she walked through the sunbathed kitchen. Carly turned back casually. "Wanna watch?"

Lauren decided then and there that she really, really liked Los Angeles.

CHAPTER FIFTEEN

The Fig and Olive on Melrose was hopping when Carly met Alika for lunch later that week. Luckily, her name was still good for a last-minute reservation. She'd worn her black suit, the sleek one with the pinstripes, paired with a starched white blouse and heels. She'd been told she looked killer in the outfit, and that's how she wanted to be seen, as a serious commodity. At The Fig and Olive, you never knew what studio movers and shakers you might run into. In fact, she recognized a couple of executives just a few tables down. They'd nodded to her politely as she'd passed.

"Well, it's certainly great to see you," Alika said. Her hair was shorter than the last time they'd met. It suited her and brought out her beautiful brown eyes.

"It's great to see you as well. I hope David and the kids are all right."

"No one's killed anyone this week, so we have that working in our favor, and that says a lot with Dynamite Davey in the mix. He's four and ready to throw down." It was truly nice to see Alika, and she enjoyed catching up. She also remembered the reason for their meeting, and it was business, but they'd get there. She'd waited while they ordered. She'd participated in small talk. She'd even taken time to admire the newly made-over restaurant decor. The live trees in the middle of the space were certainly breathtaking.

"So, here's the state of things." Alika moved them into the business lane and put Carly out of her misery.

"I'm ready." She folded her hands on the table. "In more ways than one."

"I know that. Trust me, and I've been working hard for you, Carly," Alika said, just as she was presented with her quail salad. "I have a little something you might be right for, and though the role isn't as meaty as you're used to, it's not a bad opportunity."

"Great," Carly said. Everything in her relaxed. "That sounds promising, right? Tell me. What are we talking about?"

"Seven days' work on a Richard Hennessy film. A legal drama. It's a midbudget outing, but studio backed, so it should have all the bells and whistles marketing-wise. You obviously wouldn't have top billing, but it's the role of a key witness in the case, so memorable."

"Memorable sounds amazing." She looked around and lowered her voice. "My star has fallen. I get it. I have to pay my dues before I'm on the poster again. This thing sounds perfect for me. When does it shoot?"

"In a couple of weeks. This character is the final role they need to cast, and then they move into production mode. How's that risotto?"

Carly stared at her plate absently. She'd taken a few bites but had no idea what it tasted like. She was that hyperfocused on the conversation. "Oh, um, fantastic. Here." She handed Alika a spoonful and watched her melt. "What else?"

"There is nothing else, unless you want a dog food commercial. That I could probably arrange."

"God, I hope we're not there yet." Carly set down her fork. "What's the latest on the *Starry Nights* transfer? We still have that to work for, right? I really think I'd be a good choice for them."

"I didn't want to have to tell you this, but it's a no go."

"No? How is that possible?" She wouldn't at least try to set something up? That didn't make sense. Aha. Maybe the show wouldn't be transferring to Broadway after all. "The project fell through, didn't it?"

Alika shook her head and winced. "It opens in the spring on Broadway. They cast Jenna McGovern as Ashley."

Carly closed her eyes. Of course they had. Jenna was fantastic and everyone knew it. Well, wasn't that just par for the course. "Who else?"

"Someone unknown. A ballet background, I think?"

"Dammit." Her heart sank. She ran her thumb across her napkin several times as the disappointment settled. She was glad she'd downplayed the whole thing to Lauren now that the door had been slammed in their faces. "That's more than a little heartbreaking."

Alika shook her head. "Nah, that's just show business, and you know it well."

"I guess I've just never been on the awful end of it for so long." She raised her eyebrows and dropped them in defeat.

"Don't even wallow. What I need you to do," Alika said, gesturing with her fork like a woman in charge, "is to concentrate on booking this Hennessy film. Think terrified witness. Breathe it. You have an audition on Thursday."

That was two days away. "Now that I can do."

"Good. Now pass me some of that risotto if you're just gonna move it around on your plate like a nine-year-old at an adult dinner party. Food here is too good to be wasted on you."

Carly laughed and handed Alika the entire portion. Hell, she'd sign over her soul to Alika if it meant she'd book this job. She needed it that badly. Her stomach churned, and her heart raced with thoughts of the uncertain horizon. She stared out the window, nervous, sad, and restless.

❖

Carly took another hit from her wineglass and hit play on her phone to watch the whole god-awful thing again. She yelled at the paparazzo, fury evident in her eyes, and then in a quick edit appeared to grab the camera and shove it. The extra added sound effects made it seem like someone had fallen over and had possibly been hurt. Of course, that had been their goal. The more hellacious her behavior seemed, the more clicks they'd get. Without the actual conversation intact, she looked out of control, a person with anger management issues. Another fabulous image booster.

When the video hadn't surfaced in the first forty-eight hours, she'd been naïve enough to think she was in the clear. Seeing it together like this, it looked even worse than she'd feared.

She took another gulp of wine, half a bottle in. She hit play again because why the hell not? There was the crazy woman snarling. Oh, wait. That was her. She hit stop. Play again. Her own voice echoed throughout her backyard from the speaker on her phone. *"Get the fuck out of our way, you sexually repressed piece of human waste. Do you hear me?"* She winced through the shove.

"Hey. What are you doing out here? Why aren't you wearing a coat?"

Lauren. She'd had a full day in Hollywood with three auditions and a lunch meeting with United Talent about her prospects and trajectory, as they'd put it. Carly had expected her home sooner, so that likely meant things had gone well. She turned around to see Lauren in her sweater and boots, hugging herself against the evening cold. It was dark out. Carly must have been out here for at least a couple of hours. Not like she had anywhere else to be.

"Just watching my new favorite TV show."

Lauren peered over her shoulder as Carly hit play. "Oh, God," she said as the video concluded. "That's not how it happened at all."

"Doesn't matter." Carly sipped. She set the glass on the table next to her. "My phone's been blowing up ever since it posted. Alika, Fallon, even my mom. She's horrified."

"You're not okay. I can tell."

"Just part of the game." Carly shrugged. "A game I can't seem to win anymore."

Lauren looked around the yard helplessly. "What can I do?"

"Absolutely nothing. It's a nice night, and I don't want to think about any of that anymore. Not when you're here." She held out her hand to Lauren. "Come here. We can keep each other warm."

"You don't have to ask me twice," Lauren said, allowing Carly to tug her until she sat in her lap, Lauren's back against her shoulder. "I'm happy to be right here." Lauren turned Carly's face up to hers and kissed her softly. "What a crazy day."

"Tell me about it. I want to live vicariously." Carly wrapped an arm around Lauren's midsection and snuggled in, taking a deep inhale.

Lauren laughed. "Please, I'm the one in your world."

Carly blew out a jaded breath. "Not from where I'm sitting. You're the one getting all the action."

"For bit parts maybe." Lauren's arm was draped around Carly's shoulder. She began to play with Carly's hair as they sat there, lifting it and letting it fall, which felt so amazing that Carly almost let go of the emotions that seemed to be taking their turns with her. Anger, desolation, and fear danced in a conga line of attack. The night seemed larger than she was, daunting in a new and unfamiliar sense.

"A job is a job." Carly forced a smile. "How did the auditions go?"

Lauren scrunched her shoulders in that cute and hopeful way she sometimes did. "I think they went well. For this guest starring role on *The Subdivision*, they wanted to talk the scene out with me and try different motivations and tactics in the room. I've never had that before. Back in my auditioning days, they would just say thank you fifteen seconds in, and that'd be it." She snagged a sip of Carly's wine.

"You have clout now. A quality credit from The McAllister and, even more importantly to them, UTA sent you. Everyone loves UTA."

Lauren shook her head, mystified, staring out into the night. "Who knew a stamp of approval from a reputable agency would pull such a different response to the very same person?"

Carly pointed at herself and sipped her wine. "The second I was signed with Alika, the landscape of my career tilted dramatically in a positive direction. People paid more attention."

"I can't imagine anyone not paying you attention. We walk into a restaurant and heads swivel."

"That's not about me. I wish it was. That's about the idea of me. The allure of fame."

Lauren turned in her lap to see Carly better. "You're depressed tonight. Do me a favor and look at me."

Carly did. It was the best Band-Aid in the world. Lauren's green eyes sparkled beneath the moonlight, and she suddenly had this urge to see her on Christmas morning, smiling as she unwrapped gifts. "I happen to know you pretty well after all this time we spent together, and I'm going to let you in on a secret. It's about my first few days knowing you."

Carly grinned and gave Lauren a squeeze. "This should be interesting. A peek behind the proverbial curtain and into the mind of one Lauren Prescott."

Lauren looked skyward as she assembled her thoughts. Distantly, Carly heard a coyote howling. "I was prepared not to like you. Convinced I wouldn't."

"Oh, this is off to a troubling start." Carly stuck out her bottom lip.

"Stay tuned," Lauren said and bopped it. "The rumors were awful. Then you showed up late. You didn't seem to care."

"Yeah, I'm really sorry about all of that. I feel like I've learned a lot since then."

"Not at all the point of my story. Do you want to listen or apologize some more?"

God, Carly loved it when Lauren took charge and teased her. It got her all tingly and a little turned on. "I want to listen to you some more. Please go on. Regale me."

Lauren smiled, and Carly's heart warmed. "But what happened, despite my preconceived ideas, is that I couldn't stop stealing glances at you. I watched you work. I took note of how kind you were to everyone you spoke with. Your beauty took my breath away." Carly's lips parted, and she sifted through this new information. Lauren had noticed her that early on?

"You're not making this up?"

Lauren shook her head. "The point of this story is that those heads turning have nothing to do with the fact that you're famous. I'm sure it doesn't hurt, but you need to take my word for this." Carly blinked, realizing she was holding Lauren so tightly that she had to have noticed. "You come with a life force, Carly, a presence that draws people to you. You're special in that way, and just being here with you tonight, I feel incredibly lucky. Getting to know you and seeing that what's on the inside is just as beautiful as what's on the outside has been the most amazing journey."

Carly couldn't find words, and she was a person who always had them. Hell, she rarely shut up. After spending the day feeling inconsequential and small, Lauren, in under five minutes, had managed to make her feel like she mattered again. More than that, she felt *important.* What a gift Lauren had just given her. "Thank you for that. You didn't have to, especially when I'm acting like a pathetic jerk and knee-deep in wine."

Lauren gave Carly's chin a little shake. "It's all gonna turn around. Just you wait. What did Alika say?"

The corners of Carly's mouth tugged. "She said I have an audition for a film on Thursday."

"What?" Lauren practically yelled, leaping off Carly's lap and facing her. "And you're just now saying so? Talk about burying the lede."

Carly laughed and held up a hand. "I'm not going to get excited about it yet, but the director knows my work, and if he's asking me to come in, it's a good sign. He's aware of what he's getting, right? And still asking."

"In my experience in the room with directors, yes, that's been exactly the case. I think this bodes really well for you." Lauren held out her hand, and Carly accepted it, standing.

"Where are we going?"

"We are going to your amazingly large kitchen where I'm going to cook us up some chicken carbonara while we sip wine and talk about our days."

"I have no groceries."

"Good thing I stopped at the store on my way home."

Carly shook her head. "God, you're good."

"We're not going to watch that video on your phone anymore because it's stupid and not you. And if things go well in the kitchen, we might even fool around later. Who knows?"

Carly blinked. "That sounds like exactly the kind of night I need."

Lauren kissed her hand. "I was hoping you'd think so."

As Lauren tugged her into the house, Carly raised an eyebrow. "You really think my kitchen is big?"

"Do lesbians rent U-Hauls on Saturdays?"

"That big, huh?"

❖

Lauren shifted in bed as the early morning sunlight tiptoed in. She blinked against it, slowly waking up. Her body felt heavy and wonderful and warm. God, what was happening to her? She grinned. Carly was happening to her. Carly softly tickled Lauren's stomach, waiting patiently for permission. Lauren had discovered early on that Carly loved morning sex, and it hadn't taken much to make her a believer, too. She turned her head and found Carly's baby blues. She still had those wonderfully swollen lips, a sign that Lauren had spent the night kissing them. Her blond hair fell across the pillow, and her hand circled Lauren's belly button. Carly raised an eyebrow. Lauren shook her head with a chuckle, knowing exactly the plans Carly had. Except Lauren had plans of her own.

"You're sexy in the morning," Carly said. Lauren pulled the sheet down from Carly's chest for a more fulfilling view of her body. Carly followed her gaze down to her breasts and then back up again with a *well, well* look. Carly's skin caressed by sunlight appeared so soft. Lauren wanted her.

"I'm not the only one who's sexy," Lauren said. With the stirring between her legs propelling her, she eased Carly onto her side and pressed herself against Carly's back. With her arm wrapped around Carly midsection, she had excellent access to the breasts she enjoyed so much. She cupped one, kneading it, pressing it, all the while listening to Carly's quiet gasps. She pinched the nipple. Carly hissed in a breath. She slid her arm between Carly and the mattress, which allowed her to pay the same attention to the other breast. There was a bird outside, singing to them in the middle of November, Lauren realized distantly. The perfect soundtrack for the morning. She parted Carly's legs with her knee and eased her hand between them from behind. She closed her eyes at how ready Carly already was. She pushed against Lauren's hand, but teasing her was so much more fun. She kept her touches light, fleeting, until she had Carly making the most adorable whimpering noises. Finally, she circled the spot she knew would take her over the edge and watched as her body flexed and clenched, her hips rolling in the most sensual abandon.

"You're shaking," Lauren said, gathering Carly into her arms, once she'd gone slack.

Carly smiled. "It was that good."

Lauren kissed her temple. "I think I like you."

"More. I think you have a crush on me," Carly said, turning around in her arms and touching Lauren intimately. "Oh." Lauren's eyes fluttered closed. "I think…" Heat rushed downward. Her senses overloaded, and out of nowhere, the most powerful orgasm ripped through her just like that. Her body shook, the intense pleasure washing over, fast and hard. She arched her back while Carly's hand continued to intensify her experience. The sounds she heard were from her, and she didn't hold back. She could let go with Carly. She was safe. Finally, her muscles relaxed, and she lay satisfied against the bed. "That's some kind of crush," she murmured.

Chapter Sixteen

I don't know what you want from me. I answered your questions as best I could." Carly blinked, then looked around the room, terrified.

"Did you consult with the defendant before testifying here today?"

Carly widened her eyes. "What? No. God, no. I haven't spoken to Victor since that day in July. The day we lost Amy."

"You didn't like the defendant's wife, Amy, much, did you?"

"I *did*." Her lip quivered.

"Do you always pull guns on your friends?"

"Not always."

"Perfect." Rick Hennessy stood from his chair across the room and approached her. The casting director hit pause on the video camera as Carly gathered her composure from the scene. This was the third reading she'd done for them that day She'd worked on the sides for hours to be sure she'd nail the audition, and while she wouldn't say it was her best ever, she was still quite satisfied with her work. "You brought so much more to the character than even I saw," he said and placed a hand on her shoulder. "Amazing work today. I know you're not someone who auditions anymore, and I want to thank you for doing this for me. This has been just fantastic. My brain is firing."

"I'm glad. It felt good," she said. "I love everything about the script."

"It's a smaller role than you're used to, but meaty as fuck, and I want to really highlight the character's contribution to the main's arc. Plus, there's the whole shock factor of this scene that is going to have people talking once the reveal happens. You don't see her admission coming."

"I didn't, when I read the script."

He ran a hand over his stubble. "I can see you really killing this. It's exciting. This has been good." He looked to his casting director, still seated at the table, and nodded.

Carly felt relief rise up in her chest, and she couldn't stop smiling. She placed a hand on her chest. "I feel the same way. Honestly, for me, it's not about the size of the role, it's about the character."

"Totally." He held out his arms for a hug, which she reciprocated. "Thanks for this, Carly. You were amazing, as you always are. Big fan. We'll be in touch."

"I look forward to it. Thanks, Rick." She waved to the group at the table and grabbed her bag. When she emerged onto the studio lot, she raised her shoulders to her ears and took a deep breath. For the first time in weeks, Carly felt like things just might be okay. She popped her sunglasses onto her face and headed home. Maybe she'd pick up a couple of iced coffees to surprise Lauren. After that, maybe they'd get dressed up and go some place fancy, romantic, and picturesque. She had something to celebrate.

❖

The restaurant Carly had picked out for them was breathtaking. The Orchard Inn Restaurant was just what it sounded like, a little restaurant nestled inside an inn located on an actual apple orchard. Lauren had no idea such a combination existed and had never seen anything like it. It felt like they were having dinner in the most romantic of storybooks. She'd even worn the pretty red dress and her favorite silver bracelet to make her feel fancy.

"I love you in red," Carly said. "Not that I don't like you in every color."

"I accept the compliment." Lauren lifted her glass of Bordeaux in the soft candlelight. It had to be the most expensive wine she'd ever tasted, and it showed. She touched her glass lightly to Carly's. "I missed you today. I'm glad we're doing this."

Carly's blue eyes sparkled, and matched the dress she'd selected for dinner perfectly. "I feel the same way. We were on opposite schedules all day, so I wanted to spend some time together." She looked around. "I haven't been here in years. It's a little known LA secret."

Their set menu for the evening, which Lauren was told by the server changed nightly, was New York strip with pepper cognac sauce, creamed spinach, and poblano macaroni and cheese. For dessert, they'd have bananas Foster butter cake with a petite chocolate milkshake. It really was a fairy tale.

It felt wonderful to be somewhere so quaint, so charming. Lauren's day had gotten away from her. When she'd stepped into her callback for a bit part on an action movie, the casting director had taken a good hard look at her. After her reading, which she honestly felt she'd bombed, the woman met her in the hallway. "Do you have time for one more? I can't help but wonder if you might be right for a hard-to-cast project. Something very different from this one."

"Um, sure. Of course." She checked her watch and realized it was now late in the afternoon. How had that happened?

The woman scribbled some directions on the back of her business card. "You're looking for an office building three down from this one. I've messaged ahead and they're expecting you. But hurry, because they're wrapping up for the day and have agreed to squeeze you in."

"Okay. Great. I appreciate it."

Lauren quickly read a text from Carly about iced coffees as she scurried across the lot, halfway wanting to ditch the additional audition and join Carly at home instead for that iced latte poolside. Yet she reminded herself that she'd come to LA for an exploratory mission, and she needed to use her time to do just that. Carly would be waiting after.

"And how was your day today?" Carly asked, swirling her wine from across the table. Lauren noticed a nearby table smile in their direction. They raised a glass to Carly, and Carly raised hers back. She'd been recognized but didn't miss a beat in their conversation.

"You first. Tell me all about the audition," Lauren said, resting her chin in her hand.

Carly lit up. "It went as well as I had hoped. We ran the scene a couple of different ways. They put me on video, which is customary, and by the end, I think the director was really happy." She leaned in. "Hennessy is a straightforward guy, and I don't think he would have gushed as much as he had if the offer wasn't coming, you know?"

"Of course." Lauren sent a silent thank-you to the stars, which, on their way in, had glistened extra bright. Carly needed this pick-me-up in a big way. "I knew you'd nail it. Have you worked with this director before?"

"Never, but we run in a lot of the same circles. I like his style."

"I liked the director from my audition today, too. I wound up with an extra one, which is why I was late. A casting director thought I might be a fit for another film her office was handling. So I ran over with it being so close and got to read for the part. Let me tell you, it felt like a much bigger deal than the low budget indie I read for first." She hugged her shoulders together. "I felt Hollywood fancy. It was fun."

Carly laughed and sipped the wine. "Sometimes you find the very best possible projects that way. What's the film about?"

"I'm not sure. I didn't even get the title of the film because it was such a whirlwind getting there, but the sides were from a scene in a courtroom and I read for a witness. We did some workshopping, and then they had me read with another actor who's already been cast."

"Oh." Carly inclined her head to the side. "That sounds like they really liked you." She paused and set down her wine, as if mulling something over. "You said it was a court scene you read today. That sounds like my audition for the Hennessy film, strangely."

Lauren froze. "I don't think so. The director's name was Rick."

Carly nodded, her smile now tight. "Rick Hennessy."

"Oh, wow." Lauren didn't know where to go. Had she known this was Carly's audition, the one she'd been so excited about, she never in a million years would have gone in for it.

Carly shook her head ruefully. "We read for the same director today. Can you believe that? Crazy."

Lauren blinked. "I honestly didn't realize. I'm so sorry."

Carly appeared unfazed, but almost as if she was trying for that. "You have nothing to apologize for. This town is pretty small at the end of the day."

Lauren sat back in her chair just as two amazing plates of food were set in front of them. She laughed. "I don't even know what to say now."

This was certainly awkward.

Carly took a deep breath. She stared at her plate as if she'd lost her appetite. Lauren hated that. This was their celebratory dinner. "I don't think we have to say anything. It is what it is."

"Listen, I'm nobody and you're Carly Daniel. There's no competition here. Trust me."

Carly shook her head. "Don't say that." She seemed genuinely bothered by that sentence. "You're Lauren Prescott, and you're definitely somebody important, and the only person to call me on my own bullshit in a very long time."

Lauren smiled. "I think I was the only person crazy enough to."

"So true. How is this so amazing? We need to invite the chef over and keep him."

Lauren laughed. "See? That would never occur to me, a commoner."

They ate in silence, but a weight had settled over the evening. They made small talk, smiled at each other, and marveled again and again over the amazing food. There was too much marveling, in fact.

"Are things weird now?" Lauren asked, finally, over dessert.

Carly shook her head. "No. Not at all." A pause. She softened. "Maybe a little." She offered a genuine smile. "I don't want them to be."

"Me neither."

"Okay." Carly reached for Lauren's hand and kissed it. "Then let's not allow it."

"Deal."

But when they went to bed that night, Lauren felt the distance manifest into the physical. Carly wasn't herself. She kissed Lauren good night but remained on her side of the bed.

"You okay over there?" Lauren asked into the dark.

"Yes, just exhausted. Crazy day."

"It was."

Lauren lay awake, staring across the spacious bedroom, adorned with all of Carly's personal touches: lace curtains, sage walls, soft pink pillows, and the Van Gogh print from Lauren hanging on the wall across from the bed. In her head, the questions swirled, her concerns mounting. She felt alone for the first time since she arrived in LA and was nervous about the path they were heading down. There had been a time not too long ago when she was confident what she and Carly had was a romance that would run no more than the length of their show's run. What if she was someone Carly just had to put up with now that they were in LA? Carly's life was her own, and Lauren was a run-of-the-mill stage manager with a boring apartment and a pug who liked to be fed at the same time every night. Now, in addition to all of that, it seemed like Carly was growing more and more uncomfortable with Lauren playing in her sandbox. How long would it be before Carly was done with her altogether? She recognized that her own insecurities were bubbling up, but in the quiet of the night, the unnerving thoughts were hard to swallow back. She looked to her left, to the blond hair she could make out in the pale moonlight, and her trepidatious heart pulled. Since when did Carly sleep on her own? Things were changing between them, and Lauren felt her armor go up.

It was going to be a long night.

The night before had ended on a weird note, and Carly hated that she'd let that happen. She woke the next morning with a bright new outlook, ready to make it up to Lauren and push the uncomfortable tension to the curb. She showered, slipped into jeans and a snuggly hoodie, and made coffee for both of them to drink poolside, flipping on the outdoor heaters as she passed. Thanksgiving was not far off, and she, for one, was a big fan of the holiday.

"This is what I'm thinking," Carly said, with a read-the-headlines gesture.

"I'm ready." Lauren grinned from behind her mug. She wore leggings and an oversized red sweatshirt. She was quieter than normal this morning, but still affectionate and warm. Carly woke up to find her organizing the junk drawer in the kitchen.

"I see your organizational skills are starving for exercise."

Lauren had nodded. "They are. These scissors need their own home base. I'm thinking top left, though bottom right might make them quicker for grabbing in an emergency."

"Oh yeah." Carly nodded solemnly. "I'm glad you thought of that. I have way too many scissor emergencies around here to be reaching to the top left."

"Right?" Lauren said emphatically, and the darling thing was that she truly meant it. "Bottom it is."

The organizing, Carly had come to learn, happened when Lauren was in her head, processing details, either emotional or logistical. Now, as they sat poolside, she hoped she could alleviate some of the perceived stress.

"I thought it might be fun to do a big Thanksgiving dinner here. I know I pushed for us to go out to a restaurant, but I get the feeling that it wasn't your ideal way to spend the day."

Lauren nodded. "I guess I'm a little old-fashioned that way, but I like sitting around a table with people you care about and sharing a meal." She tucked one leg under her as her passion grew. "There were times when I couldn't make it back home to have dinner with my family because I had a show to call either that afternoon or the following, and we'd put something together for just those of us in town, whoever happened to be working the show and wouldn't see their family or friends."

Carly nodded. "I love that idea. I think we should do just that. You can meet some of my friends, and of course, you're welcome to invite anyone you'd like, though it might be a longer drive."

Lauren thought on it. "Trip might come if we asked him."

Carly looked back at the house. "Yes, he can stay here. And I know the perfect company with the absolute best catering."

"No way," Lauren said, aghast. "The point of Thanksgiving dinner is the meal prep, and I desperately want to watch you race around the kitchen with me in a cute little apron." She looked skyward as if imagining a highly enjoyable daydream.

"Can the apron at least be designer?"

"I'm willing to compromise on this one detail for the sake of harmony."

"Then consider it a done deal."

The sound of a vibrating phone stole Carly's attention. Lauren's danced on the outdoor glass end table. "Yours."

Lauren checked the readout and picked up the phone. "My agent," she said, with a curious look to Carly. "Hi, Jim." Carly looked on, impressed with how busy they'd managed to keep Lauren while she was in town. She imagined that they'd lined up yet another group of auditions. "Oh, just sitting by the pool, drinking a cup of joe." A pause. "Yeah, I thought it went well. I'm glad they agreed." Another pause. "Are you sure?" Carly sipped and listened, intrigued by whatever had pulled Lauren up short. "No. I'm just surprised…Okay, sure. We can talk about it later. Thanks for calling, Jim." A pause. "Yes, all of that. I'll wait to hear from you."

Lauren clicked off the call but kept her gaze on the screen.

"What was that about?" Carly asked. "You seem confused."

Lauren finally raised her eyes to Carly again, and her expression could only be described as regretful.

"What?" Carly said. Concern flared, as a chill off the pool smacked her flat in the face. She snuggled into her hoodie and waited for Lauren to say something.

"The Hennessy film. They offered it to me."

"Oh." She paused, taking that in. "They did? Wow." The information hovered. She wasn't quite able to absorb the parameters of what it all meant. "That's fantastic, Lauren."

Lauren shook her head. "No. It's not. I just feel like it has to be some kind of mistake."

Carly sat up straight, forcing herself to rise to this damn occasion and handle it with as much grace as she possibly could. Sure, it felt like the one thing she'd pinned all her hopes on in desperation had just collapsed all around her in grand fashion like one of those buildings they implode on purpose. Step one, however, was to be happy for Lauren.

"It absolutely was not. You're good at this whole acting thing, and people are taking notice. Celebrate that."

Lauren had gone white. "But this was supposed to be yours." She stood as if needing to take some kind of action, yet not sure what. "I'll tell them I don't want it. I think that's what needs to happen. I don't need any of this, Carly. In fact, I'm not even sure that it's me."

Carly balked and stood with Lauren, taking her hands. "That would be insane. You get that, right? Of course you want it. The film could open doors for you."

"Do I even want doors open? I'm happy as I am. I like my life."

"I think you owe it to yourself."

At the same time, Carly was aware of what this meant for herself. They were outside in the open, yet it still felt like the world was closing in on her. Her sense of self drifted farther away by the minute, and grapple as she might, she couldn't quite get her stomach under control. It pitched and roiled.

"Carly," Lauren said, as Carly dropped her hands. "I don't know what to say here."

"Don't say anything," Carly said and kissed her cheek. She was wildly aware of the ticking clock, and the fact that she didn't have a lot of time before this holding-it-together thing was going to expire. An uncomfortable lump had already formed in her throat, and she needed to get the hell out of there. She retrieved her coffee and inclined her head toward her home. "I'm gonna go do some reading. I think the new *Variety* came yesterday. Congratulations, Lauren." She turned her back and headed toward the back door. She didn't get more than ten feet before the tears pooled in her eyes.

As long as Carly had known her, Lauren had been sensitive when it came to other people's emotions, and to her credit, she let Carly go.

Carly let herself into her office, her favorite place to sit and learn her lines. Well, back when she had lines to learn. In place of the work she wished she was doing, she spent the next hour watching the trees rustle back and forth. She felt unimportant and embarrassed.

"You okay in here?" Lauren asked from the doorway sometime later. She'd changed into pants, a black pullover, and short boots with a low heel. She looked fantastic, like she was ready to take on the world, which likely meant she was meeting with someone or had papers to sign on the Hennessy deal. God. Was this Carly's life now? She'd watch Lauren head out into the world, landing one new job after another, while she sat home and remembered when that used to be her? Her soul ached, and she took a moment to answer.

"I'm okay. Really. You look nice."

"You don't look it, Carly. Will you talk to me?"

How in the world was she supposed to explain that she was devastated but felt like a complete ass for it? That she wished Lauren the best but not if it came at a price like this one? That wasn't okay. As selfish as Carly had been in the past, even she knew that much. "I'm happy for you, I am. But I think the timing of all your success up against my complete and utter failure is not the most ideal, you know?"

Lauren nodded solemnly. "I get it. I hate it." She looked around, surely feeling helpless and guilty about what should have only been fantastic news. What a pair they were. "Do you want me to go? Leave you alone?"

Carly looked up at Lauren, feeling vulnerable as hell. Why did it have to play out this way? Lauren felt a million miles away, and Carly had no fucking clue how to fix that. She needed to be big and mature and an adult about this, but as hard as she tried, she couldn't muster the ingredients. "Don't you have somewhere to be?" She blinked at Lauren, and inclined her head toward the new outfit.

"Oh. Um, Rick has requested a meeting to talk through some character stuff. I can't imagine it will go too long."

Carly nodded. She knew production would start soon, and Rick was likely dotting his i's and crossing his t's. "Go. Enjoy yourself. I'm being an idiot, and you definitely don't deserve to sit in on it."

"Maybe I want to."

"Well, you can't have *everything* you want, Lauren." She hated the sentence the second it left her lips. This wasn't who Carly wanted to be, and yet, it was who she was becoming. "I'm sorry. See? You should go before it gets worse. None of this is your fault."

Lauren nodded silently, clearly feeling unsteady. Carly didn't watch her walk away, but the click of her heels down the hallway told the story. Alone now in the cold, stupid house she couldn't afford, she let the tears have their way with her. The sobs came from the back of her throat, laced with fear and disappointment in herself.

CHAPTER SEVENTEEN

The day had hit Lauren hard and fast. Pleasant, exciting, uncertain, and devastating, had all been stops on her emotion-packed day. Her good-bye conversation with Carly had been the absolute low point that now had her blinking back tears and wondering how she'd gotten so far out of her league.

For her appointment, however, she forced herself to suck it up.

Rick Hennessy had his own office on the Warner Brothers lot. He came with that much clout. Lauren took a moment to google him in her car and was surprised to see that he had directed several films she'd seen and enjoyed. That discovery left her more nervous than ever, feeling again like a second grader who'd wandered into the high school lunchroom by mistake. Surely, everyone saw she was a second grader, right?

She shook off the feeling and gave her name to the guard in the little booth at Warner Brothers, who then directed her where to park. She found the office Hennessy rented in what looked to be a small apartment complex on the studio grounds. How odd.

"Hey, Lauren. Come in. Come in." He greeted her as if he hadn't just shoved the meeting into his already packed workday and sat with her at what looked to be a cafeteria table across from his desk.

"I'm happy we're doing this," he said and ran his hand over his beard. "I was floored we found you, like it was meant to be. You know, the way it all played out? Cosmic." He pointed his finger at her a few times while he spoke, reminding her of all those really intense hipsters from college.

"I was every bit as surprised as you were," she said.

"I read about your casting at The McAllister after you left the audition. I love the story."

"Oh." She grinned. "Me, too. One of those things you never could have predicted in life."

"Right?" Rick sat back in his chair and opened his laptop. "So, let's talk about the character of Astrid." They spent the next thirty minutes discussing the script and his personal vision for her character's short arc. They had a decent give-and-take, and by the end of the session, she'd decided she really liked Rick. He knew what he was doing, even if she had no clue about what she was.

"Can I ask a question?" Lauren had to know.

"Shoot."

"What made you cast me? Cinderella story aside. I'm an unknown. You had big names you could choose from, I'm sure."

He scratched above his lip as he considered the answer. "We definitely did, and it was a tough call. I'll be honest. Lots of back-and-forth with the studio. In the end, I think there were two things that factored in."

"Okay." Lauren listened patiently.

"Your audition made it clear that you typed perfectly for the role. Physically, you're exactly what I pictured, and you brought the right energy. Next, the fact that you're a little green only helped. The character is a fish out of water on that witness stand. It all read so authentic. Now, we just have to bottle that."

She nodded. "Makes sense. Thank you for explaining." She shrugged, feeling every bit the fish out of water even right now. "And thank you for having me. All the things a person should say when leaving a meeting like this." She laughed.

He did, too. "See? You're perfect."

So that had been it. She ruminated on the whole thing as she headed back to her car. The temperatures were dropping as a cold front moved through LA. Carly had been too comfortable at the audition, too at home in her own skin. Lauren knew Carly had a dozen offers out there waiting for her. She just had to find them. In fact, maybe it was time she stepped up and played cheerleader for Carly, because nothing hurt more than seeing a vivacious, fun-loving, and kind woman behaving like a shell of herself.

❖

Carly blinked at the chip commercial on her TV screen, featuring two rival surfers. What in hell? Even surfers could land acting jobs, it seemed. That meant literally everyone but her. She'd spent her afternoon deep into daytime television, alternating with a few viewings of her TMZ video with the pap at the airport. She enjoyed the diversity of her viewing habits. Outside, the wind whipped, and the full-on cold had finally arrived in California a few days earlier, reminding her a little bit more of Minneapolis, a time in her life she desperately missed. She thought back on it now, and the sense of pride she'd had in her work. It felt like she might never have that again.

Two hours later, she picked up her phone on a whim. *What about a guest spot on that $10k Pyramid show?* she texted Alika. *Think they'll have me?*

The reply came in fairly quickly. *Are you serious? Because it's not an awful idea.*

Carly stared blankly at the screen.

That one hurt. It would be an admission of defeat to pander for any available screen time, but if Alika thought it was a viable plan, then things were now past the point that Carly ever imagined they'd be. She'd gone from headlining blockbuster films to striking out on even small roles. She wasn't ready for celebrity-on-a-game-show status just yet. If ever.

No, thanks. Was actually a joke.

Alika sent back a heart emoji. Carly tossed the phone next to her on the couch, feeling worse for the conversation.

She heard a garage door open, signaling Lauren's return from day three on the Hennessy shoot. Apparently, she'd been having a fantastic experience on set and had even received an offer for that guest spot gig on that TV show, *The Subdivision*, which had been killing it in the ratings lately. Carly knew because she read *Variety* religiously on her iPad these days with all the spare time she had. Lauren came to LA three weeks ago and had already booked two major jobs with interest mounting in more. Her agent called with new auditions daily. This wasn't a fluke. Lauren had a full-fledged career waiting for her if she wanted it. Carly was beginning to wonder if she did. Her excitement had waned noticeably, which Carly took some responsibility for.

Carly sighed and headed into the kitchen to say hello, and force herself to smile. All the while, she braced for the way the daily update would make her feel.

Lauren beamed as she entered. "Hey, gorgeous person. How was your day?" Lauren stripped off her blue peacoat. Her cheeks were pink from the weather. She seemed like someone who'd come home fulfilled, and accomplished. "Nippy out there. Who knew California could nip so effectively?"

Carly shrugged. "Day was fine. I did amazingly well at *Wheel of Fortune*, and I checked the mail. It was a huge day for me, really."

Lauren laughed and placed a soft kiss on her lips. "I suck at *Wheel of Fortune*. I aspire to your heights."

"Oh, I wouldn't advise that." She rolled her eyes. "Looks like you had a fantastic day."

"I did and I didn't. I feel more comfortable on set now. I know where all the food is and have gotten used to where to sit. I just wish I felt more like myself."

"You'll get there."

"Not sure about how I'm doing in the acting department, though. Everyone seems happy enough, but I wonder."

"If they seem happy, then you're all good." Carly pushed off the counter and wandered back to the living room. She should have talked it out with Lauren further, told her all about her own insecurities when she'd started out. Offered a few tips. She honestly wanted to participate in Lauren's journey. She just also couldn't seem to make herself engage.

"Do you want to talk about it?" Lauren followed her with a furrowed brow. She'd been shooting Carly those concerned looks ever since she'd won the film role. It was becoming almost painful to be on the receiving end of them.

"No. There's nothing to say, right? I'm not going to cry to you about poor little me just as you're arriving home from a full day on set. I'm happy for you, Lauren. You are the most deserving person I could imagine. I'm just...not myself."

"I know." Lauren sighed. She rolled her lips in, thoughtful. "I feel like you resent me."

"I know." Carly didn't offer a further explanation, which was a shitty thing to do.

After a long moment, Lauren nodded and headed up the winding staircase, deflated. Carly didn't hear anything from her for a couple of hours. Finally, she headed up. What she found surprised her: Lauren had packed her belongings.

"Wait. What are you doing?"

"I'm gonna get out of your hair." She faced Carly with a watery smile.

"What? No. That's not necessary. You're welcome to stay here."

"Welcome?" She laughed through her sadness. "That's very hospitable of you, Carly, but I think I'd want to be more than just welcome. More than tolerated. I want you to want me here, and that's not happening anymore."

A long pause. "I do want you here." It sounded unconvincing even to her own ears. The thing was that underneath all the stuff clogging her brain, she did want Lauren by her side. Why couldn't she fight for them?

Lauren nodded. "I can tell." She placed a hand on her hip and appeared to be sorting through her words. "I think you're going through a hard time, and I'm making it worse. I'm going to grab a hotel near the studio, and we can regroup later. How does that sound?"

"Lauren," Carly said softly. She hated everything about the idea but, at the same time, didn't have the emotional fortitude to wage an effective argument.

"Hey," Lauren said, coming around the bed and taking Carly's hand. "It's probably for the best. You get a chance to catch your breath from all of this without me on top of you."

"I like you on top of me," Carly said, attempting to make a joke, but not fully nailing it.

Lauren squeezed her hand, understanding the underlying meaning. "Let's get back to that soon, okay?" Carly nodded in response. Lauren tried to smile. "That's what I want, anyway."

She watched Lauren's normally self-assured demeanor fade, showing cracks in her confidence in their possible future together. That was Carly's fault. Maybe Lauren was right. Maybe if she got some space, she could pull herself out of this self-imposed isolation and work on being a confident person. Honestly, she'd settle for recognizing herself in the mirror again.

"You sure about this?" Carly asked, sliding her hands into the back pockets of her jeans. "Because I'm not."

"We're co-existing. Then snarking at each other. Apologizing. And repeating the whole process. I miss you so much it hurts all over, so I have to do something to fix it."

"I miss you, too." Carly dropped her head. "It has been a bit of a pressure cooker. My doing."

Lauren walked around the bed and closed her suitcase. "Call me when you've had some time, okay?"

Carly nodded and accepted the kiss Lauren placed on her forehead. She sat on her bed and watched Lauren roll her suitcase out of the bedroom. Tears pooled in her eyes. She thought she heard sniffling from down the hall. Her heart clenched. Yet she had no idea how to stop any of it.

❖

"Picture's up. Roll camera. Roll sound. And…action."

Lauren took her cue and slowly raised her gaze to the actor playing the prosecutor. "That's exactly why I'm here."

"Now we're getting somewhere. You're here to make sure that Victor goes to jail."

"Yes." She glared at the defendant, lacing her gaze with menace as she trembled. She blinked back tears, keeping them at bay momentarily, then losing the battle. This was their ninth take and Lauren's close-up shot. That meant she had to bring it.

"And you want him to go to jail because he killed your child," the prosecutor boomed.

"Yes," she said, eyes still trained on Victor. She blinked out of it and looked to the prosecutor. "No. I mean no."

"But you said yes. Is it true that you hate Victor for getting away with killing your child, and you've now framed him for the murder of Amy Trinidad, his own wife."

She opened her mouth and closed it again, looking around the courtroom in emotional unravel. "Killed my child," she mumbled.

"What did you say?"

"Victor killed my child and he's not getting away with it." Lauren let the angry tears fall.

"And...cut." Rick moved toward her and leaned over the witness stand. "I think that one was it. Let me check the picture and we'll see if we've got it."

"Sounds great," Lauren said, accepting a tissue from a production assistant and hoping her makeup wasn't a screaming mess, which, of course, production might have preferred. "Thank you." She dabbed her eyes and stood, waiting on word.

"And we're good," Rick said. "That was our martini shot. Thanks, everyone. That's a wrap for Lauren Prescott." The cast and crew on set immediately broke into applause for the work she'd done.

She high-fived Ben, the sound guy she'd nicknamed Benjamin Button because he was forty-four but looked thirty. Once she was clear of the set, she located her phone and anxiously checked her messages, looking for one name in particular. She'd texted Carly the night before to see how she was doing. It had taken everything in her not to text earlier, but she wanted the ball to be in Carly's court. Unfortunately, the ball remained there, as she'd heard nothing from her in the three days since she'd checked into the hotel, which left her surprised and hurt. Lauren wasn't sleeping or eating very much, and the film shoot had been a lot of tedious waiting around, which was hard on someone who thrived on action.

"You okay?" Cal Parks, who played the prosecutor, asked as he passed. "You look like someone just stole your puppy."

She forced herself to brighten. "Nothing that awful. Just hanging on to my character a bit too tightly." He laughed and headed out. Alone, her spirits plummeted. She missed her dog. She missed Trip. Above all, she missed Carly more than words could ever do justice. None of this Hollywood stuff mattered under the personal circumstances of her life. How dissatisfying it was to be given so much, only to realize that the one thing you wanted was the one thing you couldn't have. Life didn't mess around in its masterful delivery of mixed messages, elevating her professional life while trashing her personal one.

Her time on the film had originally been scheduled for five days, which had turned into seven, scattered over a two-week period due to the schedules of other actors. When the job ended, she'd planned to stick around, pick up Rocky IV, and see where the Los Angeles journey took her. The events of the last week weighed heavy on her plans.

She fired off another text to Carly. *Hey, you. If you're dodging my messages, just say so. I'm a big girl, Carly. Just talk to me one way or another.*

That night as she sat cross-legged in her hotel room watching *The Subdivision* for a bit of research on the part she'd committed to, she kept one eye on her phone. She knew Carly was in a rough spot, so she cut her a certain amount of slack. It had been too long, though. Deciding to be the bigger person, she placed a call, waiting patiently as it rang and rang. When Carly's recorded voice came on the line, Lauren closed her eyes, absorbing the familiar sound. "Okay, so I guess you're too busy to pick up. Or if I'm being realistic, you're choosing not to, which speaks volumes. Have a nice night." A pause. "I miss you."

❖

Carly could barely hear the message above the loud music. "I miss you." She lowered the phone, her heart tugging. She missed Lauren, too.

It was just before midnight, and Carly only paused her dancing for a quick drink. It felt good to get out of the house, which had been eating her alive. She needed an escape, a reset button, a lifeline. Dancing her ass off, while keeping her alcohol level to a minimum so as not to get too crazy, was doing the trick.

"From the guy down the bar," the blond bartender with the spiky hair said and pointed at a gentleman who nodded in her direction.

"Thank you, but no," she mouthed and slid the shot back. She had zero plans to get sloppy drunk and show up on TMZ all over again. *The Hollywood Reporter* article that afternoon had been enough.

You're gonna want to see this, the text from Fallon had said earlier that day. *But remember, it'll be in people's trash folders by tomorrow so don't get hung up.*

When she opened the short article and read the headline, "Daniel bested for Hennessy role by McAllister co-star," her first reaction was an eye roll. After all, it had only been a matter of time before Lauren showed up on their radar, and her connection to Carly only sweetened the appeal. The media did their research and seemed to have sources everywhere these days. She just wasn't expecting it to be so soon. "Really?" she asked her empty kitchen. "Have you not put us through enough?" And she did include Lauren in that because she'd been unfairly punished in all this. Carly was working on putting things right, but she hadn't yet found the words that would absolve and explain her unattractive behavior. She certainly wasn't proud of it and was doing what she could to learn about her own weaknesses, and how they manifested and affected others. She owed Lauren a sit-down conversation, and they would get themselves back on track.

The article had saddened her, though, and she'd decided enough was enough. It was time. She needed to take control of her own life before she lost everything, including Lauren. She refused to consider the possibility that she already had. She would face that problem tomorrow. It was a new day and would be a new leaf. For now, letting loose felt like a cool glass of water on a hot day. The music infiltrated her system, fueling her. The dim lighting and the constantly moving strobes offered a much needed feeling of anonymity that allowed Carly to escape. The aerobic exercise released her endorphins. She headed back to the dance floor where she danced with anyone and everyone.

She could not, would not be stopped.

❖

Lauren squinted at the clock in the darkness of her hotel room. The angry green numbers told her it was after two and she'd yet to fall asleep. She fell back against the pillow with a petulant sigh. Her brain wouldn't stop running through all the possible options. She touched the lonely pillow next to hers. She'd met success in Hollywood, yes, but she hadn't found happiness. She'd been infinitely happier back home, and never so happy as when she'd had Carly with her.

Just the thought of her made Lauren's heart hurt. Understanding that sleep was outside of her grasp, she sat up in bed and took out her phone. Because she was apparently a glutton for punishment, she googled Carly's name, partially because she wanted to see her face, and also because she wondered if there'd been any casting news.

When she saw an article on *The Hollywood Reporter*'s website about her taking the Hennessy job from Carly, she went still. Scanning the short piece left her hands shaking and her stomach nauseous. It was bad enough that Carly didn't get the role she'd so badly hoped for—it was worse that she'd lost it to Lauren, and exponentially unfair to have her nose shoved in it by the press. She wanted nothing more than to talk to Carly, but she'd been shut out. She shook her head and scrolled, pausing on a photo of Carly posted by a fan to Instagram. Lauren squinted and clicked on the photo, blowing it up larger, only to see Carly dancing that very night at a club in West Hollywood.

She fell back against the pillow, trying to understand.

That's when she got it. The resentment, the unreturned messages, the late night excursion. It was what she'd feared all along.

Carly was more important to her than she was to Carly.

She'd simply refused to accept it until now.

Lauren stared into the quiet of her hotel room and focused on the lights of LA just outside her window. What was she doing here? Chasing an old dream from when she was too young to know any better? Whatever gratification she got from her recent successes wouldn't last and shattered in the face of what she'd lost in Carly.

She didn't want it under these circumstances. Any of it.

Without giving it another moment of consideration, she flipped on the light, retrieved her suitcase, and set to packing for the third time in two months. She found a reasonable fare home on the internet, if she didn't mind traveling early. She definitely didn't. She needed to get the hell home.

CHAPTER EIGHTEEN

Carly rolled her shoulders as she walked through the lobby of the Hilton. She smiled at a few of the tourists who'd turned immediately in her direction the second she walked by. She posed for a selfie with a teenager waiting alongside her at the elevator bay. As she rode to the fourteenth floor, her nerves fired. She had what she wanted to say prepared in her head. She'd spent the morning at her kitchen table getting her thoughts in order, even taking notes on one of Lauren's Post-it pads.

At Carly's request, Alika had booked her on both *Celebrity Game Night* and *Pyramid*, for which she would begin practicing soon. She decided to shed her stupid ego and now looked at them as a truly fun opportunity. Why not enjoy herself a little? Maybe reminding the world that she was out there would jump-start her career. Maybe not. That part mattered less.

She knocked on the door to room 1422—Lauren's room. Lauren had texted her the room number the night she'd checked in. She waited, realizing she should have called first, given that Lauren clearly wasn't in. Behind her, a housekeeper arrived with a cart. He was an older gentleman and smiled at her like they were best friends.

"At first I thought, *I know you*, but nah, you're a movie star."

"Yes, hi. I'm Carly. Nice to meet you."

"I'm Henry. Pleased to make your acquaintance, as well." He smiled some more as he turned and opened the door to Lauren's room. He gestured toward it. "You were knocking on this one?"

She nodded. "But my friend is out, so I'll give her a call and come back later. Thank you." She turned to go.

"She checked out." He headed inside, but the cart propped open the door.

Carly frowned and peeked her head around the door into the hotel room. "Checked out? Are you sure?"

"Yep." He pointed at his clipboard sitting on top of the cart. "This morning."

"Do you know where she went?" It was a dumb question.

"Sorry. I just get a list of vacated rooms to turn around."

"Thank you," Carly called over her shoulder and left in confusion. Maybe Lauren had returned to her place, which would be ideal, because it was what she wanted anyway. As Carly waited for the valet to return with her car, she turned to the doorman on a whim.

"Did you see this woman leave earlier?" She turned her phone around and showed him a photo.

He pointed at the screen. "Ah, yep. She had trouble getting her Uber driver to pick her up in the right spot. Had me talk to him for directions."

She crouched in excitement. A lead. "Any idea where he was taking her?"

"Yep. The airport. That was a few hours ago."

"No."

He winced apologetically, sensing it was not the answer she wanted. "Yes."

Carly's spirits fell from her chest to the pavement. How was that possible? She took out her phone and called Lauren, something she now felt like an idiot for not doing over the last few days. No answer, which made sense. She was likely on a flight. She looked to the doorman again, whose name tag read *Mike*. "So what am I supposed to do now?" She had no idea why she thought Mike would know.

"I always find a nice breakfast cheers me up. I'm a flapjacks guy."

That's the sentence her brain decided to play for her over and over as she returned home, directionless. *I'm a flapjacks guy. I'm a flapjacks guy.* It was not at all helpful, but maybe what she deserved, to be haunted by one of the lowest moments in her life, reminded of it over and over. She poured a cup of coffee she didn't have the stomach to drink. *I'm a flapjacks guy.*

She sat outside next to her pool without a coat because she needed to let the cold pelt her in punishment. The empty hotel room had been a wake-up call. She saw the parallel now between her behavior over the last few years and her behavior toward Lauren. She seemed to think everyone would wait for her. Lauren most certainly had not, and why should she have? She'd never let Carly get away with her bullshit. It was one of the many things that was so great about her.

Carly called again. Nothing. She walked through each room in her home, alone with her thoughts that she sorted through one at a time. She needed a sounding board, and she knew the one person who would give it to her straight.

"How's your day looking?" she asked, when Fallon picked up her call.

"Pretty slow around here. I was thinking of knocking off early."

"Want to go out for a cocktail and knock me around a little? I've earned it."

"Hmm," Fallon said. "A cocktail and beatdown could make for a nice afternoon. Where should we gather?"

"Somewhere low key where people won't take our photo."

"So the Chateau Marmont, then?"

"Very funny. What about that place The Varnish? Reminds me of a speakeasy, and that dim lighting might be what I need to blend."

"Done. See you in an hour?"

"Prepare yourself for sad and guilty."

"Good Lord."

"I know."

Ninety minutes later, and Carly had a whiskey sour and Fallon sipped a candy-apple martini that came with a chili rim. "So what are we going to do about it?" Fallon asked.

"Do about which of the many issues?" She had laid out everything that had gone wrong as soon as they'd arrived, sparing no detail.

"Well, I think you have a lot of things going on. Some old. Some new."

"I can agree." She claimed the cherry from her drink and watched the bartender restock the sugar. "This morning was definitely rock bottom for me. I can admit that."

"Career first. So you have *Family Feud* coming up this week?"

"No, it's the pyramid one."

"Right. So your financial prospects aren't dead. They're just not what they once were. No one pays you millions to offer clues to paralegals."

"Not even close."

"Well then, let's figure out your priorities, shall we?"

"Please."

Fallon took out a pen and grabbed a spare cocktail napkin for diagramming. "We need to figure out what you can and cannot live without. Let's start with your house." She wrote it down.

Carly considered the question. "I love where I live, but I could be happy with a much smaller, more modest space. In fact, that's probably the most practical choice."

"All right, so the materials can go." She crossed it off and continued to take notes. "The luxury cars?"

"Just a bonus. I don't need them. I can drive a Nissan."

Fallon nodded and adjusted the list. "Carly in a Nissan. This is going unexpectedly well. What about your celebrity? How important is it that people see you as a high-status star in Hollywood?"

"I've loved that part of my life, but if you ripped it away, I'd still be standing."

Fallon nodded some more. "What about acting?"

That one was harder. Things weren't going so well in that department these days. She loved her job and would sorely miss it if she had to take up another career. "That one would be a big loss. I'd rather not give up acting, but I understand it may not happen at the same pay grade I'm used to."

"Would you be happy doing a smaller project, like a TV show or another regional play somewhere?"

Carly had never been happier than during the run of *Starry Nights*, which was maybe why her current existence seemed like such a steep fall. "That's actually not such a bad idea."

"Got it. Acting is a keeper, but it could happen in a variety of forms. Now, what about Lauren? If things don't work out there, will you be okay?"

"I don't want to think like that." She couldn't, in fact. The idea of going back to her life before Lauren felt hollow, cold, and unimaginable. "No."

Fallon held up a finger. "Okay, see, that's interesting. I think we've made an important discovery here."

"That I want Lauren? That's not news."

Fallon shook her head. "That's the first time you've immediately pushed back against anything I've said. And hard. Lauren was the only deal breaker you had on the entire list. You aren't willing to budge." She turned the napkin around, and Lauren's name in big, bold letters was the only word left standing with a giant circle around it.

"True. There's no compromise there for me." Fallon was right. There it was, crystal clear as day. Her response had been instinctual and instantaneous with very little consideration required.

"Yet think about it, Car. You've allowed losing your status, something that's not important to you in the grander scheme, separate you from the one thing on this list you don't want to live without. Why?" Fallon shook her head as if this was just basic math and took a sip from that candy-apple martini that Carly should have ordered.

She closed her eyes and shaded her face with one hand. "Right. I'm an idiot."

"Interesting strategy there, champ. So fix it."

Carly took another sip. "I'm gonna try. I'm not entirely sure how yet. But I'm gonna." A pause. "How about I order us another round of those," she said, gesturing to Fallon's martini, "and we come up with a firm plan."

Fallon clapped with her fingertips. "Plans are my favorite."

Minneapolis weather did not mess around. If Carly thought the place was cold in October, she wasn't prepared for late November. Her minimally lined leather jacket wasn't cutting it against the whipping winter winds. She'd honestly known better, but larger details stole the space in her mind these days. She flipped the collar up and cursed herself for not pulling a scarf out of her bag.

It had been three days since Lauren left Los Angeles. Carly knew she'd flown home because she'd posted a photo of herself reunited with Rocky to her social media accounts. They'd looked adorably snuggly, and Carly almost forgot she didn't currently have the right to take joy in that. Instead, she booked her own ticket for the following day, packed her bag, and set off for Minnesota.

On her way to the airport, a text from Lauren hit her phone, finally answering the string Carly had sent.

I'm sorry to have dashed away on you. Not really thinking LA is for me. I'm sorry things didn't happen differently. I think we want different things.

Of course, it looked that way. She'd let it. More motivated than ever, Carly knew that there was no way she was having this conversation from across the country. She needed to look into those green eyes and tell Lauren what a self-involved jackass she'd been and get them back on the same page.

In her rental, she drove by Lauren's house, but her car wasn't there. She made the quick jaunt to the theater, and there it was. The spunky sky blue Mini Cooper. How was it possible that even the car was a sight for sore eyes? Carly gave herself a mental pep talk as she walked up the ten stairs that led to the building's entrance, past the picturesque stone columns, and into the lobby, which she knew would be unlocked during the day because the box office sold advance tickets. Once inside, all she needed was for someone to open a door to the house in the normal course of their workday, and she'd be in. Luckily, she only had to wait five minutes for that to happen.

"Carly?"

She sighed. It was that Tinsley woman. She had paint all over her arms and a red bandana around her head to keep her hair back. The new set must be going in for *Falsettos*, the production that would open next.

"Hey, there." She followed Tinsley through the theater like she belonged there.

"I didn't realize you were doing any more work here," Tinsley said. "Forget something?"

"Just some business to take care of."

"Mm-hmm."

Tinsley smiled but eyed her with suspicion. Carly didn't care. She wasn't here to be friends with Tinsley, who'd never really shown her much warmth anyway. She proceeded to the stage management office just down the hall from the stage itself. Her heart thudded, her palms were sweaty, and she had a serious case of butterflies dancing a conga line through her midsection, but she was going to fall on this damn sword because it was abundantly clear to her what mattered most.

Carly paused in the doorway because, God, there she was. Lauren worked quietly at the desk, laptop open, soft music playing from the radio on the table behind her. She was a vision of beauty, focused as always as she worked. She chewed subtly on the inside of her cheek, a common occurrence when she was concentrating. Carly had always loved watching her in thought.

Finally, Lauren glanced up and went still. For a moment, she said nothing. Then her shoulders dropped slightly as if she'd been wounded. "Hi."

Carly offered a nervous smile. "Hi."

"I don't understand." She shook her head and peered behind Carly as if to see where she came from. "What are you doing here?"

"We want the same things." It wasn't the most eloquent of ways to plead her case, but it was all she could think to say, her speech having flown out the window the second she laid eyes on Lauren.

"What?" Lauren was trying to wrap her mind around Carly's surprise appearance, and it seemed like her brain hadn't quite caught up.

"I'm here for you. To tell you I disagree with what you said. We both want the same things." Lauren stared at her, clearly unsure what to say or do. "I don't know why you're back in Minneapolis, but come home with me."

"Home?" Lauren stood, gestured for Carly to come inside, and closed the door behind them. "This is my home, and it's the best place for me."

Carly squinted. "You were killing it in LA. What happened to the job on *The Subdivision*?"

"I politely asked if I could back out. They were understanding."

"Oh." Another pause. "You're really serious about this back-in-Minneapolis thing."

Lauren nodded apologetically, and Carly felt nauseous. "Wilks apparently already had me on the schedule with plans to replace me if I wasn't back. So I just slid back in."

"You're an amazing stage manager." She shrugged. "I guess I always assumed that if the people working on the production had the opportunity to be the actors, they'd leap."

Lauren smiled. "Not everybody is destined for the limelight. I once thought it was all I wanted in the world." She mirrored Carly's shrug. "But as we grow and change and get to know ourselves, our goals change with us." She looked around the office. "I really love my job."

"You're amazing at it."

"I try to be."

Carly blew out a steadying breath. There was more to say. "I realize that I got caught up in my own world, my own journey, and you paid the price." She held out her hands. "All done with that now."

"I'm happy to hear that. You were truly struggling. I hated watching it play out." She shook her head. "I felt so helpless and my heart..." The words died on her lips.

"Lauren. I want to give us our shot. For real." She tried to smile. She lost the battle in the face of such a daunting conversation that wasn't going well.

Lauren closed her eyes. "The thing is, Carly, that it was for real the whole time. Life isn't a do-over." She sighed and studied the floor as if assembling the words she wanted. "When things weren't going your way, I became an enemy to you. An obstacle on the path to what you truly wanted. That's not who I want to be to anyone, and I would fully expect it to happen again." She raised her arm and let it drop. "The acting thing was a lot of fun for a while. But maybe it's time I get back to my real life, so I can feel like Lauren again."

There was a knock on the door behind them, and not a second later, Tinsley appeared without waiting for an answer. "Everything okay, Lauren?"

Carly stared, confused. "Why would it not be okay?"

"We're fine, Tins. Thanks," Lauren said. "I'll bring you a breakdown of the move-in schedule in just a little bit."

Carly raised a hand. "Why would it not be fine?"

Tinsley took a confident step farther into the room. "Oh, I don't know, because she gave up her life to follow you out to LA, and you treated her like crap once she got there? Ruined her legitimate chance at her dream by getting in her head?"

"Tinsley. No." Lauren shook her head and closed her eyes.

Carly turned back to Lauren. "I know. She's right. All of it."

"Damn right I am."

"Do you mind giving us a minute?" Lauren asked Tinsley, who didn't move. "Please?"

Tinsley nodded and with a glance to Carly that said *I've got my eye on you*, she left the office.

"I'm a big girl. It was my decision to head to LA. We had plans, and things were feeling really good between us. I thought they'd stay that way."

"I know."

"Yes, I was paranoid as hell that you were out of my league and that you'd cast me off." She shook her head ruefully. "I guess I just didn't see the method in which you'd do it."

"I'm an idiot."

"Yes."

A pause as the truth rained down. Carly accepted the responsibility and prayed she could find a way to undo the damage. Carly took an imploring step forward. "But it was. It *was* working out for you."

"Parts were. But people change—their priorities do." Lauren rolled her lips in and leaned sideways against the desk with one arm. "I always longed to be an actress, but maybe that's not me anymore. I wasn't happy. It's easier here. Simpler."

"Lauren. Just listen, I—"

"I don't blame you, Carly, okay? Does that help? You can leave here feeling better and go back to your world with a clear conscience that little Lauren is just fine." Her eyes were watery when she said it. There was also a resolve present, and that hurt more. "You were just living your life. I was in the way."

"You were never that. I was dealing with issues of my own."

Carly wasn't able to process all of this at once. It was too much. What had she done? Turned into a petty, self-involved starlet who wasn't getting the kind of jobs she thought worthy of herself. Never before had such a startling mirror been held up to her face. It nearly brought her to her knees. She hated herself and every action she'd taken since leaving Minneapolis. "You deserve so much better than all of this."

Lauren offered a sincere smile. "I think everything happens for a reason, you know? We were a team on that show. Maybe that's what we were meant for. Now we go our separate ways."

"We're still a team."

"Sometimes things don't work out the way we expect them to, and that's okay." Lauren looked like she was trying to convince herself of that just as strongly as she was Carly.

"That's not what this is. Look at me." Lauren did and the minute they connected, Carly knew she was right. "You and I are supposed to be together," Carly said, her chest tight. "If we aren't, why would I feel this way?"

"I'm not sure I agree." She watched as the guard Lauren had in place seemed to fall away. "Do you think I don't miss you?" Her voice was strangled with emotion. She placed a shaky hand over her heart. "Of course I do. Every day. But I've been missing you for a while now, and it's become clear that maybe I'm not the best person for you. Maybe you're not the best for me."

"Are you positive of that?"

A long pause struck. "No."

"Good. Then hear me out. I'm here because you mean more to me than any job. I lost myself somewhere in a swarm of personal disappointment and didn't see what was right in front of me—the true source of my happiness was an uptight stage manager turned talented actress, and the best scene partner I've ever had in my life." She took a moment with the next part. "Give me a second chance. I promise to learn from my mistakes."

Lauren hadn't moved a muscle. "I don't think we're ready for that. I don't think you are."

"What does that mean?"

"I think you need some time for yourself, to sort out your world." Lauren was being too nice, but Carly translated. She was telling Carly to work on *herself*. It wasn't the answer she wanted, but it also wasn't a firmly closed door. She could work with a crack. She had to. It was all she had left.

"And while I do that? Will you come back to LA?"

"Not while the next show is in production. I talked to my agent about stepping back. Maybe I'll pick up a role here or there along the way in the future. Make myself a bit of a hybrid. Others have done it."

Carly nodded, trying to get past the painful lump in her throat. "I can't convince you, huh? What if I picked up and moved here? I'd do it."

Lauren shook her head, her conviction apparent. "I don't want us to go down the same path all over again. You need to gather your world. Maybe then, give me a call. We can catch up."

Carly nodded, dejected. "I'll do the work, okay? Because this right here"—she gestured between them—"was supposed to be a two-month fling, and instead it's changed me forever."

Lauren's eyes glistened with tears. "I can safely say the same."

Carly slid her hands into her back pockets. "I can't believe I'm going home without you. I don't want to do this. Please don't make me." Her own eyes filled.

"I'm sorry." Lauren touched her chest. "I have to look out for me now, okay?"

Carly nodded. This wasn't at all what she wanted, but Lauren had a valid argument. Carly had to find happiness with her new place in the world. She had to stand on her own two feet if she wanted to walk in confidence next to Lauren. "But know that I'm not giving up."

Lauren nodded and opened her arms. Carley moved into them wordlessly. The tears fell hot and free down her face as they held each other. When Lauren took a shuddering breath and released her, Carly took a step back and wiped her wet face with a laugh. "What a pair we are."

Lauren nodded. "We've come a very long way together."

"And there's so much more ahead."

Lauren didn't seem as convinced, but that just meant it was up to Carly to hope enough for the both of them. She was up to the challenge.

"Take care of yourself and Rocky and this amazing theater, okay?" She ran a dejected hand through her hair because there wasn't much else to do or say.

Lauren nodded through her tears. "You got it."

❖

Watching Carly walk out of her office had been one of the most difficult moments of Lauren's entire life. Though she knew it was for the best, she wanted nothing more than to accept Carly's offer and forgive and forget. She longed for Carly, wanted her, and almost abandoned her wits just to have her back.

"Am I dumb? I could have just gone with her, Trip. Maybe I should have." She sat on a stool in Trip's impeccably decorated kitchen. She should have hired him to do her place.

He deposited a freshly assembled cheese board between them. "I think you have to trust your instincts more, and they told you it wouldn't have been a good idea. At least not right now."

"You're right. Maybe there's a time for us. But it's not this one." Lauren nodded and took a sip of her second glass of wine. She'd been back in Minneapolis for a week now and had spent each and every evening at Trip's place, catching up and talking through all she had in her head. "I'm sorry if I'm talking your ear off—I think I'm just shaken up. I didn't expect her to walk through the door looking and sounding and smelling so wonderfully like…her. God."

Trip slid the bottle closer to Lauren, but she held her hand up to decline. "I'm sorry you were blindsided. Anything good come from the conversation?"

She lifted her shoulders and let them drop. "We agreed to take some time. I think Carly wasn't in a place where she could give of herself, and while it's nice that she said all the right things today, I just don't know." She shook her head. "Something in me couldn't seem to tell her what I actually believe."

Trip came around the island and put his arm around Lauren. "And what is that?"

"That I'm desperately in love with a woman who I can never truly have."

CHAPTER NINETEEN

The upbeat game show music played, and Carly applauded, all the while smiling at her *Pyramid* partner—Jennifer from Dayton, Ohio, who taught second grade. Jennifer had already won the first round with Carly and the second with Aspen Wakefield from the TV show *Thicker Than Water*, who—let's be honest—was not as quick on the draw. Carly was not about to drop Jennifer's chance to take it all in the Winner's Circle. No way. Jennifer from Dayton was going home with all the money if Carly had anything to say about it.

She cleared her mind of everything as Jennifer with the shiny red hair and jean jacket received their category, We're Grilled to Have You Here, and prepared to give clues. The clock started.

"Meat."

"Hamburger," Carly answered.

Jennifer tried again. "Expensive. Filet. Ribeye."

"Steak."

The bell chimed, signaling Carly had been correct. Everything within her celebrated, but she held it together. They moved on to the next five clues, all pertaining to a backyard barbecue. She and Jennifer sailed through them like pros. Finally, they moved to the last clue with only eight seconds on the clock.

"To flip something over."

"Toss."

"You turn a burger, a flapjack with a…"

"Spatula."

"Yes!" Jennifer shouted and leapt from her chair, now another hundred thousand dollars richer. Carly threw her arms around her victorious partner, and they did a little dance that pulled a laugh from the audience and host.

When the game show wrapped filming, Carly found herself on an adrenaline high. She'd shot two back-to-back episodes that day, and it was honestly the most fun she'd had in a long time. She'd made a point of going into the situation with a light heart and a plan to have fun. Both had definitely helped her release some of the expectations she had for herself.

"Ms. Daniel?" She turned and smiled at the man in a suit moving toward her. "You were fantastic today. Any chance you'd be interested in taking a turn as one of our celebrity competitors on *To Tell the Truth*? You have such sparkle that I think you'd be wonderful. More opportunity to show off your personality."

"I'd love to. Give my agent a call, but I'm in."

"Will do. Thanks again for appearing."

"I had the best time." She didn't even have to bolster her enthusiasm. It was real. When she gathered her belongings and returned to her car, she had a message waiting from her Realtor.

"We have a full-ask offer on the house. Call me." She blinked at the horizon as fear crept in. Yes, she needed to let go of the home that was way too big for one person, and also a burden to her bank account. Without that huge mortgage and upkeep costs looming over her each month, she'd breathe so much easier, decreasing the pressure on her to make the kind of money she used to. Still, the unknown was a little scary. She and Fallon had a date to go house hunting in a less expensive part of Hollywood. She'd always been a fan of the shops and restaurants in Franklin Village and planned to check out what they had on the market.

She called her real estate agent and listened to the details of the all-cash offer. "They want a fast close. Two weeks. What do you think?"

She closed her eyes, saying good-bye to her infinity pool, knowing there were many things, and more specifically people, that made her happier. "Take the deal."

"You're a smart woman," her agent said.

"Trying to be."

She clicked off the call. As she drove home, she felt…lighter. She flipped on the radio and sang along, with a smile. When she got home, she fired off a text to Lauren, who she'd left alone for the past two weeks while she did as Lauren had asked: worked on herself. Today felt like a step toward being happy again, and she wanted to share that. *Today was a good day,* she typed. *Thinking about you. You don't have to answer me, just wanted to share.*

She didn't receive an answer and that was okay. It hadn't been the reason for the text. She went to sleep that night knowing this wouldn't be her bedroom for long.

The next morning, Alika called. "You're not going to believe this, but the game show people think you're the damn bee's knees and want you for another one."

She laughed. "I had a blast. Tell them yes. My calendar seems to be open."

"They're shooting in a week and will send over some background information about what they're looking for."

"Good thing I love games."

"Is this the wildest idea we've ever had?" Alika asked. She was smiling, though. Carly could hear it.

She sighed. "I've stopped trying to run the Hollywood race. I think, Alika, it's time to be a good person and enjoy what life brings my way. That seems to be game shows, and I'm thrilled."

"Then who are we to argue?"

Carly shook her head. Who, indeed?

❖

Lauren's neck ached from rehearsal. Blocking days always did a number on her upper body because she concentrated and recorded the details of the direction for hours on end. She'd say one thing for certain, however. She saw the whole process through a different lens after having starred in a professional production herself. She rubbed the back of her neck as she flipped over the breast of chicken she was frying up for her dinner. Rocky IV whined quietly.

"You need to learn to be more patient, Rocky. I plan to give you some of this chicken on top of your kibble, but it's not ready yet." He snuffled and turned in a circle, his curlicue tail set on vibrate. It wasn't the only thing vibrating. Her phone buzzed in her back pocket. Trip.

"Hey, Trippy."

"Turn on channel six. Do not pass go. Do not delay."

She turned around and faced the TV. An old rerun of *Seinfeld* played quietly. "What's on six?"

"Oh, you're gonna want to see for yourself."

She turned off the chicken and let it sit, located her remote, and changed the channel. She sat on the arm of her couch, curious as the screen filled with Aspen Wakefield giving clues to a portly gentleman with a bad comb-over.

"Are you obsessing about Aspen Wakefield again?" she asked Trip. "I know she's beautiful, but I'm glad you chose a different Halloween costume."

"Wait for it, Lala." She did. She watched as a portly guy gave amazing clues and Aspen Wakefield spaced for half of them. Poor guy.

The shot cut away to the other duo, and when it did, Lauren slid off the arm onto the couch cushion in surprise. It was Carly, grinning and joking with the host. Lauren covered her mouth as she watched, her heart full, her eyes brimming with tears. It felt so good to see Carly that Lauren almost couldn't contain the emotion that bubbled straight to the surface.

"Lauren? You there?"

She'd forgotten all about Trip. "Yes. Sorry. I'm watching. I'll call you after." She dropped the phone and leaned closer to the TV. Carly was actually really good at the game, and she looked like a million bucks wearing a maroon sweater dress and lipstick that matched perfectly. God, she looked sophisticated and beautiful.

As she watched, Lauren placed a hand over her heart, feeling it thud away. Adrenaline coursed as she rooted for Carly and her partner, Jennifer. When they won in the Winner's Circle, Lauren leapt from her spot on the couch. "They did it," she told Rocky, who turned in a circle next to her, never one to be left out of a good celebration. She picked him up, hugged him, and placed a kiss on top of his head.

Lauren was hit with so many emotions that she wasn't sure what to do with them. She'd avoided allowing herself to look up Carly on social media, and she certainly wasn't permitted to watch any of Carly's movies. This was the first time she'd laid eyes on Carly since that day in her office just a few weeks back.

"She looks happy," Lauren said to Rocky, who'd moved back to his mission of garnering some of that chicken for himself. He stood beneath the stove, snuffling. As for Lauren, seeing Carly's face brought up a myriad of emotions she wasn't quite sure how to process. She felt joyful seeing her face, heartsick knowing where they stood with each other, and sad because she missed Carly a lot.

Lauren dished out the chicken for herself, and a little for Rocky, as she ruminated on the state of her life. She'd fled LA for one main reason—she was flat-out terrified. The jobs that she'd booked had to all be mistakes, and it was only a matter of time before the world understood that. Carly was clearly unhappy and resenting the hell out of Lauren and the clock was ticking on how long it would be before she realized she could do better for herself.

Lauren had taken off before either of those things could happen.

For the first time since she'd been home, she admitted one thing to herself. Carly wasn't the only one with issues to work through. Lauren had come to the table with her own basket of neuroses, which surely hadn't helped things.

Maybe I'm not as innocent as I thought in all of this, she typed to Trip.

Later that night, she allowed herself to watch the episode of *Pyramid* one more time on her laptop before bed. She gently touched Carly's smiling face on the screen, remembering their time together onstage and off, and wondering if there was a chance for more memories ahead.

What if...?

It was a powerful sentiment.

❖

"So, here's the thing," Alika said.

Carly held the phone to her ear and grinned from her window seat at a quaint little café just off Franklin. She had a chicken avocado salad that was knocking her socks off and a window seat that let her watch the world go by. Her new neighborhood was shaping up to be a true gem. "I'm listening."

"You're now the game show queen."

Carly laughed and paused with a forkful of chicken. "That's me. Still awaiting that crown, but the title will do for now. How many is it now?"

"You've had seven appearances air, with three more coming up."

She shook her head, still not quite believing the trajectory of things lately, but truly enjoying the ride. "I'm feeling myself, Alika. Is that crazy?"

"You want to know the *really* crazy part?"

"Tell me."

"The feedback has been way more than I ever expected. People think you're funny, relatable, and kind. The ratings for your episodes have been stellar. Not only do the game shows want you, but the phone is starting to ring again on other projects."

"Really? And what do the people on these calls say?"

"Do you have a minute? I have a list."

Carly set down her fork in mystification. "Shockingly, I do."

She heard the sound of shuffling paper. "I have an indie film script that they're ready to simply sign you up for. It's an offer, and a decent sized role, too. A couple of TV guest-starring gigs, an endorsement deal for an orange soda company, an Off-Broadway play is showing major interest, and the new Jackson Mullens film is moving into casting. They've reached out about your status. I left that one for last because I knew you'd flip out."

Carly didn't hesitate. "Tell me about the play."

"What? The play is not high profile. Jackson Mullens is."

"Tell me about the play," Carly said calmly, a second time.

"You're stubborn, you know that?"

Carly laughed. "I'm charting a new course. I have new priorities." She liked her world, of late, and had learned that what made her happy was more important than what would further her career. Status, as Fallon not so long ago pointed out, was not high on her list of priorities. Since she'd acknowledged that, the pressure had been off. She enjoyed her days, treated people with kindness, and daydreamed about a time she'd maybe get a second shot with the woman she loved. Yes, *loved*. She'd known it for a while now, but this was the first moment she'd actually allowed herself to accept what this was. She was gaga in love with Lauren Prescott and would follow her anywhere if she'd let her.

"Okay, let's see here," Alika said. She heard some clicking sounds, which meant Alika was bringing up the email. "They're describing it as a contemporary piece by a new playwright, Heather Kim. A family drama about adult children coming to terms with secrets from their past."

"I've heard of Heather Kim." Several of her castmates from *Starry Nights* had gushed about her work, and recommended Carly read her stuff. She was all ears. "What are they asking for?"

A pause. "A meeting in New York."

"Set it up for me?" Carly asked.

"Is this really what you want? More stage?"

Carly didn't hesitate. "I might have the bug." She smiled. "Honestly, Alika, nothing was more satisfying than the run of *Starry Nights*. I feel like I'm a better actor for it and want to do more."

"Fair enough, Little Miss Stubborn. I'm on it."

"Thank you."

Carly turned back to her salad, her afternoon, and her new understanding of the things that made her happy. Green eyes were never far from her mind.

CHAPTER TWENTY

The elevator ride to the twelfth floor wasn't a glamorous one. The narrow office building on Fourteenth Street between a deli and a dry cleaner's was home to the team of producers mounting Heather Kim's two-hour production of *Home Fires*, in which a daughter discovers that she and her siblings were kidnapped as young children by the parents they grew up loving. The script came with a surprising amount of lighthearted humor, given the heavy premise. Carly enjoyed everything about the dialogue and narrative when she read it and hoped the meeting would prove to be a valuable one.

She exited the stale smelling elevator and made her way down a nondescript hallway, which all served as a reminder that she was not in Hollywood anymore. The frills were gone, which, honestly, she didn't mind. The play was not a big budget outing and would instead play a ten-week limited run in a three hundred seat theater about a mile south of Broadway, which to Carly sounded perfect in every way.

An hour and a half later, and she, the producers, the director, and Heather Kim herself were seated around a table, discussing the piece in great collaboration.

"I think the scene that resonates with me most would have to be the moment Reagan brings her findings to the siblings," Carly said.

"It's definitely the scene that took me the longest to write. There are so many layers there that I wanted to be sure came through."

Carly nodded. "The brother's reaction, especially, is chilling." She'd read the script in its entirety four times now, but she'd read that scene more than ten. She loved everything about the play and thought Heather Kim deserved the Pulitzer.

The lively discussion went on like that for another forty-five minutes, until Kevin Jacobs, the lead producer, turned to her. "Listen, are you interested? Because I can safely say we are." Everyone around the table nodded.

Carly didn't hesitate. She raised her shoulders. "When do we start?"

Jeanine, the director, clapped her hands. "Quickly. We have two more roles to cast, and fast."

"Can I ask which two?"

Jeanine listed them on her fingers. "The detective at the police department, which as you know is fairly significant in this journey, and will take the right actress, and a young actor to play Reagan's son."

Carly smiled at her. "You said you saw me in *Starry Nights*?"

"I did. It's why I wanted to work with you."

"Can I make a suggestion on who you might look into for that detective role? There's just someone I couldn't get out of my head when I read that character."

Jeanine leaned in with a smile. "I think I know where you're going with this, and I'll be honest, it had occurred to me."

Carly grinned. "Just a thought. Totally up to you."

Later that night, alone her hotel room in the theater district, Carly sent Lauren one of her routine texts. She rarely heard back but that wasn't the point of them. *It's me, game show queen, saying hello.*

This time, she got a response. *Hey, there, GSQ. How are you?*

She fell back against the pillow in delight. Every part of her went warm. She sat up again, invigorated. Lay back again and sat back up, ready to type. *Good. I feel like I hit a reset button on some big items in my life. I moved.* She hit send, feeling nervous and energetic about the fact that she was conversing with Lauren, who she missed so very much. To her amazement, the phone in her hand buzzed, signaling not just a text, but an incoming call from Lauren.

She didn't hesitate and slid onto the call. "Hi."

"Hey, you." God, that voice. "Tell me about these changes."

Carly did. She told Lauren about the new home, the unexpected fun she was having on the celebrity game show circuit, and how she saw a new path for herself that surprisingly made her much happier than the old one. "I would never have guessed that I'd be happier once

I focused less on status, but I am. I'm choosing things for myself that make me smile."

"What's one of them?"

God, it felt good to talk about daily life things with Lauren again, like the most cleansing of breaths. "There's an adorable café near my new house that I'd love to take you to one day. I eat lunch there twice a week and either take a book or a play to read, or just people watch."

Lauren was quiet for a minute. "That makes me really happy. All of it. You have no idea." There was a wistful quality in the way she said it that had Carly unnerved.

"What about you?"

"The play is over and I'm taking a little time for myself. Sleeping in. Taking Rocky for long walks."

"Enjoying it?"

Lauren hesitated. "It's been an interesting time. My crossroads, I guess."

"I miss you." The words were so automatic. That's how Carly knew how deeply she meant them.

Lauren's voice was quiet. "I miss you, too."

"Good night, Lauren."

"Sweet dreams, Carly."

They hadn't spoken about their romance or a possible future, but Carly knew without a doubt that their connection remained very much intact. She smiled and slid beneath her sheets. She just had to stay the course. Patience was a virtue, right?

New York City in winter was something to behold. Lauren exited the crowded subway station and found herself in Times Square. It was getting dark out, even though it was only four p.m., but the streets were illuminated by omnipresent neon. She gave herself a small hug as she walked, inhaling the sweet scent of roasted nuts from a street vendor on the corner. In just a few hours, audiences would take to the streets, heading out in their nice clothes for the theater, a concept that always left Lauren feeling invigorated.

The trip was entirely unexpected. She'd surprised even herself when she'd agreed to the audition her agent sent her way. She wasn't entirely sure about the future of her career, but there was no way she was passing up a shot at a new Heather Kim play. She'd be happy to get coffee for people on that production. In good news, she'd felt great about the audition. She was happy with her reading and seemed in sync with the director.

They'd invited her back for a chemistry read the next day, in an attempt to match actors up with others who might complement them in the world of the play. They'd scheduled her for two such readings.

After snagging a sandwich and a giant chocolate chip cookie from Schmackary's, Lauren took in a performance of *Clean Slate*, one of her all-time favorite musicals that had been running on Broadway for years, and headed back to the hotel for a good night's rest.

The next afternoon, she met with the creatives for her second audition.

"What I loved about your reading yesterday was the way you infused compassion into what also had to be a high-pressure case for her to solve," the director, Jeanine, told her before they got started. "You took time to check in on a very human level, rather than sticking to the business of the job."

"Oh, okay, great. I can stay in that mode." She tried to remain calm, knowing Heather Kim herself sat in the corner of the room, taking notes.

"We're gonna first test you with the character of Jimmy," Jeanine said. She introduced Lauren to Freddy Hale, the young boy they'd cast in the show.

He seemed precocious and excited. "Cool to meet you."

"Back atcha," Lauren said, as they exchanged a high five. They did a short reading from a scene, listened to some notes, and tried it again.

"Perfect," Jeanine said, jumping to her feet. "Freddy, I think that's all we need from you." He offered Lauren a final high five, said good-bye to the team, and joined his mom, who held his coat by the door.

"So, your background is in stage management," Jeanine said, with an amused grin. "That's great. I used to stage manage myself. There's nothing like it."

"You've got that right. I just wrapped a show at The McAllister."

"Which is the theater where I first encountered you. *Starry Nights* was a poignant one. I might have teared up."

Lauren was honored. "I didn't know you'd seen it."

"Oh yeah. Fantastic piece. Carly's the one who thought you might be good for this. She wasn't wrong."

"Carly Daniel?"

"She's our Reagan."

Lauren was shocked.

"Hey," a voice said from the door. "Sorry I'm two minutes late. They wouldn't let me cross the street until a crane had been safely lowered. I will not be late again. You have my word."

Lauren turned and her gaze landed on Carly's. It was surreal to be in the same room with her, even more so when she hadn't prepared for it. She swallowed, rebounding. "Two minutes, huh?" She smiled as butterflies hit her stomach. Carly was standing right in front of her. "Still an improvement."

Carly smiled nervously, still as beautiful as ever. Lauren couldn't stop looking at her. "I didn't know who I'd be reading with. I hoped. But I wasn't sure."

Lauren shifted. "Jeanine here tells me I have you to thank for the recommendation."

"I just gave them your name. The rest was all them."

Jeanine stood off to the side, watching them in mystification. "It's great to see you two in the same room. Would you be willing to read the scene in the park?"

"Of course," Lauren said.

Carly slid her leather bag off her shoulder and retrieved her script. Once Jeanine settled back in with the others behind the table, Lauren kicked them off.

"You're in a unique position, Reagan. No one faults you for wanting to protect your parents."

"You do."

Lauren shook her head. "That's the thing. Not even me. I just want the information required to put this case to rest. There's a woman out there who lost her kids."

Carly nodded. "You don't think I know that? You don't think it's kept me up every night since I first found that paperwork?" She shoved a strand of hair behind her ear and met Lauren's gaze, fire in her eyes. "I can't think about her right now."

Lauren stepped forward. "She's thinking about *you*. She's been thinking about you for nearly thirty years now."

"Well, I can't. I can't just turn my back on the people I love because they did something awful once."

"This is about righting a wrong. I know it hurts. I know you feel like your life's been ripped from you."

"Everything has."

The scene played on, and the further they got into it, the more Lauren found her rhythm. It was so easy with Carly. They had such powerful give-and-take.

Finally, Jeanine raised a hand. "Let's stop there."

Lauren lowered her script. She smiled at the room, returning to herself.

"That was great," Carly said to her quietly, as the table conversed. Heather Kim pointed to something Jeanine had written on her pad and nodded emphatically, then wrote something back.

"Thanks. I'm nervous," Lauren whispered. Carly, after everything they'd been through, still had an uncanny ability to center Lauren. It helped that the read had been with her.

"Lauren, I can't thank you enough for coming back today. We'll be in touch, okay? Can I get you a water or coffee for the road?"

Lauren held up a hand. "No, I'm good. Thank you for inviting me. I had a nice time."

"Jeanine, do you need me anymore?" Carly asked.

Jeanine looked to the table. "No. I think we're all set. I appreciate you coming in, and we'll see you soon."

"Great. I'll walk out with Lauren."

Lauren lifted a hand in farewell and headed out of the room.

"This was unexpected," she said to Carly in the elevator.

"I should have given you a heads-up, but what if they hadn't decided to call, you know? You look great, by the way. So pretty," Carly said. She blinked and stared at the floor, probably feeling off-kilter.

"Thank you."

They rode the rest of the way in silence. When they hit the street, the noisy sounds of traffic and people hit. They stood on the sidewalk, dodging the quick flow of pedestrians heading to business meetings, work, lunch, auditions, or who knew where.

"I don't think I got it," Lauren said, shrugging. "That's okay, though. I'm thrilled to have met Heather Kim. It was worth the trip."

"Don't say that. You never know. I thought the audition went really well."

Lauren passed Carly a skeptical look. "They seemed unsure." She stepped out of the way so a very serious looking man could get past.

Carly mirrored her actions, stepping to the side. "There's no way to know that. They were simply figuring things out. They'll call."

Lauren nodded. She gestured behind her. "I guess I better…"

"Yeah. Me, too."

She saw the sadness in Carly's eyes as they said good-bye. Regret bubbled up. Yet she didn't know what to say. Carly was still a very scary prospect for her, but being in her presence felt like coming home. She didn't want to leave. "Don't be a stranger, okay?"

"Not a problem." Carly flashed her always beautiful smile. Lauren felt its effects all over.

She offered a final wave and headed uptown to the subway station. She didn't have to think of this as good-bye. In fact, if the job did come through, she'd be working with Carly again, seeing her every day, working on scenes together. The very concept had her heart and mind singing. So was she going to wait for that call to come from her agent, and then hope that she finally managed the courage to leap back in to something she wanted so very badly already?

Hell no.

She turned around, hurrying back down the sidewalk, dodging pedestrian traffic, scooting through tight spaces, and making each crossing sign before it changed. She passed the production office and kept going, craning her neck to see if she could spot Carly walking farther down Ninth. After scurrying another block—yes!—she caught sight of the back of her blond hair, and it was only a matter of moments before she caught up. Lauren touched Carly's shoulder and she turned. She blinked at Lauren curiously.

"Hey. What's going—"

Lauren took Carly by the face and kissed her right there on Ninth Avenue in the freaking Meatpacking District of New York City. The best part of all? Carly melted and kissed her back.

"Lauren," she whispered, coming up for air. She smiled. "You're back."

"Are we?"

"God, yes," Carly said, her eyes glistening. "That's all I want. That's everything to me."

Lauren smiled against Carly's mouth and kissed her again. And again. And again. The people rushed past. The traffic lights changed. The cabs beeped their way through the city, but in that one spot beneath the sun and moon and stars and planets, two people meant for each other found their way back home.

❖

"Ms. Daniel, the wine." The sommelier at Becco presented the celebratory bottle of Sangiovese he'd recommended. Carly nodded at the label. "Who would like to try the wine?"

Carly gestured to her most beautiful date. "Why don't you go ahead?"

He poured a taste for Lauren, who swirled it and sampled. "Wow. That's fantastic."

"Very good," he said, pouring them each a full glass.

They'd parted ways on the sidewalk earlier that day with plans to meet for dinner. Lauren arrived in a long-sleeved gray dress and thin pink scarf. Carly wore her forest-green turtleneck and swept her hair back. Sitting there with Lauren, she couldn't stop smiling.

"I'm happy you're here with me," Carly said.

Lauren reached across the table and squeezed Carly's hand. "It just came to the point where I had to be honest with myself. I want us, Carly. You were in a bad place. I was in my own head, caught up in my own insecurities, and we let those things obscure the big picture." She shook her head. "I don't want us to do that anymore."

"So let's make a plan, because things won't always be as easy as they were in Minneapolis."

Lauren nodded and set down her glass. "I think we start with promising not to shut the other person out. I never confessed to you that I felt it was only a matter of time before you decided I was boring and mundane."

Now it was Carly's turn to set her glass down. "You're the least boring person I've ever spent time with."

Lauren pointed at her head. "Sometimes we get in our own way and tell ourselves the opposite. From now on, I refuse to swallow those feelings."

"God, I wouldn't want you to," Carly said, sitting back. "The next time I spiral, and yes, there could be a next time, I will take your hand. I won't shut you out." She lifted her arm and let it drop. "Honestly, the only thing I can imagine spiraling about is not having you by my side."

"That was a really good answer." Lauren picked up her glass. "A toast. To getting it right this time."

"Take two."

"The more adult version."

Carly touched her glass to Lauren's and raised an eyebrow. "Saucy. I like it."

Lauren blushed. "I didn't mean like that."

"Too late. It's in the history books for all posterity."

After that little exchange, they seemed to race through dinner. It was almost as if they had something more important to get to. Carly commented on how amazing the pasta was. Lauren mooned over her brined double pork chop, and when they were finished, Carly paid the check, posed for a photo with the server, and they spilled out into the night. Forty-Sixth Street was bustling, and they huddled together to keep warm. A saxophonist along the sidewalk played a slow rendition of "It Had to Be You," making everything feel special, romantic.

"And now?" Carly asked.

"Take me to your place?"

She chuckled. "Not yours?"

"I know you, and you'll have booked fancier digs. What happened to the wooing?"

Carly balked. "I'm not a movie star, Lauren. I play games on TV for a living."

"Are you staying in a penthouse tonight?"

"Why, yes. Yes, I am."

Lauren poked her in the ribs, and Carly grinned. "Shall we get your things first?"

Lauren considered the question. "Well, if you think I'll need clothes before tomorrow."

Carly tugged on Lauren's arm with new purpose. "Definitely not. Let's go."

When they came together that night in the dim light of Carly's hotel room, they undressed each other slowly. They took their time with each kiss, each caress, and each lingering gaze. There seemed to be a newfound appreciation of what they'd discovered in the other. For Carly, she'd found a best friend, the love of her life, a soul mate. She would cherish Lauren and spend every day making sure she knew that she was the most important aspect of Carly's entire life.

"I love you," Lauren said, as she gazed down into Carly's eyes. She grinned and touched Lauren's lips. "So much."

"Say it again," Carly whispered, cherishing the words.

"I love you. I'm in love with you. I plan to always love you."

"I love you, too," Carly said, cupping Lauren's cheek with one hand. "To the moon and back."

EPILOGUE

"What do you think about an entirely gray and white kitchen?" Lauren asked, hands on her hips. They'd been back in LA for a little over two months now. With *Home Fires* having been met with such critical success in New York, the producers were now mounting an LA run of the show and invited both Lauren and Carly to reprise their roles. There was nothing like satisfying stage work, and with two shows under her belt now, she looked forward to more. There'd even been a few calls exchanged between producers and agents about her and Carly reprising their roles as replacements in *Starry Nights* on Broadway. The water was definitely warm these days.

"I like gray," Carly said, coming out of the bathroom. She had a streak of light blue paint on her cheek, and her hair swept up in a pink bandana.

Lauren laughed. "You look like Rosie the Riveter if she was awful at painting a bathroom." She touched the streak on Carly's cheek, but nope, it was already dry. "We can hire someone to do that, you know, if you're struggling."

"Struggling?" Carly squeaked. "Have you seen how closely I've stayed within the painter's tape? I'm the Van Gogh of bathrooms."

"Hmm," Lauren said. "Maybe more like Picasso."

"Still an artist," Carly said gleefully.

The three-bedroom home Carly had purchased in Franklin Village was everything she'd once described it to be: adorable, full of sunlight, and perfectly situated. Now that it was Lauren's, too, they spent their available days off making it uniquely in their joint style. Carly had the big ideas and Lauren reined her in, much like other aspects of their lives.

Rocky padded into the room, bleary-eyed from his afternoon snooze, and blinked up at them. Carly snatched him up and placed a kiss on his cheek. To pay her back, he offered her a tongue swipe. Then another.

"What time do you have to be on set tomorrow?" Lauren asked, giving Rocky a good scratch behind his ears.

"My call time is five a.m. Can you set a backup alarm for three forty-five?"

Lauren grimaced, not envying Carly in the slightest. The game show appearances, followed by the great write-ups on *Home Fires*, had her star on the rise. The studio-produced film offers had started rolling in once again, but to her credit, Carly hadn't jumped immediately. She'd pored through scripts, selecting the roles she'd find challenging or fulfilling, even if that meant less screen time. She was relaxed, happy, and fulfilled. It certainly showed.

As for Lauren, she enjoyed her life as a student of the theater. She'd even talked with Jeanine about shadowing her in the future, a prospect Jeanine was very much in favor of. Stage managing was a great passion of Lauren's, but maybe it was time she graduated to director. She had a lot of ideas of her own, and lots of stories to tell.

"Three forty-five, it is." Lauren shook her head. "Ouch, by the way."

"Right? Why do they hate me?" Carly stuck out her bottom lip.

"No one hates you. You're too cute for hate."

"Oh, I like that idea a lot." Carly cocked a playful hip. "Do you want to help this cute person finish our bathroom wall?"

"Hmm." Lauren made a show out of considering the offer. "Only if there is fooling around during and after. I can't see you in short overalls and not get handsy."

Carly offered an overly innocent smile. "It's the very reason I invited you. Follow me."

Lauren eagerly trailed Carly into their master bathroom, full of tarps, and tape, and paint, and brushes. Oh, my. She and Carly led a fairly exciting and diverse life by most people's standards, but the mundane moments like these were the ones that Lauren cherished most.

She looked forward to lazy afternoons by the much smaller pool in their backyard, gatherings with old and new friends alike, and the quiet of the night, when she could lie with Carly in her arms and know that she was right where she was supposed to be.

"I want spaghetti tonight," Lauren said, as she painted. "I have no idea why."

Carly pointed at her with a paintbrush. "Then we shall seek out this spaghetti and make it ours."

They painted some more with the gentle sounds of Norah Jones playing from the small speaker Carly had set up in the bathroom. Lauren swayed her hips slightly to the music.

"Hey, Car?"

"Yes?"

"I really love you."

"Good, because it's not fun being hopelessly in love all by yourself." They leaned in and exchanged a kiss over a can of paint.

"One more thing," Lauren said. She pointed just above Carly's head. "You missed a spot."

Carly glanced up and smirked. "Still the project manager. You want to grab one of your Post-its and mark its placement?"

Lauren nodded, her heart full. "Lord knows I have enough."

About the Author

Melissa Brayden (www.melissabrayden.com) is a multi-award-winning romance author, embracing the full-time writer's life in San Antonio, Texas, and enjoying every minute of it.

Melissa enjoys spending time with her family and working really hard at remembering to do the dishes. For personal enjoyment, she throws realistically shaped toys for her Jack Russell terriers and checks out the NYC theatre scene as often as possible. She considers herself a reluctant patron of spin class, but would much rather be sipping merlot and staring off into space. Coffee, wine, and doughnuts make her world go round.

Books Available From Bold Strokes Books

Femme Tales by Anne Shade. Six women find themselves in their own real-life fairy tales when true love finds them in the most unexpected ways. (978-1-63555-657-5)

Jellicle Girl by Stevie Mikayne. One dark summer night, Beth and Jackie go out to the canoe dock. Two years later, Beth is still carrying the weight of what happened to Jackie. (978-1-63555-691-9)

My Date with a Wendigo by Genevieve McCluer. Elizabeth Rosseau finds her long-lost love and the secret community of fiends she's now a part of. (978-1-63555-679-7)

On the Run by Charlotte Greene. Even when they're cute blondes, it's stupid to pick up hitchhikers, especially when they've just broken out of prison, but doing so is about to change Gwen's life forever. (978-1-63555-682-7)

Perfect Timing by Dena Blake. The choice between love and family has never been so difficult, and Lynn's and Maggie's different visions of the future may end their romance before it's begun. (978-1-63555-466-3)

The Mail Order Bride by R. Kent. When a mail order bride is thrust on Austin, he must choose between the bride he never wanted or the dream he lives for. (978-1-63555-678-0)

Through Love's Eyes by C.A. Popovich. When fate reunites Brittany Yardin and Amy Jansons, can they move beyond the pain of their past to find love? (978-1-63555-629-2)

To the Moon and Back by Melissa Brayden. Film actress Carly Daniel thinks that stage work is boring and unexciting, but when she accepts a lead role in a new play, stage manager Lauren Prescott tests both her heart and her ability to share the limelight. (978-1-63555-618-6)

Tokyo Love by Diana Jean. When Kathleen Schmitt is given the opportunity to be on the cutting edge of AI technology, she never thought a failed robotic love companion would bring her closer to her neighbor, Yuriko Velucci, and finding love in unexpected places. (978-1-63555-681-0)

Brooklyn Summer by Maggie Cummings. When opposites attract, can a summer of passion and adventure lead to a lifetime of love? (978-1-63555-578-3)

City Kitty and Country Mouse by Alyssa Linn Palmer. Pulled in two different directions, can a city kitty and a country mouse fall in love and make it work? (978-1-63555-553-0)

Elimination by Jackie D. When a dangerous homegrown terrorist seeks refuge with the Russian mafia, the team will be put to the ultimate test. (978-1-63555-570-7)

In the Shadow of Darkness by Nicole Stiling. Angeline Vallencourt is a reluctant vampire who must decide what she wants more—obscurity, revenge, or the woman who makes her feel alive. (978-1-63555-624-7)

On Second Thought by C. Spencer. Madisen is falling hard for Rae. Even single life and co-parenting are beginning to click. At least, that is, until her ex-wife begins to have second thoughts. (978-1-63555-415-1)

Out of Practice by Carsen Taite. When attorney Abby Keane discovers the wedding blogger tormenting her client is the woman she had a passionate, anonymous vacation fling with, sparks and subpoenas fly. Legal Affairs: one law firm, three best friends, three chances to fall in love. (978-1-63555-359-8)

Providence by Leigh Hays. With every click of the shutter, photographer Rebekiah Kearns finds it harder and harder to keep Lindsey Blackwell in focus without getting too close. (978-1-63555-620-9)

Taking a Shot at Love by KC Richardson. When academic and athletic worlds collide, will English professor Celeste Bouchard and basketball coach Lisa Tobias ignore their attraction to achieve their professional goals? (978-1-63555-549-3)

Flight to the Horizon by Julie Tizard. Airline captain Kerri Sullivan and flight attendant Janine Case struggle to survive an emergency water landing and overcome dark secrets to give love a chance to fly. (978-1-63555-331-4)

In Helen's Hands by Nanisi Barrett D'Arnuk. As her mistress, Helen pushes Mickey to her sensual limits, delivering the pleasure only a BDSM lifestyle can provide her. (978-1-63555-639-1)

Jamis Bachman, Ghost Hunter by Jen Jensen. In Sage Creek, Utah, a poltergeist stirs to life and past secrets emerge. (978-1-63555-605-6)

Moon Shadow by Suzie Clarke. Add betrayal, season with survival, then serve revenge smokin' hot with a sharp knife. (978-1-63555-584-4)

Spellbound by Jean Copeland and Jackie D. When the supernatural worlds of good and evil face off, love might be what saves them all. (978-1-63555-564-6)

Temptation by Kris Bryant. Can experienced nanny Cassie Miller deny her growing attraction and keep her relationship with her boss professional? Or will they sidestep propriety and give in to temptation? (978-1-63555-508-0)

The Inheritance by Ali Vali. Family ties bring Tucker Delacroix and Willow Vernon together, but they could also tear them, and any chance they have at love, apart. (978-1-63555-303-1)

Thief of the Heart by MJ Williamz. Kit Hanson makes a living seducing rich women in casinos and relieving them of the expensive jewelry most won't even miss. But her streak ends when she meets beautiful FBI agent Savannah Brown. (978-1-63555-572-1)

Face Off by PJ Trebelhorn. Hockey player Savannah Wells rarely spends more than a night with any one woman, but when photographer Madison Scott buys the house next door, she's forced to rethink what she expects out of life. (978-1-63555-480-9)

Hot Ice by Aurora Rey, Elle Spencer, and Erin Zak. Can falling in love melt the hearts of the iciest ice queens? Join Aurora Rey, Elle Spencer, and Erin Zak to find out! A contemporary romance novella collection. (978-1-63555-513-4)

Line of Duty by VK Powell. Dr. Dylan Carlyle's professional and personal life is turned upside down when a tragic event at Fairview Station pits her against ambitious, handsome police officer Finley Masters. ((978-1-63555-486-1)

London Undone by Nan Higgins. London Craft reinvents her life after reading a childhood letter to her future self and, in doing so, finds the love she truly wants. (978-1-63555-562-2)

Lunar Eclipse by Gun Brooke. Moon De Cruz lives alone on an uninhabited planet after being shipwrecked in space. Her life changes forever when Captain Beaux Lestarion's arrival threatens the planet and Moon's freedom. (978-1-63555-460-1)

One Small Step by MA Binfield. In this contemporary romance, Iris and Cam discover the meaning of taking chances and following your heart, even if it means getting hurt. (978-1-63555-596-7)

Shadows of a Dream by Nicole Disney. Rainn has the talent to take her rock band all the way, but falling in love is a powerful distraction, and her new girlfriend's meth addiction might just take them both down. 978-1-63555-598-1)

Someone to Love by Jenny Frame. When Davina Trent is given an unexpected family, can she let nanny Wendy Darling teach her to open her heart to the children and to Wendy? (978-1-63555-468-7)

Uncharted by Robyn Nyx. As Rayne Marcellus and Chase Stinsen track the legendary Golden Trinity, they must learn to put their differences aside and depend on one another to survive. (978-1-63555-325-3)

Where We Are by Annie McDonald. A sensual account of two women who discover a way to walk on the same path together with the help of an Indigenous tale, a Canadian art movement, and the mysterious appearance of dimes. (978-1-63555-581-3)